THE SAN VENEFICIO CANON

THE SAN VENEFICIO CANON
THE DIVINITY STUDENT
THE GOLEM

MICHAEL CISCO

PRIME BOOKS

SAN VENEFICIO CANON
Copyright © 2004 by **Michael Cisco**

The Divinity Student was originally published by Buzzcity Press
(Tallahassee, Florida) in 1999

Cover Art and Design Copyright © 2004 John Coulthart
Interior Design by Juha Lindroos

Editor: Ann Kennedy (buzzcity@yourvillage.com)

All rights reserved. No part of this publication may be reproduced or transmitted in any form or by any means, electronic or mechanical, including photocopy, recording, or any information storage and retrieval system now known or invented, without permission in writing from the publisher, except by a reviewer who wishes to quote brief passages in connection with a review written for inclusion in a magazine, newspaper, broadcast, etc.

Published in the United States by **Prime Books, Inc.**
www.primebooks.net

ISBN: 1-894815-67-X (hardcover)
ISBN: 1-894815-68-8 (paperback)

For My Parents

The Divinity Student

The Cloud	*11*
The City	*17*
The Car	*23*
The Dream	*26*
The Priest	*33*
The Oro	*38*
The Lesson	*43*
The Commission	*49*
The Butcher	*54*
The Mission	*63*
The Gardens	*69*
Chan	*75*
The Demons	*82*
Albert	*87*
The House	*92*
The Final Interview	*99*
The Muse	*105*
Gaster	*111*
The Last Day	*118*

The Golem

- *127*   Prologue
- *130*   The Prefect's Dream
- *139*   The Morgue and the Brewery
- *147*   The Magician
- *156*   The Golem
- *169*   Griepentrog
- *174*   The Underworld
- *184*   The Secretary and the Museum
- *194*   The Prisoner in the Fish
- *211*   The Catechism and the Ten Plagues
- *233*   The Cathedral

The Divinity Student

Chapter I: The Cloud

First black clouds dimming the sky, trailing shredded white veils in the rustle of settling audience, and, as each cloud passes framing itself perfectly in its own outlines, one especially stands out—looming like an iceberg above the others. It's moving steadily along now, coming fast and low over green canyons. It dips between the hills into a smell of water, and the placid anxious hush of rain falling on trees and grass.

    The Divinity Student, in his heavy black coat, is scaling a steep mound down in the canyon. His feet are slipping on the wet grass; he steadies himself with outstretched arms. He's wet to the skin, his spectacles are fogged and running with rain. The slope is water—softened and slick, so he's forced to scrabble at roots and stones to avoid falling. He didn't want to miss a walk in the rain. Above his head, the sky changes color from grey to black. Breathing hard and almost spent, he gives himself a last violent shove and crests the hill. For a few moments he stands bent with his hands on his knees, then he turns to take in the entire canyon rising about him on all sides like a green bowl. The sky above him thunders and blackens to coal black: a cloud iceberg high. Flushed, he pads across the green breast of the hill's crest to the highest peak. He passes a hand over his cropped hair and water rills over his fingers. He reaches the top—the sky splits above his head. Standing in tall grass, eyes lost in the distance and the wind playing in and out of his shirt sleeves and blowing up his coattails. Searing blue lightning scrapes its fingernails along his body in a column lifting him off the ground. The cloud opens a moment and reaches down, pulling him off his feet. Suspended in an infinite moment, flat in two dimensions between ground and sky, his body arching his eyes staring fingers close on snapping air white face splits apart as he turns down twisting to the dirt—stone dead. Quiet wet grass in his mouth and rain streaming over his sodden coat on his dead body, glassy eyes rigid and open, staring at one hand fixed in mid-convulsion, cupping the rain in its dead palm, his dead back shattered.

Overhead, the clouds pass by. Rain falls, time continues to pass.

Now they're finding him. Hands take him up; they make off down the slope, in the mud, with his body. The ground levels and the trees close in like clouds and spatter them with big drops of rain. They carry him away to a low building enmeshed in trees and the shadows of trees. Quickly they bring him inside, lay him across two sawhorses and start cutting at him—they gut him like a fish, cut open from throat to waist, red hands pull his ribs apart, head and shoulders hanging down, his arms lying flat on the ground, tugged back and forth as they empty him out. They dump his contents cooked and steaming on the floor, and bring up stacks of books and manila folders, tearing out pages and shuffling out sheets of paper, all covered with writing, stuffing them inside, tamping them down behind his ribs and crushing them together in his abdomen. What pages they select and what books they tear are of little importance, only that he be completely filled up with writing, to bring him back, to set him to the task. Then they suture him shut again—drag him to the tub (his arms and legs dangling and catching on things overturning tables and chairs) and dump him in the water, slopping blue water on grey stone pavings, and together they draw breath and drop open their mouths, screaming noiselessly as they shove his face under the running tap and pushing him full under the water with their red hands, under their wings. The Divinity Student twitches, lashing water over the lip of the tub. Gaping they push him down harder. He jerks to one side. They turn the spigot up full bore and shove his face into the stream—he thrashes, his body goes livid and white then his eyes and mouth snap open and gape wide all screaming without sound (they grab him and pull him out).

Clammy, bleached colorless, hauled out of the water, flopping on the ground, they hold his head as he coughs water and stares across the floor at the heap of his own guts, and recognizing them he screams again, screams himself into shadows and clammy darkness.

LATER HE'S DISCOVERED BACK at the Seminary, lying pale and unconscious in an infirmary bed. Orderlies shake their heads over him, "How did he get here?"

The Divinity Student comes to a few hours later. For a moment the memory comes racing forward like a black wave of frigid water, and he recoils and slams his mind shut. Fingers pulling, his flesh melting around them like clay, coughing water on grey paving stones—he snaps to attention and faces the windows across from his bed, reduced to a bland white smear of cloud-filtered daylight without his glasses. He stares at his hands. They look like talons hovering over the colorless blanket, something mechanical about them now. He sits perfectly still; nobody approaches or notices him, he fades in and out of consciousness with a bitter taste in his mouth and an ugly feeling throbbing behind his temples.

Disjointed he awakens again and it's the next day already, morning or afternoon he can't distinguish. Someone is drifting tall and angular down the aisle, coming to a halt at the foot of his bed like a docking ship. After a while he recognizes him—an important administrator, a teacher greatly feared in the Seminary. His face is blurred in the bland light. The Divinity Student sluggishly brings his name into focus: it's Fasvergil. As if in response Fasvergil seems to click into place in his overlong cassock, bunched frayed and torn around his feet. He looks up in pale response. Fasvergil is staring at him.

"You've had quite an adventure. Two of the boys saw what happened to you."

The Divinity Student feels a sudden weight in his chest. He tries to speak but his brittle throat cracks with the effort and he can't.

"Who brought you back here?" Fasvergil leans in close, eyes fixed as if cutting him open, searching the Divinity Student's face. "Yes, what is it?" he hisses. But the Divinity Student is already blurring, a grey haze misting over his eyes; his vision occludes until he can just manage to stare at his clawlike hands resting on the blankets. He sits mute and emptied. From nowhere Fasvergil says he will return and goes off to nowhere, leaving the Divinity Student alone in nowhere.

DISCHARGED BACK TO HIS room, he spends his days sitting at his desk watching the clouds pass through his grimy windows. Sometimes the wind moans in the chimney and he jerks in surprise, but most of all he watches the sky, and presses his hands against the panes convulsively when lightning flashes outside. Why is he still here? What's taking so long? Light goes dull in the stale air of his room, behind him his disheveled bed with sorry printed flowers waning on yellow linen. Incubating alone in his dormitory room, he gathers the clouds and swaths himself silently in them, with a jagged, glassy feeling in his head. The past few days he has seen signs and portents that something important is going to happen, and today he is preparing himself. Only just now he's fallen prey to a delusion, confusing his destination with thoughts of returning to his ancestral home, his very early childhood. He simmers in his bed wrapped hot in thick blankets and hallucinates a homecoming for himself—through the trees to his ancestral home. On either side of him the hills like low domes sit pondering in green from winter rain, trees waving him on down the street in wind that brings the smell of sweet grass and sour brush. His house is low, sitting preserved in the gelatin of memory. Overhead clouds boil and blow away, sunlight crashes down in glassy sheets shattering in glowing white aftersights floating under his eyelids. The light sharpens, dashing down, his eyes water and his vision goes pink. The house flares as he walks up to it on broken pavement, moving past the flat grey porch and chimney cooking in the heat, the air rustling close up close pressing on him like the palm of a hand. Lightheaded, he passes the house and moves to the yard behind, grass grown waist high, scorched yellow-brown and dry in spots, lush and dewy moist in others. The sun flattens the landscape dead flat, like walking into the sepia of an old photograph.

The back of the house is blazing with candles, the flames churning the air. The backyard is like a chapel. The trees above ruffle their plumage and stretch their wings, speaking up into the blue-hot sky. He sits just behind the house, the candles jutting perpendicular to the wall glowing white-orange at his back; he sits in a wooden seat, splinters biting into his legs, the corroded metal frame rusting against his fingers. He sits there and watches the light ebb and surge across the grass. This is where he came from, and the whole world will always look a little like it for him. He left this house to live at the Seminary and to train for—whatever's coming now.

Time shifts backwards, a wind winnows bricks away like leaves whittling the walls that frame the yard, the ground sprouts a white picket fence in their place. The yard undulates around him; the paving stones sink into the ground. He can hear birds, and the patter of wax dripping behind him. Grass shoots up around him and up his pant legs poking out through holes in the knees; squirrels and birds scrabble across the roof knocking leaves and acorns down on his head.

As he sits dozing, he gradually becomes aware of another presence; he is certain someone else is there. Without hurrying he looks up from the ground, unsure that he could get up if he tried, thinking that a voice or music is there, a white film shimmering over the yard, discrete from the flow of light and the dappled shadows of the passing clouds. Like highlights on pleated fabric, or a pale figure moving in fragmented light—fragile and transparent, a membrane speaking voicelessly at him, an original premonition of the future that he remembers for the first time. It gets hotter, heat closing in and descending from all sides, and he pushes it out from him again, pushing his chair back furrowing the ground—he thinks he can hear better with the chair pushed back. He opens his arms, and for a moment his heart murmurs and jumps as he sees the paleness rushing towards him, the tall grass beaten aside in great wide swathes as it comes. It's coming, it's coming for him finally.

A drop of wax lands pat on his shoulder. He looks at it as another spats his sleeve. Slowly, he looks up at the candles, and wax begins to rain gently down on him. He smiles. He opens his mouth and a tiny drop stings his tongue. Lowering his head he feels an aromatic evaporation sifting up through his head, a flavor like a continent of flowered meadows, sour-smelling hillsides, fresh grass, wet dirt, rotting leaves, dust. Wax coats him and he begins to burn in the sun like a candle. It comes down, he can see the grass curving down to the earth, the trees sagging, paint baking off the house, coming loose in flakes, then bubbling and liquefying on the pavement. The concrete flows off like mud. Holding out his hand, he sees the wax dribbling from his fingers, pink droplets. Inside, his bones glow white and expand, turn elastic, his blood evaporates, runs down his legs into the grass with a pleasant sighing sound. Heat brighter, whiteness all around, he reclines back in the chair to lose himself—and wakes, disappointed, in his bed. It's all still before him, still to be done.

THE DIVINITY STUDENT STARES out the window, oblivious, fading in and out. At this moment, he is conscious of the Seminary expanding ancient and vast on all sides—the yawning cold hallways like caverns of stone, the dank subvestries and classrooms with bubbling peeling plaster walls and a mildewed smell, frosty choirs of icy wood polished to a dull lustre by the chafing of nervous hands. Huge, gaping wide on all sides for him, also crushing inward collapsing upon him. He seems to be present in every room, feeling the students coming and going—as they learn, they come and go with greater earnestness of purpose, striding powerfully along the halls as if they were on rails.

This has always been his room; it is the center of his world, his only place. The world seems to turn pinioned on a cold-burning point in his empty chest. The other students have been avoiding him lately; he's become intimidating. It could be lightning-infection trickling in tiny courses through what's left of his body, like a minute trace of poison. He's ready to go.

Fasvergil summons him to his office. Another Prefect stands beside him, together behind a massive desk. The Prefect speaks first: "Your studies are finished—consider yourself *commenced*."

Fasvergil scans the contents of a folder with lazy eyes. "We have been preparing an Assignment in the hopes of receiving an agent of your caliber. You have been *selected* for us."

Fasvergil and the Prefect eye the Divinity Student uneasily. He makes them nervous. His eyes stare straight ahead, as if he were laying track right on top of them. Now they can get him out of the Seminary and for that they are grateful.

"You will leave for the city as soon as possible," Fasvergil says with concealed relief. "Your letters of introduction are in this folder. Further information will be forthcoming when you arrive. At the moment, certain things are still up in the air—when they settle again, we will be able to tell you what to do."

"I'll do as I'm told," the Divinity Student says, surprised despite his premonitions.

"There's no question of that. Go and pack."

"Chapel in one hour," the Prefect says.

The next day comes, and the Divinity Student leaves the Seminary knowing he won't be back.

Chapter 2: The City

SAN VENEFICIO GLEAMS IN the desert like a cut emerald on a naked sea bed. The sky is a still canopy, like the underside surface of the sea, and blue light shines on the marble walls striking patterns across the hot ground like dancing traceries of light reflected from rippling water. Sitting alone in a spacious cab, the Divinity Student watches the sweat trickle down the driver's neck, wind buffeting him from the open window. A single road lies flat on the face of the land flaring white in the steady beam of the sun, and for a moment he sees the cab from a bird's-eye view—a tiny white speck speeding along a black stripe. They pass long autos with black windows roaring hoarsely toward the city, which expands to fill the horizon. He rests his head on the vibrating door jam and squints against the dust pouring in on the wind—spotting now for the first time the famous monitors, giant lizards over ten feet long, racing with alarming speed over the dirt. One comes up by the side of the road and paces the cab for a mile or so, its oversized eyes fixed straight ahead on its coffin-shaped skull. He's heard that at night these lizards watch the city—it's said that someone looking over the town walls can see them staring back, their eyes blazing with reflected city light, the entire desert punctuated with pairs of lights, so that when the night sky is clear and dark it seems to extend down into the desert and surround San Veneficio on all sides with stars. Baked white clay streaks by, extending flat to the mountains in the distance. The Divinity Student was schooled exclusively in cold places, always rain and chill waiting outside the walls; he would anxiously look forward to the half-hearted springs and moist, wilted summers. Now, here, it's parched sharp bright heat stabbing in under his heavy coat, pricking him awake and alert and buoying him up. Only the two letters in his pocket stay sharp and white, like two rectangles of silvered glass, rigid, crisp, and cool. His Assignment is: to go to San Veneficio, obtain a position with a professional word-finder, and wait for further instructions, followed by an illegible signature. He had found the sheet under his door and brought it to his Prefect:

"Where did this come from?" he asked.

"Higher up classified—ep!" raising his hand to shut him up, "No no sorry nothing more can't tell you strictest confidence!"

The other letter will introduce him to the word-finder. He shoots towards San Veneficio, confident that this is where he is meant to go, he is starting. He has a momentum that came out of the sky. The dark marble walls draw near, black veined with green as far as his eyes can see. Beyond, the city bristles with spires and precarious minarets, lonely groups of statues standing against the sky atop copper domes, glyphed obelisks of polished basalt, gilded fountains, gargoyles; it's a city of monuments. Above, birds circle rising on hot currents watching below in lazy ascent, quiet.

"This is the Eye Gate," says the driver, raising his index finger from the wheel. A circular breach in the wall a hundred feet across looms up and swallows them, flattened at the bottom where it meets the road, and around it the Divinity Student can briefly see a pointed ellipse carved deep into the wall; huge triangular pieces of green jade gleam, smoothly radiating out to form the iris around the pupil-gateway. Lictors, in their heavy coats and blood-red gloves, silver face masks shining, turn this way and that, bored, waving the traffic into the city.

They drive up the Street of Dogs, making for the central plaza. The streets weave and twist passing through people's houses and doubling back on themselves. The buildings are old and venerable, white plaster and modest columns, flat onyx streets searing hot sunlight, smells rushing in through the window—orchards, wisteria, grilled meat, and people smells, carried on hot desert air. Finally, they make their way up the Street of Wax and into the plaza, vast and wide open, a colossal fountain at the center, buildings for giants looming all around. He pays the driver and makes his way to the fountain.

The plaza seems to curve downward as if San Veneficio is the only city on a tiny planet, hanging over the sky's open void. He weaves through currents of natives in white cotton, wealthy ladies walking pet monkeys, occasional dignitaries in loiters, and he follows in their clear wake, pardoning himself in Spanish. Now and then he checks to see that the letters are still in his pocket as he hurries to the fountain.

There, he stands a moment in the spray, watching luminous fish circling sluggishly, the level of the water surging and dropping every few seconds as if the pool is breathing. He looks back at the town, eyes smarting from the dancing reflections on the water, and then thinks for the first time to check the letters for addresses. They are blank.

Not knowing where to go, the Divinity Student sits on the clammy bank of the fountain and waits. People pass in streams and groups, cars roll by. Unthinkingly, he reaches into another pocket and produces a small metal weight on a cord that Fasvergil had given him back at the Seminary. Sheltering himself from crowd and wind, he spits in his palm and swings the weight like a pendulum above his open hand. His face drains and closes—he watches the swinging weight. Dry lightning sparks near the mountains on the horizon as the pendulum's point first swings over his palm. Even in the middle of town he feels completely exposed to the mountains and the freely-moving air. He stretches a little into the rising wind—for a moment his hand is a still point. The weight swings back and forth, each time rotating a little more to the left, until it finally stops, hanging at an angle in the air. He gets carefully to his feet and orients himself by the pendulum's direction; he starts walking. The weight floats before him taut on the end of its tether like a dog on a leash, pulling him to one corner of the plaza, down close streets, past shouting water-sellers with earthenware vats and brass ladles, air growing closer—the sky rumbles overhead, people race to hide their stalls under umbrellas or find refuge under the awnings of clay buildings. Candles burn in absentminded alcoves, spice and paraffin smells. His eyelids droop and he feels lightheaded, but the pendulum tugs at his hand, threatening to come loose. He pushes himself off the voices of the fruit vendors and shouts of old women, shuffling awkwardly among the milling people.

Finally, he staggers into a small laundry with sweating walls. Steam billows hissing in corners, more Spanish over shrieking presses. He's pulled through to the back door and out onto a catwalk above a narrow alleyway. Stairs lead up a scarred brick wall to a deepset door with frosted glass panes. He scales the stairs and goes in, pocketing the weight and string. A tiny waiting room with oak paneling and red wallpaper.

The contrast of the brightness outside and the dimness here makes him blink. A plain woman is sitting behind a miniature desk in one corner, making columns of numbers in regular handwriting on tiny sheets of ruled paper. She looks up at him blandly.

"Is there anything you want?"

"I'm here for my appointment." He rifles through his coat and produces the letters. She looks at them distractedly with two quick gestures.

"You should see Mr. Woodwind," she says, and directs him up a flight of stairs concealed behind a potted rubber plant.

The stairs are narrow and shallow, tilting down at an angle making them almost impossible to climb. He picks his way carefully up, following a series of random landings and new flights, lit always by red light through glass-filtered fixtures.

Woodwind's door is enameled, set directly into the wall, ajar and moving gently back and forth with the draught. The Divinity Student pushes it open with his fingertips.

Inside—a vast room, narrow but deep, with high windows, light filtering through a white haze, a smell of books. Shelves loaded with notebooks line the walls, their covers bulging with yellowing paper. Three clerks are shuffling about the room in excessively long robes, carrying stacks of printed pages, an occasional page spiraling to the bare wooden floor. Having crossed the room three times bearing ever larger stacks of paper, one of the clerks pauses, peering nearsightedly at the Divinity Student.

"I have letters of introduction for Mr. Woodwind."

The clerk sniffs at him dubiously and trudges off, absently waving the Divinity Student after him. Woodwind is standing at a table in the far corner: a tall whitehaired man with rolled sleeves and an apron. He is excising a page from an open book with a long pair of tweezers—dropping it into a pan of clear grey liquid. Having soaked it thoroughly, he retrieves it and plies it over a blue fire; his heavy brows knit as he reads the page's new contents to a clerk taking dictation. Finished, he brings the page down just over the fire, and it bursts into flames. Black tatters flutter up to the ceiling. After repeating this several times, Woodwind sets down his tweezers and looks at the Divinity Student in irritation.

The Divinity Student offers him the letters. Woodwind tweezes them out of his hands, opens the envelopes with a few deft strokes and studies the writing offhandedly. Then he drops both the letters into the flame and they vanish brightly, Woodwind snapping his fingers for his secretary.

"The register the register," he mutters.

Woodwind's secretary appears with an overstuffed ledger and flips hastily to a page half covered in meticulous illegible handwriting. Woodwind himself scans down the page with his tweezers, looking up only at the end.

"Yes we have an opening for a word-finder," he says in punctilious monotone.

Offered, accepted. Woodwind snatches up another page from the book in front of him and dredges it in the pan. The secretary presses a small buzzer on the wall; a thin reedy tone trills across the room. Within a few moments the young woman from downstairs appears at the door, and, directed by a hurried gesture from the secretary, walks over to him.

The Divinity Student looks back at Woodwind and his clerks, another flash of burning paper.

"I've been hired."

She inclines her head a little to her left.

"You'll be the new word-finder then."

He has nothing to say. He nods.

She is satisfied and extends her hand.

"Let me show you."

He follows her into the hall and up the stairs to the fourth floor landing. The red walls narrow until he's hunching his shoulders inwards to get past. Her perfume is wafting back in her wake, passing in currents over his face until he feels ready to topple over backwards. Finally they come to a small door in a cul-de-sac, set directly into the center of the wall. She turns to open it for him; he looks intently into her face, her bookish face, which returns his gaze calmly. The doorway is narrow, he has to brush up against her to get into the room, passing through a curtain of her perfume and the serene scrutiny of her sphinxlike gaze. He steps up onto a high scuffed floor, and she smiles as he turns back to her.

"Come on." She walks across the small office with its low ceiling to the back wall, a little window there with asymmetrical panes, shining with dusty light that seems to collect within the membrane of her blouse, making it glow like a paper lantern. She indicates a desk to him.

Slowly, he follows. There are three other desks in the room, a man at each, transferring columns of words from notebooks into codices by hand. Their presence is irritating, reminding him of the Seminary: the insect-scratching of their fountain pens, sleeves rubbing along word-wooden corners rattling papers. He steps up beside her, standing in a warm pool of light. With a modest gesture, she pulls his chair out for him, like a maitre d'.

"You should find everything you need in the desk," she says in a low voice, as if she doesn't want the others to hear.

He thanks her.

"Anything else?" Eyebrows raised, a small shake of her head. He stares blankly back

She nods pleasantly.

"Yes, that's all. Any word that you encounter in your daily rounds that's not in the dictionaries should be recorded in your ledger. New words only, please."

She stands upright again, looking down at him. She stares at him. Then she leans down close to his face and wishes him good luck. A moment later she vanishes out the door and down the stairs.

As soon as the door is shut, one of the others wheezes and snorts. His partner giggles. The Divinity Student opens his desk, finding a notebook with the first dozen pages or so ripped out, a new fountain pen and ink bottle, and a huge binder with a sheaf of paper unopened beside it. Underneath the notebook, there is a small leather-bound dictionary in impossibly tiny print with a magnifying glass tethered to it by a faded ribbon. He pockets this and the notebook and reaches for the filing drawer.

One of the other 'finders clears his throat.

The Divinity Student looks up. It's the one who snorted as the woman left. He's heavy with short black hair and a threadbare black sweater, a pale, doughy face with small black eyes like currants. He rises from his desk.

"Switch desks with me! Yours is bigger!"

The one who giggled is looking on conspiratorially, grinning.

"You deaf? I said I'll take your desk! I waited, didn't I?" He briefly turns to the giggler, who nods once, "I didn't take it right away—I don't think *you* want to give me any trouble!"

The Divinity Student fills his fountain pen calmly. He is already ignoring them.

"Hey, I'm talking to you!" The snorter says.

The Divinity Student pockets the pen and caps the ink bottle.

The snorter stares at him a moment, then sits back down at his desk again. "Idiot," he mutters.

Chapter 3: The Car

Pausing in mid-stride, two black dogs stare at the Divinity Student as he emerges from the office. Recoiling, he claps his hands and steps backwards into the threshold; they scrabble headlong down the stairs with clicking feet—a bad omen. With a rustle of papers, he recollects himself and follows them down slowly. At the bottom of the stairs there's a secondary door opening out onto a narrow street, old plaster walls leaning in to meet overhead, windows and sagging trellises, washing on lines, a thin trickle of people weaving out towards the plaza. He steps over an old drunk wordfinder, hands tattooed with old words in blue ink.

"I'm interested in rivers," he says without looking up.

Eyes on the cobbles, the Divinity Student makes his way to the corner, smelling food and garbage. There's a small cafe, two walls open to the street, scuffed white-and-orange checkerboard tiles reach to the low curb, a field of sturdy white metal tables and chairs with the occasional long-faced readers and chess players. He notes that some of these are playing against mechanized opponents.

"Chess is a game of competing algorithms," he thinks, "one piece is gradually predetermined by the action of play to end the game, either in checkmate or stalemate. And all pieces are agents, like me."

The Divinity Student navigates fast to the counter, at chin-level above glass display cases smeared with white transparent finger and palm marks. A willowy wall-eyed student takes his order and his money without looking at him, assures him it will be brought to his table, and disappears.

He turns and finds a seat close to the street, grown quiet and still. Across the plaza he can see crowds of miniature silhouettes frothing around the buildings as cloud shadows glide flexibly across gleaming stone courtyards. The city settles quiescent in the early afternoon. He turns his attention to the pocket lexicon, flipping through at random: "afflatus", "epiclesis", "soteriology"—these he knows—"ylem" catches in his throat; a kid in a coarse white apron clatters the tray down in front of him and shuffles off, drawing his nose along his sleeve. Alone again, the Divinity Student pours smoky-looking tea through a sieve over three sugar cubes. Two leathery, triangular pouches lie black and brown in grease on his plate. He cuts into one with his knife and steaming oil dribbles out; a spicy smell, tiny white curls that look like pearly onions inside, and some soft blue powder. He eats quickly, burning his tongue. For some reason he still needs to eat.

Were it not for the coppery hair thatching his head, Mr. Ollimer would be unrecognizable—of all the people he has ever met, not one of them can place him in their memories save by the color of his hair. In feature, figure, dress and behavior, nothing immediately remarkable, as empty of distinction as a technical drawing. He is the third word-finder upstairs at Woodwind's, apart from the giggler and the snorter. The Divinity Student looks up to see him standing expectantly by a nearby table, eyebrows up. Their eyes meet.

"Do you mind if I join you?" Ollimer asks seriously.

The Divinity Student raises his right hand in a small wave indicating the chair opposite him; Ollimer rushes to sit, nodding, looking down.

Ollimer toys with a napkin; he's groping for words.

"Those bastards," he finally says in a birdlike voice. "I was transferred only last week and of course I had to end up with them. They pulled the same tomfoolery with me about *my* desk."

The Divinity Student responds with another gesture, eyebrows up, a small frown, slight inclination of his hands.

"They started talking about you the moment you left the office, but I wouldn't worry." Ollimer flicked a look at him. "They won't dare give you any trouble as long as they think you've got Miss Woodwind's favor."

"Miss Woodwind?"

"Yes—the secretary—don't you remember?"

"I meant to say I didn't know she was related to—"

"—Oh yes, I'm sorry, I misunderstood—yes, she's his daughter." Ollimer rocks forward and backward as he speaks.

The Divinity Student's gaze drifts off, follows two Koreans passing, carrying a drum.

"I just met her. How could I have won her favor?" he says after a moment.

Ollimer pouts and thinks a moment. "Her demeanor around you, I suppose. She's fairly peremptory with us . . ." Ollimer leans in closer and taps the table with his finger, "You really ought to take advantage of that, if she genuinely does favor you. There are advantages . . ."

"You've never been her favorite."

Ollimer grins as if the Divinity Student had made a joke. "Oh no, certainly not me."

The Divinity Student tips his head back and gazes up past the rooftops to the sky's racing white and blue.

"Where did you receive your training?" Ollimer leans his elbows on the table and holds his hands in front of his face.

"I'm a Divinity Student."

Ollimer looks around cautiously. A car with tinted, impenetrable windows pulls up in the alley almost immediately; its idling engine sets the table thrumming. Ollimer hisses something inaudible under the noise.

"What?"

"Listen!" Cutting his right hand sideways in the air, close to the table, he speaks in a tight whisper, "You're serious? You were trained at the Seminary?"

"Yes."

"Listen! I must speak with you later! I know some people—"

The car revs its engine, backing into the alley and then jerking forward again, over and over, garbage squelching under the tires, people dodging out of the way. Ollimer casts a panicky look over his shoulder, and repents immediately.

"Oh now I've done it! I look suspicious!" he moans. "I've got to be going!"

He holds his hand out. The Divinity Student looks at it as if he doesn't understand. Panic flashes in Ollimer's eyes, he waves his hand desperately at the Divinity Student, and just barely exposes a business card concealed in his palm. The Divinity Student takes Ollimer's moist hand and palms the card, slipping it into the pocket lexicon with one fluid, inconspicuous motion. Ollimer waves timidly and walks quickly back towards the office, weaving and wiping his face. Suddenly, the car breaks its jerking back and forth and swings wildly forward, blaring its horn and flaring its headlights, onto the curb, sending tables flying; the Divinity Student runs out into the plaza knocking his table in the path of the shrieking car lurching over mangled chairs towards him. He makes straight for the nearest alley and gets clear, vanishing into a million streets.

Chapter 4: The Dream

IN DEEPENING SHADES OF blue the day burns off into space and the stars flare one by one. The Divinity Student watches the sky's well clear from a hammock he has rigged between a fire escape and a drain pipe five stories above an empty alleyway. Incidental headlights pass at the end of the alley, filtered through the slats of a makeshift fence, sending thin vertical bands of light floating left to right over the brick walls or pouring through a single window close to where he is hanging, illuminating the featureless upper corner of a white plaster box of a room. The Divinity Student can't afford a place of his own.

Lulled by these tides of light he drifts off, face upwards. Initially, he couldn't bear to look at the sky, afraid he'd fall up into the black air, falling so high he'd burst, but now he's up there already, the stars all around him, close enough to touch, humming and sparking at him like millions of brilliant little machines.

Lying there, he slowly becomes aware of a slippery feeling; he's covered with oil, clear oil oozing out of his skin, and it's soaking into his clothes—he can't afford to ruin his clothes, they're all he's got! He undresses as quickly as he can swinging in his hammock, piling up his garments at his feet, drops a sock but with surprising agility he snaps it up and tosses it back into the hammock. Naked now he stops himself, staring at his arm, and now his legs and feet, and all the rest of him—he's turned powder-white. It's pigment, like flour under his skin, white as wax and coated with clear mineral oil, dripping off his fingers, getting into his eyes and making them smart, even the hair on his head is slick with it; the rest of his body is hairless. Confused and shivering with cold, he manages to squat in the hammock, hugging his knees. The wind plays over his body and he gets another surprise—something on his back. What's happening to him?

The wind is playing over his back, delineating his form in the air, and there's something changed back there. He reaches his arm around and runs the palm down his wet skin, and feels deep fissures and ridges. He peers over his shoulder and sees his ghostly reflection in a window. Three huge dorsal vents slant down on each side of his spine, yawning open and upwards like gill slits, white skin stretched tight over powerful curves: funnels of skin and muscle held out by fans of cartilage. He crouches down and presses his hands to his head, breathing heavily and shuddering as he feels the vents twitching horribly. As he breathes he feels the vents breathing moistly, drawing air in and forcing it out through narrower openings along his sides. He screws his eyes shut and presses his hand to his mouth, filled with transparent teeth with fluorescent blue and red veins and flickering silver nerves.

He crouches frozen in place, afraid to lie down thinking he might crush the vents on his back. Panicking he starts gasping for breath, his chest is being squeezed shut, and across his back the vents jerk open, cold night air sucks in and rushes out the small openings on his sides. Faster and faster the air sluices through as he gasps for breath, stronger and stronger until the pressure pushes him up off the hammock, his legs straightening, and he rises straight up into the sky on columns of night air. The city expands below him, he passes through its lights and further into the ocean of colorless light limning the bottom of the clouds. He aims straight up, his arms at his sides, straining with effort and petrified that any moment he'll plummet to earth. A tiny white line in the sky, he keeps his body straight and slants up at the clouds. The cloud ceiling doesn't budge, muddy and silver, refusing to come closer. He charges at it with all his might; he attacks the clouds and strikes straight to the heart of them, with air running over him pushing oil into rivulets along his back and sides; he blinks it out of his eyes. With all his might he pushes himself up, scarcely thinking about what he's doing, everything fades, and he loses himself in the effort, and then moments later he remembers that he's flying and it overwhelms him, nearly sending him toppling headlong out of the sky.

Finally after an eternity of struggling, vapor closes around him like curtains of water, boding rest—he's been holding his breath, now he lets it out in humid air and breaks through. The cloud comes up beneath to support him and he falls to his knees, vomits clear, sweet gelatin from the exertion of flying.

Spectral light on a cloud landscape, a thunderhead in the distance is the highest peak in a chain of mountains from the south, wispy cloud trees stand frozen along streams of mist. Atop a nearby hill, Mr. Woodwind lies sleeping wrapped in white blankets, a white garland on his brow. Miss Woodwind emerges from beneath a tree. As she draws near the breeze brings him the smell of her perfume.

"He's sleeping," she says softly and raises her eyebrows at him. The moon emerges and her face blurs as she comes closer, hair framing a glowing indistinct face. Her hair pats her brow in a light breeze that bathes him in her milky breath.

THE SNORTER, WHOSE NAME is Householder, and the giggler, whose name is Blandings, squat in one corner of the office, shoes in hand, bashing clumsily at a rat. They've been hunting rats all day, joking with each other and drinking. Ollimer had shivered when the Divinity Student arrived; he still pores over his notes without looking up, the top of his red head jerking back and forth, from his notebook to his lexicon and back again. Householder hits on a new game, filling his mouth with ink and spraying it on the walls for fun. The giggler's running for his bottle when Miss Woodwind wafts into the office. She cocks a finger at Householder and smiles. He pats the giggler on the back and sets his ink bottle on his desk, following her out; as he reaches the door he turns once to grin back into the office, his teeth stained with ink. The giggler returns to his seat, smiling and shaking his head. The day passes.

The Divinity Student finishes his work and leaves the office twenty minutes later. He hasn't gotten down the block before Ollimer catches up with him, peering over his shoulder.

"We were interrupted yesterday. I need to talk with you."

The Divinity Student keeps going, doesn't look at him.

"I've been reproaching myself ever since we parted. I ought to have warned you about the cars the minute you told me you were a Divinity Student."

"Why didn't you? Did you think it better to let me learn by example?"

"No! I assumed that you'd know about them, or that you might have been briefed about them before you came here."

"Why did you assume that?"

"I'm sorry. I've said I ought to have warned you." He touches the Divinity Student's sleeve with a plaintive look. "Won't you listen to me now?"

The Divinity Student keeps walking with his head down, and nods after a moment. He blinks, as if noticing Ollimer for the first time.

Ollimer puts his hands in his pockets.

"I've never met a Seminarian before. It must be exciting! Do you have any, uh, *special* knowledge?"

A crash shatters along the alley walls, Ollimer starts and whirls, but it's only a delivery boy—tripped and broke a vase. Ollimer is about to dismiss it, then he turns slowly to face the Divinity Student.

"You didn't have anything to do with that, did you?" he asks, pointing at the boy gathering glass behind him.

"Coincidence," is all the Divinity Student says shrugging, turning, walking towards the plaza. They go together, neither speak.

The plaza is empty, voices are faintly audible in a distant sussuration from its borders, the babble of the fountain laughing across polished black pavement, their footfalls and the wind tugging at their coats the only sounds.

Ollimer steps out in front of him. "Listen, come with me to my aunt's house—I want you to see something."

"We're due back."

"Woodwind won't care—please."

They cross the plaza and thread their way through the vendors on Glass Street, duck into a side passage too narrow for them both to walk abreast.

"There'll be no cars here," Ollimer tosses over his shoulder.

Moving fast now, at a slow jog, the Divinity Student wonders if Ollimer isn't planning something. The walls are smooth, with no doors or windows above, the sky is a dim, narrow beam. Ollimer moves rapidly, kicking newspapers. The passage gradually slopes downwards, finally into a sooty black aperture . . . a stale, bitter smell trails out of it in gritty, gray threads, leaving a sterile taste in his mouth. Ollimer vanishes in shadow below, and he follows with caution.

The tunnel is short, light from the far end only a few yards away, a squat vertical shaft with an iron ladder stapled to a brick wall.

"After you." Ollimer graciously indicates the rungs. He's more buoyant here in his element.

The Divinity Student doesn't trust him. "I insist," he says, holding out his hand.

Ollimer nimbly scales the ladder and the Divinity Student follows behind him.

They emerge in a vacant lot bordered by a rough plank fence, anonymous buildings visible beyond, a scorched brick house at their backs, fronted by a rickety flight of steps, a spidery web of light playing over the scarred bricks. Ollimer watches the Divinity Student's face a moment, then nods and makes for the stairs. They ascend past stagnant-water windows, mostly empty rooms save for one on the third floor, where a dark-haired woman is ironing. The uppermost landing opens on a bright yellow door. Ollimer takes out his heavy key ring and unlocks it.

The Divinity Student steps into a small well-lit room with gold wallpaper and huge potted plants. Plush red furniture and shining mahogany wood, Persian rugs and aging photographs on the walls—it's like a dollhouse.

Ollimer's aunt Marigold is staring at the hearth, her smooth face and fine white hair flickering orange and gold in the firelight over a clean print dress and cameo brooch.

She turns a listless eye on him.

"This is a friend of mine, from the office—he's a Divinity Student!"

She is waving distractedly at the sideboard. "John . . ." Her voice is toneless and far away, ". . . my needle, John . . ."

Ollimer turns to the sideboard and brings her the needle and a small perfume bottle half-filled with clear liquid. She takes them with a lugubrious air and begins drawing the fluid into the syringe.

Ollimer cordially indicates a seat.

The Divinity Student takes the offered chair, while Ollimer busies himself with a tea tray. Eventually, they come to be sitting opposite each other, the tray between them, Ollimer leaning into the rising steam.

"Now I'll tell you about the Catalog!" he says with relish. "You being from the Seminary, you'll understand how important this is!"

"I'm listening."

"All right. I'm not certain who else knows about the Catalog, but I can assure you, there's none who knows more about it than me. I obviously can't discuss how I came to know about it, but rest assured it's absolutely genuine.

"What I'm talking about is a Catalog of unknown words—they're secret words, ghost-words, and completely new. I'm not at liberty to tell you who compiled it, or for what purpose, but I've been authorized to offer you some access to it."

The Divinity Student leans forward, his coat billowing around him in the chair. He stares at Ollimer.

Ollimer's aunt sighs over the thrumming of the fire.

"So where is it? Who has it?" he asks.

". . . You must understand, what's essential is to maintain the spirit of the thing, maintaining the spirit of the Catalog through practice . . ."

"That doesn't answer my question. You don't have it."

"Me? Oh, no, naturally not."

"Who does?"

Ollimer hesitates. With slow and deliberate motion, the Divinity Student produces his old black leather Seminary Edition of the Holy Book and holds it up between them. Ollimer's eyes flick between his face and the book.

"Don't forget who I am."

Ollimer looks at the book, his face pinched.

"No more games—tell me."

He lowers the book and Ollimer wavers back into his chair.

"The Catalog was destroyed . . . a few years ago . . ." he says hoarsely, suddenly unable to lie.

"Then what am I doing here?! Who cares?!"

"Please, don't be angry with me, I'm not strong enough for that!"

Tears shine in the corner of Ollimer's eyes. He wrings his hands plaintively.

"I'm sorry—they tell me so little, I really know next to nothing about it!"

"Are they from the Seminary?"

"I don't know—one of them seems to be a priest."

The Divinity Student is silent. In the dim light of the parlor his face glows faintly.

"They must have given you a fragment to show me," he says finally.

Ollimer nods, blinking. "Yes, I don't know anything about it, actually. I've had it for years—you're not the first, just the most qualified—"

"How am I qualified?" The Divinity Student's face flares white, his voice dry and spare.

"I don't know. It's all something very learned, I don't understand it, I don't have the education. Do you know what they mean? Is it that you know Greek, something like that?"

"What did they tell you to do?"

"To show you the fragment, that's all. They say things are still falling into place; they're waiting before they tell you anything more. Everything's a secret with them, no one knows more than they need to—they're afraid of the *cars*. The cars are on to you already, they suspect you, you'll have to be careful. I'm sorry if I'm talking a lot! I don't want to waste your time!"

Ollimer stands up.

"I feel such a strong desire to confide in you!" he says in an embarrassed, half-laughing gasp. "I suppose I'm a bit in awe of you. We'd better go into my room." Ollimer glances at his aunt.

The Divinity Student follows him down a tiny hallway to a boxy bedroom. Ollimer kneels on the floor and produces, from under his bed, a small tin chest with a padlock; he opens it and moves over to his desk. The light from the lamp shines up on his face, making it strange.

"Here."

He opens a leather wallet and gingerly draws out a scrap of paper. The Divinity Student accepts it from him and sits down to read it. It is half of a sheet of notebook paper, with one corner torn off, taking with it most of the first word. All that is left are the last three letters, "-nia," and the definition:

"In the middle of the night, a beautiful young woman was wakened from a deep sleep, in an empty house, by a sharp pounding on her bedroom door. Upon opening the door, she saw only the empty hallway, no one anywhere along its length, or anywhere in the house. She went back to her room and shut the door behind her, but she had not taken her hand from the doorknob when the pounding sounded again even louder, nearly knocking her over. She immediately flung the door open, and again saw no one—except for a black and white spider hanging from a thread directly in front of the door."

The Divinity Student looks at Ollimer.

Ollimer had watched him reading.

"You see? I-it's a word that can only be defined by a story. The word doesn't represent that sequence of events—but rather it names what that sequence *suggests*."

"Is that what you were told to say?"

Ollimer doesn't answer.

"The page is torn, what was the word?"

"I don't know. I'm sorry, that's all there is."

The Divinity Student gives the fragment back and stands up, pacing over to the other side of the room while Ollimer replaces everything as it had been.

"Have you told me everything?"

"Yes—they just want you to think about it. Are you interested?"

The Divinity Student is thinking.

Chapter 5: The Priest

THE NEXT DAY, A gray little clerk shuffles into the office and beckons to the Divinity Student. The others give him peculiar looks as he leaves the room, wending his way out back to the library, where Mr. Woodwind crouches over an ancient book with a miniature knife, scraping ink samples from illuminated characters. He gathers the flakes of dried ink on the edge of the blade and deposits them in glass dishes filled with different solutions, watching them react and change color. The rest he heats on a small metal pan until they glow in the flame and combust.

Eventually, Woodwind notices him. "You, you're from the Seminary? I need you to take these to the high priest of San Veneficio. His office is in the Orpheum." Woodwind withdraws a black satchel from under the table and thrusts it at him. The Divinity Student has no more than touched the handle before Woodwind turns his back and goes back to his scrapings.

Outside, the air is warm and close and still, rich with orchard smells, and, looking down, he can see the heat boil all around him, rising in curling threads, shimmering around his shadow on the pavement. Above, the sky is empty: a fathomless, midnight blue color, some dark birds circling. The streets are unusually empty, and no cars watch him go, making his way down to Calavera Street in the center of town. He can see the Orpheum approaching over the rooftops, coruscating in the hot air. It's a palace and a theater, with screens and stages; inside, cool night air coils in deep purple velvets and muted blue satins of curtains and chairs, mingling with the clean smell of water tossed from a few small stone fountains, and sometimes spiced with a faint warm breath of someone drifting in from the frying street to press his face against cool stone and sit on cool plush seats. Like a gem set in the middle of town, the first public building in San Veneficio, the Orpheum rests today as it always has at the midpoint of Calavera Street, surrounded by peppery-smelling trees, some with reddish-black leaves, others adorned only with blue flowers, petrified now like coral in the light. The Divinity Student looks at the Orpheum with difficulty, so much of it is lost in white smears of reflected light from the polished marble and the huge dome, carved from a single vast piece of green jade. Blinking in the searing light, he can see the statues hiding in alcoves, heavy basalt pillars supporting the facade: Orpheus soberly in the center—on his right, a smaller image where he enchants the animals and all of nature with his playing, and on his left, his head sings, drifting on river foam.

The sun's burden lifts from the Divinity Student as he passes into the shade of the pillars and the muted light within. He enters the main hall directly, huge and round with many doors set into its circumference both along the floor and above on the central gallery. High overhead, the dome glows green; translucent sheets of white marble set like windowpanes fill the room with warm diffused lambence. Water runs in thin sheets over the pillars supporting the upper concourse, collecting in a ring-shaped pool. On one wall, Circe is beguiling a crowd, already a handful at the edges are turning into pigs. On the other is Medusa, turning men to stone. A statue of Orpheus stands in the center of the room. The Divinity Student gets directions to the high priest's office from a young docent in a black uniform.

So, he pads up a wide, curving stairway, bypassing the public rooms to make straight for the gray, rounded service passages beyond. Soft red floors, light dapples the walls like water-reflections, a museum smell of fresh paint, and over all a deep hush, save for an occasional courier rushing by on whispering feet. He follows the passage to its end, and there finds the high priest's door set in a funnel-shaped wall. The nameplate reads: Magellan. The door is wine-colored wood with brass hinges. He raises his hand to knock, but the door is already opening; a hairless little man peers up at him with large eyes.

"Yes?" Voiceless.

"I've come from Woodwind's." his quiet reply.

"You're the Seminarian?" The words seem to bypass the air and sound in the Divinity Student's ears directly. He nods.

The other nods and gestures for him to enter. The ceiling slopes down to meet with the top of the door jam; the room is shaped like a funnel—the far wall is an ellipse three stories high into which is set a circular window with a pane fragmented into hundreds of palm-sized pieces of varying thicknesses and shapes, a gigantic eye. Immediately before this window is Magellan's huge desk and before that are seats for visitors, one of which is currently occupied by a nondescript client. A few others wait in chairs along the wall to the right. Magellan's familiar waves the Divinity Student to an empty chair and scuttles off to the wings—where racks of jars stand in static dust: later the familiar will tell his wife, "Today I saw a bottle containing a witch." A witches' ladder, a rope with cockfeathers woven in between the strands, throws curses. An impaled slug on a thorn, in a jar, withered, colorless, still, in formaldehyde. Shelves of stuffed animals, motheaten, ragged, semicollapsed, dirty, glazed milky eyes. Flat glass slabs for the invertebrates—fish, eels, worms, phosphorescent. On every surface, tiny, neatly penned labels in precambrian ink, dark jumbles.

The Divinity Student then sees Magellan. He sits almost invisible in a haze of window-refracted light; fragrant smoke curls about his head, wafting up from two braziers burning on his desk. He's of no certain age, in his shirtsleeves and suspenders, and his face is painted white, white with black marks around his eyes, and his upper lip is also black. His eyelids have been painted with two green irises and black pupils, making it impossible to tell whether his eyes are open or closed.

The client's voice breaks the silence. He's looking down into his lap, a little embarrassed.

"Uh show me what it's like to be uh—" he looks up at the high priest, "—a cat."

The familiar runs up from the wings with a large jar. Inside, the Divinity Student can see a marmalade-colored cat preserved in formaldehyde. With a slight bow, the familiar sets the jar on the desk and retreats again.

Magellan, moving for the first time, slowly twists the lid off the jar and sets it down on the desk. A thin, sour smell rises from the open jar and trickles in to the Divinity Student's nostrils, pushing him a little back in his chair as if a little had just seeped into his skull. Magellan gets ponderously to his feet and dips his fingers into the jar. He slaps the air twice with the back of his hand, spattering the supplicant's face with formaldehyde. Magellan scoops a little in the palm of his hand, brings his painted face down, and blows it in the man's face like an atomizer.

The client remains perfectly still, breathing deeply as the spray settles on his face. After a moment he begins to sway in the chair, his breathing alters, and for a time he sits there entranced. Magellan lowers himself back into his chair. The jar is resealed and spirited away, the cat inside jostling, fur pressed flat against the glass, face shrunken and vacated. The incense floats up to the ceiling, the window burns with light, the client's head falling back in slow motion . . . Magellan's fixed gaze. Watching, again the Divinity Student is overcome with the feeling that he is watching something vital to his unknown cause. He feels himself being drawn toward Magellan.

Eventually, the man's trance lifts. He rises unsteadily, struggling to speak, but Magellan isn't looking at him. So he turns, almost bending forward as if to bound off on all fours, but no, he catches himself—he weaves his way to the door and is gone.

The familiar appears again, and beckons the Divinity Student up to the desk, again without speaking, until he is within only a few feet of the high priest.

After a few moments, the familiar looks at the Divinity Student with impatience, gesturing at the satchel. The Divinity Student rustles around in the bag—empty, except for a velvet pouch, incongruously rich in the raggedy bag. He hands it queryingly to the familiar, who raises a cautionary finger to his lips and rolls his eyes at Magellan, who sits still and blank as a statue. The familiar opens the pouch, and pours out a dozen thin ivory wafers, each with a single word written on it. They are instantly sorted by the man's long, gray fingers, lining them up on the desk: verbs first, then nouns, then qualifiers, every one set in place with a single, precise tap. Then out comes a long wooden box from under his skirts that flips open to reveal an index of ivory wafers to which the new twelve are added in exact order, in exactly the right places. And throughout, he has not lifted his gaze from the Divinity Student.

"No one speaks freely to the high priest," he says, "not even myself." His voice is level and even, eyes animal-bright.

"Those who petition may only use words from this index," pausing a moment to point at the box, "so as not to profane his ears."

He snaps the box shut.

"I know all the words, I have practiced, now I use no others. It is second nature to me."

The Divinity Student looks beyond him to Magellan, unable to tell if his eyes are open or closed.

"Have you a petition? Answer yes or no."

He thinks of his flying dream, and of Ollimer's word, and in the grip of an inscrutable impulse he says: "Yes."

The familiar brings the box back out, but the Divinity Student shakes his head and beckons with his finger. He can feel the smaller man's hand resting dry and light, like a bird, on his back as he leans close to whisper his message.

With a nod and a swirl of his robe, the familiar retreats into the wings. Now the Divinity Student is alone with Magellan, smoke between them and around them, light crashing down through the fragmented window. The Divinity Student feels an inky feeling inside, a draining in his head, the closeness of the air, looking at the high priest sitting there like a monument. So, he sits too, and gazes fascinated at Magellan's silent face. He bites back a desire to ask him about Ollimer's word.

Instead, one hand on the desk, he leans in, and speaking quietly says, "Show me what it's like to fly."

Again, Magellan stands. A jar is brought to him, this time with a buzzard pickled in it. The same thin odor steams out as the lid is twisted off, only this smell is different, dry and pungent where the cat smelled almost sweet. He swallows with difficulty watching Magellan's great hands dipping into the formaldehyde—abruptly he thinks it's time to go, he doesn't want to anymore, but those hands come out dripping, thinking it's time get up and get out, too late, cool drops spattering his face, that smell burning his nose, rushing up behind his eyes, and Magellan's dreaming, painted face coming at him now, eyes open, the palm comes up, fine vapor shimmers his face, vertigo like a fast elevator, the weight of his body lifts and he's cut adrift, curling around Magellan's head like incense smoke, breath leaving, heart leaving, the light sucks him away, right away without a trace, or would, but Magellan holds him. Now he sees the window's fragments of glass and fragments of light focus through the back of Magellan's head, beaming out of his face, tinted green where it shines through his eyes, pink and white where it shines through his face—the desert white under the sun, blurring by underneath, the pull of the wind, hot air rising, motion on the plain's floor between the hills, water on the horizon. Turning and rising for a long time, getting high past the hilltops, and hungry, watching the ground, sun just rising. There's a twinge in his back. Seeing farther and farther, nothing but him and the air, the horizon around his shoulders and dwindling behind his feet. As time goes on he gets to feel the air currents, upswells and churnings on all sides and below. In a moment he sees himself as high as the sun, harmless clouds on all sides, stiffness spreading across his shoulders and outstretched wings. Lightheaded he has an impulse to fly straight up, but at that moment he spies a bleached and torn carcass on the ground, and hungrily he drops in a twisting dive his stomach lurching.

Weight, and breath, and pulse come back. Magellan sits alone and still at the desk in front of him. The familiar has closed the jar and is shuffling back into the wings with it, light dwindling with the day's passing. The Divinity Student sits without moving, looking numbly across at Magellan, until he is told to leave.

Chapter 6: The Oro

He has lost himself in the streets, wandering out toward the city limits. Eventually he comes to himself, doesn't know where he is, the pavement ends and before him a small grove of old oak trees stands in dappled shadows. There's nobody around, so he ventures out onto the grass, feels its coolness through his shoes, lets the branches brush the top of his head. To him the trees smell dusty, like a familiar old room, they dust the air with their branches and fill the grove with a white haze. He remembers the vertigo of flying, Magellan's dreaming face, sour formaldehyde smell. The Divinity Student looks back, but he can't see the pavement anywhere—there's not a rooftop or spire to be seen. He starts retracing his steps, trying to follow his footprints in the long grass. Everywhere he turns, more trees and corkscrew branches screening his view. It's quiet, no street sounds, no sign of the city at all, and with a growing sense of disorientation he breaks into a run, but his path criss-crosses itself in the grass.

He has a sensation of icy water rilling down his back and rinsing his insides, water for flesh, flesh filled with water. Panic boils wildly behind his teeth; he shakes himself, why is he overreacting? The sudden onslaught of fear confuses him still more.

Then a tree rattles behind him; he turns to look. There's a black something up in the boughs, watching him. He sees many dark limbs, leaf-green eyes, a porcelain mouth with fixed lips parted in an open grin.

He recognizes it: an oro, a tree-spirit, misdirecting him into the heart of the glade and forcing panic on him. Instantly, the cold inside evaporates, a raindrop, a single one, drops into his right eye, and his hand moves to the book in his coat pocket.

"Please don't." A voice like rustling leaves and sighing boughs. "I want to talk to you, let's not fight over a social call."

"I'll listen."

Limbs spiral around the stationary spider-head. "I've got a message for you."

The Divinity Student waits, right hand resting on the book in his pocket. "Well?"

The white mouth moves closer, the emerald eyes remain where they were, lambent in the shade. "Divinity Student, you have been to see Magellan? He showed you something interesting?"

"Yes, that's true," he replies guardedly.

"Would you like to know how it's done?"

The Divinity Student sighs and sits on the ground, but he does not take his hand from the book. Yes, he would like to know, but he says nothing.

"Magellan himself will teach you . . . provided you approach him properly."

"Did he send you?"

". . . No . . . But listen—I can tell you how to convince him."

"Who did send you then?"

The oro retreats a little into the leaves. "That's not important. I couldn't tell you if I wanted to anyway—but I *can* tell you how to get Magellan's attention."

"All right, what am I supposed to do?"

A long, skinny, black arm unfolds from the tree, carefully to set a small wooden box just beyond the circle of shadow at the base of the trunk. Then the oro gathers its arm back to itself.

"Play this in the courtyard of the Orpheum, at the very top of Calavera Street, and let him see you playing it—then he will know to call you. You must not speak to him, the box alone should be your voice. He'll send for you in his own way, and then he'll teach you how to do that trick. Rest assured!" The eyes go out, the mouth is gone.

The Divinity Student jumps up. With caution, he approaches the tree, but the oro is dead gone. Turning, he can see rooftops angling into the sky beyond the trees again, and the pavement appearing again at the edge of the grove, sunset warming the dark wooden box at his feet.

DOGS' SUDDEN BARKING AND he's startled out of his reverie—they're across the street behind a chain-link fence, snapping at some passing man, a red-haired man. The Divinity Student peers after him a moment, and then ducks into a doorway, chasing still with his eyes—it's Ollimer, walking toward the edge of town.

Dry wind sends dead leaves scattering. The Divinity Student walks through them making no sound, following Ollimer. The other man is nervous, looking over his shoulder and sometimes turning all the way around every few blocks; he's hard to follow. Overhead the sky is turning a metallic twilight color; orange lights open in doorways and windows; the pedestrians thin out; cooking smells on dry desert wind billow on his face; Ollimer turns and freezes—the Divinity Student ducks behind a gargoyle. Was he seen? Crouching in the dark, behind a hunched back and folded leather wings, he leans forward to peer over its haunch. Ollimer is staring up the street at nothing. Then just as abruptly as it came, his trance seems to pass and he gets going again.

The Divinity Student lets him go on a bit more, and then starts after. Turning a corner, the road ends, he stops—oak trees spreading in the spectral light beyond the pavement, grass white and black, the same dust shining in the air now like tiny silver flakes. Just visible in obscurity are the same domes and spires he saw over the trees at sunset; it's precisely the same place.

Cautiously, he steps into the glade, taking care to avoid the trees. With his black coat drawn close about him he blends in with the dark. Around him the trees whisper as he passes, growing quiet after him. Unsure, he makes his way to the oro's oak. Ollimer is there. The Divinity Student flattens himself on the ground, watching him, completely silent. Ollimer is still apprehensive but he does not notice the Divinity Student.

Hesitant, he starts feeling around inside a hole in the trunk of the oro's tree until his arm is swallowed up to the shoulder. His eyes look upward, the tip of his tongue visible in his straining face as he feels around with his hand. Then he pulls out a scrap of paper and steps into the light, peering at it. After reading it over several times, he pulls out his wallet, stuffs it in, and hurries back up the road.

The Divinity Student takes a different route back into town, knowing that Ollimer will approach him tomorrow with another fragment of the catalog.

THE DIVINITY STUDENT FINDS refuge at an all-night cafe. Chairs and tables spill out in a circle of orange light to fill a corner of Candle Square, lost in San Veneficio's tangle of streets and closed to traffic. A single streetlamp burns at the far corner, the walls all around are dark silhouettes before a more luminous cobalt-colored sky. The interior of the diner is a brightly-lit rectangle cut into the dark, like an aquarium in an unlit room; two sleepy waiters wearing white aprons drift to and fro, tidy up, tend a few late customers, or play dominoes on the counter.

Having given up his hammock, the Divinity Student falls into a chair at the farthest boundary of the lights, and dozes. He has a puzzling, desultory dream about lifeless mountain roads cut into shafts of solid rock and lined with boulders. Once he thinks he can see a tiny window carved in one of the larger stones, and possibly the suggestion of a door as well, with a faint strip of light along the bottom of the jam.

A noise wakes him up—somebody has set a glass down firmly on the table in front of him. Looking up, he sees a big dark-skinned man in a shabby suit of violet satin walking away across the circle of light. He sways over to an elaborate organ under an awning, sits down at the keys, turns a few knobs, and sets it going. In the light from the console, the Divinity Student can make him out—bald and heavy, baby-faced with black filigree tattooed around his eyes. A sign on the organ lights up, "The Clown Filemon" it says. Little blue and yellow lights wink over the organ pipes and keys, luminous strands of clear syrup draw a web in the air over his head, clinging to rigid silver wires, and translucent tubes, gathered around the console, glow with bubbling, phosphorescent green liquid. With slow and deliberate motions, Filemon begins playing—a mysterious, confidential humming in the pipes—but his eyes remain fixed, watching the Divinity Student. After a few minutes, he makes a quick gesture, as if lifting a glass to his lips, and jerks his head at him.

The Divinity Student looks up, and then picks up the glass in front of him—all right so far?

Filemon nods, and raises his eyebrows.

The Divinity Student empties the glass.

Filemon smiles and goes back to his playing, soft and low, for nighttime.

The Divinity Student settles back and listens to the music washing down onto him. A few moments, and then he pulls out the box. He looks up at Filemon, but the clown is watching the keys. He opens the box, and instantly the mechanism emits a clicking, hollow-timbred melody that merges instantly with Filemon's music. As the Divinity Student shifts his hands over the box, he notices that the tone bends with even the slightest change of a single finger's position. He tries the bottom, but there the box is thickest and there's no change. The edges and corners, which are singed, darker than the rest of the box, not only change the pitch when touched, but also cause a second, parallel tone, breathy and faint, to fill out the first.

As he fiddles with the box, he senses that either the random changes he makes in the melody are starting to complement Filemon's music, or Filemon is anticipating him. He starts pressing the box more deliberately, the organ follows, the notes begin to weave around each other, the Divinity Student begins to decipher the pattern of the notes, and they play together.

When he next looks up from the box, it's dawn. The music winds down, until finally they end on a single chord. They sit still a moment, listening to the sound ripple along the surface of the surrounding buildings, trickle and fade down the streets. When it is gone, Filemon shuts the organ off, smiling down at the keyboard in satisfaction. The Divinity Student puts the box back in his coat and sits back in the chair again, then looks over at the Clown. Filemon gets up without looking at him and vanishes into the cafe.

The Divinity Student takes a pad from his coat and writes at random, fragmentary notes about something: "Kill this idea by scrawling it. Happiest man, ribbon, water, droplets/griddle light, chord of music, through body in threads of water—close eye/defocus/reopen/mind-body aphasia momentary discrepancy—flash S.V." He looks up a moment across the street at a spout draining. He stops writing, it stops draining. He starts writing and it starts draining again.

Two tables over, a card game degenerates, two men fling cards angrily at each other.

The Divinity Student rests for a while, and then heads back toward Woodwind's.

Chapter 7: The Lesson

THE DAY IS LONG and slow. The Divinity Student leans over his desk, filling columns of words. Householder is absent, Blandings dozes over his ledger, and Ollimer works with typical diligence in the corner, conspicuously not looking at the Divinity Student.

"He's waiting until after work to approach me," he thinks, yawning dust. Cars race by beneath the one tiny window, rattling the pane—sometimes idling just close enough to set his teeth on edge. Every now and then he remembers the box in his pocket, gets nervous, "What if some car stops me and finds it? Bad enough I'm carrying the Holy Book—bad evidence."

It's hot in the office; he's sweating, but he won't take his coat off. He sits in a column of his own hot air, smell of wool and linen, and a fainter odor of old papers . . . an involuntary spasm jerks his arm, smears a word—remember a blast of light by a Seminary wall, jolted alive again in water? Blandings is looking at him, grinning, and the Divinity Student flips him off, hooking his thumb under his chin and snapping it at him; Blandings just laughs and turns back to his dozing. No good trying to concentrate, his mind chasing after a dozen different things, just killing time. Is Ollimer actually his contact—why wait around? The Clown was sent to teach him how to use the box, make him ready to play it for Magellan.

So he goes for a drink of water, slouching heavily down the stairs, enervated, flat warm water from the cooler flavored with wax from the cup, just transferring weight from the cup to his mouth and down his throat. Miss Woodwind walks by with her ledger. It's thick and tidy, unlike those of the other word-finders with their pages sticking out or dribbling on the floor. She's the best of the lot, has found more words than the rest of them combined, every page in her ledger neatly typed, with no mistakes. As she passes she favors him with a pretty grin and a graceful inclination of her head, fragrance trailing after, think then of father Woodwind sleeping on the clouds, her hair raining on his face in his dream.

He drags himself back up to the office again and stares at his record-book for the remaining hours of the day.

HE LEAVES WOODWIND'S QUICKLY—he doesn't want to get trapped talking to Ollimer again. Once safely lost in San Veneficio's warren of streets, he lets himself drift—today would not be right to go to Magellan, he thinks, "the time is not yet."

This day was dull, flat, and now so is he. Tomorrow will be Saturday, he won't have to go in to work, he can get right with himself before visiting the Orpheum again. The streets spiral him out to the city's limits, this time to mount the encircling wall under the lictors' watchful eyes, glittering behind hexagonal black panes set in their chrome half-masks.

The Divinity Student watches night descend upon the desert's face. The great monitors are just visible, lumbering dark shapes streaking around, positioning themselves for their night-watch. As the lights of San Veneficio come up behind him, he sees their eyes for himself, growing in brilliance like the stars overhead as they reflect the city's luminance back in tiny points. Like statues, they stare at San Veneficio, and at the Divinity Student, and the Divinity Student gazes back, amazed, at them.

Moved by a nameless impulse, he wanders over to a dim lamp hanging from one of the battlements, and draws the book out of his pocket. He reads to them from the first chapters, about the first world. The gray twilight place, trees, and rain. The trees' shadows fill with rain and the rain mixes with dirt until the shadows of the trees take substance in clay. And these shadows, having dimension and substance, begin walking around. They go to the beach, and eventually, an intermediary comes from over the water and makes people out of them, and then leads them through the water up to this world.

He stops there. The monitors' eyes shine impassively back at him, and he puts the book away with a sheepish expression on his face. Those old eyes make him feel stupid, standing there with his book.

The Divinity Student's journal from his school days: "I met a cat dressed like me on a night road—all black but for a white collar, like me in my coat. We stared at each other across the road, orange yellow gold eyes it ran off when a car came, I went into the dark feeling empowered, like an exchange had been made." More recently he added, "Now I see them all the time."

He goes, eats dinner alone, and sleeps in a grotto in the park.

THE MORNING SUN STRIKES colors off the grotto walls and fills the chamber with pale halo-light. The Divinity Student has stripped himself and is bathing in a chuckling brook that spreads its sheet of water across a bed of smooth stone. He emerges glistening white in the new daylight and goes over to the sandy part of the cave, still full in view of the sun. With care, he draws the signatures of three spirits in the sand and kneels between them. He lights a small heap of incense beneath his coat, which hangs from a spur of rock within arms' reach, to cure it in the smoke. He burns likewise a paper prayer next to each of the three signatures. He anoints his hands and forehead with a little oil. Then, he sits still.

Kneeling, he puts his hands together before him and begins a chant from the Seminary—these are words that will trail in the gaps between divine words. The glinting morning air chills his wet skin and chill blooms in ghostly waves over his body and up under the hair on his head. Now, he starts rocking, gently, forwards and backwards, just slightly, just waving a little back and forth, like a blade of grass in a weak breeze, still chanting. The air is quiet. His voice is quiet, touching here and there on the rock walls behind him and humming sometimes at the cavern's rim, just audible over the hush of the stream. The chant rings hollow, the syllables proceeding chromatic in a slow kaleidoscoping pattern of cadence rising and falling. His hands rub together only a little bit, adding a dry, regular whisper of rustling skin pacing the tones. The chant is spiraling up with the smoke from the prayers and the incense to the roof of the grotto, to linger a moment and then drift out into the open air. The sounds all mount together, something nameless growing within them, to mingle with the light that strikes stone and water like a chime. Hands pressed together, fingertips brush brow, mouth, and heart in regular, circular motion, each gesture the same as a syllable, another sound falling, and all regular, nodding back and forth in rhythm, steadily back and forth in rhythm.

The chant ends, but the light, the water, the rhythm stays with him as he gets up, stays with him as he gets dressed and covers the traces, stays with him as he comes clean out of the grotto.

AT THE TOP OF Calavera street, a small portal in the wall of the Orpheum opens onto a miniature courtyard. Above, Magellan's window is visible just beneath the dome, and within the walls, a few young trees in circular planters, the largest, an oak, in the center, and all connected by a stream that flows from a low opening in the inner wall. The paving stones are black, but three concentric gold rings radiate out from the oak-planter in the center, describing a compass. There's no one there at all.

The Divinity Student steps out carefully, coming up close to the wall. He sees movement in the water and freezes—the channels are deep, the stones are smooth and clean, and there is a column of small children gliding slowly by, faces down, propelling themselves with only the barest movements of their golden arms and legs, so that the surface above them remains calm. Startled, the Divinity Student steps back, and then forward to look again. Still they flow by in a steady stream, alone or in pairs, and without needing to come up for air. He watches them, and then he sees it—a single child breaks off and vanishes into the submerged roots of one of the young trees.

These are larval oros, enjoying the relative freedom they are afforded before pupating in the trunk of a tree. Eventually they will emerge as mature adults, varying in form depending on the tree. Oak oros, for example, have porcelain mouths.

With care, he pulls the box out of his pocket, then looks up at the oak tree—and there, rustling, maybe the wind only but perhaps some moving black limbs, a brief glint of white.

"If you're going to spy," he says, not loud, but clear and sharp, "then help me. That'll give you something to spy on."

Without waiting for a response from the oak, he sits down and opens the box, trying to remember how he played with Filemon the night before. The oak's boughs sway in the hazy light, its smell comes to him on the wind, settling in his face and lulling him into a reverie. Behind him, in the water, he can sense a change in the orbit of the oro-larva. Each one parts its lips and sends a bubble to the surface, a tiny puff of breath popping into the air, filling the courtyard with a fresh cool green odor that lingers in his nostrils and wreaths his head. Cool and calm now, the Divinity Student begins pressing the box first on its sides, then around the rim, moving languid fingers over holes in the top, the edges and corners, playing as he had with Filemon, sending a resonant wood-tone through the stones and glass and up to Magellan's office. The music grows wide and full without becoming loud, mingling as had the chant with the light and the water sounds. The trees rustle their fingers.

When he's done and turns—there's a black boat waiting for him, motionless in the narrow channel. Rock steady, it neither tips nor sways as he gets on board and sits—it's small, carved from the trunk of an ebony tree, and polished. Once he sits, it begins to move, drifting toward the black recess in the wall. As he draws near, the Divinity Student can feel spray misting in his face - in he goes. The Orpheum weighs heavily down atop the arch a foot above his head, a turn, and all light dims and vanishes.

The progress in the dark is quick and steady, cobwebs of stale air brush against his face. It's lightless and silent as empty sleep.

Presently, a dim phosphorescence limns a dirt shore before the prow of the boat. Drawing in close, a narrow beach, with cypress and willow trees beyond, stiff blades of grass, lit with eldritch yellow light. The boat glides hissing up onto blue sand, and the Divinity Student disembarks. He glides across the beach leaving no footprints, and moves cautiously through the copse to an open patch beyond. He looks up—no ceiling, around—but no walls, the light has no source. He sinks to his knees, pulls out a matchbox with a small mirror set in the bottom. He holds it in the palm of his left hand, and swings his pendulum in an arc over it. His right hand is the still point. He listens to the crickets, the cries of mourning doves from dead trees looming like spiders; in the gloom, the pendulum is a pale smudge drifting over his palm. It takes a long time, but eventually it stops, pointing straight ahead, toward a break in the trees.

Where he passes the leaves change color. Stepping over a low hummock, the grass beneath his feet shifts from yellow to blue, and up ahead—a ruddy glow, grainy at the edges, halos a boulder. The Divinity Student draws in close, and feels the rock warm against his palm as he feels his way to the light. He finds a small clearing bordered with frosty blue and purple-black flowers hiding in the lee of a rock face, crowned with flaccid tendrils of moss, and dead trees. Tombstones and crosses shine bleakly in clumps of grass all around, ringed round by a ruined wrought-iron fence. A few ghost lamps hang from posts, the grassy face of the clearing is littered with parcels, bundles. Dimly he can see small gray forms skipping over the ground like pebbles on water, carrying things to and from an open pavilion sprawling in the center of the clearing. Coming closer, the Divinity Student sees Magellan lying on a couch under heavy veils, his face still painted white and black, but now he's wearing regal garments, a yellow half-coat and long green vest, ruffles at his wrists and throat, knee-pants and white stockinged calves marble-smooth tapering into black slippers. Incense coils around his dreaming head from braziers fanned by his imps, who pour him cups of poison that he drains in contempt of death.

The Divinity Student enters the burying-ground unchallenged, lets Magellan's blood-purple canopy draw him in, up to the couch. The high-priest's eyelids are painted dark, now two diamond-shaped openings in his face, the Divinity Student feels their non-gaze settle on him. He sits down in front of the couch, an imp slipping a cushion underneath him as he kneels, and opens the music box again, slowly, letting the air calm his fingers, not talking nor trying to talk, but just playing as the oro in the oak grove had directed.

The air guides his fingers. A ululating phrase whistles out like a jet of steam, or a moth's fluttering wing, and repeats itself over and over again. Magellan snaps bolt upright; wan, hollow shapes come swirling in the pallid light around the circumference of the clearing, fast drumming follows, thundering up under the phrase, levitating it.

Magellan rises from his couch. Bringing his arms out wide, he permits his familiars to bear back his sleeves, and he cuts his white arms with a cobalt knife.

Again, the Divinity Student repeats the phrase.

Ghosts boil in the air, rustling and crying, libations fall to them on the ground, witch lights glimmer for them, alighting on branches turning trees into candelabras.

Again, he repeats the phrase.

The drumming fattens and shakes the earth, timbre deepening, growing empty and vibrant at the core, each tone dwindling to a buzzing at the corner of hearing just before the next is struck, and faster. Again he repeats the phrase.

Vague whitenesses gather about him; they open their dark smudgy mouths and exhale together, filling his head with a voiceless whispering of breath like wind in trees, whistling and yawning all around him, rising up over the thunder of the drums to lighten his head.

Again he repeats the phrase.

Sensation now of his face being pressed against something like a metal barrier, already it bends as he is pushed into it. Magellan steps forward, lifting him, lightest possible touch of Magellan's hands under his arms, as if he is only a column of air, bursting through headfirst and the metal shatters and tears, rising into a rare darkness he has seen before, frozen a moment over the earth in a column of light, the unique nothing in the shadows of Magellan's eyes, flame rilling over his body, blood and perspiration and the rustle of dry papers sewn inside like a rag doll. He's a column of air. He's a vapor. He is evaporating out of a jar of formaldehyde.

The sun settles mundane light on a courtyard filled with trees. Quiet, not busy yet, empty canals of free-standing water, the Divinity Student sprawled sodden on the pavement. A custodian wakes him, leaves him dazed on the ground and goes for a lictor or a guard. When he comes back, the Divinity Student is gone—wet footprints, sour smell of chemicals.

Chapter 8: The Commission

IN AN EMPTY GARAGE that yawns onto the street the Divinity Student wakes, lying on his side, coming to himself only after staring at the supernatural brightness outside, blades of grass poking through the pavement, looking hot enough to burn. Turning to rise, the light stays in his eyes and colors the shadows.

This morning he won't go to Woodwind's; instead he forces himself sternly through the light, to assemble ingredients for today's experiment. After two hours he finds a chemistry shop on Jack-o'-Lantern Street; it's an impersonal place, simple metal racks with bottles, a counter, a plain old man behind the counter blowing test-tubes from glass glowing pumpkin-colored. He pretends to browse awhile, always embarrassed when he has to buy something. Eventually he gets up to the counter, has to wait five minutes for the attendant to finish blowing a flask. Finally, he manages to exchange a grubby bill for six long silver cans of formaldehyde in a brown grocery-bag. A brief stop along the way back to buy some bread from a street vendor with a monkey, and he returns to the garage ready.

The first thing, he goes out back, under a tree, crumbles the bread and piles up the crumbs, kneels there nearby and waits. It's quiet. He keeps his eyes on the pile, begins rocking gently back and forth, feels his coat moving on his shoulders, blood in his temples. He does it slow, humming, burns a little prayer written on the formaldehyde receipt on a bare patch in front of him, writes a signature in the dirt with the match stick. His palms tingle, warm all the way up to the shoulder, that's good, like a little silver filament up each arm. The Divinity Student sits rock-still and waits.

A lizard appears through an overgrown gap in the wall. Expressionless with concentration the both of them watching the pile of crumbs, he's drawing the lizard with a quiet sound he makes in his nostrils, breathing the hot air out so as to make a pitch that sounds like straw rubbing together. The lizard likes that—it's brown, a foot long. Legs moving in circles it comes forward to get that bread; the Divinity Student's eyes go black; two black clouds settle over his eyes, black clouds like swarms of flies, and up comes the lizard. It starts eating the bread.

The Divinity Student's hand whips out, strikes the lizard with certainty on the side of the head, sending it sprawling on its side, legs in the air—it thrashes and dies. The Divinity Student gets to his feet and runs inside, coming out again with the bag and a bucket. Hastily, he pops the tabs on the cans and pours the formaldehyde into the bucket, all of it, and then snatches up the lizard and eases it in, coiling it at the bottom of the bucket, his eyes tearing from the sourness of the stuff. With care, he lays a board over the bucket's mouth and weights it with a cinderblock. In a day or so, it'll be mature, heated in the sun. He pauses to draw a special mark on the bucket with charcoal, and turns towards Woodwind's.

THE OFFICE IS EMPTY; the building is quiet. He's there, filling his ledger, every stroke of his pen scraping on the silence, until that is stilled too. The room is poising itself, something invisible is gathering—looking up from the page, it seems to him this place is more than empty, more than abandoned, that no one has ever been here, that he is dreaming the office, or that the office is dreaming him.

He pushes back in his chair and goes to the window, but outside the city is static and motionless; he can see no one. A set? Turning around, he examines the office, floor, walls, ceiling, furniture, all made of the same dull wood, stained black in places. The place could have been carved from a single block of wood, or maybe it grew this way naturally.

Pen and ledger rest waiting on his desk. Unconsciously, he puts his notebook into his pocket. He rifles through Ollimer's desk, looking for the Catalog fragment.

What are you doing?

I'm trying to find that bit of paper Ollimer got from the tree the other day.

What paper was this?

A fragment of a Catalog of unknown words . . . the original was destroyed somehow . . . he showed me one of the entries once. . .

Shouldn't you wait for him?

I don't trust him. What I'm looking for now, he got it from an oro, the same oro who sent me to Magellan to learn the formaldehyde protocol—don't you remember?

An oro?

Yes—a tree spirit.

Do you mean to tell me that you're breaking into his desk because you suspect him to be in league with trees? Trees that hand out Catalogs?

The Divinity Student starts slamming drawers in Blandings' desk, and then Householder's. Were they involved?

Then he stops. He's heard something. Motionless, he tries to look out through his ears, finding only the sound of his breath, his heart.

But then, another tiny clinking sound, coins flattening on each other, through the wall.

Slowly, crumpling himself up into his hearing, he draws up to the wall, placing his feet with such care that not even a mote of dust is displaced, and presses his ear to the cool wood paneling.

The coins drop, one by one or in pairs.

He feels his face go hot and red, his collar tightens, for a moment he feels something like a fever thrum in his temples and along the seams of his cheeks and forehead, and his throat constricts around his breath. Something moves in his belly; he wants to shake or fall down, but he holds himself absolutely still, breathing through his mouth.

It takes him a long time, but he gets through the door and out into the hall, not knowing what's happening to him—but there's nothing at all. Everything is as it should be, and as it always was, except abandoned.

Then he hears it again, behind him, and he looks and there he sees it. He hadn't ever noticed before, but here in this one place, the wallpaper is stretched tight over a door-sized hole in the wall. The heat and closeness of the past week has made the paper sag, and now the opening is visible. The noise comes from in there.

Dizzily, he steps forward and parts the paper with his fingers. The paper is red and velvet-feeling, opening easily along a seam, dilating without tearing to let him into the walls. The darkness grows transparent by degrees, and then he can see two candles burning on a tiny shelf set high above him. They burn before a small sepia photograph of a blank-faced woman with clear eyes, hanging on the wall, and beneath the shelf Mr. Woodwind lies, sternly sleeping, hands folded on his chest, leaning against an upright board.

Will he wake up? The Divinity Student creeps forward, but again comes the rattling of coins, very near. Then he sees Miss Woodwind, sitting smiling beside a card table smoothly set with a white cloth, with a scales and a cashbox. A Chinese lantern sheds red light down over its tassels, makes her white dress glow red. To him it seems as if a veil or shadow lay between them; he can see her distinctly and yet she is vague as a blurred photograph. She extends her hand to him.

He waves his hands. "What?"

"Your notebook!" she says with a grin, and light flickers across her features, kaleidoscoping all colors from her lips and eyes, her temples, cheek's hollow, and beneath her chin.

He hands it over, coming closer, into her fragrance, and he can see the perfume in a glassy fog around her. Miss Woodwind lays the notebook smartly on the balance. In a few moments she efficiently tallies the new weight of the book and compares it to the old, reckoning how many words he has collected by weight, and calculates his pay on a chart. She counts out seven heavy gold wheels from the cashbox and extends them, cupping the money on her fingertips, so that as she drops them into his palm, her nails brush his skin just barely, only just touching him. This is all she has to do. Now he won't forget her looking up at him through the gleam of the gold, nor the touch of her hand. She smiles at him, pleased.

ANOTHER WRONG TURN; HE looks around in anguish, lost. The streets weave sometimes changing direction; he's recognizing the buildings, but the streets don't match. The Divinity Student is following the train tracks, another passing in a blast of diesel pushing hot air and thick flakes of dust before it, electricity snapping at the synapses. These trains run above ground, their tunnels burrow through buildings, not earth, roaring through restaurants, hotels, private homes, churches, libraries, hospitals. The Divinity Student is staggering, disoriented, sweating in the wake of the trains, thinking only that he wants to sit down with her at the table and watch her filling columns of words; he'll gladly be a mirror-glass, simply to sit by her and watch, bathed in her cool breath; or a lens for her to see through, so that he could be frosted with the rays that beam from her eyes, and these ideas push everything else out of the way. Dimmed and confused, he boards the train.

Under him his seat is rocking, only lulling him further into reverie, they plunge into the bowels of some public building, lamps streak by in horizontal bars of light, a fetid smell creeps damply through the car-vents, and through his faint reflection in the window he can see the tunnel walls falling away into nothing on either side, rusted parallel tracks lying brown on lifeless grey earth, rancid pools, and occasional lamp-lit islands, a few men in construction uniforms lying idle.

He rides for a long time, people pass through the car, men in suits, lictors, old women. Some boys horsing around. Fragments, incomplete ideas, but he's sobering a little. They crash out into sunlight again, the train shrieks and complains—melancholy sighing of old metal—and stop at a tiled station with slanting roof of clouded glass. The doors hiss and roll open.

A hand seizes his arm and drags him out through the door; before he can react they shut behind him and the train drags out into the street sending a car skidding into a heap of trash cans to avoid it. The Divinity Student turns and finds himself alone on the platform, but he recognizes the station now. Outside, he can once again find the familiar streets and buildings, and a familiar city once again.

From the Divinity Student's journal, more recently: "I see those cats everywhere now. Last night I think I saw an albino cat. Led me to an infirmary I had not seen before, eerie brick houses and sodium lights. Everytime I go out at night, there they are."

THE GARAGE WAS ONLY two blocks away. He lurches in and drops onto the gutted frame of an easy chair. Now he's pulling himself together, finding that again. No more feeling whipped about, he cleans himself out—and then goes to the bucket out back. Who knows how long it's been?

He drags it inside and sits on the cement floor before it, shedding the day's last strange fragments, and watching sunset light gild his hand through a cobwebbed window. He removes the cinderblock and the plank. A cold, flat odor out of time, not emerging from the bucket but just all about him instantly, as if it was his own native scent, there it is. The monitor lies inside, already blanching, skin ribbed with folds.

He was brought here—to learn this. He doesn't know why yet.

No prayers now, only quiet, he reaches in, down, so that his fingers touch the bottom, bringing up the heaviest, richest lees on his fingertips, stinging cold and fuming on his hands and shirt-cuffs. He does as Magellan had shown him; he atomizes the formaldehyde with a blow of breath, a nonsense word, sending it out like a sneeze, tiny droplets drift like snow in space, and he lets them fall boiling on his face. He breathes it into him.

For a moment he sits, feeling the vapor creep in his nostrils and down into his chest. A shadow falls past his eyes, a dry voice dusts his ears, whisper past ears into head, dry hands tug at the back of his eyes, clap behind nose, rustle in throat. Dry warmth settles on flesh and skin, cool to the middle, low to the ground, baking earth heats his belly, eyes watching the sides all the time, dry sounds, cracks and wheezes, grass parts in front of him, dry-faced insects scrabble away, dull thud of footsteps, giants streaming all around—light falls in sheets on his face, figures blazing ghosts around him, hollow ground and hollow air, empty noises, hollow, unmoored, gray faced the Divinity Student tumbles down with his vision's passing shivering on the garage floor.

Chapter 9: The Butcher

The Divinity Student wakes with a soft head, lying on a concrete stoop. He was dreaming, a river carrying him away; now he sits up shaking his head alarmed, doesn't know where he is—walked in his sleep. Around him, a slanting narrow street with white walls flaring in the sun, small children in cotton trousers running to crest the hill kicking dust, cinnamon brown door at his back; he looks down and sees the notebook in his hand, his thumb still jammed tightly between the pages, holding his place. He opens it and looks at words he doesn't remember collecting but that touch his memory with vague suggestions—these two leapt at him out of a poolhall eight blocks from here; and that one floated down onto the page like a leaf, a woman speaking to her neighbor from a second story window, and she let that one word drop clean and clear from a stream of unintelligible gabbling. Sleepwalking, he has collected them himself, without knowing. The Divinity Student stands up and counts—he has gathered more words in one day of sleep than in any day of waking. Why hadn't he thought of this before?

With uneasy steps he navigates down the street to a crossroads, chickens scattering in his path, complaining in his wake. A kerchiefed woman beats a rug in front of her house singing "La, li, le . . " (thump) ". . . lu, lo . . ." and he asks her for directions. Red-brown face and fluttering hands heavy over her apron, her soft voice shows him in Spanish, goes back to hitting her rug.

The Divinity Student climbs ponderously up Horse Street. His body feels like a patchwork of ill-fitting parts. Tired of the desert, tired of the city, walking up the street feeling leaden and weak—make sure you survive killing yourself, that's the way to go, and the red-green light winks on in his chest like an eye in the heart and it all comes into him at once. It's too early in the story but he can't wait, he jackknifes twenty feet straight up and tears off across the roofs, rolling over steeples, around the chimneys, ripping weathervanes and antennas loose, caught in his clothes he wears them like forgotten wire hangers, bounds over streets kicking up tiles, arms cartwheeling, face set a motionless stone mask, feet planting so hard he breaks through wood and plaster and down through someone's dining room table, he smashes it in two, spilling food, breaking plates, family too dumbfounded to—he careens through the picture window taking the sill with him wrapped around his neck—strong enough now to punch through brick walls, outrunning dust clouds, his shadow so strong it's cutting through the foundations of buildings and sending cobblestones flying up after him like a wake in water, nothing in him now but city and desert. Cars watching him make abortive gestures—"Don't try it—we'd be ashes before we got within two dozen feet of him—no good while the spirit's on him."

A scent of dead flesh twists his track, he goes flying into a butcher shop, a horse carcass, pelt and hooves, eyes staring, tongue dangling a foot out of its mouth. The Divinity Student sends the butcher block flying, picks the horse up with one hand and runs outside to the trough; a single kick punctures wood, sends water sluicing out. One-handed, brandishing the body overhead, he stops the hole with a stone, just picks it up and shoves it home, empties ten gasoline cans of formaldehyde into the trough and dumps the horse in, spilling sour chemicals, weathervanes, and the windowsill, and, too impatient to wait, he jams his head under the surface and grabs the horse by its ears, ramming forehead to forehead he glares into glassy eyes and strains the horse-life in through his teeth, sucks it out in one mighty inhalation. His head rears back out of the chemicals streaming, and he staggers back against the wall of the shop shaking, a horror of dust and water and the fit that's on him, people stopping, hands on throats and mouths as he drops to his knees eyes widening to the sun—so who does he run with now, and where, eating grass warm from the meadow or drinking from that trough once years ago, rutting in tree-shade, pulling the bit down throwing the rider, now it's he who's doing the riding, the Divinity Student, his horse spirit boiling out of him as he shakes his head and droplets of formaldehyde spatter the crowd, snapping witness' heads slapping their faces with images of each others' past, and, terrified, they run like rats. The Divinity Student traces curves in the dirt with his hands and shoeheels, throwing up clouds of dust, and feels the spirit wrenching loose with a pull towards the sky. Red-green light dims and fades in his chest.

Teo Desden, the butcher, drags him sympathetically back into the shop and props him against the display case. The Divinity Student, soaked and exhausted, pants to catch his breath. Time passes, and he comes to himself once again.

So, the Divinity Student sits watching the butcher. Desden works alone in the empty shop hacking mutton; rows of sheathed cleavers and razor-sharp knives with smooth stainless steel handles hum on a white counter, making the room look like a surgery. Gleaming meathooks on a chain hang over his head, along the back wall, one red raw animal smeared with white marbling swinging in the currents from the overhead fan; smells like wet concrete and rain, a clean place, regular thocking sound of Teo's cleaver making clean bone splits, chops and ribs sliding along red streaks to nestle on lettuce in cool glass cases. The floor is checkered, the far wall one vast and spotless mirror—the Divinity Student notices that Desden stares at himself all the time he's cutting the meat, contempt drawing lines taut around his mouth, turning his glazed eyes inward. He's marked, his bare forearms and hands are scarred and cut in places, his lips and fingertips are badly chewed, and the Divinity Student sees how deliberate the butcher's carelessness is. Desden mutters something at himself and breaks the animal's back with one springlike hack of his cleaver. He tosses beautifully sliced slabs of meat into the cases, pulls on the chain to bring the next body around, gliding effortlessly forward on well-oiled wheels, pulls it clear off the hook and starts slashing recklessly at it, perfect cuts flying off and piling up neatly despite themselves next to him on the counter.

A car passes outside, the Divinity Student watches a fly zing in through the open door. With a speed that defies vision Teo uncoils, sending a four-inch steel blade silent across the room flashing once under the fluorescents and the fly runs right into it. Two black halves drop to the tiles, the knife lands on its handle on the sideboard and slides an inch to rest, just tapping the base of the mirror. Unsteady, the Divinity Student lurches to his feet.

"Don't worry," he holds up his hand and takes up the knife, "here you are."

He walks back to the counter and hands it over, a narrow streak of clear jelly marking the steel where it hit the fly. Desden thanks him, and the Divinity Student meanders unevenly to the door and brushes the two halves out into the street.

"Oh," he turns back and makes his way to the counter again, holding his head. "Your horse . . ." He reaches into his pocket for some money.

"It's not important. It didn't even belong here."

The Divinity Student obstinately starts counting coins, but Desden reaches over the scales to close his hand. The butcher's fingers are cold and dry.

"It isn't mine, one of my suppliers used to ride it," Desden takes his hand away. "He came here yesterday to sell me two sides of beef, but the moment I'd paid him we heard a scream outside. His horse was drowning itself in the water trough—we did our best to pull it free, but it ended up dead anyway. In the meantime, my supplier ran off with my money and stuck me with the damn thing."

The butcher goes back to cutting, turns a moment and says, "You saved me the trouble of having to decide what to do with it."

The Divinity Student looks to the door, his head fills with air and for a moment he clings to the counter.

"You're in no condition to go out there."

"May I stay here?" The Divinity Student turns a pale face to Teo. "I'm willing to pay."

"You can sleep in the meat locker."

The Divinity Student pays the butcher and sits at one of the tables, decorated with a small white pitcher of white and pink carnations. Eventually Desden comes out in front and hands him a glass of water, sits opposite.

"What do you do?"

After he finishes drinking, "I'm a word-finder."

The Divinity Student produces his notebook, shows it to Teo. The other man scrutinizes last night's page carefully. He points to "redactor"—eyebrows go up, "That's a good one"—looks a while and hands it back. His expression is sad.

"I suppose it's a good business."

"I collected these last night while I was sleeping." The Divinity Student looks abashed.

With a sigh and a nod, Desden goes back behind the counter and starts cutting up the bodies again. His expression hardens and he starts cursing at himself.

Time passes. The Divinity Student sits silent and dazed, not thinking about anything but vacantly staring out the door. He is trying not to think, for fear that thinking will carry him off, or exhaust him. Eventually, he musters himself enough to ask what time Desden closes shop.

"I may be going out again," he says.

"I sleep upstairs in the back, just throw something at my window if I'm not down here."

He nods and shoves a handful of meat into the grinder, sneers, "I don't have any plans for the evening."

The Divinity Student tilts out the door, street air hitting dry and yellow, just down the road and around the corner, colorless dirt road twisting down toward the middle of the city, shallow shadows under hissing branches. It's quiet. The street narrows at the bottom, silent stones bearing witness. He passes the churchyard and moves to the mouth of the Street of Wax, pulled up short by a low whistle.

Just past the churchyard, along the treeline at the city's border, he can see a column of white vapor moving, sweeping along into town; curiosity bringing him closer, he comes in, watches the train slow and pause amid the grating of brakes. Steam envelops the station, billows out into the courtyard, and gushes through gargoyles' mouths as it pours over the chapel. A group of people veiled in black darken the platform, dry hands like branches in the air, to receive a casket from a Pullman car. Six dark men in suits bring the coffin. An open carriage bowered in back with wreaths and garlands emerges from behind the church, pulled by a black mare with a high black plume.

The Divinity Student watches them load the hearse; the horse bows its blinkered head to gaze at the cobbles. He thinks of the horse, Desden's horse, and recoils himself at a terrible idea. As they load the coffin into the hearse he has an awful idea.

He measures his pace, turning deliberately from the courtyard, and following the Street of Wax once again to the plaza, and he denies that he's thinking about what he's thinking about.

Then, just outside Woodwind's, in the alley, he stops to regard a handsome cat perched on a windowsill. It's all in black save for a white spot at its throat, just like him—all black but for a bleached collar, vaguely phosphorescent peering out from his heavy coat. The cat is green-eyed, as is he, just sitting there, just looking at him. It tosses its head once toward a building off to one side and bounds past his shoulder, across the alley, disappearing. A hot wind snaps the tails of his coat; he looks both ways, up and down the boulevard, but there is no one. He slips into the building.

The lobby opens to him, scented with her fragrance, turning, and suddenly she's there, within inches of his face, watering a potted rubber plant. Looking at him, her eyelids flare a moment, head inclining slightly to the side; she can see something's happened. Then she relaxes, eyes almost closing, their color changing to purple, their luster deepening into distant facets, and she smiles brightly at him.

"You look different," she teases, and shakes her head, light strands of stray hair tapping his face like drops of rain. The Divinity Student looks down at her pearls and grins faintly.

Miss Woodwind seizes his ear, "Tell me what happened!" just cajoling him, still smiling; her breath spreads twin crescents on his spectacles.

"I walked in my sleep," a mock wince, his hands flutter at his side.

She releases his ear, but the contact brought her close. Her soft fingers had pinched his ear; her voice hummed through him.

The plant across the room needs water. He wanders up the stairs.

Householder and Blandings are playing dominoes in the corner; they ignore him—Ollimer rushes up.

"Could you do me a favor? I wouldn't ask otherwise, but I don't know who to turn to . . ."

The Divinity Student tells him to wait, sits down at his desk and copies out his ledger, Ollimer all the while running fingers through his copper locks, cleaning his glasses, rubbing his palms on his vest, swaying from foot to foot. The other two rattle their dominoes and mutter to each other in subdued voices.

He finishes quickly and strides out the door, Ollimer following closely. "Please accompany me to the house . . ."

He knows what to expect. They pass through the empty lobby and out into the alley, shooing dogs away from the door. With a furtive casting about for witnesses, Ollimer leads him back, quiet, glancing over his shoulder, nervous, and sad.

OLLIMER'S PARLOR. THE DIVINITY Student enters slowly, expecting the other man to trot out the wallet, produce the next fragment of the Catalog. With a stricken look, Ollimer gestures vaguely to the corner of the room; his aunt's body is leaning up against a chair, stiff as a plank. Her eyes and mouth are open, her flesh looks like blue cheese. She's been awkwardly dressed in a fraying grey terrycloth robe, twisted, plastered, and strangely wrinkled in her nephew's haste to cover her. Her feet are curled up like two pillbugs.

"I'm terribly sorry to trouble you, won't you please give her the last rites? You're the only religious person I know."

Ollimer cuts him off as he opens his mouth, "No priests—they all hated her, she wouldn't want a priest."

"All right. Does she have a bedroom?"

"Thank you so much, at the end of the hall, the door's open" Ollimer's gratitude pours out, meanwhile the Divinity Student hauls the old woman into his arms and turns in time to see Ollimer heading for the door.

"Get back over here!"

The other man freezes.

"Idiot! I'm not going to do everything for you! Now get in there and shut the curtains, and get the damn bed ready!"

Ollimer bolts down the hall like a scared rabbit, the Divinity Student swaying behind carrying the body. She's heavy-soft like a cushion, all save her neck, her head stiffly upright, eyes pasty and dull, turning blue about the lips. In the dark of the hall a dim light shining through doughy flesh becomes visible just at the center of her head; he can see drifts of shining dust in her mouth and nostrils.

Just at the threshold of her room her weight seems to double and the Divinity Student stops, almost losing his balance. Her dead eyes roll in her head and the corners of her mouth turn up. She stares at him, winks an eye and grins wider. He steals a glance at Ollimer, who's lighting candles with his back turned, then looks back at the body—she follows his eyes and draws air through her gums with a sticky sound, hushing him, a little secret.

"Quiet, stupid," he says and slams her head hard against the door jamb. Her head drops, she goes still.

The room is small with rose wallpaper, the floorboards taken up in the corner, water rushing far below breathing mist up into the room. With care, he lays her down on the bed and straightens her robe. Not a large woman, wouldn't take too much formaldehyde to pickle—and that's enough of *that*!

"You," he takes Ollimer by one shoulder and manhandles him to kneel at the foot of the bed, "stay."

He leaps onto the bed, pulling a hammer from his pocket, and starts pounding nails all along the top of the headboard. In a moment, he turns and drives another row of nails into the footboard, Ollimer wincing as the hammer falls within an inch of his face. No time to waste, the Divinity Student withdraws a fistful of wires and some pliers from his pocket, and starts stringing wire from nail to nail over her sodden body. With much slicing of fingers and screeching of metal he draws the last one tight.

Then the Divinity Student stands over the body with the Holy Book in his hands. He sets himself on his feet, kneading the cover a moment with his hands, then opens it, to watch letters flicker on rippling pages in wan yellow light. He lets the words out into the room, lets them hum through the wires strung across the bed like a tone across guitar strings.

Air trickles out around her teeth and the hollow of her mouth humming in the walls and bedframe, rattling the windows, buzzing in the cords strung tight above her, draft reeking of stale ice, words bubble from her lips, shaped somewhere deep in her chest—but Ollimer doesn't hear. The Divinity Student bends down to listen . . . only silence, wires blurred but quiet. The room goes dark, he can see her head lit up like a paper lantern, thin curtains of flesh shining orange from inside, out of her gaping mouth, lights shining on the threads, passing up and down their length like mercury in a thermometer. He passes his hand over her face—the words stop, the light winks out. He signals Ollimer to get up.

"Thank you." Ollimer is fumbling in his pocket—the Divinity Student knows what he's got. ". . . here," a familiar-looking scrap of paper.

Ollimer insisted that the two fragments stay together, that the Divinity Student could not keep it; the point wasn't pressed. Later, the Divinity Student couldn't recall the word itself: "mermeral" or "mermarescent" but definitely with "mermer" or "mermar" in it, with this definition, handwritten:

"A prince, or a prisoner, on his deathbed remembered for the first time a childhood incident. Wandering in his ancestral home, he found himself in the dining room. Up until that time he had only seen it at night, in the company of adults, and now, daylight revealed it to be a false—the windows were plain white paper, the furniture, decorations, even the plants, were all props, hastily slapped together, where they had seemed so fragile and elegant before. Upon leaving the room he found the house was empty. Then he died. The boy is a man remembering, on this one occasion, he is dying."

Again, the same disorientation, vertigo on the edge of the paper, words written as a guide toward an obscure center—

"This is my payment?"

"Don't put it like that!" Ollimer comes up to him, hands open in supplication. "I'm very sorry—"

He brandishes the Holy Book and seizes Ollimer by his collar. "You're going to be sorry for real this time if you don't tell me who's putting you up to this!"

Ollimer squirms. Perspiration oozes on his forehead.

"Baiting me! What is it—is there a schedule, do you give me a fragment a week, and more and more? And then what happens? What happens then?"

"Let me go!" Ollimer casts fearful eyes up at the book, "There was only one left to go after this one! They're getting ready to tell you everything—you know as much as I do! You can't possibly blame me for this!"

The body on the bed emits a high arching wail, the Divinity Student hurls the book at it hard, striking it across the forehead. The wailing stops. Dragging Ollimer with him, he staggers over to the bed and reclaims the book.

"Well, I think we're going to wrap this one up ahead of schedule. I think I'm going to go straight to the source this time!"

Ollimer actually relaxes, "Yes, all right, that's a good idea."

The Divinity Student releases him gingerly. Ollimer looks as if he'll faint.

"I'll relay your wishes and get an answer—"

"You'll tell me now."

Ollimer deflates. With an effort, he turns to the desk and scribbles a name and address, sweat spattering the wood and scattered notes.

"Here," he croaks, holding out a crumpled paper covered in botched handwriting.

The Divinity Student puts the book away, takes the paper, and walks out the door without looking back.

Chapter 10: The Mission

So the Divinity Student whittles away the daylight hours in Desden's meat locker, alternately watching the Saturday crowd marketing up and down the road through the doorway and playing hide and seek with the address Ollimer had given him. He puts it away for a while and then picks it out of his pockets again, stares at it without seeing, then folds it up, making shapes, being bored, paper gets rattier and more crinkled until he can barely read it in the dull glare filtering in from the shop. He avoids making a decision by counting tiles on the wall and calculating how many checks there are in the floor, then how many black checks and how many white checks and trying to reckon their length and breadth measured in hand-widths. It won't be until sunset that he'll make his decision, whether or not to go. He's been missing night time, and being able to look up at the sky without burning his face, so he'll wait.

Watching Desden he notices something. Every time a woman comes into the shop he tenses up, and just as she's turning to go out the door again he'll raise his hand and just wave at her a little. He waits until she's almost all the way round with her back to him, but not so far that she couldn't possibly see him, only enough to make it improbable that she would see him. The expression on his face—he'd jump under the counter if he was caught. But every time, like clockwork, that tiny wave at the turning head, hair and shoulders and curve of her cheek, a glint of her eye framed with lashes, then he goes back to his cutting, always watching the mirror as he cuts, staring hard into the glass.

Eventually, the Divinity Student gets up and meanders into the shop. Teo is sitting on a folding chair, knees spread over a bucket, plucking chickens with a sour, bored expression. It's dimming outside, orange lights coming on at crazy angles along the street; pedestrians pass in glowing white cottons.

"I'm going out for a while," he says.

"After I close up I might be able to find you a cot."

He thanks the butcher and swings out the door into wine-colored air, his collar goes phosphorescent blue-white, and he looks up into cool azure sky and first pale lights, air stirring slightly with spare desert smells. He settles down, and sets off to meet Ollimer's contact.

Behind him, a mush-faced little girl is watching the shop, sees him leave. A fly is buzzing in and out of her mouth.

He dawdles and hangs about, taking time to investigate back alleys, cockfights, musicians; he stops at a corner to eat bread and cold water, indulges himself with a stale plum-sized sugar skull branded with his name.

The address belongs to a house standing alone at the edge of an athletic field, an oversized brick box with one door in the middle of its face, and one narrow window immediately over it, resembling nothing so much as a cyclops. No lights nor mailbox, only a chain link fence and concrete path. He knocks on the door and it swings open before him on an empty hallway lost in a vast unlit building. With a little investigation he discovers a pair of fine fishing lines running from a hook on the back of the door to a motor, poorly concealed behind a bust on the hall table. The cobwebs on the bust are artificial.

Swift footsteps herald his appearance: Fasvergil floats up out of the unlit murk of the house into the paling orange light of the single window.

"I was told to expect you. You have been extremely impulsive." Fasvergil's voice is dry; it rustles along the walls like dead leaves.

"The power went out only a few moments ago." He deftly lights a storm lantern, a column of light touching his saturnine features. Fasvergil is wearing his ordinary black habit. Chalk-dust still powders his sleeves and shoulders. Beneath, his thin ankles descend from the hem into small dark shoes.

"Shut the door."

The lamp draws him in after Fasvergil, and as he immerses himself in the depths of the house he can see that the entire place is one vast chamber separated by high partitions, supported like stage flats by chains hanging from the ceiling. Their footsteps echo over their heads, and meet an answering tick of a hidden clock. Emerging into the vast central parlor he sees it is a lumberyard of carnival haunting-props from cannibalized ghost-trains, mired half in shadow, in failing light, like shipwrecks: dressers' dummies leaning in the corner next to a skeleton, glass eyes on a shelf, chain-bound books with uncut pages next to a crystal ball on the table, all cluttered with deliberate disarray and aged with tea stains and fake dust. A heavy grandfather clock raps solemnly in the corner, and a dull bread smell comes from Fasvergil's dinner, sitting in a pool of light from a wine-bottle candle on a card table; he pulls a Chinese screen across that corner of the room and brings the light out, setting it on an endtable.

"Sit," he says, indicating a ponderous armchair. The Divinity Student obeys. Fasvergil takes his seat and fixes him with a baleful look.

"Looking there on your left, just on top of that pile of books there, you'll find the third fragment Ollimer told you about."

Fasvergil points obligingly with a long, weary hand—the Divinity Student looks around and pulls a thin sheet of folded paper from between two featureless volumes. The page has been prematurely aged with tea stains. He looks up and sees Fasvergil watching him, and while he knows he is being manipulated he cannot resist reading the page. Silent in his chair he reads a word meaning:

"A very aged man finds again the love he lost as a youth. As he moves to embrace her, he is suddenly transported to a lightless place. He can feel a cool, sterile wind blowing upon his face, a numbness in his limbs. Nearby are shrieks and mutterings, unseen yammering things surrounding him on all sides. After an infinite time he wakes beneath a tree, when a raindrop, a single one, drops into his right eye. When he understands that all he had just experienced was merely a dream, he walks into a river and drowns himself."

He reads, and he feels Fasvergil trying to read him. A headache developing, the page turning gray and blurring a little as he reads. The Divinity Student is struggling to keep the vertigo from showing. Inside he feels a yawning sensation, waked and tantalized and he wants to seize Fasvergil and shake the rest out of him sheet by sheet, scrabble into a corner and roll himself up in them; these unknown ghost-words leave him clutching the air. Catching himself swaying he throws a look at Fasvergil, "What have you done to me?"

Fasvergil's look of surprise is unfeigned, "What?"

"Where does this come from?"

Fasvergil collects himself and says, "Ollimer may have told you that these are all fragments of the Catalog of Unknown Words, compiled by a man named Schroeder and a small team of mediums, word-finders like yourself—this was many years ago—at any rate, from what little evidence endures, we know that Schroeder destroyed the Catalog just before he committed suicide. The other word-finders were dead by this time, or died shortly thereafter, and it is possible that Schroeder may have killed some of them himself, presumably to keep the secret of the Catalog."

The Divinity Student feels a weighty, obscure pressure fasten upon his head, and clutches at the armrests. All his powers of concentration are focused on Fasvergil's words.

"The fragments to which you have been exposed were found among the possessions of a man named Chan, one of Schroeder's word-finders, who was found dead in his hotel room." Fasvergil is nodding his head and steepling his fingers, reciting, "I acquired them myself, and I've been rationing them to Ollimer to give to you."

"You were baiting me . . ." and now, slowly, it starts in his throat and fans out cold at the edges settling into him, ". . . You want me to resurrect the Catalog for you."

Fasvergil's face goes dead-sea calm, remaining just affable enough. "With the training you have received from Magellan, you could walk directly into the memories of any dead man, and bring them back—specifically I mean the words, that is, you of all people can bring them back again."

Even though he doesn't trust Fasvergil—he's been set up: go into Magellan, find out how it's done and then bring that back, now do it for *us*, young man, Magellan wouldn't, but *you* will, won't you?—even though he has a dirty feeling of being used and puppeted by his own teachers—there's a cold tang that billows through his head like frigid, early morning light. For this he came to San Veneficio, and the job as a word-finder, everything has been preparatory to retrieving those words. Now, understanding everything for once, he is in a position to choose with open eyes. The pressure at his temples spreads to mantle his shoulders and flatten his arms to the chair.

"You've read about the Eclogue," Fasvergil says, hanging his words carefully in the air, "These unknown words of Schroeder's are its vocabulary, we believe. 'Eclogues' are dialogues between shepherds. *The* Eclogue is the dialogue of the shepherds of *men*. That is our conclusion. You are in a position to prove it."

Fasvergil seems oblivious to the Divinity Student. He sits motionless in his chair, his large, colorless eyes fixed on empty air. He speaks as if he were reciting his catechism.

"The Eclogue is the essential substance, or first cause, of creation, and is the source of all renewal. It is much like an invisible fundament that buoys everything up. Also, it is the communion or synthesis of all natural forces."

"That's what *you* think," the Divinity Student says to himself.

"It is a mystery and will forever be unfathomable to mortal understanding—our purpose in sending you to find these words is not the deciphering of the Eclogue. That is not our goal, and regardless it is an impossibility. Rather, we at the Seminary feel that a more comprehensive semantic understanding of the basic qualities of the Eclogue will enable us to convey the essence of its mystery to the uninitiated more precisely. We must, in short, strive toward an apprehension of what the Eclogue is *not*, and by filling in the darkness around it, develop a corresponding conception of what it *is*—without pursuing the folly of a direct definition. Then we may create a precedent, whereby the knowledge of the mystery of the Eclogue may be transmitted in such a manner as to preempt misunderstanding or heresy. Do you understand?"

The Divinity Student nods. Fasvergil has just named the stream that runs through his head, right through and behind, just obscured by himself, in his blind spot. Whether he understands or not, Fasvergil is asking him to remove that blind spot for both of them, as if that were possible. The Divinity Student will get closer to the Eclogue. He tries to dissemble, appear disinterested and force Fasvergil to bargain with him. But even as he hides his feelings he knows he must not refuse—this is his mission.

"Will I be allowed to keep what I find?"

"Provided I receive copies of *everything*," he gives him a frosty look, "that you find, naturally any notes you take are your own."

Time passes. They look at each other, clock ticking, dust gathering, this is what he came here for, and heart in his mouth the Divinity Student says, "I'll do it."

Fasvergil nods at a foregone conclusion.

"If you will look to your left, in the upper drawer of the end table, you will find a list of the word-finders and where their bodies are buried. Your procedure in probing them is of no consequence to us, but I am under orders to exact from you at this point your most solemn promise that, in the event of your capture or arrest, you will not under any circumstances mention your affiliation to the Seminary or the Mission with which you have been entrusted."

The Divinity Student takes the list and swears.

As the sun settles overhead the Divinity Student steals away from Fasvergil's house. He's walking quickly, holding his legs out stiffly, and his face is pale and drawn. There are dark blue circles beneath his eyes. He imagines himself growing a second pair of eyes, ghost eyes, animals with the power to see the future, look into a mirror to wake yourself. A maze of streets opens before him like a jigsaw puzzle, and he meanders in and out of alleyways and private homes, beneath balconies and gargoyles, but the city walls seem to close in tightly about him, crushing him in a thin envelope of space, and reducing his path to smaller and smaller circles, going about the same landmarks and places again and again faster and faster. Fighting vertigo and intimations of nightmare, he pushes himself harder, trying if possible to force his way through the streets, but they catch at his effort and pull him down to the pavement. For a moment the buildings swim and dodge away from him and his head goes light, and then he is tumbling head over heels, unable to trace the course of his various parts to the ground. Before the blackness swells absolute, he can dimly sense low music muttering around him.

When he comes to himself again, he is looking into the seamed face of a stranger. Other faces peer over the stranger's dark shoulders, thinly draped in a frayed linen shirt. The man is speaking but his language is unfamiliar. Whoever it is has retrieved the Divinity Student from the middle of the street and set him leaning against a wall, cradling his head with his hand.

The Divinity Student looks dazedly from one face to another, and then in a moment is filled with gratitude, and from this gratitude he gathers his wits again. He draws himself to his feet sliding upwards along the wall, and follows the men toward the music. There's a sizable circle of people down one alley, playing instruments. One man has a guitar that he is playing upright. The rest clap and sing in their language. Standing there in their music, the Divinity Student feels calm. The feeling is intense; it reminds him how long it's been since he's felt calm. Like a rush of involuntary memory he recognizes the hymn, which he learned a long time ago in another language. He tries to sing it himself, but his voice is rusty and unpleasant. He stands silently to one side and rests, listening.

Chapter 11: The Gardens

EARLIER, THE DIVINITY STUDENT had encountered those two dogs at Woodwind's again. He had been called in to meet with the old man himself, who had commended him on the sleep-walking words, and given him a bonus. Coming downstairs again, they had been there waiting for him, tongues hanging out, one a bitch, the other not. They had stood there, watching each other, the Divinity Student poised on the third step. Then he had let himself fall forward, just falling forward with his arms out, with his hands straight and flat stretched out like blades, and just falling as a tree would fall he had driven his fingers down, impaling them, splintering their spines. He had risen unhurt, and then spirited them downstairs and out of the building in a sack. He ran all the way to Teo's place, pickled them and then, behind the butcher shop, he had taken them both at the same time, while the sun set over the roofs, and he got to know everything they had been together.

The experiment finished, now he's clean. He's washed it away, no formaldehyde smell left, he had scrubbed it away in a spasm of restraint. He'd wanted to get another horse, or maybe a bird, but something bigger—even one of the great monitors in the desert—but perverse discipline had told him to keep off. Chan would be his first assignment. Fasvergil had explained:

"The human memory is vast and obscure; specific recollections of any kind beyond the most basic experiences are extremely difficult to locate under even the best circumstances. Therefore, as the last moments are the most immediately accessible to the investigator, it's best to start with Chan—while his role in the compilation of the Catalog was minor, he's the only one who seems to have died thinking about it, so the desired information will be closer to the surface with Chan than with any of the others on the list. Going to Chan first is also advisable in that he's also the most recently deceased, his memories will not have sunken as deep as those of the rest."

Eyebrows rise, index finger lifts:

"Moreover, Chan will provide you with a test, whereby the use of your training upon human subjects can be evaluated and criticized. I have it on the best authority that his body is in an excellent state of preservation, no significant decomposition. I shall expect you to report to me by the end of the week."

"Too many reasons," the Divinity Student says to himself. "Who is he trying to convince? Let him tell me what to do and forget the reasons."

Wrapped up in his thoughts, he wanders around San Veneficio, pays his way into the Gardens, and wanders there. Small paper lanterns and candles are hidden in tree boughs and bushes, throwing webbed shadows across the paths. It's busy, people milling on their evening constitutionals in a soft night-time darkness, humming with sourceless cricket sounds. The Divinity Student skulks along the edge of the grass in his heavy coat, remembers haunting the bushes as a child, choosing his moment and ambushing, then running off through the plants, impossible to pursue. He'd have been happy to see himself grown up in this park, large and black like a spectre lurking at the edge of the path.

Incongruously he remembers the Seminary as it was for him when he was alone—dappled tree shadows on buildings waving at night, blue light in high little windows where magic was being done, a faint whispering above the world that would sometimes drop tiny leads down like cut wires live with current. The Divinity Student waves on his feet.

People drift by in evening-clothes, with parasols. Not a few children run by and give him a gratifyingly wide berth—being taken for a spook amuses him in a bitter, spectral way. Looking around, everyone looks ghostly in the shaded witch-light from the trees and lamps, drifting fluorescent whites and darks fading in and out of the greater patches of shadow, voices now sourceless like the crickets, but sometimes breaking off, becoming discreet, and passing him, often with a trace of scent or a brush of air stirred by passing bodies. It's as if the pedestrians and passers-by are shaded from him by a thin tissue of luminous color, and they pass behind it throwing flickering lights across its surface.

At the center of the garden there's a pool cased in a basin of perfect glass, one hundred feet across at its diameter and three feet of water at the perimeter, deepening to six in the center. Beneath the clear glass floor there's a huge kaleidoscope with powerful lamps underneath, spangling patterns across the water and up onto trees leaning overhead, sending patches of light gliding from leaf to leaf and across limbs, skimming over outstretched faces and hands. At night, translucent or luminous fish are released into the water, and freak freshwater cuttlefish three feet long changing color to match the dancing lights beaming up at their bellies, no sooner camouflaged than the pattern changes and again they change, free drifting memories of the former colors and patterns shifting again and outmoded again. Finally, at the center of the pool, a large freshwater octopus sits immovable, stirring the water with his tentacles, watching the people watch him with blank bilobed eyes; a single valve in its side opens and closes languidly—it's the heart of the pool.

Miss Woodwind is watching the octopus. She's by herself, leaning on the glass rim, lights filtering through the water to catch in her hair and flicker in her eyes and off her teeth, tracing like fingers the contours of her face and body, tinting her nails and soaking her clothes. The Divinity Student smells her before he sees her, soft on soft air, her fragrance sweeter for not being boxed in the office. Not moving, she's staring at the octopus, meeting its gaze directly.

She doesn't look when he comes up, "Would you look at it?" pointing, "Look at the way it hovers there."

Now she favors him with a bright face—"How beautiful it is!" —and goes back to watching it.

The Divinity Student nods absently, looking at her. She's dressed like a schoolteacher, but excited like a little girl. All alone and she comes here; he's never seen her outside the office like this, nor has he ever seen her with friends, although he had assumed. He looks closely, and he finds on her face the kind of enthusiasm that is cultivated alone and rarely displayed to anyone but strangers, and he feels honored to be given access to her privacy. She watches the water, and he watches her.

Then she notices him again, "Oh, you!"

He turns his face to the pool and the water lights, puts his hand on the cold glass, but he's trying to think of something to do. Already, she's muttering to herself and drifting off; he has an impulse to plunge his head into the water. Instead, he immerses his hand and brings it out, freezing with cold water, letting it spill in long clear festoons from his fingers. Unsatisfied, he does it again and again, staring at ropes of water encrusted with lights.

"Looking for something?"

"You're a word-finder," he says, gasping because the cold makes his fingers hurt, "you're the best of all of us . . ."

"You're flattering me?" She looks like she's getting ready to grin.

He shakes his hands, sending droplets pattering on the glass, "You were looking at the water, so I thought perhaps some of your talent could have rubbed off." That sounds desperate.

"Rubbed off into the water? How superstitious of you."

"I only want to be as good as you are."

That was bald enough to evoke a grin of surprise. Her face opens a little in curiosity. She mutters a response; he doesn't hear. He sees her interest reawaken. Papers rustle in his chest.

And so they walk together. Her eyes fixed at some vanishing point on the horizon, walking with her hands behind her back, and he is following the changes movement makes in her, as the lights pass and fall behind, and she changes all colors, reminds him of the kaleidoscope. She's speaking to herself under her breath all the time. Then out loud she says:

"You know, I shouldn't worry if I were you—the last few batches you've brought in were remarkable."

He nods.

"It must be difficult, or perhaps you've found some special place where the words dangle from the trees, waiting to be picked?"

There's something suggestive in her tone.

"Playing dumb?" She still isn't looking at him. ". . . I know where you get those words."

He hadn't submitted anything from the Catalog, he'd forgotten each word as the fragments left his hands—but he might have remembered them in his sleep.

"You walk in your sleep, so you hear words that people say without knowing they're saying them. I've seen you in the plaza mooning about like a ghost. You stop every few moments and scribble things in your notebooks that no one else would have heard. I know your tricks."

She hasn't turned to him once, but she walks beside him as if she knows exactly where he is. Headlights sweep over one corner of the gardens; they flash in his spectacles and then he's speeding invisible down a side path chased by a wild car horn blaring from the street. Birds burst shrieking from the trees overhead. But the light passes; unsatisfied, the car pulls away. The Divinity Student looks around for Miss Woodwind, and she's right there beside him, smiling pleasantly up at him, with her arms crossed.

"You're right to avoid them—they're driven by demons."

"They've been after you?"

One eyebrow raises. "No, but I've seen them do their business. You watch out!" She taps his chest with a finger.

For a moment they sit still in the shade, listening to the crickets, her lips moving quietly to herself. Her face is mostly hidden. Lights from the street shining between the leaves illuminate one high smooth cheek, garlanded with wisps of glowing hair.

"Come on, I'll show you something!" and she hurries off over the grass, under the trees.

They follow the course of a stream along a rocky path overgrown with vines, Miss Woodwind knifing through the bracken unhindered, the Divinity Student shredding and tearing behind her. No matter how he tries to catch up to her she always keeps ahead of him; his feet feel like blocks of clay dangling awkwardly at the end of his feet. He redoubles his efforts and presently walks directly behind her. By planting his feet precisely in her footprints he avoids the pitfalls.

One by one the lights dim and vanish, along with all sound of voices, wood and the smell of wet earth close around them, the city melting far behind. He follows her smell and the whispering of her voice with a sensation much like shifting from one dream to another. Trees get denser on all sides; he senses that no one has ever been back here before, pressing in toward an oasis older than the city.

A wind comes up and a roaring sound. She points. "There!"

She turns her brilliant face to him framed in a halo of hair, "It's the source of the stream!"

Just beyond her pointing finger a great spiraling channel of water gouts up out of the ground, cutting straight for the rocks and the gorge upon whose rampart they are standing. Trees stand all about the waters' edge following with their branches the flow of current, the air curiously stirred here by the speaking of the water at the center.

"I'll show you the way." Miss Woodwind's voice is perfectly audible over the noise. She weaves along the bank of a small tributary up to the main pool, an eddy where the flow is quiet, where the water is filtered through old tree roots and between rocks. One boulder shows a flat face and that's where they sit down, both turned to confront the stream bursting shouting out of the ground. Miss Woodwind looks at the Divinity Student for a moment, and then favors him, bending to cup her hand under the surface of the pool, bringing it up full, a bowl barely dripping.

"If you really want to soak your head, you should dunk it in here." She offers him the water, and when he hesitates she grabs the back of his neck and shoves his face into her cupped hand. He drinks soberly, and all the while she watches him with her lips moving, speaking softly and warmly to herself. She draws more water and he drinks from her hand again, motionless, bowing over her palm, and Miss Woodwind turns her face up to see gray sky and metallic stars through a black web of tree boughs, and sees the talking water flashing by like smoke and lightning from its source. The Divinity Student laps droplets from her palm, and draws his face along her fingers, and she finds her hand still resting on his neck, and it goes soft and strokes his throat a little. He looks up and she turns him toward her, drawing her water across his face with her hands, and bringing him in close, the things she tells him, she tells him, and tells him.

Chapter 12: Chan

Slabs of crushing heat fall and shatter on San Veneficio's shoulders, boiling back from the empty ground outside its walls to surge up the streets, churning into doorways and bulging against grey window glass like sheets of mercury. The great herds of giant monitor lizards are shut deep in the desert's recesses, where the blast of the sky's open oven is only a thin whistle of stirring dust and broiling plants. All along the city streets green leaves wither yellow-brown, in cracks, and, overhead, copper domes and gilded spires slant blazes down onto the streets, refocusing the sun. Magellan swings back and forth before his fractured window, while his familiars rub their velvety hands dubiously, watching him. When his couch swings forward to the summit of its arc, Magellan's wax-white face is only a foot from the glass, and as he falls backward he brings another part of the city back with him; San Veneficio trickles down vines of incense into his ears and the corners of his painted eyes. He can see the lowing, shrieking animal-souls of magicians pacing invisibly on walls and rooftops, or weaving unseen between pedestrians' feet.

The Divinity Student can see them too, now, for the first time. He's walking down the center of Monument Street, so named for its many statues, some set on high pedestals, others standing on the curb, leaning against buildings, trees, and store fronts, or sitting on benches. Out from the shade, the Divinity Student stands full in the heat's hammering in his heavy coat, defying the sun, the passing cars, buoyed up, the cool water in him and running down his face. A cattish ghost-familiar wauls from a monument's bronze shoulder, seeing him see it, and he shrieks back in its own language, pulling a face so horrible that pedestrians scatter out of his path, their white cottons flapping. The spirit's eyes flash and it bolts down a drainpipe, and somewhere an old misanthrope, brimming with bitter malice, poised over some catastrophe, gasps and stumbles, shivering off to hide in a corner. The Divinity Student laughs a silent witch laugh after it, and multicolored throngs of animal-souls up and down the street fan out to avoid him, peeping at him in fear, irritation, derision. They, none of them, they don't challenge him.

At the end of the street he drops out of sight. Today he's getting ready for Chan. This morning, as he had passed beneath an oak tree, a card addressed to him had dropped into his hand from the boughs, inscribed with the location of Chan's grave, so he's heading for the chemist's—he's a regular by now—puts the two barrels of formaldehyde—"very fresh, this imported you know"—on account and takes a cab back to the butcher shop. Teo's retrieving a carcass from the meat locker. The Divinity Student walks in hauling the drums and shoves them into a corner.

"Assignment from the Seminary," he explains.

"You live an adventure," Desden says, retreating into the shop with the meat.

The Divinity Student zigzags across town buying specimen jars and surgical instruments, special saws, a shovel, bags, and a rickshaw handcart with money he'd received from Fasvergil, comes back a piece at a time and dumps the stuff by the barrels, in the locker, with the exception of the handcart, which he chains outside by the broken horse trough. Eventually, the day's baking is done, the sun going down runs crimson over the town, air thinning, and he draws up to rest a moment. Teo comes out of the shop.

"What are you going to do?"

"I need a favor."

"For your assignment?"

"Yes."

"Anything."

"The use of your shop, or a private room . . . I don't know for how long."

Teo comes closer, "What for? Secrets?"

"Yes." The Divinity Student leans forward off the wall. "What I did with your horse I'm going to be doing to people. I'm stealing the body of a word-finder tonight . . . I'm supposed to dig through his memories and find certain things he took with him."

"These things being special words? I would assume that, since he was a word-finder."

"Yes, that's right."

"This is going to involve more than one corpse, isn't it?"

The Divinity Student pauses. "Yes, possibly as many as twelve."

Teo suddenly gets excited, "Listen, the bodies, what are you going to do with them when you're through?"

Shrugs. "I'd dump them somewhere. Perhaps rebury them if I've got the time."

Teo comes closer still, eyes bright in the alley-lights, "But you don't need them for anything else?"

"I have to keep their brains, that's all, everything else is waste as far as I'm concerned. None of them is going to be very fresh."

Now the butcher pauses, his stained apron humming blue-white in the thinning sunlight. "You can use my shop, or my apartment upstairs, whatever—provided you let me help you."

The Divinity Student remains silent.

"I have the shop and the rooms, I can be very useful to you. Just let me help, you won't regret it, you'll see—I'll dispose of the bodies myself."

The Divinity Student looks at him.

"Let me have the bodies when you're through with them!"

"Why do you want them?"

"I'll dispose of them for you! You can't simply dump them, they'd be found and traced back to you. Reburying them would be just as obvious. If you let me help, I can get rid of them. They'll vanish as if they had never existed."

The Divinity Student grinds his knuckles against his head thinking.

"Please!" Teo hisses.

"All right . . . Provided you help with everything."

"Yes!"

"May I use your apartment?"

"Yes!"

"And anything else I ask, you'll do?"

Desden gives a small bow with shining eyes, "Your servant."

"All right, 'servant,' help me load up the cart."

Desden ignites like an engine, tossing shovels and equipment into the cart. He closes the shop early and runs after the Divinity Student, pushing the cart in front of him.

Together, they walk streets that weave crazy patterns, passing dice games and weavers' looms on front stoops clacking out across the curb. And here's the church quarter; the street is lined with small chapels on all sides, some of them tucked into alleys, makeshift enclosures for tiny shrines, and booths selling incense, candles, prayers, offerings, flowers, nurture fires, and hymnals. With eventide approaching the crowds come out before dinner; in some places songs already rising out of doors and windows, but the people make way for the Divinity Student unasked. Hurry along quickly, out of the way and down to the cemetery.

A large, L-shaped building squats on that block, with a heavy black gate and yawning arch in place of a front door. Beyond, the graves lie marked, spread haphazard under dead grass. The gate's locked—the Divinity Student takes a metal rod out of his pocket, coats it with pink rose-water from a little vial and starts rapping it against the lock. Suddenly, the rose water congeals and the rod freezes to the lock as solid as if it were welded there; the Divinity Student pulls the gate open using the rod as a handle, motioning Desden inside.

Chan's grave is marked and shaded from the street by an old oak. Desden points to the tree.

"I hope its roots haven't gotten into the coffin."

The Divinity Student cuts into grey dirt just in front of the tombstone, sending lizards hissing through the high blonde grass. The soil is loose and dry, crumbling to dust and clods, insects, smells like smoke. He's moving fast—his form smears, hard to see in the failing light—tearing up the soil like a machine. Teo looks around, but they can't be seen from the street, then he takes up his shovel and starts in behind the Divinity Student, pausing every few moments to catch his breath and scan the windows overhead, waiting to be caught. Twenty minutes later, in a rain of dirt, a spade grates hollow on termite-pine. The Divinity Student scrapes the lid clean and motions Desden up onto the grass, gives a single heave and throws the coffin out of the grave. He follows it out a moment later and wedges his shovel blade under the lid. One ratchet of his arms and it slides off, splintering desiccated nails.

Mothball smell and sweet stench, Chan's suit is too small, deflated in the box but still a little damp, a white gecko stares up at them—he's been licking Chan's ear. The Divinity Student shoos him away. Reaching down, he embraces Chan's waist, hears a gurgling sound beneath his closing arms.

Desden hisses, "There's someone here!" and presses himself against the oak.

The Divinity Student dumps the coffin back into the ground and leaps down with it. A light blazes in the twilight building looming by the gate, two people alternate passing by the window—two men, pulling on jackets, one packing his briefcase at a desk.

"The bag!"

Desden tosses the bag down.

"Get down here now!"

Desden casts a fearful glance at the window. One of the men is laughing. The butcher slips quietly into the grave and helps bag the corpse.

"Just do it fast!" the Divinity Student says.

They toss the body back up out of the grave and leap out themselves. Teo dusts his apron but the Divinity Student seizes hold of the bag and drags it onto the cart, tossing the tools in besides. Above, the light goes out, stairwell lights flare in a column down one side of the building.

"Any other exits?"

"That gate is the only one!" the Divinity Student is spitting with anger. He kicks most of the dirt back into the grave and then tackles the cart, flying across the yard, with Desden running to keep up. Ramshackle, he tears up the earth over the graves, overturning tombstones and crosses, kicks a wreath out of the way, making for the gate. He bashes it open with the front of the cart, tearing the metal rod off in passing, and Desden shuts it behind him, the lock snaps. The Divinity Student is already halfway to the corner, Teo can hear voices ringing hollow, and nearby a door rattling—he sprints up the street and slams into the cart, together they send it hurtling up around the corner and down Rat Street.

Turning, they run down a service passage along the train tracks, their faces flashing messages to each other in passing orange work lights. Low thrumming sound, and the earth hums beneath their feet, the Divinity Student points, they duck into an alcove with benches for maintenance men as a train hurtles by like a thunderbolt only a yard away, earsplitting and spitting flying windows. Once it's gone, they pull out and make fast for the nearest access tunnel disgorging them into night streets.

"Too many people here," the butcher says.

"I'll get in the cart, they won't bother us."

The Divinity Student leaps up onto the cart and sits beside the bagged Chan, putting his feet up on the corpse.

"You said you'd do anything, so push."

Desden squares his shoulders and pushes the cart through the crowds. Finally, as the moon rises over the level of the rooftops, they draw up to Teo's street. The Divinity Student jumps out and together they rush their baggage up the pavement and around to the back. Teo practically dismembers himself flailing with the keys, he finds the right one, shoves it home, opens up, and the Divinity Student rushes Chan into the shop. Teo runs past him, draws the blinds and pulls a heavy flat across the front of the store—even peering through the cracks, it's impossible to see anything. He clears off the cutting board and heads back into the locker. The Divinity Student already has Chan out of the bag, stripped and ready, together they carry him out under the fluorescents and slap him down on the board. Teo puts on a fresh apron and starts rinsing the corpse, the Divinity Student runs out, comes back with a heavy jar filled with formaldehyde, mingling that sour smell with Chan's new wet sweet smell.

"Just the brain—the less tissue, the faster the fermentation."

Desden nods, yanks a cleaver out of his knife rack. With a few deft moves he shaves the front of Chan's head, then swings up at arm's length over his head and brings it down right on target shearing off the top of Chan's skull with one stroke. A muddy, metallic odor is decanted, curling sluggishly in their nostrils. His sense of smell already powerfully sharpened, the Divinity Student quickens and leans forward, takes a good long whiff almost getting it right then and there, the whole thing, but no no it's not enough, the formaldehyde is needed.

With the genius of natural grace Desden whips out a small, wickedly sharp blade and stabs in through the back of Chan's neck, putting his weight on it, driving between the vertebrae and then shifting his weight bringing the knife up—a sound of dry fibers severing like old corn husks. The spinal chord is cut. A few more dextrous disconnections and he puts away his knife. His cutting board and apron are stained with black tarry stuff, rancid bad-milk stink from the body. With care, Teo slides both his hands into the aperture at the top of Chan's skull, feeling with his fingers for the base of the brain. Then, easy as bobbing for apples he draws the dripping, only slightly shriveled organ out of its case, complete and undamaged, with a thin queue of neatly-cropped spinal chord at the bottom. With all the gentle concern of a doctor birthing a newborn he slips it into the jar. The liquid takes its charge in silence without a single plip, closing solemnly over Chan. Gratified, the Divinity Student nods wordlessly to the butcher and steals upstairs to Teo's rooms. With grim pride, and a secret delight, Teo turns to watch himself in his mirrors. He starts hacking the body to pieces. This hand to his hand, this arm to his arm.

Desden has a few small rooms just past the uppermost landing, clean and bare, an odor of metal desks and office supplies. The Divinity Student sets the jar on the desk, turns on the desk lamp and sits in a cone of harsh blue light. He pulls his pen and notebook from his pocket, and uses the pen to stir the formaldehyde. Eyes locked on Chan, he can see thin filaments of yellow essence swirling out of the tissue, mixing—the smell is strong enough now to disjoint his body, intensify a feeling of being stitched together and soft in the head, of half-emerging from his own head. Shaking badly, he dries the pen and sets it aside for fear of dropping it in, staining Chan with ink. Clammy in pit of his stomach and cobwebs threading down his arms and legs, he sits, barely contained, waiting for the fermentation to hold. Not much time but forever, thankfully the last memories are all that's needed, and he dips his hands into the blend—cold puckering his fingertips and boiling vapor off the nails; breathing hard now, he raises dripping palms and sprays sour fluid into his eyes, bedews his face—coming at him it's coming at him, blue light flickering out and it's got him, he's going into it, wrench and pull and for a moment hanging over the grass suspended between sky and ground tied to a cloud by a shining line flooding body taut and crushing the back of his skull cracking him open shrieking and nothing pulling at him to go into nothing passing through the nothing and he's nothing—and comes out the other end in a cheap hotel room, floor and carpet stretched on his face, his insides being hammered with a tapeworm thrashing in his stuffing, or Chan's, bones turn to white hot glass and bend to ropey twisting arms and legs and ribs collapsing, re-expanding to collapse again. The Divinity Student pushes back in time, now Chan is breathing and he can feel something like hard bubbles drifting up through the floorboards, passing through him with cold angry pressure, and there in his arms and legs coming up through his abdomen, all of him going glass then marble then wood and carpet then back to glass going brittle and aching and acid searing in bone filaments and bubbles bursting out his back and through his head rolling like a ball clearing columns through his body. The Divinity Student screaming and pushing, he's got the tearing at his throat, the air channel collapsing and shredding like tissue paper, trying to push further back, and as he rises free and watching Chan slobbering out his last breath beneath him, face all eyes and gaping mouth, as he's getting out, he latches on to one tiny part, he draws back just a little, only just a small bit, to Chan at the desk, Chan writing his notes, and the Divinity Student copies these notes, and watches a dark-haired lady drift in and leave many times, an empty thing day and night, all of life on the page, in the pen, sad writing at the borrowed desk, pause and stare at the bricks in the wall across the street, then turn and spread ink again, and sad, and write, and dark-haired lady, and eat, and sleep, and sad, and write—and Desden's room.

Back: returned, the Divinity Student sitting and staring, new magic words humming on the pages of his notebook, and sad Chan's dead memories rest again on the desk in front of him, in a cone of harsh blue light.

Chapter 13: The Demons

The Divinity Student scowls through the window at a metallic sky turning cobalt-colored at the end of the day, strange high clouds moving fast. Behind him, Miss Woodwind is measuring his notebook on the scale, her neat hands setting weights with care on the balance. She comes out from behind her card table, moving toward him, holding the book in front of her and stabbing at him with it.

"You've torn pages out, I can't get its proper weight."

The missing pages, covered with Chan's words, are wedged in the Divinity Student's inside right upper coat pocket. Their typed duplicates were delivered this morning to Fasvergil, who received him sitting on a plywood tombstone, mending costumes. He had extended his hand and let the sheets drift to his palm. They had seemed to catch and spin in the air as they dropped. Fasvergil had settled his needles and deposited them on the small shelf of a lectern behind him. He had said nothing, looking candidly at the Divinity Student, and then turned his eyes down to the costumes again.

"Sometimes the words get mixed in with gibberish. I thought you wouldn't want them."

She cocks an eyebrow, "Whatever it was you collected last night weighed more than this notebook and everything in it. Gibberish or not, we need those entries."

"I threw them away."

"You're working for someone else."

"I'm working for myself."

Her face distorts, "I say you're working for someone else!"

"Think twice before you accuse me of anything," he says quietly.

For a moment Miss Woodwind returns his gaze, muttering under her breath. Air hisses through her nose as she hands him back his notebook.

"I suppose next time you'll at least have the decency to keep separate notebooks for your separate jobs." The corners of her mouth turn up, the air around her is getting warm.

"Next time I'll bring you everything," he lies. "I'll bring you my old exercise books from the Seminary."

"Really?"

"Some of them."

"Oh." It's not what she wanted. She looks off into a corner, listening to the office buzzing around them, the rustling of the wallpaper and the rattling of the windowpanes. Dust rains down on paper reams and book spines. Outside, he can hear cars roaring up and down the street and squealing across the plaza, swarming across the city like rats on a corpse, looking for him. He follows her eyes. They drift back towards him, then lock on his. He drinks her fragrance in, and the warm column of air in which she stands.

"No," she says, "not when you ask me. Never when *you* want, only when *I* want, that's the way it works."

She raises a finger, looking like a schoolteacher admonishing. "Only when I want. You're always working for *me*."

And she turns to go, when he asks her to go walking with him. She rubs her hands a little. "I'll finish a few things here, and join you on the corner."

Later, she meets him, and together they march down through the plaza and into a part of San Veneficio he'd never seen before. Until now, it had seemed to be exclusively composed of hallways and lighted porches, low buildings. Now he is surrounded by towers, lights kaleidoscope as he passes, leashed to Miss Woodwind. The avenues are broad and black, fewer people, trains howl by on creaking trellises over their heads. She's got him; he's just realized the emptiness she makes him feel, as if a space with shimmering edges is yawning in his chest. It's filled with vapor that emanates from her in thick gouts, pulling him along with her. Her breath, and the moist corners of her mouth, small, shining in the streetlights, rolling out silent words, and parting over her even, white, filmy teeth. Her fragrances, particularly from her hair, the close parts about her ears where her skin is especially delicate, where the scent goes dark and rich.

"Tell me about the Seminary."

"It's old. It was commissioned by a king . . . the last one to be canonized, I think . . . There's a marble statue of him in the hall. Every year, we had to pay our respects on his birthday."

"What classes did you take?"

"Languages, literature, history, what you'd expect."

"Theology?"
"Of course."
"Many different kinds?"
"There are thirteen disciplines."
"How many did you take?"
"All of them."
"What disciplines were they?"
The street passes, they turn a corner, no reply.
"I would have thought you could tell me."
No answer. The Divinity Student lays his hand upon the Holy Book, holstered just below his shoulder, under his coat.
"Did your father train you in word-finding?" he asks.
"Yes."
"What does he do now?"
She bites down on the words, but they won't be dammed, even by her, "He still works—he finds words in books."
"Hidden words?" He remembers the pages Mr. Woodwind was soaking, how carefully he watched the color of the flame as they burned away. "Words written in secret?"
"Yes."
"Had much success?"
She's trying not to answer; she can't understand why she does.
"None."
He takes his hand away from the Book. Miss Woodwind relaxes.
"You learned to do that at the Seminary."
No answer. A cat, dressed in black and white like the Divinity Student, watches them passing.
"Don't do that again," she says, just quietly.
The Divinity Student nods his head.
Time passes, and she brings him up short before a billowing steam grate; delighted, she steps into the white column and beckons him to follow. In a close alley, with no one to see them, he follows her, and she's smiling at him again, her face in condensation glows right in front of him. His face alights on hers. She's smiling at him, indulgent and she bares her shoulders, collarbone spread-winged and delicate, he kisses her throat.

She turns and leads him into the building—the office, they've come full circle—invites him inside, embracing him, murmuring happily to herself.

AND LATER THE DIVINITY Student is walking among white houses, shining like bones in the moon's arid light. Dampening every sound, their black lawns soak in dew by the road, their curtained windows are flat against their closed and dozing faces. When he looks up, there are two seven-year-old children in dirty shorts walking toward him on either side of the road. They freeze—air closes around the Divinity Student like a hot wet hand, chalk stuck in his throat, and he strains forward, his lungs pulling to open but drawing only vacuum. The moon goes impossibly white overhead and the sky darkens and turns transparent. He can see them, one a boy, one a girl, shaking with silent laughter, standing rigid by the side of the road, and the air around his head is crumbling into black pellets. In the distance, a pair of headlights stab into his eyes—there's a car coming fast down the road, still far away but speeding toward him. Pushed down by a weight, the Divinity Student stumbles against a wrought-iron fence, feet slipping on dewy black grass, seeing now that flies are swarming from their noses, burrowing out from the corners of their eyes, crushing themselves pushing between their teeth until their chins run with threads of black juice.

He can see more now. The children's teeth are clamped shut, their lips pulled back but not smiling, leathery fixed withered lips like mummies, skin on their faces brownish-black and cracking, silent, the laughter still bubbling up inside them making them shake. And now the flies are coming toward him, the Divinity Student, clutching at one of the rods of iron. He forces his mouth shut but the cork in his throat slams down harder and his limbs coil back on themselves whipping around him, muscles snapped tight as piano wire, but he's struggling. The children laughing harder now, he can hear it, high pitched and hysterical, and the cackling getting faster and faster until they seem ready to fly apart, twisting at the knees, but his feet are rooted in place, and their fingers bend back and then snap one by one like wet twigs—the Divinity Student can see the stumps of black bone and blood popping out to splatter scattershot on the pavement, a drop of blood spats on his cheek, and, in a brief moment, he sees them, strangers to each other, emerging from their homes, running to the waiting car in obedience to a wordless command to be used as instruments against him, moon intolerable, blinding now, and flies all around him matching their whine with the laughing boy and girl. In a moment the demon will be on him burrowing, and they clench their teeth so hard their jaws break lopsiding their faces with two synchronous wet snaps and their teeth are driven up right into the gum, blood coming out thick with bits of flesh, the rush of the car's engine thrums louder pounding in his ears and rattling the ground, and with shaking voice the Divinity Student suddenly starts reciting Chan's words. He speaks to unravel them and push himself free, without understanding what he says.

A fence rod tears free in his hand, and around him the flies begin to burst and spark like firecrackers crashing around his ears. The Divinity Student breathes again and starts to run away. The two children shriek and pound the street with their fists, but the words strike and rebound from their skulls and faces with a sound like metal striking stone. They stop laughing. They've been dead now for a while. The car's voice dies, the lights wink out. For a moment, they turn around on their toes slowly embracing the air; then they run as fast as they can, past the Divinity Student. But what they run from can't be outrun, and holding hands together they fall and blow away.

Chapter 14: Albert

Weaving his way over half-sunken pavings, a priest assigned to the chapel of St. Sulpice walks among eroded tombmarkers, pacing toward the listing shadow of his rotting church. St. Sulpice squats immediately adjacent to the city's lowest point, a convex basin at the base of a funnel, whose walls are a prison rampart of derelict, scarred brick buildings with broken windows. Hissing sewer grates flank the churchyard, bordering it on two sides with foaming gutters—a flimsy wooden bridge spans one of the sewage-channels connecting the churchyard to the street; the priest had used this bridge himself a few moments ago. The chapel itself, foundering into the mud, is abandoned, smells of rotting stone and wet ivy leeching the walls. The priest is here to inspect the grounds, insure that the place still stands inviolate, and with cold hands he inspects the padlock and anchor chain that seal the doors, then turns to wipe thick sweat of rust from his palms. Stepping gingerly on soft earth he follows the perimeter of the walls, peering in the windows, but his eyes find only decay and hollowness inside.

He follows the convexity of the apse and picks his way along the other side of the nave—the silence breaks with the ponderous rattle of a handcart receding over the bridge. Dashing around the other side, muddying the hem of his cassock, he sees two men pushing away up the street, one man in grey, the other hunched in a heavy black overcoat. They are fleeing the torn grave of Albert the word-finder, open, still steaming beside a pile of dirt.

The Divinity Student hears the priest shouting after them and curses. He has a bottle of ethyl alcohol in his pocket—he tears off Albert's pant cuff, gags the bottle with it and lights the fabric, tossing it onto the bridge behind them. The fire bursts blue in the gloom, fire flaring purple-hearted over the wood. The priest has his pistol out and fires; bullets ricochet over their heads. Teo flashes him an inexplicable look. Up the street empty and striped with intermittent street lights they racket with a sodden bag sloshing in the cart, and the priest's curses fading into nothing behind them.

TEO HAS SCAVENGED A small air-pump from one of his discarded refrigeration units. The Divinity Student now rigs it with a hose and a hollow ring of metal perforated at regular intervals. He drops it to the bottom of the jar of formaldehyde, and Desden settles Albert's gluey brain gently on top of it. The air-pump purrs quietly on the desk, sending up a coil of bubbles in thin mercury columns that babble at the surface. Teo withdraws downstairs, reluctant to leave. The Divinity Student—having correctly guessed that the agitation of the bubbles would speed the fermentation process—watches already the yellow ropes of Albert's memory oozing from the tissues, mixing thickly with the chemicals. He rolls up his sleeves in the fluorescent light, and makes himself ready.

Downstairs, Teo is segmenting the soft, seeping body of Albert an inch at a time when he hears the noise. Rushes upstairs and throws open the door. The Divinity Student is crouched by the open window, chin and eyes running, glazed, oblivious. The pump and ring lie on the table, dribbling. The Divinity Student is holding the jar in one hand. With a horrible face he raises it to his lips to drink, and then vomits out the window, and drinks again and vomits.

"What are you doing—you're drinking it?"

The Divinity Student's voice is hoarse and thick, his nose is clogged. ". . . he's been dead longer than Chan . . . the words won't come clear enough . . . I have to look *closer* . . ." He shakes the jar in frustration, "I'm not getting enough!"

Desden looks at him. They look at each other, and then the butcher thinks of something.

"Wait, don't try it again yet." He holds up his hand and runs back downstairs. He whips a blade from the rack and walks up to Albert, neatly cuts off a strip of his liver and carries it back up to his friend.

"Swallow it."

The Divinity Student eyes him blearily, blinking water down his face.

"It may help you digest . . ."

He's waved forward from the floor. Desden gingerly hands him the morsel, and with a sour face the Divinity Student shovels it into his streaming mouth.

"Whole, don't chew it at all."

Throat working violently the Divinity Student nearly gags a moment but forces it down. Teo puts his hands on his shoulder.

"Wait a moment or two for it to settle, and then try again."

Time passes. Teo retreats to the doorway. Compulsively the Divinity

Student masters himself and drinks again. Teo watches his eyes roll back, smells the rancid chemical rasp his nostrils, while the Divinity Student turns inside-out drinking. Then, suddenly calm, he rises, carries the jar back to the table, and sits, and stares, and is quiet. Teo goes back downstairs.

Much clearer this time, sensation of magnetic repulsion and slipping along fields, edges pressing and grating inside, not painful, and slowly going in no direction. Many bodies pinwheeling out from his, maintaining single pivot points of contact, a knee, the neck, his collarbone, he turns around to face what's coming, like a lightless world roaring there and drawing him in, but he eases around the edge and spirals through an orbit before sliding into clammy vapor to preset occasion, then jackknifes straight down into the heart of the cold, and unseeing a million miles away he picks up his pen.

This one, Albert, works in fits and starts, disconnecting periodically from memory, disjoint, platforms at the edge of sight are walls and curtained windows, frequent beds—breakfast time now, but they serve dinner instead, dark outside, so yes it must be dinner time, only I'm sleeping now, bathing, lunch, but which day again? Shadow music and ghost rooms, pretty wife in care maintaining him. Words coming now and then, writing them down, getting ready, just getting ready to go where they come from, windows blur to clouds and lightbulbs to dandelions, pretty wife to pull up the covers, and son watching over him at night, smiling pretty wife pressing cushion coming down again she holds it close, soft pressure hot against his face and feathers clogging his mouth, then, no feeling in his legs, no feeling in his arms, a snowball bursts in his chest, and nothing again, like the Divinity Student's lightning-caught nothing, but too late, it's gone, it goes away, a full notebook and he's missed the most important thing! The medium, falling back in his chair, the medium, running his fingers through his hair, the medium, he wipes his chin, looks at the jar and the wallpaper refracting through yellow fluid and the glue-smell old Albert's brain. It's already going clear.

But the medium, press through and try again to get back to the medium. Incline his face into the clammy mouth of the jar, sour chlorine chemical smells thrusting fingers down his throat and up into his head, shooting down his nose, boiling behind his eyes, atomizing the stuff into his face, drinking more of it and feeling it burn heavy down into him. Now it's diluted but any memory, anything at all, passing through nurseries and locker-rooms, dim haze of family outing and hateful weather, tossing on vomit-colored oceans that stank of vomit, swam with it and shrieked it at him, and all the time the Divinity Student is there on the deck, or under the crib, or loitering reflected in the eyes of his friends, pressing in at the borders, pushing at the edges of those memories, pushing out, get out past the frame into the blackness memory floats in, the place the words come from, but grinning faces hand him books weighing him down, pinning him in place, a ring on his finger weights him in place, blankets tie him down, years pile up on him and the Divinity Student is fighting to get out from under, or dig down deep enough and push out in all directions. Everywhere, no break, no stop, Sunday school and cooking, laundry, talk, eat, sleep, breathe, tedium-exhaustion.

Now the Divinity Student is only fighting to get out, just to get out, he punches the friendly faces, he kicks down the bookshelves and throws the plate, the bed, out the window, and cuts the ring from his hand, and leaps off the roof, puts the whole pencil in his mouth and eats the lead like candy smacking his lips, he tears up the calendar, and shreds the clothes, and pulls the house down around him, and now only an instant there it is—that same place the lightning showed him, only for a hair's breadth turning of a moment, and then back again in the same damn room and the same damn chair, and he rushes down and out of the shop, lest he destroy that, too.

DESCRIBING A WIDE ARC, the Divinity Student weaves back towards the shop. He's watching the sky so intently that he knocks into lamp-posts and stumbles over paving stones. Slowly it's building, the sense of staring down into limitless openness, until his head reels back and he has to catch himself. The moon's gone new, dimly visible, a black ball drifting just past peaked rooftops and gutters encrusted with carved star-lit faces—it's a huge closed eye trained on him.

Teo's street appears to his left. The shop is ruined.

The Divinity Student sprints snapping broken glass under his feet and bounds through a gaping hole where the door was once. Inside, the refrigerator cases lie uprooted against the far wall, meat and machine entrails strewn across the remaining scarred tiles. He looks down; sees tire tracks smeared on the floor.

Desden pokes his head out of the meat locker with wide eyes. He comes up fast, still in his apron with a holster of knives.

"Two cars came while you were gone." He makes an aborted gesture at the shop. "I managed to get rid of the body before . . ."

"What about Albert and Chan?"

"Safe in their jars—I packed everything up after they left."

"Did you get a look at them?"

"Windows were tinted."

"Are you all packed?"

"Not much to pack."

"Wait here." The Divinity Student stalks out into the street, stepping over some beams that used to be in the ceiling. His throat's gone tight like a slow vise clenching down on him. The city has an undersea look to it—he goes down to the pay phone on the corner.

"It's me, I need a new place, the cars got Teo's shop."

Fasvergil says nothing for a long time. Eventually, he disappears behind the receiver, comes back in a few minutes with an address.

"Itemize the damages. I'll expect a report on this."

Dial tone.

Food-smell and people-buzz and then the rubble again, Desden standing alone in the shop with a bitter look on his face.

"This is very bad, very bad," he says.

Chapter 15: The House

High weeds around the house bristle like a frightened cat and surge against the fence. As with the rest of the place, its paint flaked away long ago exposing old, grey, seamed, desiccated wood fresh only for new splinters. The porch is fifteen feet off the ground, with broken wicker screens between the supporting beams, and behind, the foundation settles into the slope of a low mound, brackened with wiry impenetrable desert brush and short oaks. The Divinity Student carries a bag that sloshes and chimes occasionally with a rich tone of ringing glass. He's following the banister up to the porch, which is also banistered. The entire front of the house is railed with banisters like rows of bones stripped bare and fossilized. Teo passes him and holds the door open, biting his lips, and inside, the core of the house—a vast central shaft with tiny rooms radiating out on all three floors, and separate stairways along the walls with direct access to each floor—more banisters, and ribcage shadows along every wall.

The Divinity Student is a little relieved to get out of the sun; he's been feeling it more lately. A sick, disinterested uneasiness in direct sunlight, making him screw his eyes up and walk stiffly along the street, like an old man. With care he selects his staircase and carries Albert and Chan up to the third floor room where they'll be working together. Teo goes back out to the cart and brings in another knife-rack for the kitchen, then sets about installing the last refrigerator unit.

The two spend the evening pacing the porch and kicking dust and dead leaves down into the weeds. Across the street is a somnolent congregation of desultory houses and yawning warehouses. The wind blows warm brown air baked all day in desert earth and grazed by the monitors. Desden absently flicks one of his knives at a spider—he follows the blade with his eyes, then cocks his head, and the Divinity Student looks.

The point had bitten deep into the wood-rusk, the polished steel handle still humming, but the spider is not there. Nor was it ever there. Teo shrugs and retrieves his knife.

Later, Miss Woodwind comes to visit. Teo opens the door for her. In the vacant expanse of the house's heart, she is pushed by invisible currents from one staircase to another, finally caught and pulled upward by a conveyor-belt of banisters. She holds her arms against herself, but her eyes shine like venom, and she is not afraid.

The Divinity Student's room is directly under the roof. He's there, at work in his shirtsleeves building a divining machine out of an umbrella. She walks in and pauses a moment; there's a great suspender "y" sprawling across his back, darker against his fading black shirt with its bleached silver sheen, frayed cuffs, and worn through at the right elbow, which is cool white and hard, like a water-smoothed stone.

She says hello. He's predictable; he's forgetting about the agency, and Miss Woodwind has taken it upon herself to remind him. He looks sheepish and surprised to see her in the house, digs out one of his notebooks. As she sits on his cot to read the new entries (none of them from the Catalog) he goes back to his invention, impatient. The shaft of the umbrella, sawed off close to the support beams, is attached to a variable set of gears and a single lever with a numerical dial. The spokes are cut to diminish in length according to random intervals within a preset range, between three quarters and one half the length of the previous spoke, and each is tipped with a small tin reservoir atop a fountain pen nib and a spigot. The Divinity Student is currently stringing clear plastic fishing line from each spigot down the length of its spoke, and tying them to the central gear.

She finishes reading and leans back. The cot sags almost to the floor in the middle. One blanket, no pillow. Yellow chemical stains on the sheets. She sits up again, watching him work. Presently she comes over with his notes.

"More sleepwalking?"

He nods. Her fragrance envelopes him.

"This will be acceptable for now, but . . . I have a bad feeling." She wrinkles her brow a little. "You're . . ."

She slaps him across the forehead, and startled he jerks back.

"You're getting a bit remote," calm voice, "wherever you go, you must always come back to me." After giving him a significant look, she turns her attention to the desk. "What does this do?"

"Nothing. It's a divining machine, but it's not finished."

"How does it work?"

"You set it in a circle of paper, fill the spigots with different pigments, and turn the crank without looking at it. The configuration of the gear engagement is random, some unpredetermined gears act to wind this spring," and he points to a copper coil in the midst of the cogs, "others rotate the entire apparatus to a starting position, while others open the spigots. Then you flip the starting lever, and the machine begins to rotate as the spring uncoils, clockwise or counterclockwise, starting and stopping, fast or slow, all randomly."

"And meanwhile the pigment is dripping down onto the paper from these arms" She points.

He spreads his hands. "When it's all finished, you take the paper out and examine the pattern."

She smirks, pouting her lips a little. "How do you read the pattern?"

"You look at it."

"What a hobby!" She laughs

Why take this from her? There's no choice. He opens his mouth, and something flickers across his features, just a flaring on the rims of his spectacles and the briefest instant of momentary sadness, or sympathy. His eyebrows draw together slanting upward, sending curled ripples across his forehead, his eyes widen and seize at the corners, his mouth pulls open downwards, his throat strains against his collar, all for a moment, then his features melt in confusion—Miss Woodwind has him by the shoulders.

"What's the matter? What are you doing?"

He shakes his head, slumping to the floor half-conscious trying to point.

She turns her head, her eyes probe the attic's darkness and then turn forcefully back to him.

"You're being ridiculous. What did you see?"

A light had gone by very fast. He shakes his hand in front of his face. Everything had looked different in here, for a moment. The Divinity Student had seen someone staring at him from the dark.

"I don't see anything. Would you stand up!" She shakes him hard.

"I don't know."

"Well?"

He saw only part of the face, only eyes and an open inky mouth, no one he knew.

She throws up her hands. "You're making all of this up, it's clear you're not up to getting anything done today." She heads for the door.

The Divinity Student follows her and pulls her back, muttering, "Making things up I'll show you who's making things up," and, clasping her belt, he drags her out the door and along the top floor landing. She leans away but does not protest, mumbling distracted to herself, always curious.

The only door on the other side of the landing bears a heavy latch and an eyepiece, set slanting down—someone on the other side of the door could presumably use it to stare down the staircase. Still holding Miss Woodwind about the waist, the Divinity Student throws the latch and pushes the door open, then thrusts her inside.

He tells her to "look!"

The chamber is vast, reaching its two wings to claim almost all of the upper floor. It is infested with crawlways. Just enough floorspace remains to allow the door to swing open into the room; the rest is heaped with overlapping tunnels, coiling about the room on the floor and hanging from the ceiling, sometimes angular, sometimes curved like a hose, punctuated by small doors and landings, portholes, chutes, and in one case a miniature spiral staircase. At their feet is a terminus, with a wooden door and a small white porcelain knob, just large enough for an adult to creep through on all fours.

"No one knows what this is for. It was built into the walls. Now listen!"

They stand listening for a moment.

From deep within the room comes the muffled sound of someone crawling.

Miss Woodwind is silent.

THAT NIGHT, SHE GOES with them to find Niffruch and Dreyfic. The city morgue is a squat octagonal building situated near the Orpheum, with a green copper dome and thick marble walls. It's windy tonight, sending showers of dead leaves eddying by streetcorners and rattling empty branches. The vault of the sky is swept clean, so clear that the moon, though new, is still dimly visible as a ball of shade floating above the horizon. The street is quiet save for the hissing of the breeze. Silent, they, three now, fan out and submerge in the shadows flanking the morgue, searching for an entrance.

Miss Woodwind signals. She had walked directly to an open door set deep into the eastern wall.

The Divinity Student gives her a nod. "I knew *you'd* find the door."

Inside, a narrow passage plumbs into the building like a mineshaft, the ceiling merely inches over their heads. Its walls are yellow, the floor padded with dark green carpet sponging up their footsteps. At regular intervals, pallid, anemic lamps link wall and ceiling, but cast almost no light. They walk for a long time, and the corridor slopes gently downward and begins to curve in on itself, until abruptly they turn a corner and stumble out into the main holding area.

Under girders and swinging lightbulbs are rows and rows of vast cabinets, fifty feet high and white as bone, milky gloss of porcelain doors hinged in tile facing and chrome handles. Once in a while something creaks or whines off in the distance, as if the whole place were adrift on the ocean. The Divinity Student rushes forward and begins looking for the N's, while Teo and Miss Woodwind search out the D's. Labels penned in the same meticulous handwriting spell a legion of names, up and down the ladders and through the aisles, stirring long-stagnant air redolent of rubbing alcohol and boiled metal. Then the Divinity Student calls them. His voice is quiet, but his whispers are carried by the vastness of the unstirred space.

They find him before the special cases, drawing a broad drawer open. Niffruch and Dreyfic lie there together, hand in hand, rigid faces upright at attention. Shreds of tenuous white mist flutter about them or plunge feathering to the floor. The Divinity Student draws a deep breath of stale ice-musk through flared nostrils, then he pounces, trying with all his might to tear their clasped hands apart. Frozen solid. They don't move.

Desden says, "We can't carry them both—we've only got one bag."

The Divinity Student scowls. He turns and fixes his gaze on Miss Woodwind, stabbing a finger at the spiderweb of catwalks overhead.

"You keep watch."

She stands off, watching, smiling back at them from time to time, lips moving, voice droning silently.

The Divinity Student turns back to the bodies. For a moment his eyes flick from one seamed marble face to another. Then with speed prompted of pure bile he seizes Dreyfic's head and wrenches it viciously to one side, snapping his neck. He exhales and throws Desden a look.

"Now cut it off," his voice is low.

Desden decapitates Dreyfic with three simple strokes, the cold flesh cuts with a sound like tearing cloth. A watery trickle of thin purple blood drips from the neck wound, but the butcher is careful, and spills nothing getting the head into the bag. The Divinity Student is already dragging Niffruch out of the frost; the ice whines and crackles on the dead man's suit. Teo comes over to help, and when Niffruch stops short, his hand caught in his partner's grasp, down comes the cleaver to hack off the hand, and Niffruch slides into the bag.

In the passage again, Desden stumbles; the bag clonks against a wall leaving a broad smear of carmine blood reeking like rotting fish. The

Divinity Student is against leaving evidence—the pieces in the drawer would go unnoticed for weeks, months probably, but blood on the walls will bring inquiry the next day. With care he nicks his left eye with a sharp fingernail, and squeezes out a small pearl of clear fluid. As Miss Woodwind and the butcher stare, he seals the wound with one hand while flicking the liquid at the stain. Where it hits, the blood goes clear and begins to run, and this spreads until all is innocent water coursing in small droplets toward the floor. In the cool dry air it will sublimate away, no stain, no trace. With a look of warning to Teo, he squeezes by them and heads back to the street.

DIVINATION MACHINES ARE NOT the Divinity Student's only project. He's devised a new method, more effective than drinking the preservative fluid. By adding a special reagent to the formaldehyde, he can cause the fermented memory-infusion to rise to the surface without requiring agitation. Strain the liquid off the top, that's the next step, and collect it on a small metal plate, under a glass dome, with hoses attached through a tube at the dome's apex. Electric current runs through the metal plate, vaporizes the fluid, which condenses on the interior surface of the dome, and is channeled up through the tube, which ends in a breathing mask.

Now he's shut in the room. Miss Woodwind is still in the house, on the next landing down, wondering out loud to herself at the light under his door. It's late; he's rigging up two assemblies—he plans to read Niffruch and Dreyfic together. She's anxious, could have left hours ago, but there's something irresistible happening. Eavesdropping earlier, she had heard the Divinity Student reporting to someone on the telephone, someone who didn't want him to take Niffruch and Dreyfic at the same time. The Divinity Student had agreed not to, then went ahead with his plans anyway. What happens next?

It's quiet. Teo is downstairs with his mirrors, dissecting Niffruch's body just a little at a time, occasionally bursting into a frenzy, carving deep, straight incisions, but he's quiet now. There's no way Miss Woodwind can guess what's happening.

It's still quiet. Coming back, bringing the body into the house, the Divinity Student had frozen, staring at a window for a moment. Another flash had flickered across his face.

It's even quieter still. She feels smoke in her chest, something frightening like a slow kick in the stomach. Whatever it is, she sneers at it and pads up the stairs and right up to his door.

She can hear something. The door is locked, but she can hear a noise through the door, a windy, scratching sound. For a while she fumbles for what it could be, what's making that noise? Then he stops to take a breath, and she understands she's hearing two sounds. A pen scratching paper, and him. Reedy, and whistling, and hollow, and only a veil over a silent nothing so that even when she stops her ears with her hands and runs downstairs, she hears him screaming without a voice, whisper-screaming, without stopping.

Chapter 16: The Final Interview

MISS WOODWIND TALKS IN her sleep. She wakes in mid-sentence—she's in the house, the Divinity Student is curled asleep at her feet. He's rolled himself up into a ball in his heavy coat at the other end of the bed. She didn't hear him enter the room, didn't remember when she'd fallen asleep. His spectacles are getting bent, pressed up against his face. Light from outside is bursting on the windowsill and glaring at her from burning patches on the floor. She blinks, dazzled, and windows and carpet corners flicker in green and purple under her eyelids. Getting up, she nearly steps on a cloth-wrapped charm that the Divinity Student had made for her—anyone entering the house in which it is hung must close his eyes and keep them shut until he leaves. She picks it up and picks a little at the rough string binding it shut—he's told her that if she unwraps it to see what's inside it won't work. Impatient, Miss Woodwind plunges through the door and into the central shaft of the house. Here in the gloom the light-doubles turn to blurred black blind spots hovering immediately before her eyes, and she follows the banister railing downstairs, sloughing off curled scales of paint with the edge of her hand. There's the front door. She stands looking at it for a moment, then thinks again of the Divinity Student sleeping upstairs. What is he doing? She decides to stay longer.

She goes to the kitchen, drawing back too late, remembering what lay there cold on Desden's cutting table—but Niffruch's body is gone, the butcher had already disposed of him. The marble top is antiseptically clean, the knives are racked and shining, cuts of meat, expertly prepared, glow red in the display cabinet under shining glass, unmarred by so much as a single fingerprint. Miss Woodwind purses her lips and walks out. There's the front door.

She wanders past and into the living room. The windowpanes are grey with dust, admitting only the shrillest light glancing hysterically across peeling walls. The furnishings look like bundles of twigs, elongated spiny chairs and listing endtables on precarious spindly legs. She sits for a moment, perfectly still, and stares into space. After a few moments she hears, for the first time, a faint low sound—a yawning rumble from an indeterminate source, either far above or far beneath the house. Its tone is so low as to be more a sensation than a sound. Not constant, but intermittent, she can only just feel it as a current passing through the floorboards. The house emits no other sound, nothing coherent or discrete, no creakings or settlings, only that sourceless roaring. She mutters a little to herself, stands, and weaves back into the rooms, passing through each and not lingering. In this house, it seems to her, the spaces are always the wrong size, either too large or too close, and everywhere the same disrepair and neglect. She feels it closing around her like a shell, and she longs to burst it apart and expand into the opening. Apart from the furniture, spare and fragile and seeming to be parts of the house themselves, there are no artifacts, nothing left behind, except the things they brought with them.

There is the front door again, but she won't leave yet.

WITH THE PASSING DAYS she stays with them, goes with them at night to cemeteries and churchyards, holds lanterns over straining backs and flashing shovels, keeps watch while they curse and drag bodies heavy with rot to the cart, tries to read undistracted while lights flicker under the door upstairs—she always goes to the landing; she always stares at the door; she never goes in.

The Divinity Student is changing. He speaks less and less. Miss Woodwind can see him being drawn not so much into himself as outwards into something else. He's getting pale and moist-eyed, he complains of strange pains, he can barely stand in the heat of the day. He has ceased perspiring altogether—to keep cool, he must spray himself with atomizer filled with formaldehyde. Eliot was the next target after Niffruch and Dreyfic, and after Eliot came Penfield, then Mira, then Gomes, then Carrasene. He sleeps in the same room with them all, dimly shining glass vats wired to the distilling chamber. He takes all of them on at once; he can do that now, easily. She watches him go out every day, tilting down the street with his rolling gait, now much slower than when she met him, easily distracted, more particular than before, bringing in fresh barrels of formaldehyde every day, and she knows he's stopped going to see Fasvergil (whom she now knows by name, from the telephone), that he's been out beyond the city walls, walking alone in the desert with the monitors. He knows which body to collect next without having to consult with Fasvergil or his agents—the divining machines tell him everything. Sometimes, he'll jerk abruptly back, as if he'd been called by name, or turn, with a flickering expression, to the windows of the house, staring at something invisible over her shoulder.

When she sees him next, his great coat is so black and terrible it's almost leaking darkness, it smudges the air around him like a pall of coal smoke. Even Desden, the devoted friend, will stare at him in disbelief sometimes, when his eyes disfocus, and he'll be slapping himself, struggling to finish a sentence. When he does talk, he stifles every other word, and she knows jealously that he's fighting off *their* words—the dead minds upstairs.

Miss Woodwind wants to see his notebooks, but he refuses to show them to her. She wants to go to her father, but she doesn't. It's what she doesn't understand, it's really nothing that keeps her in the house. She spends her days reading in her room, and feels the current of the house tumbling through the floorboards.

THE DIVINITY STUDENT DRIFTS in twilight under the trees. He can see the oros clearly now, poised and silent, some asleep, others staring at the road and wailing to each other in low whistling voices. Pedestrians mill about aimlessly; they've gotten harder to see clearly—occluded, indistinct figures. Much sharper are the others he had never seen before. Carried along by the sight of them, he can do nothing else but look. Not just familiars and animal souls, the street is a reef, inhabited by insubstantial things skulking under the pavement or flitting effortlessly above the people's heads, coiling between their legs, lashing out at each other from windows. There are shades like torn umbrellas convulsing up through the air, past the rooftops, like jellyfish, long white smears and clouds of tiny multicolored phosphorescent shapes with jagged edges. A flat manylegged object exhaling odorless blue smoke scuttles over his left foot; he's not disgusted, he doesn't flinch.

The house floats into view like a shipwreck, rocking gently in the air. An inhabited wreck, there are lights on inside, just dimly visible yellow lambence strained and diluted by silvery windows. The Divinity Student pushes through the long grass beyond the fence, barely touching the ground, then flows to a stop at the bottom of the steps. A thin veil of blue light flutters across a windowpane. The room beyond is empty. The shutters frame a blue face crying out the window, black mouth drawn wide and cheeks pulled back, eyes two shining crescents, wet brow—it slips away. He watches those features fill with shadow and retreat—they submerge. Something's happening; he's seeing them all the time, every day he sees them. Ghosts. Desperation seethes in him; what's happening? Run, but no, he won't run, this feeling's not worthy of me, I've got things to do. He goes up into the house.

WHEN THE SUN SETS, he tests his newest divining machine, an afterimage light-scribbler, inspired by a note he'd taken earlier: "arrange lights at random in a dark room, enter dancing, read the afterimages in your eyelids. Takes practice and long study." He turns out the overhead light, and sits in the dark in front of a wooden box with a single gear on the right side. Turn the gear to the first cue position with the gentle pressure of fingertips, a muffled report, and a series of tiny shutters in the box's face fall back into dark openings of all shapes and sizes, some interconnecting to form irregular grooves and channels, at random. The Divinity Student presses the lever to the second cue position, and tiny multicolored lights wink on inside, either staring out from single holes or poised at the top of a groove or channel; from a slot just below the "lid" of the box, a broad black damping bar clunks into position, hinged to pass at regular intervals down over the face of the box. The Divinity Student pulls the gear a few more notches.

The damping bar rolls down, disappears through a slot at the bottom of the box's face, the lights shunt back and forth, some moving at random, others trace the pattern of the shutters, the damping bar reappears through a slot at the top of the box's face and sweeps down again. Watching, he then shuts his eyes and reads the residual streaks beneath his eyelids, the afterimages, scribbling notes on a pad by his hand. He pulls the lever a few more notches.

Another dull wooden clack, the shutter configuration changes, the lights get a little brighter, they accelerate under the passing of the damping bar, and the Divinity Student shuts his eyes and takes the next reading, one after each pass of the bar. After a few moments, he pulls the lever down again. Faster, brighter, and some lights change color, shutters reconfigure, behind him, and unseen, his shadow flares against an angle of the ceiling. He takes more notes and pulls the lever down.

Grains of light billow behind him in the dark like wind-stirred snow, but the Divinity Student keeps going, staring at the box until his eyes hurt then grinding them shut. He's trying to write what he sees, writing so fast his pencil tears the page. He jerks the gear and the box flares like a match drawing streaks along his face and on the walls, drawing flecks of light into patterns swimming through the room. Adjust the gear and the box spins faster making a rattling sound, and turn the gear and the room goes brighter, long figures resolving in the room, behind his blazing face, arms hanging useless at their sides, drawn faces like cracked shells of blue light with gaping eyes and mouths listlessly watching him at work.

No time for notes, he's gradually speeding the box by increments until it buzzes and rattles and shakes on the table. Wide green eyes, fixed and colorless, trying to swallow the patterns whole, while all around him figures mill and weave, taking any shape and color, while cracked blue faces slacken and nod like faces at asylum windows, fixing empty vision on the back of his head, the careening rasping patterns spinning around his face. Breathing hard he grips the gear as tight as he can, turning it bit by bit under white knuckles; the damping bar fans his face so fast it's little more than a grey blur between him and the lights. Then suddenly the Divinity Student shuts the machine off and screws his eyes shut, falling backwards, even as he hears the engines' wheezing halt, into a black ocean of stars and streaking bolts of lightning.

On the street below, Fasvergil turns his face, saturnine in moribund light, toward the house. He folds his hands. Overhead, stars retreat and the constellations yawn apart, the wind rattles the grass at his feet, and, behind him, empty buildings gape and dribble streams of dead leaves from their gutters. Drawing closer, the house tips precariously, balancing to fall on him, but Fasvergil's concern outweighs his doubts. All in black with his frayed belt and soft cat-burglar slippers, he pads up the stairs on thin crepe soles and raps his long dry knuckles on the door.

A woman answers; surprising. Miss Woodwind scrutinizes him carefully, bringing her face right up to his and staring directly at him, as if memorizing his features. He can tell that she wants him to go away. Her expression is disdainful.

"I am Father Fasvergil. I'm here to speak with the Divinity Student. We have some words for each other." His face creases softly and mildly, with real priestly reserve.

Miss Woodwind becomes more annoyed. It's dark inside; he can barely see her, but it seems her mouth is moving silently. Talking to herself. After pausing to think, she turns and walks stiffly into the house, leaving him to shut the door behind him. In a patch of light falling dead from the neighbor room she turns and indicates one of the stairways with an offhand gesture. He sees her better in the light. She looks tired and pale, and she is talking silently to herself.

"He's on the top floor." A quiet, rich voice, though sighing with fatigue, perhaps she's ill. He thanks her sepulchrally and slips past, mounting the stairs.

Miss Woodwind watches him vanish into banister shadows, squinting a little. Behind him he leaves a smell of mothballs and library dust familiar to her.

Fasvergil knocks and waits, and knocks again. He has a long wait. Finally, the door falls silently open before him, and he steps in quietly to confront the Divinity Student.

"You haven't been reporting to me. You've been missed."

He scans the many silver-shining jars watching from shelves, tables, and mantles. "Nevertheless you clearly continue with the project."

The Divinity Student stands mute, disheveled, his face gone soft and pale as wax, his flesh turning translucent. He stands in the middle of the room as if he were hung there, twisting slightly on his feet.

"I can only conclude that you have decided to pursue this entirely on your own, and that you are keeping your discoveries to yourself."

The Divinity Student crosses to the desk with a single step, surprisingly strong and decisive for all his weak looks. He seizes a handful of paper and hurls it in Fasvergil's face.

"Now leave," he says.

"This house belongs to the Seminary. If you withhold information from us we will be compelled to evict you."

"Leave," the Divinity Student says.

Fasvergil opens his mouth to speak again, but the Divinity Student is already by his side, seizing him, his breath clouding in Fasvergil's dry face.

A single dry gasp of formaldehyde unfurls from between the Divinity Student's lips, and in it boil a hundred gaping blue faces, and infinitely silent watching things, and many other ones stirring along the ragged edges of the Divinity Student's breath, and more—a deep empty nothing, spreading behind the walls and surging through the floorboards and shimmering inside him. Fasvergil is stunned. The Divinity Student has a stronger claim on the house than he does.

That dead hand falls from the back of his neck; the Divinity Student retreats into the shadows. Faltering, Fasvergil is consumed with a new feeling. He struggles to address the Divinity Student, but his words crowd and trample each other, muddling in his mind until all meaning is consumed.

Then the Divinity Student's face turns back upon him, fixing him with a gaze as steady and impersonal a star—he sees the Divinity Student's face silhouetted against itself—and staggers back as if struck, not recognizing anything human in that face. Fasvergil finally backs out onto the landing, looking at the Divinity Student in a convulsion. The Divinity Student stares at him from the far end of the room. The door slams shut between them.

CHAPTER 17: THE MUSE

CRAMPED IN HIS ROOM, the Divinity Student shakes awake in the middle of the night. He rolls over and takes his head in his hands, but now even sleep is strange—falling and waking with blunt headaches, half-dreaming all the time in weird fragments, dragged away and thrown in the river, or held down and screamed at, wordless, voiceless howling. Tearing the sleep from his head in shreds, he turns to look out across the expanse of floor toward the wall and its windows. Suddenly, he comes sharply awake, alert, the air seems to vanish, and his gaze accosts the furniture, objects, flowing their outlines into each other in the dark. Caught, they snap back within their borders and their borders go rigid.

He's on his feet. Things scuttle in the corners; they whisper to each other, and the Divinity Student is beginning to understand them. One window in particular is asking for him, shining bright blue in a black wall. Padding across the floor, he can hear tiny scrabbling footsteps dodging out of his way, rustling like grass at his feet. He stops, resting his hands on the sill, and looks out.

There she is! It's a woman, standing far off on a roof top, looking in his direction. She alights on a chimney and vaults impossibly high, landing on a neighboring gable as lightly as a falling leaf. Dancing bright bounds and leaps, she hurtles from one house to another, always coming closer and moving faster and making no sound. Even at a distance the Divinity Student sees her clearly: compact, a white pinafore with skirts like sea foam and black bands around her waist and throat, each hand gloved in black, fluttering in a lace cuff like a spider in a white blossom. Her long legs are also pitch black and likewise her hair, wrenched back in a tight knot on top of her head. She's still far away, then suddenly she cartwheels along one roof's spine and hurls herself out into the air like a thunderbolt, flashing through the air. He hears her touch down over his head, her two feet landing as light as birds. Footsteps tap up and down over his head—she seems to be dancing.

The Divinity Student throws open the sash and thrusts his head out the window, craning his head in time to see a flash of petticoat. Then suddenly her face appears between his and the sky, peering down. She smiles, and her smile strikes him with a tangible shock, like a hammer blow. Her teeth are jagged as a mouthful of venomous broken glass, her eyes, black and glistening like deep wells, narrow to two happy crescents. The Divinity Student steps back from the window, and in a flash she flips down, hanging from the eaves, slipping lithely into the room. Now she is immediately in front of him, silhouetted against the window. She puts her hands on her hips and looks at him, and her teeth flare in an awful grin when she notices jars on shelves and tables. She takes a step forward; one of her gleaming shoes crackles a spare page lying on the floor; she squats and looks it over—it's one of his notebook pages—her eyes snap back up to him again, and they shine this time deeper than water, pinning him on the spot.

The page drops straight to the floor like a stone. She walks up, making ghastly delightful faces, and stands right in front of him, breathing cool air on him; she's rustling and cool with flesh like tissues of liquid air, pulls a serious face and raps on his head with her knuckles. He jerks away but does not retreat. She raps again, gravely. Then he reaches for her, and she reaches for him, and what happens next—words fail, words fail . . .

Now he's always dreaming, and so sensitive to the slightest excess of sensation that daytime is too much for him. He remains inside all day, quailing with a sense of brittle fragility that threatens to erupt in splitting pain, and when night brings him relief, he wanders the streets, passing cemeteries filled with spirits gently singing, "Oh see us," after him, eyes closed; hands pat the air. His eyes close and his hands pat the air just the same. He then leaves San Veneficio altogether to walk outside in the desert. The monitors ignore him, lying motionless in rows, a petrified forest of black shapes against the horizon, eyes staring reflected light back at the city. He still sees strange things, but away from the streetlamps he can't make them out clearly—they're much larger and slower out in the desert, sometimes whispering past him just a few inches away, whale-sized or larger, and glacially silent. At other times he'll look up at the stars, or a gibbous moon, and a vast shadow will swim by overhead, diving between the clouds, occasionally sinking low to drift along the ground.

As he wanders there, sometimes he turns and looks at the city, and his eyes water and smart. Glowing, San Veneficio blurs into a jagged coppery smear along the horizon, shimmering at its base, its penumbra of lights dotted with spiraling shapes circling over the Orpheum, the plazas and spires, his house. Lustrous people-shaped things sail around the walls like uprooted anemones. Gazing at the city repels him, disorienting, making him giddy, and he turns away before too long.

Returning one night, sleep steals over him with such force that he drops to the ground directly, like a scarecrow.

Sunlight lances red-grey through his eyelids; the shadows of people fall across his face. He covers his face with his palms against the light, until, after blinking a few minutes into his hands, he becomes accustomed. The Divinity Student looks up, squinting. He's lying at the end of Box Street, just inside the border where pavement gives way to bare dirt and trees. It takes a long time for him to make out the dim figure hovering against a wall nearby.

The Divinity Student drags himself up into a crouch and starts to move toward the other man—then stops. There's a line drawn in the dirt in front of him. It curves around . . . it's a circle. Someone had drawn a circle around him while he was sleeping. The Divinity Student surges forward and then staggers back. He pushes out to the sides and all around, but it's no good, he can't move past the perimeter. Every time he nears the edge a greasy nausea rolls over in his stomach, and the physical burden of the sun's light becomes a sort of sucking pressure snapping at his legs, making him tumble to his knees again.

The one against the wall is coming toward him. Now the Divinity Student can see him, the curious expression on Ollimer's face, that he had not genuinely believed it would work, still doesn't believe it.

"Now listen you," he says quiet and timid, "just stay where you are."

"Break this line and get me out of here." The Divinity Student's voice is harsh and disembodied, and for a moment Ollimer almost looks ready to obey. He straightens instead. "I'll let you out, provided you give me reason."

"I don't have my notebook and you wouldn't get it anyway now break this line!" he points to the ground.

"You have to turn over the house! You made a commitment and now you have to give us the words!" It's beginning to dawn on him that the Divinity Student really can't get out of the circle. "You'll hand them over or stay right where you are!"

Time passes. Ollimer stands with strengthening resolve at the end of the empty street. The Divinity Student, squatting in the dust, glowers malevolently back up at him.

Suddenly he's knocking back and forth inside the circle like a caged animal throwing dust in the air, howling and barking curses, and Ollimer jumps backwards startled. The Divinity Student freezes and stares intently at Ollimer, and for Ollimer it's as if two black gulfs yawn in that face. This time the Divinity Student speaks quietly, "Break the line."

Ollimer is trying to twist himself free, screwing his eyes shut against the two icy fingers that press out of the Divinity Student's face onto his own.

"Come here."

"You owe us those words!"

"Come here and I'll give them to you."

Ollimer takes a step. "You don't have your notebook."

"I was bluffing, I have it right here." He shows the book, holding it between his long fingertips. "Let me give it to you."

Ollimer is coming toward him now. "And the house? What about that—"

Ollimer has permitted his hand to stray over the circle's border. He's staring at the way his shadow falls across the circumference he drew on the ground, his head cocked to one side, gazing with the look of a daydreaming schoolboy at his hand's shadow, realizing too late, in slow motion—and then the Divinity Student seizes Ollimer's outstretched hand and drags him forward nearly tearing his arm from his socket. Ollimer's feet gouge two long grooves over the circle's outline, breaking it.

The Divinity Student explodes, hurling Ollimer down the street, sending him flying down the block, touching the ground roughly on his side and then Ollimer skips and spins along the pavement like a stone skimming the surface of a lake, slapping the ground with his palms trying to steady himself. Finally he manages to get to his feet and runs in panic down a side alley. Behind him the Divinity Student is angrily scuffing the circle out with his feet, and when he's done, Ollimer is just disappearing ratlike around a corner.

"Ollimer I'll murder you! I'll cut you out of your head and give your body to the butcher!"

His black coat bursts open in a cloud of dust, and springlike the Divinity Student sprints after Ollimer, his long legs reaching out and snapping back so far he nearly grazes his back with his heels. Almost out of control he ricochets down the alley. He windmills his arms seizing garbage cans and debris and tossing them out of his way, and he's granted a glimpse of Ollimer at the other end of the alley, pale panicking face under flight-disheveled red hair. The Divinity Student bellows horribly at the retreating back. Redoubling his efforts he leaps over crates and heaps of trash, rappelling off of windowsills and fire escapes to keep himself in the air. He rounds the next corner, and Ollimer is vanishing down another alley, showing his heels like a scared rabbit.

Ollimer leads him toward the town center. Presently the routes widen, more people appear, until they're both of them fighting their way through crowds, Ollimer weaving with agility enhanced by fear, and the Divinity Student stiff-arming pedestrians and cars out of his way. They're murky shadows to him, scarcely recognizable. All he sees is a flash of red bobbing like an apple a few blocks ahead. But as time goes on his rage abates—he gets confused and worn out. The burden of the light and the enervating presence of other people seeps into his joints and saps his strength and determination by degrees, until he has to forget about Ollimer. He's started dreaming again, getting a soft head, half-blinded by the obscure shapes milling around, their murmuring voices humming up and down in his mind. Something like a jackal is peering at him from a window. It throws its head back and its mouth tears wide, yellow shoots and leaves sprouting from its throat, so the jackal seizes the vine and pulls it, coaxing it to grow with its hands. The Divinity Student watches the blind drop between them, and a sodden depression closes on him. Further down the block, a long black car belching exhaust pulls up and disgorges a large black dog, disappears into a building. The engine stands idling, fumes catching in the Divinity Student's throat, nauseating. Later, the dog comes back out again, back into the car, the door slams and the car speeds off, odd smell emanating. Feeble and lost, he wanders with arms outstretched in front of him like a blind man, trying to find his way back to the house.

He blunders up the Street of Wrought-Iron Workers, deserted now—it's midday, and too hot to work with fire. He passes them drinking their tea on the corner. The street curves as it goes up, and soon they're out of sight; he's invisible, soaking with sweat. He stops, pulls the atomizer from his pocket, and sprays formaldehyde on his face. The Divinity Student stares around at the twisted black iron gates and rods in the shop-courtyards, and it seems to him as if he's wandering among strange oversized letters glistening in gullies and nooks to either side, limned in flickering inky fire. The impression of walking through a printed page becomes overwhelming, disarming, and he sprays himself again, taking comfort in the familiar bitter smell and searing vapor.

A shadow falls over him from above, and in a moment he finds that his vision is suddenly less foggy, and that the heat has abated a little. He looks up but the brilliance of the sky blinds him to the descending shade—someone's coming down out of the sky. The shade is presently standing beside him. And now black gloved hands, like spiders in lace cuffs, take hold of his arm, clamping down vice-tight through his heavy coat, and guide him up the street. And out towards the edges of town. And up the steps to the house.

Once under the eaves his vision finally begins to clear. The house exhales cool air on him, and he basks in it. His head, plagued by slabs of day-heat out in the sun, turns glassy clear, and the swaying dizziness of the street is arrested as decisively as the motion of a pendulum is stopped by the clockmaker's hand. A shade ascends out of sight behind him even as he turns to it, vanishing with a rustle of petticoats.

Chapter 18: Gaster

The Divinity Student falls out of his cot, lies on the floor, jarred but only just barely awake. He has dreamt the dream he'd dreamt before, in the hammock, but this time he changed more completely, into something impossible to remember, and it was the woman who had come through the window who was waiting for him in the clouds. The ugly, ginger ache behind his eyes wakes up, too, and he holds his head in his hands, yawning until his jaw hurts. He's graduated to a new level of pain; his muscles feel like they're being rubbed with sour stinging fingers and his joints shriek against each other like glass on glass.

Still exhausted, he pitches himself forward and drags himself to the chair. Tonight they're going after Gaster—the last of the twelve word-finders. Tonight the Catalog will be complete. Gaster is kept on permanent display in a public building, but the place empties out after hours and they can take him then. The biggest obstacle is a tight noose of guards present twenty-four hours on the premises, but Teo has remedied that now, with the help of a forger he knows in the Street of Clockworks. For a small sum and commission he has happily faked three passes for them as "security inspectors." The Divinity Student lays his head on the desk, feeling blunted and feeble, wanting only to rest and rest. Over and over he relives the dream, seeing clouds parting in front of him and half-remembering being drowned by a feeling he couldn't describe. Relapsing the sky is black before him, a gaping absence—but all the same it's reaching out and spanning the distance to snare him, and all the time he's reaching out his hands to meet it. He comes back to himself, and realizes that Gaster is the key, Gaster and then rest. Gaster, and then the mission is over.

There's a lighted candle over there on the windowsill. The blade of flame is tiny and dwindling, poised at the tip of the wick between empty air and a lake of liquid wax steadily rising, strangling the fire. The Divinity Student stares at the candle with a sense of recognition, falling against himself back into reverie. He stares at it from under his eyelids, until everything around the light dims and wavers, and although he's smothered and weighed down with exhaustion, he's thinking clearly; he knows the candle is burning away its own substance, sublimating itself invisibly into the air. It's eating itself. Swaying slightly back and forth he realizes that it's hollowing itself out, and going faster and faster, that it will either drown in its melting flesh, or shrink starving away to nothing. Then —snap—and he's out of it again. He catches himself with his mouth open, blowing just gently toward the candle, but it's all the way on the other side of the room, and his breath isn't enough. The Divinity Student sneers at himself. He gets up, walks over, and pinches the candle out with his fingers. Outside it's getting dark—he pulls on his heavy coat and heads downstairs.

It's when he's doing something important that the pain changes. He still feels like a walking scrapyard, but the leaden, crushing vise at his temples relents a little. It doesn't vanish, rather it changes character, and focuses into a sweet toothache pain, and all his senses light up like a window display. He feels as unreplenished and unrefreshed as before, but at these times his machine parts take over and carry him along where he directs, like servants tending a bedridden invalid.

Miss Woodwind emerges from the kitchen and meets him there in front of the door, puts a black doctor bag in his hand. She says something to herself and fetches Teo, who's in the basement grinding his knives. Outside the air is dry and cooling, night's veil drawing across the sky again, San Veneficio lighting up in front of them, orange streetlights and wan porches, rolling in rows up and down and at all angles, making the town look like a tangle of frozen rail cars knotted together in big strands crisscrossing the desert. It's exhilarating. All together, they go quietly, avoiding main thoroughfares where they can and sticking to the slums, smell of stale frying fat and old cabbage. Now and then, drawn wasted faces peer out at them, but something in the air the Divinity Student carries with him keeps them at a distance. The three of them are charged. Teo carries a knife ostentatiously in his belt, but people scrabble aside from a mere look from the Divinity Student. His face is scoured with death.

Miss Woodwind guides the Divinity Student across the big boulevards—otherwise he'd get disoriented, forget where he's going and what he's trying to do, walk through a wall, make mistakes. She doesn't look at his face: she'd made that mistake before and seen his eyes darting this way and that, peering at nothing, and, following his gaze, she'd almost seen . . .

Presently the crowds thin out, the exodus from the business end of town is over for the night, the people are already lost elsewhere. The Seleucid building is at the northernmost corner of a small, star-shaped square, a big blocky thrust with circular portholes lined in brass, and now that the people have gone, each is a blank, placid well of suggested space inside. The lobby is a glass-fronted box, with a couple of guards pacing around between the ashtrays and potted palms. Miss Woodwind leads them to a nearby alley where Teo has stowed the handcart earlier, and they retrieve the rope from it. They cross the empty plaza to the lobby and stand mute in front of the glass doors.

A dough-faced guard walks up. The Divinity Student holds up his forged pass. The others follow suit. The guard's eyebrows rumple and his mouth stretches a bit at the corners in an unconscious ingratiating grin—he doesn't know whether to ignore them or curry their favor. The doors sigh open, with a gust of antiseptic, air-conditioned air. The other guard approaches.

"I wasn't told about any inspections."

The Divinity Student glowers at him, and the guard backs away. For a moment he wavers, then nods and lets them pass. They head straight for an open freight elevator and instinctively the Divinity Student presses the button marked "five." The door slides shut on the guards' flummoxed faces.

Fifth floor. Miss Woodwind is the first in the corridor, jumping ahead of the Divinity Student. The hall is dark and empty, a double set of swing doors set directly into a far corner.

Now they're in a big room with long transparent white drapes hanging like ghosts at the windows. Arranged along the walls are the skeletons of monsters glossed with lacquer to prevent evaporation, encrusted with precious metals and gems. The younger, or naturally smaller, varieties leer from dim alcoves and display tables. In the center of the room, still slowly rotating on a pedestal rigged with ribcages of struts and gear-clavicles, is Gaster. Among other things, and beyond his duties as a word-finder, he was also responsible for the collection of old bones that stands watch over him now. During the day he meets his admirers, revolving in a pressurized case filled with invisible preservative gases. The visitors mill around, read the little plaque, and peer morbidly at his slack face and blanched hair.

The Divinity Student strides directly up to Gaster, and, as if pushing air before him in a solid sharp mass, a crack whips across the front of the case, and with every step he takes, the fissure widens and spreads. There's a hissing sound; Miss Woodwind and Teo cover their faces, for their noses and eyes are already smarting and burning with the hot, buzzing, non-smell of that gas. Even Gaster himself looks singed. The Divinity Student reaches out his hand and taps the case once, and the front panel collapses like wet paper. Teo and Miss Woodwind stagger back to the door, then drop through. Taking a deep breath through flared nostrils, with relish, the Divinity Student steps into the case and draws Gaster tenderly to him, carrying him out of the room like a baby, head cradled on his shoulder.

Then, in the hallway—footsteps are coming, a few flashlight beams scratch across walls and framed pictures, guards coming from around the corner. Teo grabs the Divinity Student, who stands gazing lost in Gaster's face, and pulls him along, following the bend in the hall, and Miss Woodwind starts trying doors. Finally, she kicks one open and they all pile into a small office with a window facing the street. She slams the door behind them and barricades it with a desk. Voices call from the elevator.

Working fast, Teo pulls the rope out from under his apron and ties it to the radiator, tossing the other end down to the street. He looks to the Divinity Student, but he in turn grabs Miss Woodwind by the arm and sends her through first, then Teo after. Flashlight beams itch by under the door; knocks and bangs up and down the hall; the lock rattles and starts to give. The rope breaks. Down below, Miss Woodwind is already on the ground, and Teo drops only half a story; he's safe, coils of rope spiraling down on top of him. The Divinity Student gently presses Gaster's face into the folds of his overcoat and bounds out of the window.

He lands square on his feet from five stories, stamped on the pavement a sound like a gunshot. For a moment he's perfectly still, then, exhaling, he straightens his legs. He walks, limping only a little, and tenderly places Gaster in the handcart. Teo, moving very slowly, goes to help him push the cart up the alley. Miss Woodwind follows too, also very slowly. Above, lights flare in the empty office, heads pop out the window and stare, stabbing their lights down the side of the building, up and down the radiating streets. There is no sign of the Divinity Student. They are getting away.

OVER THE PAST FEW weeks, Teo has become more and more thorough, his technique now demonstrating a decidedly greater degree of precision and skill. Now he's dissecting Gaster slowly, piece by piece, flaying him first with exquisite care, and always watching himself in the mirror, imagining himself on the table. Periodically, he sprays Gaster with a bottle of formaldehyde to keep him fresh; now he too finds the smell refreshing. If he takes his time and breathes the mist in deeply, he can feel the more acute sensations inflicted on the body—sharp decadent pain welling up like foul water in his limbs, pocketing itself inside him, making him wince and recoil from the body and then step up and carve into him again, like someone endlessly inspecting a painful wound, or someone whipping himself. Desden still curses to himself, but he's taken to cursing quietly, muttering all the time under his breath, almost as an afterthought. It's the cutting that seizes his interest, and he knows this time will be the last, at least for now. As he walks around the table to start on Gaster's left side, passing the empty skull, he thinks of the Divinity Student at work upstairs, and wonders what will happen.

EARLIER THAT DAY, MISS Woodwind found a fragment, transcribed in the Divinity Student's handwriting, in the attic room:

"From dictation: A degree of self consciousness so acute that it is impossible to be lonely. One does not feel lonely so much as one becomes sick for want of distraction from oneself. One does not encounter others directly, but only through a blind of observed personal reactions. One is a ghost chasing after and spying on oneself, a lesser part. I correspond to San Veneficio in this way. It manifests reactions interpretively prompted by events external to this world, translated into fictions in this world, and this fiction and its reactions are reported directly to me by winged saints who are my eyes and ears. This is not a function of my mind, but a representation of my mind's function. The only release is apocalyptic, where reaction/sensation overrides (or better, out-shouts—a Divinity Student suggestion) the observer, incorporating and embodying him, giving freedom through absorption."

She knits her brows and shakes her head.

THE DIVINITY STUDENT IS beginning. Hoses curve in the air around him, one from each of the twelve jars, drawing formaldehyde through an air pump onto an aluminum plate on the table. Each hose adds a different color of fermented memory: grey-green, yellow, brown-orange, tea colored, and clear—they collect in layers without mixing. When the plate is filled, the Divinity Student turns the pump down to a trickle, empties his lungs, and fits a mask, connected to a porcelain dome suspended just above the plate, over his mouth and nose. At the same instant, he drops a catch and sends current running through the plate. The formaldehyde hisses and vaporizes, boiling up into his face, and with a single breath he draws it all into his lungs. His head snaps back against the chair and his arms fall stiff over the armrests. On the table, a thin trickle of chemicals dribbles from each hose onto the plate, skipping in beads over the electrified surface and melting into steam, breath drawn into the Divinity Student.

He loses all sense of his body immediately, his limbs go warm-numb and seem to fall away, and then his senses fall away, too.

The first thing is a clear cycling chime like a ringing glass that passes through at intervals. He's got nothing else but that and a feeling of something like a lightless explosion—solid and frozen . . . not warming but still melting into wind or waves. He's going very far. Although he can't see, there are shapes around him, darker shadows looming against the dark like cliffs and frothings like sea foam. There are things that seem like panels of transparence, windows, lightless as everything else but looking as if he's peering through something, from one dark to another. At first he thinks they're moving past him, but no . . . their positions are fixed, he's the one who's moving. Gradually, a low thrumming sound becomes audible, from no particular source, as if all the surrounding landscape rests on a blurring membrane. He continues to move "forward," and then he starts smelling a warm, sweet, acrid smell, like wood alcohol, but it's a secondhand sensation, from far off or somebody else. Now he can feel ropes whipping around him, or maybe flying stones, but it seems more like taut ropes spanning vast invisible distances, whipping through the air with a low whistling sound, dropping tiny currents of air or water, small disturbances in the air.

Albert is the first to arrive. He just appears, although he's not actually visible—it feels like light hitting blind eyes, a physical touch. If he's anywhere he's just above the Divinity Student and to the left. One by one they appear—after Albert come Niffruch and Dreyfic together, and then Chan after that, and the spectrum fills out piece by piece. Gaster comes last, and he's right beside the Divinity Student, so close he can feel the "waves" or "wind" berthing around him.

As they speak together he begins to forget their names, recognizing them only by their manner of speaking. The first one has a shrill, wan voice, and shrieks; two together make rustling, whispering sounds; one is almost wholly silent; here coughs and barks; and there the patter of fingers flicking together; this one hums, stuttering "mm" or "mm mmmuh"; from that one—a bubbling hiss and sneeze; a bestial lowing and shouting on one side; on the other a flat uninflected voice muttering on a single fixed tone; laughing or sobbing; and the last speaks by dancing in an awkward, heavy circle, invisible yet sensible. Together they're all speaking the Catalog-language, the Eclogue-language, about everything, and behind everything.

The strain is terrible; the longer he stays the more tenuous he becomes. Vaporous hot flashes shoot from underneath to curdle up and around brittle sensations of obscene toothache pain and he's being whittled away, flying off in pieces that flutter away in high-pitched sounds like flocks of frightened birds. Pushing in farther it's only more obscure and much deeper than he's ever been, drawn into wide expanses filling with cold fibrous structures unraveling outward with no horizon visible only as greater shadows against dark fields, veils or endless surfaces both fluid and brittle, less moving than expanding—he's the only limited thing—him and the twelve with him, but they've been gone a long time, they're less limited. Only ghost sensations now, like tingling in phantom limbs, clinging together but strained to a point of tearing fragmenting and flaking away in flecks that reflect the dark—he's still trying to remember enough, the twelve word-finders drop away completely —he's looking for the medium, and what words they *really* use. The pieces twist around him in orbit, brittle weak feelings crumpling and collapsing pours over smooth planes searing hot along the edges and collecting in boiling beads, wash back into the Divinity Student wracked in his chair on waves from an empty-foaming ocean.

Chapter 19: The Last Day

THE DIVINITY STUDENT KNOWS this day will be his last. The divining machines verify it. It. The twelve jars that stare at him from all corners of the room tell him, the daylight that ebbs and flows in slow tides of color tells him, and the lightless patches in corners and along the edges of his room—they, in particular, tell him. He's found the Catalog. His studies are completed. He sits at the desk, rocking back and forth just a little, feeling only empty waiting for more dreams. The house around him is expanding to let it in. The air around his shoulders draws in frozen, painful needles in his fingers and down his legs, deep tooth-rattling shudders. With an absent feeling, he practically throws himself from the chair and out the door.

Miss Woodwind is reading in her room when the Divinity Student comes in. He sits down beside her, says nothing. She finishes the paragraph and puts the book in her lap.

"Well?"

He's staring at the floor. Again she becomes conscious of the house's low thrumming, fluttering hard under the floorboards—has it gotten louder?

"What is it?" she asks, but he only starts wavering gently backwards and forwards. Miss Woodwind gets up and grabs the arms of his chair.

"What are you doing now?" she says it loud, trying to get through, "come on, answer me! I've been here all this time waiting for you, at least you could tell me what's happening!"

Either he's dreaming again, or ignoring her, or he can't understand her anymore, because he still says nothing. She throws up her hands, they land on her hips as she goes to the window.

"What am I doing here?"

Outside, she can see a car idling at the corner. It's windows are dark; it's impossible to see inside. Eventually, as if responding to her angry gaze, it drives off down the road in a bleary cloud of scattered paper. She thinks of her father slipping pages into developing pans and the heavy magnifiers he'd use to study them; she thinks of the office and misses it. Finally her thoughts spin out beyond her attention and she finds herself peering at an empty street. When she turns around, the Divinity Student hasn't moved.

"You don't even realize I'm here," she says quietly.

She looks at him across the room, crumpled in the chair like a scarecrow.

"I know you're here." His voice is repulsive, it nearly pushes her back against the windowsill. But she screws up her determination and approaches his chair, his splayed feet in heavy shoes discarded on the floor.

"So tell me what you're doing! If you're not collecting words anymore then why do you stay here? You're looking for something else!"

She brings her face down until it's only inches from his. For a moment he weaves, barely able to find her eyes.

"Yes, you're right."

"Then let me in on it! Tell me what it is! I just have to know what it is!"

This is wearing him out. "I would tell you if I could."

"What's that supposed to mean?!"

He's waving at her, trying to fend her off. "I can't tell you anything more . . . it's not for telling."

"Liar!" She's keeping after him, thin lipped and bright-eyed. "That's nonsense! Nonsense, nonsense, nonsense!"

But he's already fading; his eyes are glazing and his mouth goes slack, his head falls back against the chair.

Miss Woodwind's eyes bore into him a moment, and then she goes downstairs.

There's the front door.

After a moment, she bites her lip, looks up the shaft framed with stairflights; her heart's in her mouth, something awful pouring up into her. One last thought of him as he had looked, standing talking to her father for the first time a few weeks ago, and then she remembers him at the fountain in the park. Then she walks out the door.

CARS HAVE BEEN PASSING up and down the street all day trying to distract him, or trying maybe to shave off pieces of his thoughts as they go by, fragmenting his concentration. Sometimes they'll idle directly in front of the house, and the Divinity Student will stand perfectly still, feeling the house shake to their engine hum, smelling the exhaust, the lingering outside pressing like a weight on his chest. Then, for no discernible reason, they'll pull away. Then the pressure lifts like a fading headache. He's come to suspect the insects, too. There aren't many Teo doesn't manage to kill, not just with knives, but with all manner of poisons and toxins tracing the edges of the house, baiting every door, window, crack. Those who do get through must have a reason, a powerful drive to get into the house, and seek out the Divinity Student. There's no telling when a pair of tiny eyes may be watching, and the Divinity Student is constantly on the alert. He can't let anything go wrong —just a little longer, until it comes. Once or twice a mosquito bit him, only to be killed and embalmed instantly with its first sip of his formaldehyde blood, and the Divinity Student suddenly felt the tug of its tiny mind as it perished, living its death along with it, connected together along a thread of formaldehyde. He smiles when that happens.

Teo is leaving. He's disposed of Gaster's body, and he's packing his things. Teo can see the time ahead unspooling like a short ribbon striped with days and nights, and at the end the Divinity Student's failing body will lie pale and curved on the ground with shadows over his face. However much longer it will last, he knows that the Divinity Student has no use for him anymore. So he puts his things away, and sends for a cart to carry off the last remnants of his shop. There are relations of his in town who will put him up until he can open a new shop, and pace in front of his mirrors again.

The last time Teo sees the Divinity Student, he's standing on one of the landings on the middle floor, leaning on a precariously tilting banister and staring out into space. The butcher waves his hand a little, and says he's going. The Divinity Student barely notices, inclining his head down only slightly, swaying. One suspender strap falls from his shoulders. He manages to unwrap a few waving fingers from the railing and makes a painful effort to grin, but his grin looks like death. Teo turns to go, and all feeling washes out of him, and he's all but forgotten his friend by the time he's out the door.

COMPLETELY ALONE IN THE house, staggering from room to room without point until he can barely lift his feet, then sitting with an empty head, staring at the wallpaper for a while, and getting up again. The place is empty. Wake up and there are cars going by outside, there's a fly watching him from a windowpane. He crushes it with his notebook and cracks the glass. Despite the effort he rambles up and down the stairs over and over again, increasingly coming to rest up in his room, staring at the glasses gathering dust all around, and his rickety, derelict divining machines. Time runs out. Fasvergil and Ollimer fade away. He has the Catalog, he has translated it and now it is translating him. The Catalog was not intended for them. He has destroyed his notes.

Sitting, and with evening falling, the Divinity Student feels himself settling in his chair, dropping further and further, and he has no strength to resist. As the day fades, his eyes refuse to become accustomed to the dark, everything blends behind a screen of tiny, shimmering motes of increasingly diffused light. Months pass without the lifting of that curtain, the window beyond remains as black as if it were painted black. Over time, cobwebs gather across the panes; dust blankets him, the room, the whole world; and he sits without stirring a single finger, his breathing the only sound and movement, growing shallower all the time. In imperceptible increments the house begins to fade, each fiber of the wood, the glass, the plaster, all of them starting to blend into the air with a faint dying glow. Older, much older vistas are coming through now. Luminous forms swim in and out among the furniture fanning the air with spectral plumage. Others sulk in shadow corners coiled ready to spring. Still others hover basking in dull, motionless inertia. For the first time their voices are audible to him, the inarticulate noises and weirdly-voiced half-words recited almost like verse in the air, which has become thick with things previously unseen. Cold draughts skitter along the back of his neck and roll in tides over him as he sits like a stone in place. Gradually, he begins to sense even the residual presence of the twelve word-finders gathered here, faint like people in weathered old photographs. This is where they came to find the words. There's a feeling like autumn leaves piling on top of him—he's become a piece of furniture himself, unable even to give the impression that he can move. With a hollow feeling he shrinks and shrinks, his insides ebbing away from his outsides, knowing implacably this is precisely how it has to be, to freeze and freeze, it's all part of the story. A cold aroma gradually fills his nose and expands down into his chest, pressing down farther into his empty cavities and numbing his limbs, making him even drowsier, and even colder, and even less concerned with himself, and he wants to embark, finally, sink into the weight and rest. It's a smell of repose and relaxation. It's a smell of peace and quiet.

No, it's the stink of wet dirt and rotting leaves—his eyes fly open and he instinctively recoils pushing the chair over backwards and tumbling out slamming his head against the floor. Twisted dark shapes trailing shadows had flocked around him like buzzards, looming together wreathing him all around; they scatter fast back out of sight blurring. The Divinity Student, his head ringing like a copper bell, drags himself across the floor like a man plucked from a freezing river. His bones are groaning like rusting machinery, but with every movement he gets going faster, shaking the cold, panic searing at him instead. He still has to finish properly, see it through or fail once and for all. Outside the cars are howling, their tires are whining on the pavement, their horns are blaring—and there's another noise. Slithering on his belly like a snake the Divinity Student slides out the door and down to one end of the landing, near the windows. Muscles complaining he lifts himself on the lower lip of the sill and peers out. There are three cars swerving drunkenly on the street below, jumping the pavement and splintering fenceposts, gouging furrows in the yard, spinning their tires and kicking up paving stones through the porch windows. The air is boiling with shadows ducking in and out through their windshields and doors, shadows with vicious bent figures and low whistling voices, whipping elastic through the air like clothes on a line.

Downstairs a crash that could only be the front door, slapped flat to the floor. Barking dogs and heavy padding with clicking claws in and out of the rooms, scaling the stairs, filling the house, baying, fighting each other. The Divinity Student is on his feet, the din getting intolerable with a dozen answering voices in every room responding in every register until the floor shakes and the walls rattle and the ceiling cracks. Black dogs the size of calves loping through doorways, and things beyond describing prowling, flying, dancing, swimming, lurking everywhere until they're all he can see. The Divinity Student runs up and down the stairs batting them out of his face, running from room to room, trying to escape. The cars are roaring in the yard horns droning like sirens, and inside the babble and the shriek and mutter surging louder like bedlam, so keep running from one room to another, keep running, stop and turn back and run again, rescue, rescue, breathing hard in a panic but never stopping going round the house, looking. Run and watch the house dissolve before his feet, the last tenuous fabric going translucent dark and fading away until wooden floors turn cobble streets and plaster walls of stripping paint and bubbling wallpaper go marble and stone and ebony with wrought-iron fixings, lamps to streetlights, tables to monuments, bookshelves to shops, curtains to trees, windows turn from inward to outward and the ceiling yawns translated into an endless void lit with huge heat-distorted constellations where minutes ago there were gaslights. The must of an old house going to earth and stained with formaldehyde turns to the many-colored spectrum of a city's smells, and the streets of San Veneficio burst out on all sides cutting between looming houses crammed with people, and around him, still weaving things and shapes like an army rushing around him in the dark, voices broadening too to a dizzying variety until the vastness of the sound homogenizes into a seething drone and the kaleidoscope of silhouettes and luridly-colored luminous things blends together into a transparent, boiling cloud.

San Veneficio comes clear again. The sky is a hurricane of still black clouds like the swirled cone of a cavern-roof, from horizon to horizon save for the storm's round eye immediately overhead. There the pupil-less moon stares down, and strange shadows move on its face; its light dapples the city blue and red. Where it's blue, San Veneficio is a ruin. The streets are empty and quiet, the buildings crumbling and bleached like ancient grave markers, the air turns chill and thin. The Divinity Student's breath steams acrid in his face, his feet stir plumes of dust powdering the ground like fine snow. Where it's red, the streets buck and shift like the deck of a doomed ship; the air rises in hot transparent coils so that the city distorts, as if viewed through a window of wrinkled glass. The outlines of the buildings around him billow like smoke. They hide enormous roaring engines, legions of enemies. In passing from color to color he can feel his wake in the air reflected back on himself, as if he'd run through a doorway where no walls or door had been. He looks down at himself and, like looking into a convex mirror, his body distorts, curving down to the ground, legs tapering to points, his pale hands like a doll's hands, his own pale face startling him in windows, and the rest of him lost in heavy folds of black coat.

For one hundred years he's making his way toward the center of the city. Dark and heavy the world falls away. San Veneficio is a maze, dead-end and then turn to dead-end again, but always a column of smoke rising from the center, and that's what he follows, running toward rest, toward rescue. He sees all but the largest now, those that rush by whale-sized, glistening in corners chirping and muttering to each other. The rest blend into the air. A train passing screams at him with a woman's voice. Somewhere on a back street he meets a man he'd met before on the floor of a hotel room. He drops from a melting fire-escape and stops in his tracks to stare at the Divinity Student. That single inexplicable look masks his eyes, so that when he looks again, the man is gone. Passing the cemetery, he sees huge pulsing trees burrowing into graves with their roots, their branches forking like capillaries into fleshy clouds. Another time he is stopped by someone else, someone who dances in an awkward, heavy circle, and vanishes into the corner of a building. Two men pass him on a rooftop holding hands, and passing, they greet him and wish him welcome. He never stops long, but keeps making his way toward the center of the city. He doesn't count the twelve men that he meets, one after another. The closer the column of smoke looms the faster he goes, and once he enters the inner district, he moves fastest of all. Now he's all but flying, feet barely touching the ground, streaking dust behind him in blue light, dancing along the uneven cobbles in the buckling red light, suspended between the ground and the air. And once in a while, he'll look up, to see someone pacing him along the rooftops, vaulting from chimney to weathervane, skating on gutters, using roof-slates for her stepping stones, and her black-gloved hands flutter in their lace cuffs like spiders in white flowers. Dark and heavy, the world falls away.

He gains the inner city at last, coming to San Veneficio's heart, the Orpheum and its great empty plaza milling with a thousand invisible shapes, sounding with a thousand hollow voices. Here the light is pure, the moon shines like an iceberg in stark white sterile light; the Orpheum is neither smoke nor ruin, but it blazes like a second moon, cool and unsearing. The dominant voice comes from deep inside, a disconnected, businesslike voice chanting inside the Orpheum, and a column of smoke dissipating across the city now that the Divinity Student has arrived. A lone white figure with long black legs whips through the air like lightning to plant her feet firmly atop the apex of the Orpheum's shining dome. She raises her two arms high in the air and turns her face to the Divinity Student, she bows her head to the Divinity Student, who is coming through the plaza to stand directly before the palace's great doors, between the statues of San Veneficio's greatest poets and a dry fountain filled with earth and blossoming night-plants, where dark and heavy the world falls away.

Voices rise again on all sides and shapes outlined in the dazzling light take on substance again, altogether a vast soundless noise and lightless light suborned and controlled by that one dispassionate chant from the Orpheum. A terrible feeling takes the Divinity Student, like a clod of dirt lodged in his chest, and branching through his limbs. He clutches his chest and falls forward, acid pain scalding him inside. The pain climaxes as the chant reaches its crescendo and he then raises his head despite his agony, because he recognizes the words, they're Eclogue-words. Now he knows the words, and the language, his own language, finally roots in him. A dark place he's seen before collapses all around him, and in darkness the Divinity Student catches with creation on the air, hooking his teeth, the sky clothes him and strips him in divinity and takes him like a messenger, he is drawn up into the sky.

The Golem

Prologue

THREADS COMING TOGETHER AGAIN with a racing, vertiginous feeling, speeding down a tunnel, hands thrown up in shock and dismay: it's time again, and space again. Where, for the moment, there were no dimensions, now there is at least a lightless below, and one dropped from a temporary nothing into it.

Read: white room, wide white pallet, a long window with blinds, closet, one door hanging open, a mirror on the inside of the door. Mild, milky light snowing across the thick carpets and across the walls, everything quiet. The room is empty; no one is here. Turn to leave with a tearing disengaging feeling and see in the mirror a collapsed figure, the nearer hand sweeping heavy as stone and slow as he turns to go, hanging his head and turning like one turns to run from a nightmare, straining inside against his body as it petrifies into grey film and slows . . . without stopping altogether, but helplessly jammed in foreign, artificial time.

Miles beneath this white room, may be a dark doorless black room, embedded in rock; lined with control consoles, hands and eyes fluttering like bats above illuminated displays. Now and then a hand or an eye flaps up to make control adjustments, and the keys thrill again to the purposive touch of icy fingers. Turning from the mirror, dimension again opens at his feet and he drops stupidly into it, fixed in an endless shift of equilibrium, arcing forward hands thrown up to protect but so slowly that he feels his body ticking through distinct increments of space. When he finally drops it's as though a hand had turned him out of its palm, and he falls, spinning, closet light and mirror winking out in space above him.

Now—this is always difficult—boundless space on all sides. His pupils dilate until the iris splits, his back arching headfirst downward, neck whipping helplessly right and left in the onrush of air. Repeated pulses of nausea, he vomits from an empty stomach, stinging bile churns in his teeth, up his cheeks, over the chin, into the nose and ears, hair, splattering the throat, searing the eyes. Doubled-up spins faster bellowing without hearing his own voice, cries of alarm unheard by anyone. A sudden cold sensation on a wet face, a struggle to breathe through ropes of mucous, eyes tearing uncontrollably, a stink, unraveling body. Wild attempt to catch hold of something, a pawing out with hands. Very soon, there is no more sensation, only an intensifying forward tilt of falling, expansion of a body, weightlessness, rigid and uncoupling, crumble through soap-bubble panes of space like icy glass. This falling body now proceeds to trope through all its forms.

In the darkroom, hands on controls.

The outer surface of a skin comes first, bleached opacous white, then raw red eyes, raw as raw meat in hot eyesockets, thin hair—the color rilling out of it draining transparent fibres, finger and toenails flick past, teeth turn clear over incandescent nerves and blue and red blood vessels, oil beads appear on the skin and then spread in the force of the wind writing trickle-patterns across skin tightened and painful. His back hunches and splits into seams, distending in funnel-shaped white loops of manta-ray flesh; these are the jet engines of his body with air intakes in front and angled jets along his trailing legs, blurred chalky and white like fish under murky water.

Burning cold air knots in his muscles as he gnashes his softened teeth, angling himself up to push himself up off the air and stop his fall. His body restored for the first time, rigid in its full weight, he retches again and it pours down out of him, tan jelly mixed with tiny threads of blood, caustic against his oily skin. His ears pop and then crack, and his eyelids squeeze together oozing tears that steam off his cold cheeks, his hair prickling. He is strangling and toppling unconscious—turns in midair, end over end, slower and slower, like someone turning in a nightmare, clicking through separate increments of space, spin down through clouds and a dimming night sky. Below him, a desert landscape ringed with mountains, a city gleaming with light, and beyond its walls a sea of reflected lights shining in pairs, watching.

Elsewhere, hands flutter and adjust the controls, and then *hold*.

To be read another time:

There are two kinds of priests or priestly people. One sort are linked by tradition to the lives of their parishioners—they perform socially. These are the kind who organize charities, who extend aid to the needy, who regard the well-being and happiness of all their flock as personal responsibilities.

The other variety exists in mortal terror and loathing of the material world, and recoil from every object as if it pricked like a needle; that pin-prick is an inlet for a withering current of anguish that flows from contact and which floods in like an infection and a lingering illness. This second type will take what limited refuge it can in the cloistered, monastic life, where everything is assiduously marked and branded with the icons and names of the divine, giving these objects an elevated status as corporeal components of ideas, making the fact of their material existence less chilling. But once begun, the process by which these priests shrink from the physical world is difficult to arrest. Many will eventually recede so far that they stare out in horror at the boundaries of their own bodies, feeling at every instant the impossible weight and degradation of their filthy garment of flesh. They walk cowed and bent, with their heads drooping to one side, their eyes screwed up so as not to see too much or too clearly, and their bodies are dwindled and transparent, as if they've begun to evaporate in the rarefied air of their retreat. All the force of their faith and expectation is directed toward the moment when they will finally lose themselves once and for all in limitless absolute noumenal perfection, and anything not also touched, and flawed, by the idea of perfection, is forever beyond their grasp. The Divinity Student is one of these.

If there's ever a film . . . clouds and sun, sunlight ebbing and flowing in clouds.

The Prefect's Dream

Arms fling the curtain apart, and darkness pours out. No moon tonight; the desert exhales powdery ropes of darkness, as glacially indifferent and absent as the sky, with a positive substance of darkness. From horizon to horizon the only light comes from San Veneficio. I feel that spiced breath from mummified lungs once more. The marble domes and brass onion-shaped minarets, high glass ornaments and quartz monuments, all gleam in a field of diffused light, concentrated here and there at the bright points from whence it issues. Overhead the stars collect that shine without radiance, and out in the desert giant monitor lizards, the size of horses, have emerged from their daytime hiding places to watch the city as they do every night, standing completely still, the city lights reflected in their enormous eyes. Looking out from the city walls, one is hemmed in on all sides by blankly staring eyes, beaming in pairs from the desert floor below. The beam from each eye is a thread in a web they weave out of San Veneficio's light, which strains the desert's exhalations through its mesh, and binds the city to the ground like a net, to prevent the desert from releasing it into the sky.

From a distance, looking back, the city is hemmed in only from behind, because the monitors in front have their backs turned, and their eyes cannot be seen from out here. Now, one pair of eyes detaches itself from the others and begins to move in this direction. They pass the city and continue out into the desert, without dimming or changing in intensity, although they flicker as the car goes over a bump in the road—those are headlights, not eyes. The car is following a pale ribbon of compacted clay, heading for a low hill outside town. Now it stops at the base of the hill, pointing its weak lights up toward the peak. They shine on a few desultory dead trees and collapsed iron fencing, and on a flat broken stone thrusting up from the ground.

Somewhere, within the walls, the Prefect of Police is awake, sitting in his nightshirt by the telephone. One hour ago, he started from sleep, his mind a chaos of dream fragments. He often has these especially alarming, unspeakably shocking dreams, which invariably prove prescient. Even in the alarm of his first few waking moments, as his eyes swept back and forth over the contents of his dark and sinister bed chamber, a familiar feeling of satisfaction came over him as he recognized the tell-tale signs of an oracular visitation. Within a minute or two, he had perfectly regained his composure; he suavely resorted to the telephone, summoning his two principle detectives, like two pet devils, from their sleep.

Now, three men emerge from the back of the car and open the trunk. The pet devils appear from the front to watch. Picks and shovels are shouldered, and the five of them make their way up through dead, waist-high grass. The grass rattles in the wind, rather two winds mixed, one warm and one cold. The two detectives have no tools because they're in charge, and they are moving back and forth among the tombstones now, peering at inscriptions with a small lantern. Their seamed, impassive faces loom down in the feeble yellow light of the lamp, and for a moment hang suspended in black space above the graves—the air is very clear. From grave to grave until they've seen them all, and then they pause and put their heads together. The wind comes up again, and the dead trees scrape their branches. The two men make up their minds and wave the lantern at a grave with a blank stone.

One of the workers carves an X in the baked-hard ground, and then together they plunge their picks into the breast of the grave, breaking up the clay and dragging it aside. Their overseers stand and watch, and yawn and check their watches. The car's headlights blanket the hilltop with a tawny spray of dim light, barely enough to see by, or to obscure the sky, which also yawns. They drop their picks for shovels because soft loam lies beneath the upper clay. There is no sound except the scooping and choughing of the shovels and the hiss of the wind in the grass.

As the grave deepens around the digging figures, the wind catches in quick eddies around their feet, stirring the dry soil and whistling in the small tunnels and burrowings that the shovels uncover. The wind brushes away the last thin veil of dirt. Wedging their feet awkwardly around the sides of the coffin, they work the ropes underneath and then step gingerly up onto it, kneeing themselves back up into the stiff grass overhead. The detectives, Pracke and Kipe, approach, and look down into the grave. Its walls are lined with tiny colored lights embedded in the dry dirt, flickering in little pools of blue, green, red, and yellow, dappling the white ropes with regular patches of color. Kipe nods to the others, and they take hold of the lines. The coffin seems to float up to the surface; the lights winking out as it comes level and then passes them, leaving all dark below . . . streaks of tiny colors gliding across the unvarnished sides and lid, the iron handles . . .

With an effort, they lay the coffin down gently beside the grave, and no sooner do the lines fall slack than two men rush forward and start pulling the nails out of the lid. The wind carries the sound of complaining wood down the hill and across the road. The last nails pop out simultaneously, one at the foot, one at the head, and the workers turn their eyes to Kipe and Pracke. Kipe nods again. The others look at each other, and then they ease the lid off. A lizard sits on the body's chest; it jerks its head up, staring directly at the two detectives. Pracke steps forward, languidly shooing it back into the grave. He moves slowly, standing over the open coffin, gazing steadily at its occupant.

Kipe comes up behind him, peering over his shoulder. With two fingers he nudges his partner in the back, and Pracke reaches into his coat pocket and brings out one of the Prefect's fragrant handkerchiefs. Carefully he handles it with the yellow ends of his long fingernails. He holds it up against the night sky to flutter in the wind for a moment like a flag, showing an all but luminous unstained white square with initials in one corner. Slowly Pracke bends, turns in space over the body, and lays the handkerchief over the dead face. It settles there, creased along the middle.

Together, Pracke and Kipe stand and wait. The others have retreated a little way off, watching the open box, intent and anxious. They are all attentively still. The hissing in the grass abates, and suddenly the sounds of the city far off in the distance are just audible again, and the long low breaths of the monitors who are also watching, still as standing water.

A dark spot appears near the center of the handkerchief. It spreads as they look and start—others appear, the cloth begins to sag inwards a little with a new weight of bloodstains and then *his* hand reaches as he sits up to lift it from his face, crumpling the cloth in his fingers. He's sitting up, staring at it intently, with all his concentration. The momentum of his forward motion levers him to his feet in one continuous slow upward curve, his heavy black coat brushing the edge of the coffin. Pracke recoils without moving, feeling his body sinking into itself, an uncontrollable shuddering inside, his throat tightens and he feels a hot, weird pressure behind his eyes—Kipe also feels this way, Pracke can tell even without looking. All *he* did was step out of the coffin, hovering a little above the ground, looking at them, the light from the headlights reflected in his glasses. The figure looks as if it was smeared there like a smudge on a pane of glass—except for the shining spectacles. Kipe makes a convulsive gesture meant to signal one of the men to turn off the headlights; those two disgusting reflections, angled to one side with the tilt of its head—Pracke imagines them gone, the figure occluded by ordinary shadows, and the thought merges with a hysterical impulse to shut off the lights so that he won't have to keep looking at him, or *it*. He imagines their relief if the figure, crying out or dropping to its knees, would take sadness and hopelessness back into itself. But they're paralyzed—Kipe realizes it's looking back at them.

Then the figure abruptly settles his feet on the ground, the full weight of his body returning. A moment later he's gone.

Pracke runs to the edge of the cemetery and scans the slope. Down below, a dark figure is bobbing through the grass. He turns to Kipe and the workers, telling them to bring the car, and then he takes off down the hill. Lights sweep drunkenly behind him as he hurries, and then, turning round the incline and onto a narrow dirt path, he's out of sight of the car. In a few moments, he is walking beside the Divinity Student. For the first time, he notices that the Divinity Student has a ponderous metal brace running the length of his right leg, which nevertheless appears to support most of his weight as he walks, trailing dead earth from his shoes. Pracke hadn't seen it under the coattails at first, or perhaps it hadn't been there before. The Divinity Student is gasping with the strain to keep moving with eyes fixed straight ahead, set on San Veneficio, and clouds of torn bits of paper flutter out from between his lips. His shoulder slams against a tree and he spins to one side, careening over a rock by the side of the road. He crashes down into the dead grass, flailing his arms and legs. His head rears up, eyes twitching back and forth, and his legs and arms writhe underneath him in a completely uncoordinated attempt to get him back on his feet. Kipe pulls up on the running board of the car, jumping off lightly and rejoining Pracke. They are accustomed to handling dead bodies, but they hesitate to approach the Divinity Student, who is seething back and forth in the tall grass like a broken machine. Eventually, Pracke musters himself and steps forward. Seizing one shoulder, then Kipe the other, together they drag the Divinity Student toward the car. Under his coat he feels like a bag of sticks, his joints poking out in all directions, his flesh like wet cardboard. He coughs up a few more bits of paper with a retching sound and goes limp. Pracke and Kipe push his chin down onto his chest and load him professionally into the car, accidentally battering his leg brace on the fender and front seats a few times. They crumple him against the opposite door and clamber in swiftly behind, shoving the broken leg underneath the front seat to make room for their feet.

Riding back into the city, the two detectives avoid looking at him, sitting close together against the opposite door. Occasionally, Pracke glances at the other side of the car, but there is nothing to see but a vague patch of denser darkness against the blue-black desert flashing by the window. Motes of light from the city start to accumulate in the car as they approach the walls, condensing into an almost invisible haze around them, dusting the Divinity Student's face and hands so that they glow the color of sour milk. The car passes through the city gates and the Divinity Student lunges backward like he's just touched a live wire striking his head against the ceiling with an alarmingly loud bang. He twists to one side, crashes once against the door, and goes still again. Everyone in the car turns to look, Pracke and Kipe staring mutely from the other end of the seat—it took only a moment. The Divinity Student is cluttered across the door, his right temple against the window, looking straight ahead. The driver shunts through traffic with anxious efficiency, closing on the police annex.

From the window, the Divinity Student watches people passing in busy streets. The streetlights peer down overhead, and the people's faces and clothes are folded, with heavy shadows pointing down. The thick glass of the window muffles their voices, so that only a melodic hum is audible, like an orchestra tuning up. Standing in doorways, sitting outside on patio chairs, pushing vending carts with hanging strings of bells, alone or with another or in groups, walking pets, standing against walls and posts, entering and leaving buildings, chasing across the street, each with a valence and a wake like a fan of cords woven out of each gesture, and each wake mixing currents in the street with the lights and traffic, a flock of pigeons scattering in front of the car and swimming around the window where the Divinity Student sits, drawn down the street in the closed car. It veers to the left and stops on an empty side lane with steep iron-faced buildings looming up on either side, and then rocks as they get out. Kipe opens the opposite door and the Divinity Student staggers forward off-balance; he stops himself, planting his heavy braced leg. While Pracke and Kipe pay the diggers, he shambles out into the middle of the cobbled street, his head lolling forward.

A car with blazing lights careens around the corner. The men look up. It accelerates down the street, howling and shrieking, steering for the Divinity Student, who stands facing the other side of the road, oblivious. He buckles and flies upward bouncing once on the hood and again across the windshield shattering it with his leg brace, his body spins over the car beneath him and then dashes to the ground—the car wheels around the corner and disappears. Pracke and Kipe run over.

"Is he all right?" Kipe is bending over him.

"He wasn't all right to begin with," Pracke kneels by the Divinity Student. His body is bent, face down, palms up, the legs twisted to one side. They take him by the shoulders and help him stand, steering him toward one of the gaunt doorways on the nearer side of the street.

"The Coroner ought to have a look at him," Kipe suggests, trying to get a better purchase on the Divinity Student's shoulder.

Pracke appraises the Divinity Student's condition with a cursory glance, then nods. "I don't think he's fit to speak with anyone right now, anyway."

They pull him through the door, into a tall, narrow lobby with white walls and a polished wooden floor. Pausing a moment to shove the Divinity Student's feet into position underneath him, they turn down a long, narrow hallway off to one side.

The door at the end swings open with a kick, and they drag him across the threshold. The room beyond is a warehouse of huge banks of tall freezing-cabinets for the storage of bodies. Each one is divided into compartments with shiny steel trapdoors and tongues of metal on rollers for holding the corpses. Aluminum ladders glide along metal tracks atop each cabinet. Luxurious fans hang over the broad avenues between the freezers, spinning slowly in the thin air near the ceiling. The floor is gleaming white tile, glowing in the dim light. Here and there along the walls are small offices with corrugated steel walls and small-paned frosted windows. Pracke and Kipe head for an office in the rear corner, with a gurney and a few racks of surgical and garden tools, resting in glass cases filled with green sterile solution, out in front. With a final effort, they drag the Divinity Student into the enclosure and toss him into a swivel-chair, which rolls backwards under his weight until it raps against the flimsy corrugated wall. Pracke sits down by the desk, and Kipe goes to find the Coroner.

The Coroner is there a moment later, still dressed in his white autopsy outfit, rubber gloves, apron, and skull-cap. He has a young face with an earnest expression. He radiates energy. Kipe stands in the doorway and indicates the Divinity Student with a theatrical gesture. The Coroner steps in and begins studying the Divinity Student immediately, peering into his throat and ears, listening to his chest, tapping his knees. He works silently, with sure, steady hands. He takes a big embalming syringe from his apron and drives the long, thick needle into the Divinity Student's neck, angling down toward his shoulder. Holding the syringe in his left fist, he strongly draws the plunger back and a thick, clear fluid flows viscously up into the dropper, threaded with tiny grains of black. The Coroner pulls the needle out abruptly and squirts some of the liquid onto his fingertip, holding it up to the single lightbulb in the room, hanging over the desk, looks at, and then smells it. He frowns and wipes his hands on his apron. He steps forward and pulls back the Divinity Student's eyelids, staring at his eyes.

"He's blind."

". . . He didn't act blind."

He produces a little flashlight and shines it in the Divinity Student's face. Then he looks around at them.

"I don't see how these eyes could possibly work."

Then he seems to think of something. He presses his palm across the Divinity Student's forehead, and then lays the back of his fingers against his right cheek, leaving behind fading purple bruise-marks on the Divinity Student's paste-colored face.

"He's got a fever. A high high fever."

"Contagious?"

"If it is, you've already been exposed plenty." He puts his hands on his hips, "But I suspect it has more to do with decomposition."

With his right hand, he gently touches his first two fingers to one side of the Divinity Student's throat. "Yes he's very sick," he says, almost to himself.

The Coroner is distracted; his eyes wander. Then, abruptly turning his attention to the legs, he kneels and starts fiddling with the brace.

"I didn't expect he'd have that," Pracke says.

"It's welded on," the coroner says, rocking the hinges in his fingers, "-tight as a vice from his ankle to his hip."

"Is his leg broken?" Kipe asks.

"It would have to be—in at least two or three places. Permanent breaks, most likely. I'd have to cut the brace off to find out." He inclines his head and thinks. "I'll leave it," he says, "unless you insist?"

They shake their heads no.

The Coroner steps back and looks at the Divinity Student as a whole. He takes a flask of formaldehyde from his back pocket, sets it on the desk, and sits down, still looking at the Divinity Student. Suddenly, the Divinity Student springs from the chair, his eyes wide open, and he seizes the bottle. He bashes the top against the edge of the desk, breaking off its short neck and spilling a little onto the floor, filling the room with a familiar smell that neither Pracke nor Kipe have smelled before. The Divinity Student jams the jagged mouth of the bottle against his lips, tips his head back, gulping convulsively, his eyes jerking shut and tearing. The Coroner's face is only inches away, watching him, motionless. The Divinity Student drains the bottle and drops it on the desk; it clunks and rocks back and forth; the Coroner's hand stops it. They're all staring at the Divinity Student, standing with most of his weight on his braced leg, wet mouth hanging open and ragged from the broken glass, but no blood, no gasping. He curls backward, settling into the chair and silence again.

"Well, is he OK?" Pracke asks after a moment.

"I suppose. Is that all?"

"Well, will he be able to speak with the Prefect?"

The Coroner produces a tongue depressor and gingerly applies it to the Divinity Student's mouth. Wrinkling his nose at the smell, he peers down the Divinity Student's throat as Pracke obligingly angles the hanging overhead light.

"As far as I can tell, he is physically capable of speech," says the Coroner, heading for the door. "Whether he has anything to say is none of my look out."

Now they've given up trying to question him. One sat on his right, and the other on his left, alternating their tones and modes, threatening, cajoling, promising, enticing, waving the formaldehyde bottle in front of his face—nothing. A voice on the telephone informed Pracke that the Prefect had already returned to his bed, and would inspect the remains in the morning. The detectives went away, locking the door behind them.

The Divinity Student has been lying on the desk for several hours, in the dark, motionless. With a single jolt of one shoulder he now rolls to one side and collapses to the floor knocking the desk chair over. Using his cane, produced from the lining of his coat, he tries several times to get to his feet, repeating the same useless, spasmodic motions every time. Finally, he somehow levers himself upright and propels himself out the door, knocking it open with his weight alone. His surplus momentum carries him down the corridor between the freezer units, shining ghostly blue in the dark warehouse. He blunders out into the street, and reels drunkenly on the pavement, flapping his desiccated arms like a mummified bat. The Divinity Student shambles down the street.

Nearly blind, with painstaking effort he traces the textures and shapes of each facade with his heated fingertips until they cool against cool stone and thick polished wood, cool as if it were saturated with cold water. The wood glides silently back into the shadows on rough iron hinges and the darkness of the chapel swallows him. With spidery steps he crosses the nave and pulls up before a stained-glass window gleaming faintly above him, suspended, shining, in shadows. Scaffolding scales the pillars—the ceiling is being restored. There is a length of rope among the tools by the base of one of the pillars. The Divinity Student picks it up, works it for a moment, and then looks up. He can now see. With his shaking hands, he throws the line up, and it catches in a hook-like projection of stone at the top of the arch. The rope hangs in silhouette against the window, its dangling loop encircles an angel's face. The Divinity Student pulls himself up the scaffolding with one arm, holding the end of the rope in his other hand. He gets to the top of the scaffold, and with a single gesture swings himself onto the platform. He ties the rope to the trellis, leans out, seizes the swinging noose, and fastens it around his head. Then he climbs back out on the scaffolding, taking up as much slack as possible. He kicks out with his braced leg, dropping a few feet straight down and then stopping abruptly. With clement eyes, the angels watch him swing back and forth.

The Morgue and the Brewery

Of course there is a circus in San Veneficio—open warehouses with dirt floors and straw on the ground. The nightly audience sits hushed and excited in fleets of folding chairs on graduated risers, with their backs to the open air. In the center ring, Teo rises up from over his table gleaming with knives to face racks of mirrors, one in front of the other, lined up forty feet away, with small spaces in between, several side by side. They catch his reflection like the knives on the table, blazing with the white of his spotless uniform. With nimble, scarred fingers, he raises one blade and then another, hurling them with lightning speed at the mirrors, snapping them faster and faster, his right hand does all the throwing, his left hand feeds the knives one after another, until Teo's hands are a blur eating knives from the table and flashing each one a shining reflection of Teo's tense face to dash through the mirrors and plunge through his face, his hands, his chest and abdomen, arms and legs, a blazing stream of spinning knives buzzing from his hands and chasing each other into the mirrors, breaking them in sequence and crowding after each other in their haste, thunking solidly into silvered glass and plywood backings. As the last knives leap from the table and across the room, his face is twisting, his lips furling up, baring clenched teeth. Shatter the last of his reflections and turn to face the crowd who gasp and nearly forget to applaud. The Desdens have produced a number of that daring breed of knife fighter whose representative image has become part of San Veneficio's glamorous reputation. Blink-memory of his cousin Ernesto teaching him how to whip his short cape around his left arm with a single deft motion.

Now Teo heads home, an old shed, now his place to stay, in a lot adjacent to the circus. His uniform blazes white in the gloom. Without putting on the lights, he steps to his closet and looks inside, by moonlight, at his old spotless apron. He brushes it with his fingertips, and pulls two big knives from his belt, holding them tight, one to each hand, bright and sharp against the dark.

Then an uncatagorizable impression—a low, uneasy chord received like a tactile sensation. Or also like the minute flux of a small earth tremor, registered in his stomach like a jarring loose, or a glancing blow, the clumsy superimposition of a previous self. Teo thinks a moment, but the feeling is gone. With care, he takes down his apron and puts it on, and then, pocketing his knives, he leaves the shack and the circus grounds.

Overhead the sky is a patchwork of clouds stitched with bright silver borders where the moon shines above them. The air is clear and still, warm and cold evenly mixed, frictionless. The streets are empty, small stone buildings with little onion-shaped turrets and leaning gables, all lightless and quiet. No streetlights. No sound. Everyone is sleeping. He travels along the perimeter of the city, weaving over uneven streets, muted and expectant. Presently he turns down a narrow side street, heading for the smooth stone wall of a tiny chapel a few doors up from the corner, with two recessed stained-glass windows and a heavy wooden door, set into a telescoping, arched doorway. It glides open with a touch on rough old hinges, and inside all is dark and still. Teo passes through the door and steps down into the chapel on steps worn smooth as brook-pebbles, and he scans the room in the dim half-light from the short, wide colored windows that punctuate the walls just below the flat roof. As he looks, he sees one window is broken by a shadow, slowly turning.

He approaches the far wall, and sees scaffolding against the pillars, and a twisting form dangling from a cord. Teo stops and looks at the body, and recognizes the heavy black coat and large white hands. Then involuntarily he begins to weave toward the body, its feet bobbing in scuffed shoes over the paving stones. He stares up at it, the toes almost scraping his nose. The Divinity Student's head hangs at an angle on his breast, his face is discolored purple and swollen. Teo stares at the creased face. Blazing white in a dead face the Divinity Student's eyes flick open and focus tremendously on Teo. The hands open outward in an image of blessing, and then point with irritation at the noose. Instantly, Teo mounts the nearest scaffold, nimbly scrambling across the trestle to peer down at the Divinity Student, just below him. With a single slice of his knife he severs the cord, and the Divinity Student falls noisily to the ground, landing on his braced leg. Teo climbs down and comes up to his side.

"It doesn't work does it?" he asks.

The Divinity Student draws his broken cane from his coat, plants the tip firmly between two paving stones and says, "It's not what you think."

Teo moves to help him up, but the Divinity Student says, "Don't touch me. I'm very sick. If you touch me you will surely die."

He shifts his weight onto the broken leg and levers himself ponderously to his feet with a grinding, reluctant creak of his brace. He leans on the stick. Teo can see his face again—clear and wan as always, but now it's moist with sweat and clammy across the forehead and cheeks, pulsing with waves of dry sick heat, palpable even from a few feet away. There is a fading band of livid red around his neck.

Teo hefts the rope. "What was this for?"

The Divinity Student squints at it, "I don't remember," he says in a hollow voice. "Ah. Now I remember."

He starts to hobble toward the door.

"I needed to find you."

"You sent for me?" Teo asks after a moment.

The Divinity Student says, "Yes."

Teo walks up beside him and follows him out into the street.

"You and one other."

"Who?"

After a moment, "Let me stay with you again."

Teo decides it would be all right.

"...The sun will be up soon," he says.

"I wouldn't notice. It doesn't bother me any more."

"Congratulate me," he says quietly, "I'm in the circus now."

"I'm sure you are. You're the knife-thrower."

"Will you be needing my help again?"

"Yes. I'm having trouble walking, and I can hardly see. Perhaps, if I had a rest..."

They come to Teo's door. Before going in, the Divinity Student turns to Teo, his head shaking with an uncontrollable tremor.

"Are you still unhappy?"

Teo peers at the ravaged face, obscured by thick orange rays of light from the setting sun.

He shrugs and says, "I'm less unhappy."

The Divinity Student's face and posture do not change, and still the tremor wags his head for him.

"I wish I could help you," he says in a ragged voice. Then, without straightening his arm, he points up at the sky, looking Teo directly in the eye.

"Just do not question," he says, and turns to enter.

TEO IS STANDING OVER the Divinity Student, looking down at him in the light of the setting sun. He still lies collapsed in the corner, radiating a parched, sooty heat like a cloud of hot dust, and the slatey cathedral light of grey days. Teo is staring at a oblong white spot on the Divinity Student's head, just above his right temple. At first he thought it was a speck of paint or a crumb of plaster from the chapel, but then he saw how the skin puckered around it, and realized that he was looking at the Divinity Student's skull, where the skin had worn away. He's still looking at it now. But he can see where the Divinity Student's hair is sloughing off, and how flimsily his ears adhere to his head. The tips of his fingers are slightly shriveled, and the fingernails seem ready to drop off. His skin is coarse and flaking, his eyelids, transparent membranes like a single thickness of onion skin.

The Divinity Student looks slowly up at him, with a rustling of neckbones. His face is a mummy's face, the whites of his eyes are turning yellow-orange and the irises are fading, smearing, turning a wan clay-colored grey. He looks directly into Teo's face.

"I'm not perfect!" he chokes, and waves his hands over his body, "I just can't hold this together much longer!"

"Are you planning on doing anything about it?"

"I need to build a new one, a proxy, to send down. I'll need you for that . . . and we'll have to find a nice, cozy private place to work." The Divinity Student gradually musters his extremities, dragging himself upright by inching along the wall with his back until he can get his brace underneath him. He places a desiccated, tarantulalike hand on the wall and locks his other elbow, pressing down on his cane. "I'll direct you," he grunts. Teo looks at him for a moment, and then leads him out the door, limping, rickety and cadaverous, along behind and beside him. The Divinity Student seizes fragile blades of heat out of the air with his mind, not with his hand, so as not to snap them . . . smell of his fingers, smell of his own dry, dirt-choked body.

They return, after hours, to the Morgue, down streets of dried weeds and leafless twigs rattling in the wind. For the next few days, they have the run of the place, checking the cabinets one by one, row by row, closely attended by Teo who stands ready with a dolly loaded with cleavers and saws. From time to time, the Divinity Student calls him over, tapping at a body with the tip of his cane, and, with grim satisfaction, Teo brings down the knife, lopping hands, feet, ears and the like, comparing them to the corresponding parts of the Divinity Student with a tape measure. He raises his eyebrows and frowns, reckoning their similarity, making his selections and rejections, and then takes the chosen parts back to the dolly where they are stored in glass jars filled with formaldehyde. The grosser structures are found first, then comes the more difficult task of finding matching eyes, a proper skull, the right-shaped teeth, and the components necessary for constructing an identical face. This last obstacle requires Teo to make a chart of the Divinity Student's face, with exacting measurements of each muscle and tissue element. He has to invent his own system for categorizing degrees of muscle tone and skin tightness to insure accuracy, until he is certain within several hundredths of a millimeter of the precision of his chart.

After the first two days, the Divinity Student is no longer able to navigate the aisles by himself. He is almost completely unable to walk, and Teo must bring each selected part to his seat, leaning against the flimsy partitions of the Chief Coroner's office, for inspection. The Divinity Student is deteriorating rapidly, carefully budgeting his strength. Teo runs up with a dripping piece of cartilage and holds it gingerly before the Divinity Student's face. With effort the Divinity Student focuses his eyes, now caked over with a sulfurous yellow powder, on it. His purple lips part over dry, black gums and a single tooth rattles to the floor.

Teo hollers at the top of his lungs, "Will this do?"

"Not DEAF yet," the Divinity Student rustles in a voice like paper cinders. He seizes the cartilage with two long skinny fingers, bruised nails peeling from the tips, and holds it to his nose, sniffing vigorously. Hot, dry, sick-room air boils up from his coat as it falls open, and for a moment he sits still, a pensive expression on his green face. Then he tosses the hunk of cartilage to the floor with a frown—"No good, doesn't match, find another." Splat. His face caves in and he shrinks into his seat, exhausted. Teo returns diligently to the stacks.

Finally, he emerges with a dolly bowed and creaking under a heavy load of anatomy. He sweeps his instruments into a small black bag and then stands back as the Divinity Student, now little more than a mummy, painfully climbs onto the top of the dolly. With care, he administers a fortifying sip of formaldehyde between the Divinity Student's lips. The Divinity Student slumps to one side and seems to fall asleep. While the rest of his body is as inert as clay his right arm moves with electric, nervous energy, as though all the life in that body had momentarily concentrated in the right arm. It rummages his coat pocket and extracts a scrap of paper and a pencil nub with a rusty iron cap on one end. His hand scribbles a series of discrete numbers on the paper and then clumsily tears the paper to bits, dropping the pencil stub on the floor. Jerkily, his hand collects the paper fragments and squashes them together in his palm, then extracts a series of four at random, laying them out on his thigh. The hand flops down to his side and his head rises, his eyes rolling around until they find Teo, then flick down to indicate the numbers. He tries to speak. Teo brings his ear close to the Divinity Student's mouth—he learns that the numbers are an address, an empty place on a street he knows, a safe place to work.

Turns out to be a derelict brewery on the outskirts of the small industrial district; a cavernous stone building with extensive underground fermenting rooms carved into the bedrock. Above ground, the walls are a thick shell around a vast open room lined with staggering or collapsed copper brewing vats. One of the four corners on the floor plan bulges out into an enormous stone tower, most likely a sort of silo, but with a windowed observation deck at the very top. An arched aperture nearly twenty feet high and fifteen feet wide opens at its base, gaping at the empty brewery littered with defunct machinery. Teo wheels in his carts of body parts and deposits them beside the operating table, isolated in a pool of light in the center of the room. Although it's on the opposite side of town from the Morgue and the chapel, Teo nevertheless has the feeling that they are all connected, as wings of one colossal necropolis branching its dark, yawning hallways and limitless storage houses through the city and into the unending distance; and at every turn he half expects to see again the limitless ranks of freezer cabinets and covered gurneys, or to hear the businesslike tread of the thousands of morticians and coroner's assistants who attend the bodies. An abrupt clatter of metal wheels distracts him and he looks up to see the Divinity Student approaching the table, dragging an IV hanger on wheels along behind him, a bottle of formaldehyde draining drop by drop into his arm.

He mutters something about lightning rods and clumsily pulls a sheet of white paper the length of the platform from a roller at its foot. Teo turns and notices a bundle of lightning rods and wire at the foot of a column nearby. As the Divinity Student starts rummaging noisily among the containers and machine parts, dumping organs out on the table for a last-minute inspection, Teo gathers up the rods and heads for the tower. A flight of iron stairs bolted to the inside wall of the tower circles upward to a dome a hundred feet above, but he turns off after climbing only halfway, taking a side-door out onto the roof of the brewery. Stepping out into the wind, he can see dark clouds slithering ominously over the mountains, drifting across the desert toward San Veneficio. Standing before him is a plain, wooden block with a plaster bust on it, representing the tutelary angel of breweries. He picks his way across wide green copper panels to a row of exposed knobs on a rail, and fixes a rod to each knob, trailing the insulated wires behind him like the stinging tendrils of a jellyfish. This task completed, he gathers the cables into a bundle and trails them back down the stairs to the operating table. The Divinity Student is busily cobbling together something enormous, hydraulic, and many-armed, with an attached magazine of glass cases filled with formaldehyde and pieces of bodies. He glances up briefly and points to a huge pair of contacts, to which Teo affixes the cables.

When he straightens up, he can see that the Divinity Student is loading spools of surgical silk onto rows and rows of bobbins, each attached to a spidery pneumatic arm. His face is greener and thinner than ever, the skin on his brow stretched tight as a drum across his temples, and small blisters beginning to form at his hairline. He threads a bundle of needles, using his palm as a pincushion, and then screws each needle into place. He jerks his head up at Teo.

With an effort he says, "Now install the array." His body buckles a little forward and he steadies himself on the edge of his stool, milky yellow-green discharge frothing at the corners of his mouth. Hands trembling, he increases the dose of formaldehyde from the IV, reaches again for another needle. Teo looks at him closely.

"You're burning with fever. Isn't there anything anyone can do?"

"*I don't want to get well!*" the Divinity Student snaps.

So, Teo climbs to the top of the tower. From the observation dome he looks down over the lip of the inner wall at a shaft like the inside of a smokestack. Cautiously he picks his way around the edge, threading among piston machines, regulators, pumps, siphons, receivers, transmitters, all pressed up against the base of the dome. Finally, he steps into position. Using chains and a pulley, Teo winches a steel ring, almost as wide in diameter as the tower itself and bristling with dozens of in-pointing telescoping metal arms on all sides, to within a few inches of the base of the dome, at his feet. Locking the winch, he moves slowly around the periphery, fixing the ring in place with thick steel coils, and then around again, attaching the ends of the telescoping arms to the diverse machines on all sides. When he's finished, the array looks like a wagon wheel with spokes but no central axle, floating horizontal across the mouth of the tower. Teo checks the strength of the ring, pushing and rattling it, then returns to the lab chamber below.

He emerges from the shadows in time to see the Divinity Student slump forward—his IV is empty, black ooze is backing up into the bottle. Shocked, Teo rushes over—the Divinity Student's brace is locked, keeping him propped upright. Teo jerks the bottle from the hook and unstoppers it, oily black ooze spouting out of it across his apron and onto the floor. Moving quickly he grabs a full bottle from the gurney and moves to reattach it to the catheter, which lies dribbling and writhing on the floor.

"Wait . . ." the Divinity Student's voice comes drifting weakly from somewhere ". . . until it runs clear . . ."

Teo slaps the hose against the ground trying to squeeze out the black stuff, and in a few moments a clear glycerous gelatin begins to trickle out of its mouth—the fungal syrup that saturates the Divinity Student's tissues in lieu of blood and lymph. One of his crooked fingers taps an empty petrie dish lying on the gurney beside him—disembodied, the Divinity Student's voice speaks again, "Save it—and culture it!" Teo drains some of the clear gelatin into the dish, then plugs the tube into the fresh supply and hangs it again on the frame.

After a few moments, the Divinity Student's body begins to shudder and list, then rights itself—hands clasping the edge of the gurney in a vice-taloned grip, the head floats up, trailing knobby shoulders and withered torso like a stillborn animal trailing its afterbirth. Wheezing and sputtering black saliva, he fumbles blindly for a screwdriver and begins adjusting the machine's alignment.

"What do I tell him when he comes to?"

The Divinity Student doesn't look away from his work—"Don't worry about that—he will know from me . . . I will be in him . . . but he will not be in me . . ."

He gingerly turns to look at Teo.

"I can't tell you anything about it—you're used to that . . . When it happens—don't stay—and don't come back . . . when he has finished—I will be free again . . . and then I can protect you from any consequences . . ."

"What if he wants my help?"

"Then help him," the Divinity Student turns back to his machine ". . . just don't stay with him."

The Magician

CHRISTINE DALMAN, THE MAGICIAN, moves to the center of the stage seeping autumn perfume, her serenely concentrated face suspended in tissues of faint red light, her hands float at the ends of rustling red silk sleeves, pale and bright against the carmine draperies behind her. She produces a Chinese fan and waves it, her other hand splayed in the air above it, and butterflies gush up between her fingers from behind the fan, fluttering up to the ceiling, to fall again as scarlet rose petals. White face with pointed vermillion lips, and two thin streaks to elongate her eyes, and black hair, pinned up, fine strands aloft around her head, and a red silk dress and trousers with embroidered flowers, black slippers skimming her across the stage like skipping stones. She has an eager following and many admirers because she is so beautiful.

Expectantly brief applause. She bows, curving to one side facing forward, her white face level and placid like a mask. Clapping once, with authority, she turns around, her long fingers pulling invisible lines in the air, bees spin off from her palms and dance around the stage. One by one they zip through the hoop of her looped thumb and forefinger, turning as they do so into fireflies. They return, pass through her fingers again and turn into precious stones, agleam with the same green firefly-light. These tiny beacons drift out above the audience, hovering in neat rows above upraised heads, until each spectator has his own companion. She draws her sword and chops the air—the shining chrysolites break and shower down on the people, evaporating at a touch with a sensation like the brush of dewy new leaves, and the theatre fills with scent of orange flowers. Gasps of pleasure, the applause is more warm than strident.

She whistles, and a small troupe of cats file onto the stage, rolling glass balls before them with their forepaws. While obedient to her commands, these cats are obviously enjoying themselves. Christine gestures to the audience—the cats grip the balls and leap down into the aisles with them.

She gestures to the audience—the cats, without needing to see what she does, roll the balls up the aisles, leaving them in a row in the middle of each aisle. Swiftly the cats vanish through small curtained cat-sized doors in the walls of the theatre. Christine, who all this time has been making a quiet singing sound in her throat, opens her mouth and emits a soaring, pure tone—the glasses break and send plumes of fire into the air, plumes that rise and spin like pinwheels and then burst in clouds of coruscating pollen. The curtain has already fallen.

After a moment of silence, applause, the audience files out talking. The theatre is empty. Christine is still standing in the middle of the stage, looking at the back of the curtain, eyes with pin-strut umbrella irises.

Her face goes wan blue and her body turns to vapor and condenses solid again with the distant beating of her heart. Her staring, golden eyes fix in space. She shuts them, and when she opens them again, she is on the street walking, as she does every night, down the streets of San Veneficio. She haunts the little plazas and open spaces and the crowded busy thoroughfares with the glowing white plaster of the tiny coffee shops, and the battered white wrought-iron chairs and tables, the white cotton shirts and pants on bronze and tan skin, glowing in the fading daylight and the waxing platinum beams of the street lamps. She passes through a city that rises around her like an architectural forest, hung with lazily flapping white muslin sheets that are film screens on which the people and the city are projected, rolling and swaying with the shifting of the sheets. They split to let her pass, one after another, and the thin cellophane tails of frayed cloth stroke her face as she goes by with a touch as light as a bubble, dewing her face with their faces and bodies. The brown-red and yellow-orange gold of the sunset and the lights of the streets and shops and the reflections, all mingle into an image of her face, her body moving forward, like the intangible wall of a bubble, an extension of her image cast in mingled light and color; and she occupies this image from moment to moment, stepping up to press herself into it, like putting on a mask, with the sensation of tiny electrical shocks criss-crossing her in waves, or the icy-hot sensation of a bubble bursting on the skin. Every moment it is renewed, every moment she steps forward to occupy it, and her ghost or her angel walks beside her and whispers to her, the gentle brush of her own lips on her own ear. Everything reacts to her, people, buildings, sky and ground, like reactants to an acid they come open and dissolve, and she completes them with her presence, arcing out from her in curved panes like wings or the tail of her shawl. Christine scans the crowds, and from their heavily flapping screens they watch her pass with flickering projected attention and a silent-movie indicator closing her in a circle. They look to see who she is looking for, as she searches one street to the next, finding no one. The same sinister, dreaming face, the same glinting gaze of shadowed eyes, the same impersonal, vatic presence, like a somnambulist, a sleep-talker, filled with secrets she urgently wants to discover. As always, he is never quite there, although everything invokes him. He would not approach her from the dusty projector beam, but out of the lightless expanse of the theatre itself, where she is, although lost for a time in the endless kaleiding attractions of San Veneficio in desert sunset, the imaginary stars, the odor of partial phantoms. He would emerge from the source of all these things, and also from the darkness on which they are projected. He would emerge, but he hasn't. Christine continues to patrol the streets at every sunset just as the exquisite portrait must always rise to occupy its frame, to meet or evade the viewer's gaze.

The bargain was struck some time ago, in a dream. There were ten strange, real dreams. The first night, she dreamt she was a child again. She saw her mother, who has been dead for many years. Christine, barely taller than the ornate doorknob she turns with both hands, makes her way into her mother's bedroom. The room is a silhouette against the sunset sky, which shines through two gaunt french windows; the walls are invisible. Her mother sits before the mirror on the opposite wall, her face lit by the reflected light of the sunset and two miniature lamps on the table before her.

Christine's mother is in her dressing-gown, pale and long as a stalk of celery, cool and fresh and Junoesque, beautiful still, though she hadn't long to live. Christine remembers standing by the generous curve of her thigh under her long red gown, looking up at her long-lashed face. Her mother was a stage magician and her room was filled with props—they had all been stage magicians, her family and a whole covey of other women as well. Christine was to be her successor—she would follow her mother's ivory hands and imbibe the lesson in red tea from hibiscus petals—and she would replace them all in the future. Christine was the only child any of them had ever had, and they placed all their hopes in her.

Christine understands all these things right away, as one does in dreams, but the words her mother speaks to her are never fully intelligible. Something like this encounter in her mother's bedroom takes place in dream after dream for many nights, and in each dream the words become a little clearer, the room a little darker, the hour outside the windows later and later. This is not a past moment revisited, this is a present moment—her mother is dead and has been making arrangements. A far better knowledge and a far better power than she or any of her colleagues or ancestors had ever had was somehow being offered to Christine, in exchange for a service. Some part of that knowledge, an essential initial clue only, but more than she could ever have discovered on her own, and which would surely lead to a better magic, was on offer.

Her mother has pulled out a developing pan filled with red, the lights in the room flick red, and she slides a paper in the pan and held out her hand to Christine. Christine feels her mother take her hand, and a sting as her mother pricks her finger and squeezes a drop of blood into the red . . . presses her hand down into the red.

"Yes, it must hurt, I'm afraid," her mother says, swirling the tray.

Slowly a picture appears on the paper. Christine's mother pulls it out quickly and looks at it, then shows it to her. An irregular, dark figure peers out at her.

"He will teach you. The training must hurt, I'm afraid."

And on another, later night, when the sky outside the windows is indigo and black, her mother, sitting in a tall golden bathtub with a turban binding up her heavy hair, says, "I will find him for you."

Dimly, Christine sees her mother talking with someone, a dark and ominous figure at the end of the paved walk outside their house. She stands on one side of the fence, and he on the other. This is the figure in the picture, too dark to see. Her mother pulls something from her pocket—although she is too far away, watching from an upper-story window, to see what it is, Christine knows what it is: a picture of her. Reaching across the fence, the phantom places a bright red book in her mother's hand.

The last night is the tenth; she stands at the fence, no longer a child but fully grown. Her mother is dead, Christine lives in the house with her father. It is dark, crickets are chirping, and this is odd because she doesn't normally hear such incidental sounds in her dreams. She stands at the fence, where the light cast by the porch lamp grows weak—and suddenly he is there, as though sprung from the earth. She sees his appalling face, looks at his eyes, and at once knows entirely what she is being asked to do . . . and what she stands to gain. He warns her of the danger, and then asks. With a cold flash she agrees, bracing herself against any violent transformation to follow, but everything stays the same. Still he is standing before her, on the other side of the fence. Speaking strange words, he instructs her to wait for his signal to act. For him and for this signal she searches in these nightly excursions.

When she fails again to find him, she always returns home. She walks between the trees and feels their cool, moist breath hazing the frictionless air of morning, their boughs wave and fan her in passing like royal attendants. She glides over the steps to the porch and bobs noiselessly through the front door. In the left-front room, wide open beside her, her father used to sit in the center of the room, used to watch the sun rise, the window's projected rectangle of light inching up his cotton shirt, illuminating his vacant, placid face. She would change her red dress for one of Quaker grey, and lightly step into the room, to stand behind his chair. He had been schizophrenic. Forever in the same chair watching the same sun rise over the horizon, the identical rays playing over his same features and body with the same intensity, warming at the same rate. Time bends and resutures itself to loop this moment outside of time, for him. To her, he eventually ceased to be a person. He had become calm, indifferent, and open, like the trees and the grass, the ground beneath and the sky overhead, and like the sun also. He had radiated ocean-deep calm. Christine had liked to settle her weight on the chair's arm and rest her head on her father's chest, to be included in his vast, vacant calm. It wasn't ocean-deep. It was shallow. Everything beyond a shallow depth vanished without trace or memory, and when she had been like this, all but the moment and the attendant sensibility were occluded, endowing her with new vitality and incredible strength, refreshing her like a full night's sleep. Presently, as the sun-window would pass to the wall behind him, she would raise her head and go upstairs to sleep.

She always rises the moment night began to fall. As the sun sets, it reflects into her room, multiplying its gleams on the cut glass beads that fringe the ceiling lamp, and lighting constellations of hanging glass ornaments, spangling the wallpaper with fading pumpkin-orange diamonds, but she remains asleep until it has set, and twilight turns everything to blue. The setting sun dapples her face smokey orange through her windows, but she doesn't wake up until twilight limns her face in pale fluorescent blue, like a patch of sky in the midst of high-piled cloud-white cushions and fog-white linen. Then her eyes snap open and she bolts upright like a jack-in-the-box.

She throws the sheets into the air and in a rustling flurry of flying cloth she rises to her feet, now in the center of a small hurricane of cloth, and in a moment the sheets settle again as silent and calm as a slow page turning, the words passed into forgetful darkness again. As they drop past her, she emerges fully dressed in grey, watching the bed fall into place as if she'd only just come in, hadn't slept at all, was ready to undress and retire—the Magician. Outside it's getting cold and dark, but she doesn't turn the lights on right away. Instead she sits on the settee by her bed and looks around her, at the walls. In a moment, they light by themselves the color of light under deep water, rolling in synchronous waves across the walls, timed to her slow heart beating. A few hours to kill before the show begins, her father has been dead for several years now, she has nothing to do and no one to look after, empty hours of waiting strung out behind her in endless reels of unspooling film of action taken and repeated and modified in infinite recordings.

Although she cultivates regular habits this next element is always introduced outside of any pattern. She opens the drawer of her nightstand and withdraws a doll, roughly eight or nine inches tall. It is a man, wrapped in a thick coat of black cloth. His face is pale, mutable, familiar and indistinct like faces in old photographs. She looks at it from time to time and to her it looks like an old memory—air rustles in the trees playing cool air over her bare arms and legs as she hides savagely in the bushes, tracing her glances between a pack of kids on the far side of the park and on the picnic tables, and she tries to catch the particular smell of sandwiches warmed by the sun and exhaling the stored breath of a dozen different kitchens, or the smell of upholstery, lying very still in the back of her father's car, hiding again, and watching in mute delight the faces of her friends passing by the windows again and again, rolling by with the sun glaring off their hair and faces as they squint and turn their heads searching, and all the while she's inches away, inside the car. She waits for them to come back, suddenly desperately hoping they'll come back and discover her this time. But the face that appears above her, framed in the window of the car, and dark with the shadow that falls over its features as it leans forward to peer into her eyes, is one she has never seen while awake.

Christine looks up into its eyes and says, "I understand." She wakes up, her eyes already open, staring out the window at clouds in the night sky.

AT THE MORGUE THERE are steel tables and cold air, bodies covered with sleek white draperies, and Christine is there, too. Unerringly, she threads her way among the tables to the center and spins slowly in place, her wide skirts flaring across the floor. Then she moves from spot to spot, lifting sheets, exposing blue faces. Here, a young woman, her age, with black hair. Flick of her fingers in the air, the woman's eyes open—the same color as hers. Roughly the same height and weight, the livid purple stripe across her throat: she had been throttled to death. Quickly, Christine draws the sheet over her again, bundling it underneath her with swift, businesslike motions, until she is completely wrapped. Then she draws a large brass hoop from beneath her skirts and, holding it in one hand, she waves the other, palm down, back and forth above the body, as if caressing it in the air. Her face hovers over her gliding hand, tight and intent, pushing out through her opaque eyes. The corpse rises a few inches off the table, still tightly wrapped in its sheet. Moving only her arm, the rest of her rigid as a statue, she passes the hoop along the body, right through, stopping just at the waist. Then she pulls the hoop slightly, toward her, experimenting, and the body moves with it, remaining perfectly stable in the center of the hoop. She pulls it gently off the table, pulling it easily across the room with small tugs, as if coaxing it to drift across a pool. She pauses only to pluck a scalpel from an tray.

She checks the street outside with two craning twists of her head. Then she pulls the body out with her and right into the coach, a spectral white figure glowing faintly like a filament in the dark interior of the coach. Without a word, Christine taps the ceiling, and the carriage instantly jerks into motion, sweeping silently down the street, with no driver.

She disembarks onto her front porch evening wind across her back. Easily she brings the body inside, dismissing the carriage around to the back of the house. Now she is working quickly, heading upstairs first, angling the corpse up the stairs behind her, grasping the top of the loop. She gets it into her bedroom and withdraws the hoop, letting the body settle onto her bed. Immediately she strips the sheet off and begins dressing it in her clothes, working hastily, but she is thorough, taking the time to collect its hair properly, trim the nails and buff them, the file rasping against the silence of the room. When she is done, the body looks like her. Now the hoop again, and downstairs to the back room. There she lays the body on a high table, flicking on a dangling, hooded light bulb. Gently, she turns the face to one side, and taking the scalpel, she starts to cut the face, carving deep gashes in the bloodless, soft flesh, like cutting clay, it falls away in even straight edges, and all the while that face gazing up, smiling at her with the blissful, rapt look of a nursing child, up at her own face—still intent, forcing its way out through her eyes. She cuts the face until it is no longer recognizable, not anybody's face. She checks the teeth, and pulls out the ones with fillings with a pair of pliers. Then she fetches her fountain pen. With a few deft strokes, she draws a silver-headed cane on the skin behind one of the ears—a sign, as instructed. When the ink dries, she is finished.

She takes the nail parings, the teeth, bits of hair and flesh and bundles them neatly into a cloth with the scalpel and the pliers. Then she drops the bundle into a wooden case she uses in her magic act, closes the lid, and taps it once with a black wooden wand. When she opens the box again, the bundle is gone. Satisfied, she carries the corpse into the front-left room and arranges it carefully on the floor.

It lies there now, staring straight up, absolutely still, its ruined face still placid, radiating ocean-deep calm.

THE COURTYARD IS LINED with pillared Greek facades and broken paving stones scattered at the periphery over the dirt. There is a large oak tree in the center of the yard, its spoon-shaped leaves fluttering in the wind high in its boughs. In the shade of the tree and to one side is a rough wooden park table made of dry grey wood, bristling with splinters like a porcupine. She can make out the secretary sitting in the dim, yellow light of two old storm-lanterns, glass chimneys cataracted with a layer of milky grime. At first, the secretary's mousy-blonde hair, piled up on her head and just barely reflecting the light of the lanterns, is the only thing visible underneath the tree, but then the rest of her emerges as Christine draws nearer. Then, suddenly, she seems to snap into focus, carefully toting up accounts in a thick ledger, writing briskly in a neat flowing hand so fluid and graceful that simply watching her fingers flicking the pen back and forth is a pleasure. Christine has the impression that there are other people lurking about in the shadows, possibly a line standing in the shadows by the opposite wall. Ignoring them, she approaches the table, the wind rustling overhead like the hiss of silk cloth.

The secretary looks up at her and nods once, primly. She puts the pen back in her inkwell and closes the ledger, leaving it shut on the table. With a quick finger to her lips, she leads Christine out past the rear wall, pointing her down an alley to an open door with a dark frame in the center of the right-hand partition. Then, with the same darkly mysterious air of exaggeratedly scrupulous discretion, she withdraws.

Within the doorway is a small room, not ten feet square. There is a single fluorescent high overhead, a pay phone on one wall marred with graffiti, and an extremely large confessional against the opposite wall, to her right. The door to the left-hand side is closed and latched, but the right-hand door is slightly ajar, not quite clearing the jam. Christine steps inside, her small boots thudding muffled on the wooden floor, and draws the cabinet shut behind her, latching it with a small iron hook. She sits. The door in the partition falls slowly open away from her, silently. Within, she can just make out a few spangles of light from the outside, spattering the interior in the other compartment, where they fall on a fold of a white shirt, or a single white cheek—perhaps the gleam of a fixed eye.

She whispers, and her words stream through the door like a gust of snow. She explains everything, perched by the door like a bird on a windowsill, and waits.

A pale, white hand floats up through the opening out of a black frame, holding a small vial of blue liquid between thumb and forefinger. Gingerly she accepts the vial, and the hand snaps back again the door slams shut. She pauses only a moment, then puts the vial away and leaves the cabinet, slipping out and down the alley, invisibly, into the city.

The sweep of her broad grey skirt and a blur of windows and streetlights passing to a rusting iron lattice crowning a tall, polished, bottle-green building. Wisps of hair are blown around her face as she looks compulsively down at the foundations, obscured by straight-edged shadows from the surrounding rooftops. In the light from below, her face stands out white and tapering in relief against her dark clothes. The light catches in her brimming eyes, reflecting sharp and clear around irises that grow hard and dense, staring down at the fall.

She pulls out the vial and drinks. The instant the thick fluid drains into her mouth she is disoriented and her knees buckle—she reaches for a crumbling metal beam to keep from toppling forward, and already her hand is miles away from her, her body is coming apart, her limbs go warm and numb, expanding away from her, going to sleep, sensation reduced to unconscious whispering diffused by great distance. Suddenly, she realizes she's leaning out too far and somehow pulls herself back, but a moment later her equilibrium shifts and she leans over the edge again. She's becoming a dummy, extremities connected by flimsy wires, dead weights. She wants to drop the burden of her heavy body onto the infinitely yielding air below. She jerks her arm and her body pulls back. Now her torso is vanishing, disappearing in a spreading cloud of warmth, her neck starts to droop. Her eyes feel cold, fixed. Then she leans out again, and the weight of her body pulls her distant fingers free. She falls, passing through a shaft of moonlight on her way to the ground, conscious enough to be thankful to see it once more. Her arms are blown up in a Ballerina's halo around her head, her legs bend also with the skirts billowing among them. Then she is absorbed by the shadows below. She approaches the ground like a transparent object brushing a transparent surface, hanging a moment impossible to see, and then, ghostlike, she passes through the ground and disappears . . .

The Golem

Black clouds gather among San Veneficio's minarets and boil down low, rumbling and flooding the city with their clammy breath scented with rain. Quickly, precisely, and with a minimum of faltering, the Divinity Student makes the last few modifications to his construction machine and reviews the condition of the surrogate body parts. In the meantime Teo checks the electrical connections, nodding sagaciously over his tools. Together they load the machine with exact reproductions of the Divinity Student's clothes and shoes, and with a reproduction leg brace in two halves, one of which is outfitted with a miniature receiver tuned to a transmitter in the Divinity Student's brace, and a small scroll. The gelatin culture that Teo took from the Divinity Student earlier has thrived in solution to a volume of several gallons; this is loaded into a special pump. Teo loads a magazine with pages of the Divinity Student's writing, all in Catalog-words, in Catalog-grammar, clamping them in place against a metal panel inside a machine resembling a film projector. It's beginning to rain outside.

The Divinity Student looks down. His right hand is crawling with ants, gnawing at his fingers, and carrying tiny crumbs of flesh away in their mandibles. He does not feel them. He imagines for a moment dissolving into so many fragments to be carried away by legions of mechanical ants. Then Teo is beside him, brushing the ants away with an outraged expression on his face, a doubled-up towel in his hand. The Divinity Student gives him a long, penetrating look. Then he glances up; he is directly below the spoked ring in the observation dome. The rods protrude from their circular frame like the feathery threads of a pin-strut umbrella iris around an empty pupil, staring down vacantly at him.

Teo backs away to a safe distance as the Divinity Student starts throwing switches on the instrument panel, setting the construction machine to work. Teo in a corner, the Divinity Student at the base of the tower, and the machine.

A torso swings into view on a platform, lungs and a heart are installed, held in place by one pair of pneumatic arms while several other, smaller praying-mantis arms, tipped with spinnerets, snake around into the body cavity on tiny hinges, busily suturing veins, arteries, and organs into place. The arms then retract, another pair staples the diaphragm into position, and then the Divinity Student's pages are sewn up inside the abdomen. A pair of tongs pinches the muscle together while a spinneret travels the length of the seam and sews the two halves together, its needle buzzing violently. While this is going on the legs and arms appear, dripping with formaldehyde from the tanks, and are held precisely up to the joints and sutured in place by a many-headed suturing array, dozens of tiny, whirring accelerating sewing heads flashing up and down with the deliberate motion exclusively characteristic of living things.

Above and to the left of the platform, which rotates back and forth as needed, tiny struts rework and rewire the jaws, the skull gaping in midair as the teeth are repositioned, pulled, inserted, filed down. Miniature files and sanders grind puffs of powdered bone from the cheek and jaw-line, and around the eyesockets, while the top is sawn off and lined with tissue-paper. An intolerable, nerve-wracking bone-friction whine of saws and files. The individual muscles are bolted on with artificial ligaments and steel welds. Meanwhile the brain is prepared for insertion—threadlike probes sink in and out of its folds like hummingbird beaks, delivering minute pulses of current to keep the neurons active, playing over the entire brain as it swings out, cradled in a contoured steel basin at the end of a great boom arm, into position above the skull. The boom lowers it down slowly into the skull, the eyes—dangling deflated from the optic nerves like shrivelled prunes—are tugged forward into the sockets by loops of metal, then reinflated with hypos of vitreous humour when in position. Meanwhile, whip-arms the gage of wire hangers work feverishly around the brain, soldering connections, hand-over-hand clamps opening and closing, threading the spine down through a small tail of vertebrae. The skull cap claps down and welders seal the join, and a hood of skin, attached to the throat, is pulled up and over from behind. The face, stretched on a metal ring, emerges from an ornamented compartment and is pulled taught across the muscles and sutured beneath the chin, hair is tweezed into the scalp and eyebrows and eyelashes strand by strand by tiny repeaters. Flashes of lightning flicker through the windows, skip across the floor.

Now the head, a perfect likeness, is lowered and joined to the body, the spinners sewing crazily, the surgical silk singing through the runners.

The Divinity Student watches the body assemble itself dreamily, nodding back and forth on his stool. The head is attached, the body is complete. Corpulent needles puncture the skin and pump the veins and arteries full of the Divinity Student's gelatin-culture, the body becomes somewhat less flaccid-looking. Then strips of cloth, sleeves, buttons, the soles and tops of the shoes are brought together around the body and sewn together—the body is fully dressed. It bobs and weaves back and forth, lowered and raised from one station in the machine to another with smooth mechanical regularity trailing flutters of winding and unwinding synchronized armatures. Finally, the right leg is lifted and the two halves of the brace clap shut around it and are spot-welded in place with loud raucous buzzes and little plumes of smoke. The leg is lowered smoothly. The body is ready. For a moment the Divinity Student waits, his face uplifted, the transmitter in his brace winks on, the receiver in the Golem's brace winks on.

Then a blast of lightning strikes current up a wire like a neon tube—the iris of rods in the apparatus over the Divinity Student's head extend downward—with the speed of striking snakes the tips of the rods thrust into the interstices of his limbs, supple control wands coil around his spinal cord, coolly self-possessed fibers spread through every part of him; all of this in a single second. The rods retract with equal suddenness, carrying him aloft with them; he sails passively up through the air as if he were falling into the pupil of that eye overhead, the rods radiating out from him like a metal web, his body hanging in space, turning him by increments upward toward the sky. At the same time, a curved glass lid has already dropped out of the gloom over the machine, down over the body on the platform, and a pair of curved glass sections swerve up from underneath, and all come together to form an ellipsoidal glass enclosure around the body, like a clear egg. The hiss of gas as halogen and argon and supercooled formaldehyde vapor isotopes come flooding in, invisible, rustling through the body's hair and clothes, and the lights over the platform go out, leaving it in darkness; the machine is cringing back into itself.

Another blast stabs down out of the clouds and the wires snap against the floor like whips, tiny lights wink on around the Divinity Student in his ring of support rods, and the connected machines start to take measurements and administer medications and chemicals, small doses of current. Below, the chamber flickers searing white and inside the alembic Teo can see the body intermittently frozen in convulsions, and more lightning arcing down, the body is jerking and reeling in an egg of white-blue light fed by glass coils candescing under the platform as more wires flare and crackle, throwing curves rigidly, streaming smoke from burning insulation, lightning again and again and the body jackknifes in angular twists like the wires, clattering against the inside of the enclosure. Then the glass lid rises, the two segments beneath drop away. The gas inside turns blue and opaque when it comes into contact with the outside air. The Golem swings both legs together over the edge of the table, pivoting on his hip and pushes off as he comes upright to land on his feet, standing, white vapor oozing from his clothes and steaming body. Without hesitating, he marches to the door, loping firmly on his broken leg, enormous discharges of static flaring from his brace as he walks, like camera flashes popping in the air around him—he steps outside. And in the tower, sighing, the Divinity Student is rolling over as the dome slides open above him, sparking flashes of static electricity like miniature sheet lightning. Outside, the Golem stands in the street and looks up at the clouds, feeling the rain pouring down over his head, his glasses, rilling in refreshing sheets down his face and across his heavy coat, cool trickling streams across his burning temples and in his charred eyes. The clouds come down within twenty feet of the street and seethe directly overhead, as if on his convection. Inside, the Divinity Student stares up into a limitless expanse of frigid blackness and tiny stars glittering like puny flashes of lightning. In them he sees a thousand years from now San Veneficio buried by volcanic ash, and the new citizens of the new city walk past the observation dome protruding from the ground, a hemisphere of thick glass filled with formaldehyde, and the Divinity Student is still there, barely visible, far below in the murky depth of the tower, resting on his bed of untarnished metal rods, his flesh bleached colorless, white, and shriveled by the preservative, his skin folded and seamed, clothes and hair drained of color hang motionless around him. Every few hours, his sunken eyes twitch in their sockets, following the movements of the hazy, tea-colored shadows undulating over the surface of the dome, across miles and miles, from the city beneath the city. The moon, a visible other world, lifting him past the ground, pulling him up with it as it rises, lowering him as it sinks.

Far below in a welter of confused double impressions below and behind him, Teo's last goodbye gutters out.

THE COLD AIR WASHES over his face like alcohol, interrupted by warm shafts of dawning copper-colored sunlight up the tree-lined, unpaved drive to the house. The Golem is walking on his own, still leaning heavily on his brace, and waving his cane in a slow arc in front of him. It has a curved silver handle, and the shaft is thin and painted black, ending in a long diagonal fracture where the tip is broken off. Steam still spills in tiny threads from his face; more from between his eyelashes—the sunlight is so brilliant it blocks out sound. He moves as if he were under deep water, his blank eyes fixed on the small gabled house with peaked roof and peeling white paint. As he looks up, the features of his face begin again to cohere, resolving into an expression of mute, unsettled anticipation. To his right, beyond the trees, is a wide lot with dewy grass growing in thick clumps, in a smell of wet dirt. To the other side are a row of charred-black houses with their backs turned. His path is a minor deviation from the main road where these brick houses huddle. He has come to find a woman named Christine Dalman, she was promised to him in marriage a long time ago. Now however he knows he must find this woman, homespun advice about keeping promises, plain simple values. In his memory he sees his mother talking with a dark man on the other side of the fence, he sees the bargain being struck, he somehow receives her name, her image. Gleaming skin and eyes, gleaming lips, shining teeth, shining hair. While he is no longer exactly fit for the task, he must keep this long-deferred appointment, and determine what is to be done. He knows the Divinity Student made him for this purpose.

The Golem's movements are random and unconscious, but chemically vigorous; his nerves fire through numb dead limbs, but as he steps up to the porch, he experiences a feeling—a strangled, plaintive sensation ignites in his chest and steams up into his throat, leaves his head smouldering. This place is familiar. He's feeling waves of weirdly disembodied nostalgia and dread. Turning around the rim of the hedge he sees the two detectives, their names warble in his head from unfamiliar memories, recorded through distorted senses—Pracke and Kipe.

They start when they see him: he knows they recognize him, and see that he has changed. Instantly, they turn and disappear into the house with the air of bearing urgent news. The Golem steps heavily onto the porch, and through the swinging front door.

There's a hallway directly before him, with a narrow staircase to one side and doors to the right and left; police inspectors are scurrying all throughout the house. The door at the end of the hall is open, framing, perfectly, the Prefect of Police, reclining with crossed legs in a leather armchair, in the room beyond. The Golem accelerates down the hall, drawn toward the Prefect as if he were at the end of a string looped around the Prefect's little finger. The door looms wide and swallows him; Pracke and Kipe are standing in the corner their faces blank with stupid astonishment.

The Prefect of Police, his name is Griepentrog, is sitting directly across the little room from the door. Behind him, the rising sun strikes the heavy curtains, and they glow the color of a honeycomb, illuminating him with a soft, caressing glow. He is dressed in a spotless, pressed white suit with a high starched collar, his legs crossed across the knee exposing a long thin ankle in a gray stocking. Looking up at them, his face is the color and texture of yellowed newspaper; his hands are small, soft, and pink, like a baby's, with gleaming, manicured fingernails. He grips a long white cigarette at a crisp angle next to his face. It oozes a heavy blue smoke that rises like slow-moving air bubbles in deep water, a line of smoke like a strand of resin depending from the cool shadows of the ceiling. He takes a languid sip from the butt, drawing the last thread of smoke between his parted lips with a small circling motion of his pointed red tongue. His thin eyelids hang low over his amber-colored eyes, floating in limpid orange nicotine jelly. When he exhales, the smoke trickles from his nostrils into the curling edge of his nose, eddying in the pits on either side; then the two tributaries of smoke stream up through his eyebrows and fan out in a thin, barely-visible membrane over his broad, impressive forehead, nestling in his thick gelatinous hair. His hair is the color of powdered charcoal dusted with lead, and spreads from his temples like the head of a mushroom. He gazes at them with catlike contentment on his girlish face, his pursed lips framed by two small moustaches, like crossed brooms, above, and a comma of beard below. Out of his happy complacency, he welcomes them with an inclination of his head.

"Well, hel-lo!" he says, another dream come true. "Have you come to help us with our investigation?"

The Golem jerks the corners of his mouth up and drops his lower lip, returning the Prefect's false smile.

"Yes!" says the Golem in a clotted voice.

The Prefect grins wider. "Good! We could certainly use someone like you!"

The Golem's face is flushed and hot. The acid, unnatural body odor that emanates from beneath his coat is filling the room, deadening the florid aroma of the Prefect's cigarette. A cavity of sick dread is opening up in him—the emotion is *his* and nightmarishly painful—sucking at his quickening sense of expectation, his face is turning bright red radiating palpable waves of heat that rustle across Pracke's face and Kipe's face like a cloud of flies, his odor getting chokingly strong, and the Prefect is still smiling and calm, with his spotless suit, and his eyes slitted in satisfied crescents in his papery face. The two detectives shuffle back into the doorway, trying to draw clean air from the hall and the draughty wakes of the other inspectors as they stream from room to room to room behind them. For a moment there is no sound except for the rhythmic thud of their footsteps all throughout the house. Then the Prefect speaks again, in the inflections of a playschool teacher.

"Would you like to work with the Police?"

The Golem nods erratically, his hideous grin widens in his red face. "Yes!"

"Fine. Then why don't you assist the detectives here. When you're finished looking at the house, Pracke and Kipe will take you to the station, where you can examine the records we already have." He is speaking slowly and carefully. "This case has been very difficult for us," he puts his hand to his chest to indicate *us*, "and you have talents that we need very badly. It makes me very happy to know you have decided to accept our invitation."

Griepentrog pulls a photograph from his jacket with elegantly tapering fingers, and holds it up.

"This is the vic-tim."

The Golem looks at the picture. It's like watching a ghost appear in a column of white smoke, black smoke writhing up from the embers and twisting into the sharp M of a mouth, the curling nose and nostrils, the black pits of the eyes with glowing whites and dark iris. He stares at the image and inside he collapses, and throbbing like a terrified heart, dislocating and fragmenting into shards of nameless sensations—"Where is she?" he asks in a shrill voice and trembling hands outstretched. He's recognized her—this is a memory that was driven out of him completely, shocked out of him, and it has returned now for the first time, somehow he knows this.

"Her body was found in the parlor, the left-front room from here," the Prefect says, and the Golem turns and bolts down the hall throwing open the door, and he falls forward into the emptiness of the room as if it were a pit, as if he were stepping down onto a step that unexpectedly wasn't there, snipped out, tragic all-aborted future, a dead end. This is narrative shear, when the story is suddenly amputated. Wan wallpaper, iridescent white drapes and a wide view of the trees and the walk beyond the porch, simple furniture against the walls, a single chair slouching in the center of the room, and the air full of the grimy haze of abandoned lost empty murder houses and protoplasm of blank crime photographs, and as he looks around muddy tears overflow his eyes and run thickly down his convulsed face, crying incoherently he stumbles around the room clutching at furniture, drapes, dragging his palms over the walls and carpet in torture of successive blasts of loss . . . "Where is she?" appears ghost-written on the wall soldered with absence crashing over him like heavy waves that pin down the drowning only inches from the surface, and he runs from the room, and up the stairs, and from room to room, and everywhere, the same absence, the same void of blazing light and drifting dust churned by detectives tweezing evidence into plastic bags and with his mouth wide open, "Where is she? Where is she?" wracks out of him in grotesque sobs. It's as if he were a child, coming home from school and finding his house stripped bare to the four walls and his parents vanished, nothing left, not even the child who crosses the threshold into the vacant house and fades away into an odor of damp roots chewing wet dirt.

The Golem, from room to room in the tiny house, weakly tearing the air with his hands and voice, and returning again and again to the front-left room until he stands turning in the center. He falls to the ground, arcing a moment from the ceiling to the floor, and pressure enough to burst his eyes explodes him, like a string of firecrackers down his spine, throwing him to the ground and hammering at his head—his limbs go light and jerking wildly he tips backward, slammed down by a blaze sheet of light and then another and another. They strobe, he collapses, strobing on the corners, flood of dead pieces hurtling away leaving nothing behind, frothing at the mouth and bashing the floor with his brace. The furniture in the room all flies into the center and collides in midair above him, clatters down on top of him.

Pracke and Kipe run in and pull the tables and chairs off and drag him out of the house, his limbs locked, his eyes gone white, foam on his lips, torn face red, burning, unrecognizable. Slabs of oblivion scissor his ribcage shut like the door of a tomb, all the sterile weight of the future slams shut and squeezes him out—a single dark edge sharp as a razor, as the borders of your vision, squeezing down to compress him into a single point of endless repetition, and wink out like a dead star, drained and disappeared. Pracke and Kipe pull him over the boards of the porch and down the steps. He lands thrashing in a stone gutter full of stagnant water. After a moment he seizes up, petrified. The same sense in slightly different words spills out on a paper tape—She's not there, not waiting for him, nowhere, dead, not there, not waiting for him, nowhere, dead. Nowhere, not anywhere—a memory brought back to him as a weapon turned against him, a photograph he was given by his mother or father or by someone, "this is your fian-cee", everything founded on that exquisite clockwork face that would be his face, the only meaningful promise, every trace of it had died out of him, while her face hadn't changed, had grown only more painful to see. He won't be carrying out his purpose.

Pracke looks at Kipe. Functionaries and bit players, they remain characteristically unaltered by narrative shear.

"Perhaps you should brief him now," Kipe says. "It's as good a time as any."

Pracke licks his lips, takes a deep breath, and begins, shouting his words at the smashed meat of the Golem's melted face: "The victim Christine Dalman was discovered dead apparent homicide at 4:15 PM by the postman the victim lived alone and has no surviving relatives she worked at the Orpheum Theatre as a stage magician—"

At this time, the Prefect of Police Griepentrog is walking away down the lane, stretching his legs without pain. Behind him, trails of wafting photographs, police reports, affidavits, statements, appraisals, records, warrants, letters, court orders. . .

MAGELLAN'S SECRETARY, CROSSING A small, boxy courtyard covered by a stone vault—

"Excuse me, miss."

She turns, her feet grating on the cobbles echoes in the vault—a man's voice—a man in a cassock stands there just a few feet behind her. Handsome, catlike face with creased cheeks, thick dark hair; he flashes brilliant white teeth and takes a step or two toward her.

Wary of this bland appearance, she fixes him with green eyes like crackling electrical contacts, "Well?"

"I'm an officer of the Seminary—my name is Dulem."

"So?"

He is now a few steps away—he stops, still basting her with warm reassuring rays from his gleaming teeth and athletic tan.

"Don't worry, I'm not going to try to get you to say anything about Magellan," he spreads his hands in front of him, kind of laughing, all friendly personable bonhomie.

She gazes back at him stonily. She is completely there.

"Actually, we're interested in a former agent of ours—you might have known him?" Keeping things diplomatically vague, there.

"Perhaps you should ask Magellan about him. I'm just a secretary."

"You know I can't—Magellan won't speak to us."

She shrugs, "He's my employer—if he won't speak to you, I don't see why you'd think I would."

"There are more important things to you than your job."

Still smiling, he pulls a printed white card from between the gilt edges of his beautiful prayer book, and offers it to her. "I can tell you all about them—just call at this address."

She eyes the card a moment. The smiling man drops the card as her hand reaches out for it, allowing it to flutter to the ground—he turns with a brief laugh and walks away.

TEO WAS BUYING A newspaper—as he handed the man his coins he glanced up, and saw someone he recognized at the head of the street. The Golem is loping along painfully on his bad leg, his jaw clenched. He starts to pass by, then pauses and peers at Teo dubiously.

They stand in the street for a moment. The Golem nods at him ambiguously, and looks up at the sky—overhead, the ragged clouds are grey and purple, their undersides lit with vermillion streaks, and the horizon glows like a furnace. Teo is watching—the Golem already looks different; the purposive affect is gone. For a moment he feels a sense of graduated relation to the Golem; both of them have changed in essentially identical ways. It throws him off his stride for a moment, and the Golem walks off, his shoulders rolling with his loping gait. His momentum pulls Teo after, the steps seem to be taking him, falling again into place as he did before. He notices that the air around the Golem is rigid, a perfectly transparent envelope like a clear force-outline. Like the Divinity Student, the Golem has an air of rottenness about him, but without the Divinity Student's decrepitude—the Golem is vibrantly rotten. Like a lens, his rottenness magnifies and clarifies a narrow tunnel of vision around him, but its boundaries are almost invisible against the air. Teo takes his arm and leads him back to the morgue, a few blocks away.

As the daylight grows feebler the Golem walks more and more swiftly, with mounting assurance. The morgue comes into view just as the streetlights wink on, and the two of them scurry into the shadowy alleys, lined with modest lean-to kiosks selling shabby, inexpensive wreaths, black armbands of greasy fabric, darned second-hand veils, and other furnishings of mourning, that surround the morgue.

A heavy truck, with a canvas top, thunders down the narrow street rattling loudly over the potholes. Belching a cloud of exhaust and lacing the air in its wake with sickening traces of foul meat, a smell familiar enough to them both, the truck lurches crazily over the wildly uneven road and jerks its way around the corner. In the resounding silence it leaves behind it, the Golem rushes to one of the side doors of the morgue and raps the lock once with his cane. The lock clicks open and the two of them duck swiftly inside.

"Leave the light off," the Golem rasps.

Teo stumbles behind the Golem, little more than a lurching patch of darker black against the lightless warehouse. He drags and scrapes across the tiles and nearly collides with a freezer. Awkwardly he paws the metal door and gestures to Teo to come up close, tapping the card on the front of the door. Teo moves in to read it: "Christine Dalman—d. 02/29 / 03/01."

"The murdered woman?"

The Golem makes a noise.

The Golem slides his face down beside the door, peering through the dark, and claws open the latch, shearing the padlock's bar clean in two. He sweeps Teo aside and behind him with his arm as he pulls open the door and a tiny refrigerator light winks on inside.

Staring with furious impatience into the compartment, the Golem hauls the steel drawer out to its full length and imperiously hurls the pall to the floor.

Leaning forward, the Golem props himself on the shelf and peers at the body. Its face is badly disfigured, long slashes running deep across the features. Teo regards the cuts professionally.

"Scalpel work," he says.

The Golem is scanning her face and throat with birdlike jerks of his head, and then he reaches up gently and pulls her hair up away from her face, and, despite himself, he makes a little sound.

"There!" he says, tapping the spot behind her right ear with his fingertip.

Teo looks, and sees a small ink drawing on the skin. It's a broken, black silver-handled cane.

"This isn't her," the Golem says, grinning horribly; and, when Teo doesn't understand, "—*my fiancée.*" He points at the card on the door, "Christine Dalman."

"This—" he taps the drawing again, smearing the ink, "—is a sign, meant for me. She's still alive." His face flushes and turns up towards the ceiling as he straightens up, settling himself standing upright, not hunched, eyes flashing. His fever dapples his face white, red, and green at the edges, the skin blazing hot as a furnace. He looks once at Teo, and then turns aside to go. Teo pauses a moment to look at the body.

Teo can't believe he's engaged.

"I *knew* she wasn't dead," the Golem says to the ceiling. "She mutilated her 'own' face," he says, and his grin flickers once in the darkness as the freezer-door light blinks, "She did just as I, uh, just as *he* did."

"What for?"

"I don't know," the Golem says, looking again at Teo. For a moment he puzzles over the question, and then a light flickers in his eyes and he taps his own neck behind the ear, "But now I know why he made me . . . he *knew*. Only a double, like me, can follow her."

Teo shakes his head, shrugs.

"She's down there," the Golem says with unaccountable certainty, banging the ground a couple of times with his foot, "hiding, and doing her research. You can't go down there without a reason, and you can't go down there in the ordinary way—you need a substitute, either above or below. She left hers above, he sends his below—that's *me*."

"Why would she hide? I mean from what?"

The Golem thinks—"You know Griepentrog, don't you?"

"Ugh."

"Yes, ambitious in all the wrong ways. He wants knowledge of certain things."

"Her research?"

"Whatever she learns. If he knows where she's gone, (and I think he does,) he wouldn't know how to follow, but he would certainly be waiting for her when she gets back."

"He's been watching her?"

"Of course. He's not in his line of work to enforce *the law*."

The Golem stoops painfully to retrieve the pall, and drapes it again over the body.

"A dream told him to dig me, uh, *him* up. He didn't know why then, but he knows why now."

"You'll go after her, and he'll follow?"

"He can't—he'll string me along, as the next best thing."

The metal door snaps shut, the substitute body locked away in the dark.

As they turn away, Teo is struck by something—"Griepentrog is an agent of your old Seminary, isn't he?"

He's talking to the back of the Golem's head, which nods twice, "I knew it the minute I clapped eyes on him—he's got a diploma somewhere."

Far from leading, Teo follows the Golem back to the circus grounds. He is still loping on his braced leg, but he's taking longer strides, and the heat shimmers around him in the growing daylight in a halo of shuddering threads, his red-green face blanching blue-white in the twilight before dawn. One day, the chord that binds him will snap him back into the sun.

Now they're back at Teo's small house. Without waiting for the lights, the Golem lurches to a corner and collapses, clattering down into a sitting position with his braced leg sticking out in front of him. Then he sits still and is silent. His eyes are open, blank.

IMMEDIATELY BENEATH THAT SPOT in the sky where the sun makes an orange X in the caverns of the clouds, in the weak and uncertain light of a phone box one can make out the face of Magellan's secretary. She impatiently asks the operator at the exchange for the police.

Griepentrog

The Golem is making his way to the cemetery—it's very important. The wall along which he is walking is very white, dazzling in the noonday sun. The muscles around his eyes are stiff with squinting, when he looks away from the wall, a pink haze sidles over everything. Through this pink haze he sees, standing on the corner by an idling car, the two detectives, Pracke and Kipe. Pracke nudges Kipe.

Kipe clears his throat several times, "You'll have to come with us."

"Now?"

Kipe nods.

"You see, I'm a busy man."

Pracke raises his eyebrows. "What difference does that make?"

"Does it absolutely have to be now?"

Kipe nods, rumpling his face as if to say, "I wish it wasn't so."

Pracke says, "We are all at the mercy of our superiors."

Pracke coughs. He coughs again, and clears his throat.

". . . Appointment time, big fella."

He and Kipe walk swiftly, side by side, up to the Golem. With a peremptory heave they drag him up by his shoulders and pull him along to the door, his leg brace screeching on the slate paving. They pitch the Golem into the back seat of their car. With an affected sigh, he gathers his complicated limbs together and just out of the way of the slamming door.

Police headquarters—the Golem shuffles inside, tiresome as ever. Powerful aura of futility, inertia. The walls are smooth, cool plaster with wide arches and bristling red crescent tiles, red cobblestones worn smooth as rocks under a riverbed. Detectives in light overcoats spill past, crisscrossing the buildings and grounds, giving him a wide berth. They keep him waiting for over an hour in a dingy, airless room the walls shellacked with thick glossy tan paint. The usual routine, trying to get him riled and impatient before the big meet.

Finally, he is admitted into Griepentrog's office, and it is spacious as a barn, with potted plants and ceiling fans. A phalanx of desks guards the outer office, each one attended by a secretary in a simple white dress like a modified lab coat. Pracke's head pops out of the doorframe and swivels on his collar, inviting the Golem in.

The inner office is frozen in warm gelatinous orange light from glowing window shades, drawn down against the direct rays of the sun. Pracke and Kipe stand before the massive oak desk, flanking a wooden chair with leather cushions riveted onto its frame. Griepentrog, gleaming like a marble statue, sits motionless behind his desk, steepling his fingers, silently cuing the Golem to sit. A cigarette sits poised at the rim of the ashtray like the barrel of a cannon, smoke laddering up past his face in a rolling, funnel-shaped stream. Griepentrog waits a few moments, permitting a heavy mantle of powerful silence to settle about his shoulders in a passive gesture, waiting for the fruits of machinations that, once set in place and motion, need no maintenance.

"Well, what have you got for me?" he asks, languidly transfixing the Golem with his oleaginous eyes.

The Golem's greenish face now contorts again into a repulsive false smile.

"You haven't been honest with me," he says.

"In what way?"

"Why didn't you tell me you were watching her?"

"Why should we have told you that?"

"Why did you have her under surveillance?"

"It isn't important. You really ought to confine yourself to investigating her death."

"You had three cars on her almost all the time."

Griepentrog turns his chair slightly to one side, himself still as motionless as a statue. "I can only say that we felt it was necessary that we keep an eye on her for a while."

"You know where she is, but you can't get to her."

Griepentrog is silent.

"I can bring her to you," the Golem says with a nauseating grin, redolent of steeping fever and the moist haze of general infection. His face looks fibrous and drawn, in places the skin is white and dead like a webbed membrane over his flushed cheeks and forehead.

Griepentrog also smiles, a slow, infectious smile, that spreads from his lips across the room to crease Pracke's and Kipe's features as well, dreams coming true again like a golden boy can do no wrong. They are all smiling and their smiles get broader and broader and he flushes redder and redder as he explains his plan, and Griepentrog leans forward, his eyes on the Golem as he doodles a string of elegant loops of ink from a gold fountain pen, his smile still stretching, chiming into the room and coloring it deeper and deeper shades of orange. And as the Golem leaves, they watch his loping back through the closing door and glance at each other, smiling and nodding with an unspoken air of accomplishment, as if to say, "We finally brought him around." The door shuts silently on their smiling nodding faces, and the secretaries sit and type without looking up as he passes.

As the Golem heads for the door, he engraves in his memory the image of Griepentrog's smiling smiling nodding face, thinking all the time about the cars, the hounding, the chasing, the hectoring, of Christine, how far she ran to escape them—*they are capable of doing anything to her, to learn what she will know, or hopes to know.*

He carries a sample of the Divinity Student's tainted saliva in a gelatin envelope beneath his tongue. Pausing only for a moment, he lifts the ceramic lid of the water cooler by the door to the office and spits, dexterously squashing the gelatin bubble and ejecting its contents like a cobra. (The envelope seals again the moment the pressure of the tongue is lifted: a skillful practitioner need never worry about self-contamination). The clear dollop of saliva dissolves instantly, infusing the entire volume of water in the tank.

MAGELLAN'S SECRETARY HAS THE habit of eavesdropping on her employer; she is enterprising, she reads more of his documents from time to time than she is, strictly speaking, permitted to. She works at home, in her free time, and after a number of failed secret experiments, she hits on a preparation of paste, clear glue, pectin, and chemically very pure, very expensive wax in her bathtub. Stirred in hot water, the preparation gradually settles to the bottom of the tub; she skims the water into the sink with a bread pan.

Careful not to disturb it, she reaches down and feels the warm, doughy wax with the palm of her hand. Satisfied with its consistency, she seals the room, leaving only a small aperture, outfitted with a filter, in the window. Now, she lies on the floor, on her back, immediately alongside the tub, and recites from memory until she falls asleep. After her eyes have closed, and her breath has become shallow and slow, her voice continues to sound . . .

When she rises from the floor the next morning, her wax double rises from the bottom of the tub. Miss Woodwind stands facing her double, which reproduces her in every particular, down to the buttons on her blouse and the threads that fix them there. Studying the pale, white-yellow eyes, whose irises and pupils are delineated by fine grooves, she opens her mouth; the double does the same, opening a colorless mouth filled with facsimile teeth and tongue. After a thorough investigation, Miss Woodwind leads her obliging double through the door and conducts her to her bed. The double stretches herself out on top of the covers. Without pausing to look again, Miss Woodwind snatches up a few of her things, and is gone.

AND NOW, WITH EYES everywhere, the Golem is biding his time, waiting until he can get away unobserved—wouldn't want to give away any trade secrets. After a few days, he's picked up again. Initially too busy trying to disengage himself from the car he doesn't notice at first that that they are not parked in front of police headquarters. Pracke and Kipe spent the brief trip coughing and making liquid sounds in their throats, and now they assist the Golem through the glass doors of a small private hospital.

Prefect Griepentrog is on the sixth floor, lying in a small bed, hemmed in on all sides by a white linen curtain hanging from a track in the ceiling. A lurid green has crept into his pink complexion, and his oleaginous golden eyes have sprouted crystallized droplets of amber at the corners. His breathing is wet and labored, filtering through curtains of mucus in his lungs and throat. He lies propped up in his bed, hair graying against the stark white pillows and sheets, his hands lying flaccid and hot in his lap, his throat protruding, like warm ruddy parchment, from the collar of his white gown. Kipe approaches, whispers something through a handkerchief (to prevent further infection), and the Prefect turns his wasted gaze, now diffused and colorless, on the party. The Golem stands at the foot of his bed, leaning on the metal frame. He eyes the Prefect with a dire, exhausted look, as though he were about to collapse into a heap of dusty fragments.

Griepentrog opens his mouth, triggering an attack of convulsive coughing, eyes screwed shut, squeezing out thick orange tears. Pracke hands him a cup of water.

The Prefect tries to speak, his chest heaving. He rolls his head on the pillow and strains his wan face—". . . you . . ." he says, feebly waving a finger toward the foot of the bed. ". . . water . . ."

Kipe hands him a cup of water. The Prefect knocks it aside, spilling it on the floor, and jerks forward shaking, lips writhing, glaring hatefully at the Golem.

The Golem bends down over Griepentrog's face. With an expression of exaggerated sympathy he makes a glistening funnel of his lips "sshhhh . . ." a gush of cesspool breath. Griepentrog hacks and gags, reeling over to the opposite side of the bed, greenish-black filth and gobs of tissue welling from between his clenched teeth. The nurse dashes in round the curtain and insists that they leave, holding Griepentrog's head in her hands as he noisily fouls her uniform. As he turns to go, the Golem's back straightens, the feeble act drops away.

The Underworld

HAVING FOUND HIS TIME, the Golem picks his way through the graves—under the bones, under the stones and the caskets, in deep ruts between the plots. Weathered old groundskeepers trickle dust from their footsteps along the ruts, nodding over him as he passes, moving their cold hands weakly from their pockets, into the grass, by the trees. Pickled old men with thousand-year voices wandering on dwindling pathways, in the tombs, on the stones, their frail gramophone voices eddy in stone corners in cobwebs, broken glass of boarded-up tombs, gingerly creaking iron gates rusting off their hinges, cobwebs of rust and water trailing smeared powder of flowers, dried and crumbled, streaking the slabs, running in cracks. The Golem finds his way in sunken paths worn down by mourners' feet, stopping at a stone scroll half-collapsed into the rank grass. Miles away the Divinity Student nods, the Golem pulls the scroll aside, exposing a withered coffin on a bed of dried heather and woven round with white hawthorn. The Golem pulls the coffin open, the nails give way in softened wood, and inside the body is already falling away . . . he can see water dashing miles away, a quivering streak of reflected light at enormous distance, nearly lost to sight at the bottom of the coffin. The cadaver, dressed in its sentimental best, fragile and light as a dried corn-husk, has already vanished down a spiral flight of stairs, moving at unnatural speed owing to the greatly favorable ratio between its weight and its size. The almost-silent brushing of its feet on the steps is vanishing without echoing, is already almost inaudible. The Golem drops his head dubiously into the coffin and sniffs—the air is invitingly moist and cold, scented with dust and mothballs and fossilized flowers, perfectly unique, flawless scent.

The Golem raises his braced leg and lunges forward—it clatters down on a metal landing that bobs precariously under him. With care, he brings his other foot down and begins to descend, holding the rim of the coffin, releasing clouds of pollen and pulverized heather. The darkness closes around him and he goes down slowly, the stairs coiling and uncoiling as he shifts his weight from one step to the next, swinging a little, the Golem feels weak old metal straining through his hands. The light from above is already far away, obscured by the stairs. Then it's gone. The shaft is dark and silent. The earth presses in on all sides and there is no stairway, no river. The earth presses in and crushes him, fills his mouth and eyes, his ears, cold and silent. The Golem flexes in space, murmuring, and the Golem reaches and finds the railing, descends, feeling the steps surely under his feet, listening to the sound of the water coming closer. Nearby the cadaver rattles in its throat—no matter what, the dead always laugh.

Then the Golem lunges wildly forward into space, there being no stair there for his foot. He holds onto the rail and thrusts himself backward even as rough, papery fingers claw at his hands. He says, "Get away!" and the hands pull back, behind them a dry rattle in the dark air, then nothing. He gets his feet back above the amputated step and stands there thinking. He can hear the water beneath him, a huge volume of water making no more sound than a hollow, tinkling chuckle where the current wrinkles along the banks of the channel. There is no light anywhere, the water is blackest of all. The Golem leans forward and peers down anyway, feeling only the finest brush of spray on his face. He thinks, resolves himself, and tips himself forward—the stairs snap back upward like a released spring, and the Golem drops straight down into the water, plunging down through the surface into biting cold, tortured blackness of uncontrolled spins in speeding current in water black as oil. His body locks, a half-tumbled half-uncurling ball spinning in vast black water under a glowing ceiling of blue-white ice, curtained round in a sheath of tiny shining bubbles that rise slowly and collect in silver-edged blobs against the pack. The Golem, petrified, shoots down the stream forever, curving round on himself in ice-water, turning round on himself in ice-water, curving round on himself in ice-water, turning round on himself in ice-water, driven like a stone through chutes of ice-water, down channels of ice-water, through chutes of ice-water, down channels of ice-water, turning and staring, turning, slower and slower over infinite time, churned out in underwater froth into an underground lake, infinitely deep, boiling out in underwater froth from a stone channel. He drops in bottomless water, sinking in the cold, where no light is, his brace pulling him down like an anchor. Finally, the water becomes crushingly heavy, he stops sinking and floats in place, his flesh turning to water, still water in his flesh.

After a time he is aware that he is moving laterally on a weak current.

He feels himself bump up against something, an unyielding vertical surface. The current holds him there, eventually pressing him face-to-face with it, something like a stone pylon. With effort, the Golem reaches out to his arms and legs. He has to call them over and over until they come. Blindly fumbling over the surface of the pylon, he finds it is roughly-made, covered with protrusions. He finally manages to take one in his hand, find another with his foot, and he begins climbing. Passing in and out of consciousness, he draws himself in the direction he hopes is up. As time goes by, the water seems to become less heavy, he begins to feel the weight of his brace, he begins to feel his own buoyancy. He climbs. Over time, he gradually begins to see his hands in front of him, he can make out a faint radiance, but no surface as yet. He climbs with his neck craned back. Like a man half-asleep he begins to see a surface far away. He climbs, and he can make out a thin line running across the surface, one that will intersect with his column. He can dimly make out other pylons in the water, miles off in either direction.

Then in a moment his head breaks the surface, which is still, and he freezes, feeling as if his head will burst in thin air. Stunned, he hangs there a moment. Then, he climbs out. The air restores his weight but relieves the pressure of the water. He climbs up, pulling himself over a stone railing onto an elevated road. He falls forward onto his face and lies there, staring beyond exhaustion at the surface of the road.

After a while, the Golem gets up and begins walking. The road stretches off in either direction in an endless series of bounding arches, from pylon to pylon, only a few yards beneath the roof of the vault. The water stretches off into a misty, horizon-less distance, completely still, not even lapping at the pylons. The Golem walks pointlessly, with his head down, moving in one direction, although the road begins to branch almost immediately, spreading out like a web over the surface of the water as far as he can see.

Suddenly he has bumped into something—looking up he sees a tree growing in a huge clod of earth, sitting by the side of the road. A man is hanging from the tree; this is what he bumped into. Looking more closely, the Golem can see that the rope that hangs the man is not suspended from the branches, but extends up past the top of the tree to vanish into the vault's ceiling. Looking more closely, the Golem can see that the hanged man is the Golem, upside-down. The Golem stares into the Golem's face, slack but not discolored, for a long time. Then, he reaches into his mouth and pulls a little on the end of his tongue. The stitches that hold it there writhe out of their holes and the tongue comes loose in his hand. The Golem gently turns the tongue over and slides it into the Golem's gaping mouth, caked with dried blood, showing a stump where his tongue had been. The sutures in the Golem's tongue bore into the stump and cinch the new tongue firm . . . the Golem kneels, and places his ear to the Golem's mouth. The lips move against his ear—the tongue tells him which way to go, where to look, then falls silent. The Golem retrieves his tongue and puts it back in his own mouth; it tastes of bitter blood and rusty shears. The Golem wanted to cut the Golem down, but the Golem had told him to leave right away, and he does. When he looked back several hours later and much farther down the road, he couldn't see the tree, the rope, or the Golem behind him.

WHEN THE VAULT OPENS out in all directions, the Golem can see the city spread broadcast on the water, floating on a vast raft of creosoted pilings. The city is only barely visible as a complicated three-dimensional constellation of dim lights. Nearby, the road opens out onto a shelf in the cavern wall, which closes in around the road as he approached, a puncture in a larger bubble in stone, the walls rushing in from out of limitless distance. There is a small rail-yard laid out on the shelf, lit by tall sodium lights, shadowy, charcoal-colored figures moving in and out among the heavy cars. The road leads into the yard, and then out again the other side—from here, the only way into the city. The Golem comes closer, and the figures seem to withdraw, having lined up a set of empty cars on the tracks. By weaving in and out among the cars and piles of empty crates, the Golem is able to avoid being seen. He walks out onto the center of the platform, crossing behind the line of cars, heading for the darker edge of the shelf. The platform is sheeted with oily steel; his footsteps rap on the steel as he crosses over past the rails. The cars are cable-cars, pulled along by heavy chains set in grooves in the steel platform—the chain presumably attached to a winch at each end. As he crosses behind them, the line of cars begins to move, rolling down toward the city.

The Golem suddenly looks down at the groove beneath his feet in time to see the chain snag his leg brace as it slashes by and he is torn from his feet and falls half-turning and flying over the ground. He lands on his arm, his hand held out a little reaching and crushed back against his chest—his head whips on his neck, batters against the ground. His brace still caught he is dragged along with it, slicing along the platform and then out over pummeling wooden ties. He is dragged unnoticed behind the cars, which tilt down over a rough concrete ramp with steps cut into it and the Golem is pulled down behind them and into the water at the bottom: he cannot lose consciousness. In the shock of the water he feels himself nearly twisting free from his caught leg. The weight of the water stretches him; he tries to reach up over his locked knee to the snag in the brace but the force of the water is pushing him back, his arms are shattered and torn open. The cars yanked themselves out of the water and the Golem is rammed against a concrete embankment, his unbraced left leg trails behind him nearly bent double at the ankle: he still can't pass out. He can't come apart, he even has to keep jerking to the right to keep his body from being caught by the other end of the chain, which is going in the opposite direction. If he were caught on both chains he'd be ripped in two at once. A steel shelf comes up and chops at his left hip, he is flipped backwards but he is still conscious, the sutures hold. His back is burning with friction against the shelf, the cars turn a corner and again he nearly twists off his braced leg, his whole body ready to come apart but the sutures won't give way even as the flesh around them tears. He is dragged past a platform and his head snaps back against one of the supports, his left eye clawed by a rivet, and as he is flipped again he sees they are crossing an embankment. The storehouse is up ahead, the cars disconnecting from the chain as they come in, the chain is speeding up as it is less and less encumbered, heading for the huge toothed gear that turns it and the Golem realizes he'll be shredded by that gear if he can't get loose. As he is pulled over a small bump his upper body flips up into a sitting position for a moment and, with his left arm, which is less mutilated than the right, he seizes his locked brace and holds himself in place, upright, pulling in a frenzy at the brace. The brace miraculously unhooks, and he goes tumbling down the embankment to land face-first in thick mud and cold water. He has not lost consciousness.

With pain, he begins to paw at the bank with his left arm, the right floating useless in the water. He paws at the bank for a long time, without thinking, eventually realizes that he's caught hold of a root. Almost inert, he pulls weakly at it, drawing himself slowly up the bank. His braced leg, wrenched but working, flounders a little in the water and against the bank, finally finding enough leverage to push him forward. By pushing off with his leg and pulling himself with his arm, he is able to drag himself up the bank, holding his head up. Every now and then he stops, dropping his head in the antiseptic mud. If he could get into the water, he might be able to pull himself along more easily, but his leg brace is too heavy, and would bear him down to the bottom. So instead, he struggles along in the mud, occasionally turning his face up to look at the high bank overhead. He doesn't know whether he should waste his energy trying to climb it, or keep going along the water's edge in the hope it will level out further on. He hauls himself up onto a small mound and sees the city lights stretching out in front of him, and up to one side. He can see he's on the edge of the gargantuan raft on which the city rests, on a lip of pilings. The mud is run-off from the earth heaped on top of the raft. Pivoting on his stomach, he angles his body up the bank and starts climbing—if he loses his footing he could slide right down into the water. His grip fails once, but he turns as he slides and digs his brace into the muck, anchoring himself. Then he hauls himself up over the edge, feeling like he's passing through a mangle, and comes to rest on top.

He can see a few buildings across a narrow, empty street. He's lying on a thin strip of park by the water. Presently, he starts scrabbling along on his belly, the wet grass lets him slip along without too much trouble. He can see smudged figures moving in the street—they ignore him. He keeps his head low to the ground, turned toward the street, the grass brushing by against his cheek. With his one working eye, he sees a surgical supply store across the street—actually down a short side-alley opening onto a bigger boulevard on the far side. Mechanically, the Golem begins slithering toward it—the cobblestones tearing at his underside, the cloth of his shirt worn away, he narrowly misses being run over by a huge, clattering shape. He manages the sidewalk and batters the door with his left arm—it's unlocked. Inside, bleary figures shriek and draw out of his way, he can hear echoing protests from someone standing over him, nudging his broken ribs with the toe of its shoe. The Golem ignores them, his eyes have fixed on a bottle of formaldehyde on a conveniently low shelf. He knocks away the stopper with a swipe of his arm, falling forward off-balance, then rolls over onto his back, tilting the bottle off the shelf with him, splattering the formaldehyde into his mouth. With his left arm he heaves the bottle downside-up and pours it in, feeling it chime through his limbs: his ruined left leg straightens, the back of his head uncollapses, his ruined right eye inflates in its socket, his body's form is restored, although still badly rent apart. The bottle drained, the voices now silent, the sounds of footsteps rattling out the door, he seizes a second bottle, rolling over onto his back, much stronger now. He balances the bottle on his back and seizes an IV stand by its base, pulling it along with him as he crawls out through the back of the store into a courtyard, open to one side, littered with rubbish, machine parts, an old car. The Golem navigates through the clutter and crawls into something like an old chicken-coop. With increasing pain and irritability he props the bottle on a ledge over his head, dragging the bottle down from the IV stand. He knocks the stopper off the bottle of formaldehyde and jams the stopper from the IV bottle in its place, catching up the few splashes of formaldehyde with his mouth, as best he can. The formaldehyde runs down the tube and trickles out the needle. The Golem fumbles impossibly with his sleeve a moment, then gives up and jabs the needle directly into his neck. He drops his head back on the planks and passes out.

WHEN THE BELL RINGS, the Golem is shocked awake. He turns the bottle upright and plucks out the needle from his neck, then wanders unsteadily out into the street. A series of chimes are being hung in the air, one at a time, ornamentally reverberating from the dingy storefronts, trickling around his feet. He cranes his ears in a circle and begins to follow the sound toward its source, not so much the bell as the hand ringing it. Streets swivel around him, figures run by or sit and gnaw illusions like praying mantises. The city is scored across with fissures where the segments of the raft are caused to float side by side, by means of heavy girders, bearded with seaweed, and by curved bridges. Small channels help divert the weight of the water beneath onto the top of the raft, making it more neutrally buoyant. Large, flat, sluglike fish cruise by in the channels, nibbling at the tarred lining and glancing girlishly up at the Golem with their dead eyes. The bell makes them wince and shrink back into themselves.

The street the Golem is following opens out. The museum occupies one side of the deserted square. He wanders toward the museum portico haphazardly, and looking up only a moment he notices a pair of golden eyes watching him from a quiet corner of the bell tower . . . and a small coral smile in a pale face . . . This figure, who seems to be wearing his clothes, grips a painted fan, and vanishes back into the shadows of the bell tower to the laughing cries of its birds. The Golem rushes up the steps and knocks the heavy bronze doors open, staggering into the lanes of the endlessly radiating galleries. His brace bangs on the hard floor, the noise carols through the dark, into the corners. Phantoms everywhere pull back obscurely, through patterned ravelings of shade in the lee of looming windows and curtained foyers, bewildered and discomfited by this uncouth man and his noise. Under glass in every exhibition, the bell's softest note is still humming in place, biding itself without diminishing, below the threshold of audibility.

There: skittering along a railing, or flashing by at the far end of the room—fluttering wings, the glint of a perfectly round, webbed eye, the dry scraping of claws on marble floors . . . The Golem follows the bell tower birds, clambering after as best he can, always late, missing his chance to see something. Unable to move fast or adroitly, he is only just able to catch a glimpse of her before she disappears again. On several occasions birds erupt from the dark only a few feet away from him, he hears the rustle of her skirts, but so fast do these eruptions come and go he has no time to move at all, even to jerk back in surprise. In the dark, he can't see them coming—but here, in this corner, he sees a woman's foot. There on the banister, a woman's hand. . . . and her fragrance, blown here and there by the energetic flapping of birds' wings, lingers everywhere in the air, stronger and less strong by turns. This fragrance materializes from time to time in tiny flurries of bees with bright yellow stripes, and the humming of bees' wings and the rapping of birds' wings grows louder as he searches, but only by barely perceptible degrees.

The Golem is getting impatient. He is now standing on one side of a partition wall running the length of an enormous room. This wall is broken through with windows at floor level, and the other half of the room is several feet lower. When he sees the flash of her teeth in those windows on the other side, he bashes the glass in with a few light knocks of his brace and ducks through the window, landing on his braced leg, this coils beneath his weight like a spring and then rebounds, shooting him along the partition, following the cooler, less dusty contour in the air left by her body as it passed a second earlier. He is brought in this way to the base of a flight of stairs, which he climbs. There's another gallery at the top—the trees have thrust their branches in through the empty windows, their silver-dollar shaped leaves wiggle along the ceiling. In the light of those windows, shining for the most part beneath the branches, he can see a deep gulf in the floor, opening on to a vast orchestral pit far below—there are heavily-curtained boxes on the walls facing him across the gulf. As the Golem peers down into the darkness, the idea that she is present, watching him, begins to grow in his mind.

Night has fallen above ground, and Miss Woodwind has slipped stealthily into the park. Nimbly picking her way through the dense bracken, beneath the wiry black limbs of the barren trees, she pursues upstream the course of a flickering, talking brook, whose slick rocks shine like opals in the moon's waxing light, whose fragrant billows fold along the edges of its bed with a crinkling sound. Now, close to the source, she kneels beside the stream.

In a box furnished with two elegant, white-upholstered, gold-painted chairs, and hung all over with heavy golden ornaments, he sees a magnificent, queenly woman: her skin is as white as paper, her hair is as black as ink; the fiery roll of her black bangs shines like a polished oil drum; her pointed lips and nails are scarlet as the red of my binding; her mistletoe eyes are maned with black lashes coal-sable; her dress striped gold and blue like quire-stitches. She appears beneath an arch, because the arch is our symbol for the dream.

Miss Woodwind slips her left hand under the water, along its bed, until, lying on her side, her entire left arm cradles the stream like a bolt of cold cloth. With dreamlike slowness she brings her right arm up through the air and down to rest on the surface of the water.

Christine smiles into space at first, her face gleams. Then she seems to notice the Golem. Her eyes widen, whitening their sockets, and from her lips escape the inverted white arch of her gloating grin: a baroque grin glistening with venom, a grin you want to suck like hard candy—a jaw breaker. Her throat is girdled with a garland of beautiful paper flowers, which promiscuously offer their jasmine and orange blossom perfumes to the engorged air.

Miss Woodwind's softened senses tell her that her left shoulder has slipped a little—and with a gradual inclination forward, she then tilts all at once and slips beneath the stream, holding it still in her arms and borne off by its current into the dark. As a cold dream presses its lips about her form, the water turns dark, shivers and divides into randomly-mingled ribbons of black and white, scribbling across each other, form lines, illegible words . . .

A spur of desire, new to him and alarming, penetrates the Golem as he first lays eyes on Christine. From now on, his cane is also a sword with a broken blade, upon which every word he speaks will be in elegant handwriting finely engraved. He ransacks his mind for some way to cross the gulf separating them, but knows already that she will not stand still to wait for his crossing. But her eyes are glimmering with light like a madwoman's, her purring face is all opalescent syrup on the cold, lightless air, the tresses she indistinctly shakes are as splendid as a crown, her teeth are sheathed in a membrane of dewy saliva, like oil-of-glass, which gives luster to her coral lips, her chalcedony breath sifts across the breach to alight on his face.

"*Go away!*" she says. Did he hear those words, or only find them written inside? They are associated with the echo of a far-away and thrillingly low voice—but her lips didn't move. Again he hears, or somehow receives, the caressing words "*Go away!*"

Still wracking his brains for some way to cross to her—even as her eyes, her presence, rivet him to the spot, stops his arms and legs. Her breath, her perfume, the air throbs around her like a pulsing mouth, a soft and trembling babyish lip . . .

Now she seems to laugh at him, or almost—"Haven't you gone yet?"

The Golem is beginning to feel lightheaded. He shouldn't have tried his feet so quickly, he hasn't healed properly. He feels the puncture in his neck and wishes for the IV. But he doesn't take his eyes from Christine.

She hasn't stopped smiling. If anything, she's smiling more and more. It hasn't been more than a moment since she last spoke. Her hands, which up until now had been clasped demurely in front of her, now rest on a lever protruding from the floor.

"All right, catch me if you can!"

The lever is pulled—although Christine still has not moved. With a dull rattle of wooden cogs the walls of the museum unlace around them like unmeshing fingers and spread to either side like wings, galleries and hallways scrolling smoothly past, and Christine, her face now streaked with tears, her mouth livid and pale, the lips compressed, drifts past in an alcove lined with vermillion fabric, and out of sight. Her bowed neck will become an arch passing over him. The Golem stares weakly around at the moving walls and scanning doorways, finally bolting through an aperture at random, and from there trying to thread his way out again. The museum churns, swapping floors and rooms, basement for attic and back again, shifting in all directions at once like a moving labyrinth, but eventually the Golem manages to navigate out into the square again. Behind him, the museum withdraws into the shadows, still disarticulating and sliding through itself like an elaborate explosion. He can tell that she's already far away.

The Secretary and the Museum

Christine never takes the same street twice, but she knows that she will inevitably be seen. He lurks everywhere, setting up precisely-timed "spontaneous" encounters, parting the city at every corner with his skulking, waiting to meet her again. She keeps her eye on the dripping eaves overhead as she weaves across short bridges and suspended walkways toward the heart of the city, where the monumental buildings rise directly from the water. Some nearly brush the roof of the cavern, while others penetrate it, and rise higher still. As she moves into their shadows she can feel a cold exposed feeling shiver across her back, and turning she catches a momentary glimpse of him before he melts again into shadows of his own. The same loping silhouette, where had she seen it before?

She turns and slips around the corner onto her street. The desultory lighting from hanging lamps and unshaded windows fills the street with a pale glow the color of watery milk. Without running, assuming she is even now under his gaze, she hurriedly glides through the doors to her building and into the elevator. As the doors glide shut she remembers how she'd seen him, looming ominously over her open windowsill from across the cavernous distance of her bedroom. She had hidden herself in the tiny milk-drop compartment in the wall and watched him come creaking through the door and scan the room with a slow sweep of his leaden, pasty face. It had seemed to her that his face telescoped out into the room on a stalk, peering into corners and behind the drapes, but nothing like that had actually happened. He had simply failed to find her and left hastily, perhaps in the hope of catching her outside.

She had moved house right away. She'd rather negligently arranged to have her expense money sent to her directly—but, after a narrow escape in the mail room, she now picks up the plain yellow envelopes filled with the charred-black paper coins with ghostly white letters that are the currency here—at the post office. Now he is after her again; he's found her new address somehow. She wants to get a few things from her apartment before she moves on again: and it wouldn't do to cheat him of these precious few glimpses.

Something batters faintly against the floor of the elevator, directly beneath her feet. Christine jerks away—another blow, harder this time, and the thin plywood panel pops up, a dent appears in the metal floor. Christine presses against the doors watching the numbers change. Another blow and this time she can hear the metal tear and the sounds of the shaft come echoing through. Behind her she is listening to his hands scrabbling along the edges of the rent he's made, pulling the metal wide apart. The floor light shifts, the bell rings, and the doors swing open; she flits out into the corridor even as she hears the floor giving way, the doors clicking shut.

He'll catch her on the stairs: her door, even locked, wouldn't stop him— it hadn't the first time. So, she runs to the window at end of the hall. Stepping out onto the ledge she estimates the distance to the next building. Glancing back—he's stepping out into the passage, silhouetted in the light from the elevator, bent with his hands hanging down and his arms curved in beneath him like a spider. With all her strength she stiffens her body and rises in the air, her skirts twisting around her legs. She sails, patting down her pleats now on this side now on the other, across the gap, glimpsing water flashing hundreds of feet below where the foundations sink out of sight. Gracefully tilting back onto the cushions of the air she drops feet-first through the opposite window. From there she need only trip the length of the hall to the opposite stairwell.

The Golem follows only moments later. Step onto the ledge, then simply lean forward and drop like a sack of concrete, but at an angle, toward the building opposite. Crash down onto the fire escape which bends under his weight with the sound of protesting metal, the rivets pulling free from the wall. The slats snap beneath his feet and he has to pull himself through the window by the jam—his weight nearly wrenches the frame loose, the glass in the panes squeezes then shatters, but he lunges forward in time. He has narrowly avoided getting tangled up in the fire escape and plunging with it to the pilings far below. Christine is already at the stairwell. Loping after her, he pulls the door open so wildly it comes clean off of its hinges and slaps the floor. From the landing, he can see her face staring placidly up at him, smiling, spiraling down into the blackness. She's sliding down the banister, circling round and round out of sight, lit intermittently by the windows in the fire doors.

The Golem leaps down to the first landing, scattering broken tiles where he lands. Using the banister poles to sling himself around he leaps again and again, from landing to landing with jarring force, whipping around to pounce once more, sending cracks up the plaster walls and deafening reports rebounding along the shaft. Far below, Christine's shining white face recedes in concentric circles, trained on him, and smiling . . .

Down a dark corridor and across the ensuing room; large, damp, irregularly lit, many doors, oversized packing crates stacked high on its floors, and immediately before her, a short flight of plank steps. She stops for a moment puzzling which way to go, the door swinging shut behind her—he's coming, thud thud thud down from story to story.

Someone emerges from behind the plank steps opposite the door, holding her arms folded across her chest. She is plain, with blonde hair piled on top of her head, and wearing a heavy coat, buttoned, with the hood thrown back. It's Magellan's secretary.

"Go on, up these stairs and out that door—here, I'll unlock it for you," she's pointing to the steps where she'd been hiding, pulling out a rusty ring with a number of keys.

"Why Miss Woodwind, whatever are *you* doing here?"

Miss Woodwind trips up the plank steps, unlocks the door at the top and throws it open, revealing an arched passage of dank black brick.

"There's a train station just beyond the end of the passage. Don't hesitate, but go as quickly as you can."

"You still haven't answered me—why are you here?"

But Miss Woodwind is looking past her, over Christine's shoulder, across the room. The pounding on the staircase is getting louder. She rustles down the steps again and takes Christine's shoulders in her two weightless hands.

"I've managed him before, don't worry about me. I'm here for *you*, Miss Dalman."

Christine's eyebrows pop up.

"Don't waste time!"

But Christine lingers, as though transfixed by the suspense between going and staying—to watch them together.

"He cannot be stopped," Miss Woodwind adds, bringing her face in close, where Christine can feel her feathery breathing on her face, and smell her perfume. Miss Woodwind's fingers are strong on her shoulders.

"You're not going to let him catch you?"

"What are you playing at? Who sent you?"

"I'll hold him off as long as I can—"

Miss Woodwind's eyes sputter a dense stream of sparks that bores into Christine's face. Christine seems to be thinking about saying something, now thinking better of it. She's smiling.

Miss Woodwind isn't sure she likes that smile or this woman; she makes a curt gesture toward the door, and Christine, moving deliberately and according to her own will, spirits herself swiftly through and runs down the passage. Miss Woodwind shuts the door behind her and hastily locks it, rushes down the stairs and back into the room. She hangs the key on a hook attached to the banister and crosses the room again, pulling crates down, knocking them into an impromptu series of barriers. Already she can hear his jangling step. Casting about at a moment's notice, she takes her belt from around her waist, holding it up in one hand, and, seizing a crowbar from the floor, she hides by the door.

It flies open and the Golem ploughs through, making straight for the opposing door with unerring intentness. Miss Woodwind leaps up and outstrips him with effort, interposing herself in his path, standing on a crate. The moment of recognition she was waiting for doesn't happen; he keeps going. She lashes at him with the end of her belt, snipping it across his cheek, but the moment it touches his flesh it bursts apart in crackling cinders like a string of firecrackers. He evades her and presses on for the steps, batting crates out of the way with smashing swings of his braced leg. Miss Woodwind leaps onto his back with the crowbar in her hands, swinging its hook down under his chin, pulling back with all her might, trying to crush his throat. Without slowing down he bends forward and grabs a fistful of her coat at the back, plucking her off his shoulders with one hand and tossing her across the room like a rag doll. She crashes gracelessly against a metal pipe, nearly shearing it off, and the end of the crowbar smashes a glass panel that had been painted over, making it look like part of the wall. A fireman's axe hangs inside. Recovering herself (the Golem is already at the top of the stairs, raising his fingers to shiver the lock apart) she seizes the axe and charges up behind him, burying its head between his shoulder-blades.

The Golem collapses. His coat seems to fall empty across the steps, then liquefies and oozes down between the planks like black syrup. She can hear meaty splats below the steps. For a moment she stands still and thinks, gnawing her lips, her eyebrows pressed down and together. Then, rushing down the steps, she kicks the crates aside in time to see the Golem's sections, having unsutured themselves, neatly queued up and slithering one-by-one down an open drain. The black coat-ooze is just draining its last before she can get over to the hole—her fingers clutch at rustling cloth before it snaps out of her hands.

That drain opens on the other side of the door. She turns and runs back up the stairs—he hadn't shivered the lock apart when she struck him, she'll need the key.

On the other side of the door, the Golem's disembodied hand flicks the grating off the drain. Another hand pops out and, like spiders, they scuttle across the floor, pulling the black bulk of a sleeve, with an arm in it, after them.

Miss Woodwind has the key; she leaps down from the platform, barging through heavy crates and rough wooden barrels, snarling with frustration, her eyes fixed on the keys hanging by the door on the other side of the room.

Now the coat is lying flat on the ground on the other side of the door, two hands fluttering around trying to fix themselves to hidden wrists up inside the sleeves. A rib cage and spinal chord spring out of the drain, flickering forward on the rib ends like a scorpion, the vertebrae coiled threateningly overhead, the pelvis being the stinger. It raises the hem of the coat and crawls underneath. Already, anonymous undifferentiated tissues are slurping after it like creeping vines from the drain.

Miss Woodwind is across the room now. She snatches the key ring from its hook, lunging back again toward the stairs like a swimmer forcing her way into a raging surf, kicking and punching obstacles out of the way.

The full body is sitting by the drain now. It holds up one leg, brace included, and a foot in its shoe pops out of the hole like toast from a toaster and drops into the stirrup of the brace, the ankle knitting with the end of the calf with an audible click. Naked eyes in a skull face watch with expressionless satisfaction as the ankle flexes twice to demonstrate the soundness of the articulation, before the next stump is held up.

Miss Woodwind finally makes it to the steps only to come up short at the landing—which key was it?

Finally, the Golem shoves his skull face into the drain for a moment and then rises to his feet in one hydraulical motion. His cane jumps up into his hand. A heavy wardrobe is standing to one side of the door, its back to the same wall in which the door is set. The Golem reaches out with the tip of his cane and pushes the heavy wardrobe over. It lands on its side, across the doorway. His face still slithering into its sutures around his jaws and forehead, he lurches off down the passage after Christine.

Miss Woodwind tears the door open at that moment, in time to see the wardrobe barring her way. She claws at its adamant wooden back but it's far too heavy even for her to move. The Golem's footsteps echo indifferently back to her, diminishing, down the hall—she shouts curses after him and ineffectually butts at the wardrobe with her shoulder.

. . . The train is sitting empty and open at the station. Christine takes her seat by the window and waits anxiously for the doors to close, staring back over her shoulder for any sign of the Golem. The bell sounds, the doors close, the train tugs gently forward. She is alone in the car, watching the lights spin out from the windows as the train climbs into the sky on suspended rails, snaking along between the buildings, stories above the ground. Tilting backward against the inclination of the train, she walks down the aisle to the window at the back of the car so that she can see down the rails, but there is no train following this one. She goes back to her seat, cocking her chin up thoughtfully.

Offices flash by at her level, and later on descend again. From moment to moment, gaps between the buildings reveal vistas of the black lake beyond, visible only as a darker patch against the perpendicular banks, striped with broken gleams of reflected city lights. The tracks hang on steel cables fixed to the roof of the cavern itself. Last stop: in the center of the city. The doors sigh open. Christine steps out onto the concrete platform and crosses under the tracks, through a featureless passageway whose walls glisten with a vile, pallid, yellow color like the inside of an esophagus. From where she emerges she can see the broad square beyond, with a dead fountain, broad swaths of dewy grass, and she can smell their cool green breath on the lake-breeze. An electrical crack sounds from the track behind her. She turns and looks—the electrified rail had grounded to the Golem's leg brace as he stepped over it, walking toward her out of a limitless windy night behind him. He is unhurt and lists forward, knocking clumsily against the raised platform on which she stands. He slaps his arms down straight in front of him on the platform and levers himself up onto it. She can see the blackened welts on his hands (a very satisfactory testament to her beauty,) where he had clung to the bottom of her car.

Christine turns and runs down the other side of the platform and across the square. First, the snicker of her boots on the cobbles, and then a moment later the swishing of her feet through the grass. The Golem is coming up fast behind her, mechanically bolting into the square on her trail. Christine runs to the closest open building—the titanic central clocktower. Through polished doors, resignedly mounting the red-carpeted stairs with extraordinary speed. She can hear his footsteps outside. She watches to make sure he's following her, and as his shadow falls across the broad steps, she sends a massive bronze urn tumbling down the shaft to greet him, then resumes her climb without bothering to watch, already knowing he won't be deterred, that Miss Woodwind was right—he can't be stopped.

She passes swiftly through a partition into the works, scaling the metal steps that hug the walls. The soft white glow of the clock face is the only light, a brassy gleam in the workings. A faint breeze pulses across her face at intervals, and staring up she can see a gargantuan pendulum sweeping back and forth only a few feet away. Even though it doesn't touch the stairs, she still times her own passage to avoid it. Its weight is a perfect brass ball, bigger than she is, polished as bright and reflective as a mirror. She rushes on, guided by the whirrings and clickings of the clockwork massed at the top of the tower.

The Golem blunders in and starts up the steps behind her. By now she's moved through the clock itself and is ready to step out onto the roof just above the face, but she pauses to watch him climb. He moves as regularly and unconsciously as if he were a part of the works, the tapping of his feet blending into the buzzings of the clock, shadowed by the sounds of the clock. But she is not ready to be captured. She steps out onto the roof, and over the partition onto the narrow ledge beyond, raises her hands. The Golem lurches to the top of the steps and out onto the roof. Christine stands on the ledge, her arms raised. He moves toward her, but as he draws near a flock of birds drops out of nowhere and swarms around her, like a curtain of flapping wings. The next moment, they are flying off together, with her suspended in their midst, dimly visible in silhouette among a scintillating screen of beating grey wings.

The Golem watches her go, thinking furiously, shuffling his feet, feeling stupid. Then, with unfailing intuition, he strikes the roof with his cane, and in that instant the roof turns transparent, and he can see the cogs and gears whirring smoothly beneath his feet. Taking from his pocket a small battery kit with tiny platinum pegs on curly wire he plugs the pegs into sockets set into his cane head. The Golem kneels, with pain, and presses the silver head of his cane to first one eye, then the other, over and over again, the tip of the cane planted on the roof, like an upward-ended extension of the pendulum. He repeats the gesture until he is synchronized with the works, and then opens his eyes. Now the invisible portions of the machine are beginning to appear, adumbrations normally secret to the soul of the clock, and he can see how it radiates its works all throughout the city, how all the city is regulated and run on the unwinding of these coils, the shifting of these weights, the regular swing of the pendulum, the ticking of the gears through increments of space. Unseen arms, like the boom of a crane, telescope out over the streets and span the distance all the way to the lake, and from each arm wires and control rods spool and extend and retract like spectral puppeteer's cords. Now that he can see them, the Golem clambers on to one of the arms and crawls along its length, after her—she is a distant, warbling cloud. The arm sweeps out in her direction like the outstretched arm of a giant, with the Golem creeping on it, eyes on her, confused by her corona of fluttering birds, receding away from him.

Their grey wings flicker in blue light—they're mourning doves, just like the ones who used to sing morosely to him when he was attending the Seminary...

He's hot on her heels as she disappears into the safety of the museum's cavernous galleries. Still animated, from moment to moment the museum shuffles its rooms like cards in a deck, wooden cogs dully rattling underground, rearranging huge sections like the blades of a fan, positioning and rearticulating them most of all like the glass plates of a magic lantern, etched with wan motionless statues and charming pink-and-white portraits. But, always watching, she can see the Golem is threading through the rolling doorways after her, following the extremely subtle traces of her track without fail; the vast clock-works don't seem to confuse him anymore.

She enters the Egyptian wing, which is not moving like the others—its mechanical foundations are broken. There are more stairs at the opposite end of the wing, but the Golem is close behind her, and she's getting bored with running. Catching sight of her, the Golem suddenly stops short, wrenches the lid off of the nearest sarcophagus and leaps inside, sifting down through the mummy's wrappings like mist through a screen. A moment later he bursts through the stone cap of the sarcophagus immediately to her left, his body seething up through the linen as the lid shatters to pieces with a fantastic racket, and, as he does this, his movements send the mummy's gold mask flying through the air. Christine, recoiling from his clumsy embraces, catches the mask dexterously and cradles it tenderly in her arms. She recedes into the shadows, pressing the mask to her face.

Now she can see as the Golem sees, with dead eyes for the pathways of dead footprints across the floor. As she moves in and out of the shadows, her face is sometimes the mask and sometimes the mask subsumed into her own face, gold where the mask is gold, blue where the mask is blue, and shining clear quartz-coral eyes. She is lost, vanishes in among the glass cases.

The Golem stalks after her carefully. He can no longer track her—not while she is wearing the mask. He weaves silently among the exhibits, moving toward the rear wall diagonally. Then their eyes meet, hers staring out at his, from the mask. There are reeds around the base of the urn, and she is hiding there among them. He can hear her rustling and splashing to keep out of sight, but for the moment he still sees her eyes in the watching mask. As carefully as he can, he presses his hands against the side of the urn, but he cannot touch the rushes. They wave behind his hands in a breeze he can't feel, and the water ripples under his fingers but he can't see the bank. Christine is every moment escaping farther and farther away.

The Golem looks around for something useful. A rigid, sleek stone dog nods its head and up-pricked ears at a jar standing alone in the corner. For a moment the dog's chiseled features seem precariously balanced, the grooves poised to expand and draw him inside its stone blackness like hinges. He tears his eyes free and walks to the jar, thinking. He taps it lightly on its sealed mouth with the head of his cane.

The jar topples without breaking, and winged scarabs blow out of its yawning mouth. The scarabs fly in among the reeds, whining and clacking their black parts, confounding Christine in her hiding place. She is presently forced in vexation from the cover of the reeds and back among the exhibits, haloed by whining scarabs. The Golem chases after her, but he is slow and she is fast—the mask still cool and gold on her face. Her one hope is the cache of Canopic jars huddled together on a plain marble block. She fiddles with them, touching them, trying to find the one with his organs in it. Swatting beetles with one hand, the fingers of the other flicker across the limestone jars as if they were cards in an index, searching the cartouches carved on their sides for the one that spelled the Golem's name/ the Divinity Student's name. But she is confounded again by the cyclone of bugs, growing thicker with every instant, pouring in blasts of hot air out of the jar. The Golem is coming, she's run out of time. She takes down her ankh and flail from the wall and opens a sarcophagus with them, causing billows of water to sluice out, lifting off the lid and carrying it speeding on the current. The heavy basalt lid torpedoes the Golem, sending him flying off to one side.

The water is rising quickly, flooding the room. A moment later it bursts the windows and flows out onto the garden bank beyond, heading for the lake. The Golem hurtles out on a curtain of water, catching for a moment a glimpse of Christine, her image kaleided by tiny balls of water and a curtain of foam, multiplying her into a thousand grey shapes with shining, laughing faces of blue and gold. The current carries her out as well, and through the foam and flying water she sees the Golem multiplied into a thousand black shapes with wan, sad faces and invisible halos like black holes behind them.

The Prisoner in the Fish

The Golem wakes, draped around a bronze horse rearing in the square. His leg brace had somehow locked in the crooked position, and the hook of his leg had entangled him among the legs of the statue as he was swept along, unconscious. He reaches one sopping arm and unlocks the brace, dragging his stiff body off the pedestal, clattering to the cobbles. The streets are deserted and silent—she is still lost. She is somewhere in the city, but now he is cut off from her by the mask she wears. For a while all he can do is make feeble, abortive gestures reaching out to somewhere, for her, falling back each time in confusion and dissolution—she is impermeably curtained off. Now his strength is melting away soft and disabling like a slow punch in the stomach. He only stands where he is, holding his nose up in the air, like an abandoned dog. Feeling the heavy weight of his dead flesh and soggy clothes, the Golem staggers off randomly, still forlornly spying from side to side as he walks, looking for any signs of her. On all sides, the city raises blank and ruined, hollowed and burned-out, all vacant. Its streets are strewn with rotting clutter drooled from doors and windows, and the breeze stinks of old soot and moldering wood, dust from falling plaster. The Golem trudges through this desolation dragging his cane over the scarred cobbles and his head downcast.

Gradually, without knowing when he first notices it, he can hear a man's voice, groaning from somewhere. He looks around, but none of the houses seem to be inhabited. He walks in a circle, his eyes squinting and unsquinting, trying to make out the source of the sound. A narrow alleyway formed by two slanting walls of blackened bricks sweating slime—the Golem picks his way through the litter down the passage, tracing the intermittent groans to a battered stone building with bars on its windows.

The front door opens smoothly on its hinges, without a sound, and instantly the groans become louder and more distinct. A narrow hallway runs to the back of the house, without a single door along its length—

nothing but dull, featureless wooden panels. The Golem walks down the tiled floor to the back, where the hall opens on a tiny parlor, with a sofa in the opposite corner. It's brown-grey, with rough upholstery and a stern wooden frame, with no movable cushions. Just around the corner there is an opening in the wall, with a cell door set in it. Someone, clinging to the bars as the Golem enters, springs back in shock and surprise into the shadows toward the back of the cell. The Golem can barely make out a whitish figure pressed against the stone wall with its single, tiny, barred window.

"You!" the figure cries incredulously. "You!"

The Golem's brow furrows. He stands a few feet in front of the cell door, staring.

"Have you come to release me?" the voice comes again, and the figure rushes forward and throws itself on the bars. It's Ollimer.

"What are you doing there?" the Golem asks.

"What am I doing here? *What am I doing here?!* Don't you remember?" his eyes are starting from his head, his grimy face contorts in sorrow and contrition. "You *put* me in here!"

The Golem ponders for a moment. Then he wanders over to the sofa and sits, not looking at Ollimer.

Ollimer waves his arms, the frayed ends of his shirt-sleeves trailing from his elbows. He cannot see the Golem from where he is.

"Please—let me out!"

For a moment there is no reply.

"You mean to say you've been in there all this time?"

"For eternities! I'm begging you, unlock the door!"

Ollimer reaches through the bars, trying to bend around them enough to catch a glimpse of the Golem.

"Has *he* been here?"

"Who?"

". . . You were locked away here—when?"

"I don't remember!? It's been forever—years!"

". . . Why did I lock you up?"

"You don't remember?!"

"—No. I'm not the same as you remember me."

". . . You never told me why! . . . I was only doing as I was told—I can't be held responsible if I didn't have a *choice*, can I? Whatever it was, it wasn't my fault! It's not fair! You're just being cruel—please relent, set me free!"

Nothing.

"I implore you!"

Ollimer implores empty air for a moment. Then the Golem speaks again.

"I don't have the key."

Ollimer brightens.

"You didn't take it with you—you left it hanging there on the wall by the divan! Look! It should be on a wooden peg beside the window. Do you see it? Are you really going to let me out?"

But the Golem says nothing. Ollimer is petrified—as if his fate hung in a balance so frail that even an injudicious breath or motion could tip the scales against him.

At the other end of the room, the Golem is run down, like a stopped watch. He's confused, but he can't think things through . . . although he hasn't turned his head, he gradually realizes that Christine is watching him. Her gaze has descended on him. Beyond Ollimer's cubicle, through the back door standing ajar, and an irregular rhomboid hole in the rear wall, her face is framed in the far distance, dimly beaming blue and gold. He leans forward slowly, bending only at the waist, and his coat is getting blacker, dripping blackness on the floor, and melting into the darkness of the wall.

Ollimer waits, and the Golem leans forward getting darker all the time.

Then, a long, spindly limb, like the black leg of a spider, emerges from the shadow of the Golem's back, as if it were a hole in the air. Another follows, and another, without sensation for him, curving at their joints to touch the floor, and the walls, and ceiling.

Finally, Ollimer, who can't see him, swallows painfully and speaks—"Are you there? Have you found it?"

But there is no reply. The Golem is sprouting more legs sheathed in glossy black chitin, while his body curls into a ball, his head back against his shoulders, and he stares straight ahead with a motionless face. He's sitting in the corner like a cushion stuck with shiny black needles.

Ollimer, panicky, speaks again: "What's happening? Where have you gone? Let me out of here!" and he rattles the cage.

The Golem suddenly scuttles by, passing the door swiftly on his many new legs, body rolled up and head staring forward.

"Wait! Where are you going?!" Ollimer screams.

"I don't know," the Golem says quietly, as the legs take him smoothly and silently flashing past the bars of the cell door, out into the matted, rank mounds of weeds in the back yard, and up to the opening in the rear wall. In its center, he can see her mask staring at him out of the blackness, like a beacon, or a gold coin tossed into murky water. A wire runs taut from some point below her face to the base of the wall's opposite side. The Golem's new legs carry him nimbly through the hole, and he can see where the wire is bolted to the perspiring brick foundations of the house with ponderous metal fastenings. Humming a little in the breeze, the wire is as straight as a razor, and the mask hovers in a circle of sourceless light off in the distance, directly above the point where the wire disappears. With effortless accuracy, the legs whip one in front of the other, carrying him along the wire, up into the "sky," his eyes fixed forward, watching for any sign of a trap.

A pair of tapering white hands appear first, below the mask, resting on a dimly-lit level horizontal bar. The fuzzy gray of her dress materializes next, bisected at the waist by a railing. He doesn't notice the wall impending until he passes through the oversized window and into the colossal interior. She is standing directly in front of him, on the lip of titanic storm lantern made of polished brass. The cable is a thread knotted around the base of the lantern, where it sits on a gigantic table. As he comes nearer, she backs away from the railing, leaning against the lamp, her hands splayed on its curved surface beside her hips, and her expressionless golden face craning down and forward on her long neck, waiting. Reflexively sure, the spider legs undulate alternating right then left, perfectly balanced, so that his body does not sway at all.

He can see the surface of the table starting to heave up and down, rolling like a boat in the water, and he can hear waves splashing against a breakwater, and he smells water below him—very deep, very cold, very old, old water. Christine the Magician is staring directly into his eyes—her eyes are clear blue, lined with blue and startling white, pressed into a gold brow and sealed with a puff of frigid air, the cold hollow breath of something dying. They froze then and they freeze now; the Golem freezes in mid-stride, off-balance, and tips off the wire. As he turns in the air, toppling down off the wire, he can see Christine slumping against the lamp, exhausted. Then the shock of the water, and the sensation of stabbing needles of cold as his body sinks quickly down into shadow and silence.

A rumbling, gurgling sound rattles through the water—he twists and sees a huge fish rushing toward him, blank gaping black eyes and a huge yawning mouth opening onto bottomless, fathomless blackness. He flailing uselessly in the heavy water, churning his arms and many snapping legs, but its shadow is already enveloping him, and the jarring bow-wave preceding it rolls him over, slashing ripples of deathly cold from the fish's mouth over his body as the black hole of its mouth swells and closes around him, the faintly-lit irregular circle of light between its lips dwindles . . . winks out.

THE GOLEM FOUND THE fish's inner chambers familiar, but the memories they recalled were not wholly his memories; they were the Divinity Student's dog-eared, shopworn cast-offs. Specifically, they snagged on the way time passed inside the fish, but the Golem was for a long time unable to trace where that time, that flavor of time, had happened before. Eventually, sitting on a fleshy stump in a small, igloo-shaped enclosure, he gathered it together in his mind. The walls sweated a white, milky oil that congealed in pearly drops around the floor, so that, as he sat there, a glistening, pebbly ring would slowly begin to form all around him. Then, at long intervals, a low tide of brackish, tea-colored froth would flush across the floor, dissolving the pearls instantly and carrying them off down an intestine, and the slow accretion of a new ring would begin again.

The white drops reminded him of white glue, the kind that had been endlessly doled out to younger students at the Seminary—and he jolted back with the force of the recollection. Time passed in the fish precisely as it had at the Seminary—it was like a fall of dust, silent and steady as snow, or a shower that soaked everything, seeping in everywhere. Nothing changed, time only made things heavier, more solid, more dense and fixed. Both here and there (although *he* had never been there), he felt no more real than a superimposition, or a wandering film image. He puzzled over it a while.

It wasn't dark—everywhere the fish's interior was lit by bundles of flabby tubes filled with yellowish gelatin that glowed like sodium lights. These nodes clung to the walls of the passages and sprouted like topaz chandeliers from the ceilings of the larger rooms.

The spider legs had stopped working shortly after he first regained consciousness inside the fish. They hung limp and useless, and he dragged them along behind him like a heavy train for a long time until they finally began to break off of their own accord. Something was corroding them quickly, so that their black chitin turned a blotched grey flecked with green; in time, the discolored leg would snap off with a sickening click. He examined the end of the first leg when it came loose—it was a hollow tube of thin metal trailing a few colored wires, and smeared here and there with minute traces of oil. The dead legs made exploration of the fish impractical—as he lost them, he was able to go further and further, through narrower apertures, until he could make his way around with the same facility as he had the Seminary. The airless atmosphere exaggerated all motion, giving him the abrupt and awkward appearance of a puppet, but the absence of air pressure and friction made even the most strenuous activity easy, allowing him to climb almost effortlessly through the lattice of arteries and intestines connecting the habitable cells. The vacuum also deadened all sound and smell, and permitted him to see at all times with complete clarity.

The fish's single, centrally-located lung was its most spacious cavity. It was a long oblate cylinder lying on its side, tapering toward the forward end, where water would silently collect in an enormous clear bi-valved bulb covered with arabesques in fine white veins. The water would pour into the bulb from the outside, swirl in a wide, sluggish funnel down into the second opening at the bulb's base, and flow from there into a space between the outer and inner membranes of the lung, causing the sulfur-yellow interior walls, floor, and ceiling of the chamber to undulate rhythmically as the fluid passed beneath. The oxygen was absorbed by the lining of the outer lung wall. The exhaust gasses were channeled out through the back portion of the lung, through a screen of interwoven brownish-white cartilage crescents, resembling a chaotic fleur-de-lys pattern. The Golem liked to walk along the walls of the inner membrane, through the alveoli, which were trefoil-shaped porphyry indentations that opened into each other, separated by rigid bony pillars rooted in the floor and ceiling, raised slightly above the level of the central atrium—forming a sort of cloister along which he was able to stroll comfortably.

He spent most of his free time in the cavernous stomach, where he had first been deposited when the fish swallowed him. The lining was bluish-white, pulpy, and fibrous like the inside of a gourd, and folded tightly upon itself everywhere in ridges pressed against each other. He would search through these for undigested leavings like himself, prying the folds apart and peering into the pocket behind. After a while the floor was littered with junk—a pair of old shoes, a traffic horn, a fishing rod, large clots of water plants, an empty tortoise shell, a wooden carving of an elephant playing a white saxophone, a glass eye and a wooden leg with matching monograms, a tin cup, a sepia daguerreotype of a toothless old man with a weedy beard and a baggy ill-fitting suit, a pile of driftwood, a pink plastic Sphinx, a few magazines and newspapers, an axe, a dartboard, three small stone intaglios and an ivory cameo all with the same design, and a random assortment of bottles and cans.

Toward the rear end of the stomach, he could see the fish's previous victims lying stacked, one atop another, in lozenge-shaped pouches of semitransparent tissue attached to the wall. Most were people at varying stages of digestion. They all were lying on their backs, with their hands crossed on their chests, steaming off tiny plumes of white vapor as they dissolved. The pouches were cold to the touch, and the bodies seemed to be freezing as they withered and shrank. A few were almost totally gone, leaving only a rumpled set of clothes and a few twigs of ashy, inmetabolible tissue. These were closest to the ceiling, leading him to believe that the sacs formed out of the floor and slowly ascended as their occupants were digested until finally being reabsorbed into the ceiling. Radiating out on all sides were thick, translucent screens of tissue stretched on frames of flexible bone. The zonate screens were patterned with irregular, rounded patches of gemlike color, separated by tiny gray ridges, and resembled stained glass.

Occasionally, the Golem would glance up at the screens and catch sight of a spirit, presumably belonging to one of the victims, lingering behind one of the screens, close to its body. They had no color of their own, taking on whatever hue was projected on them from the screens, wavering in outline as they rippled across blobs of color. The Golem tried repeatedly to approach them, but they always fled—turning around the edge of the screen and vanishing. Sometimes, though, he would be resting quietly in some corner, and happen to look up for a moment, and he would see them standing nearby, watching him, their shadowy forms drooping and limp, their faces obscured by blank expressions. Several times, upon waking from a dream and finding himself still in the fish's stomach, he would detect a faint fragrance of orange flowers hovering around his face, as if someone, only a moment before, had exhaled it there. The smell would rapidly expand and fill the airless cavity, dispersing utterly in a few seconds—footsteps pad away, and then stop, abruptly.

Further to the front, the canals converged around a ponderous domed chamber with mottled arcs of bone growing along the walls in symmetrical rows. The arcs were broad and serrated, and could be used as stairs to reach the braincase overhead. The walls were pink, marbled with wide bands of white, and here the topaz lights hung on sinewy cords, of greatly varying lengths, that depended from the pedentives supporting the dome. It reminded him of the library at the Seminary, which had long curving staircases, heavily ornamented with cherubs holding scrolls and musical instruments. The place was also much like the Orpheum in San Veneficio.

It was colder in here, although everything was visibly palpitating with slow, syncopated pulses emanating from above.

Up there, he could ride along on a shelf above the rear portions of the fish's brain, which pressed up against the edge of the shelf like a wall, curving away from him. An indentation at the bottom of this false wall revealed a crawl space down into the channel separating the brain's two hemispheres. He had gone down there only once—the intervening space between the two halves buzzed with a prickling low frequency that slammed against his head and chest like a lead weight, making him vibrate so that his outstretched hands blurred in and out of resolution, and his body felt ready to shake apart. He ducked back out again the next moment and kept his distance from then on. The atmosphere in the skull seemed even more rarefied than in the rest of the fish, and he found it difficult to remain there for any length of time. He would become dizzy, nauseated, and disoriented, and stagger down into the warmer, more habitable compartments further back.

He forced himself to return, however, because of the eyes. By slipping between the base of the horizontal occipital plate and the base of the skull, he could thread his way down into the fish's eye itself. It all but filled the wall of the socket—a thick convex lens as tall as he was. From the first moment he was fascinated by the view: a clammy, pitch black dome of soft gelatin opening onto a featureless depth of empty water, stretching off into infinite distance. From time to time, uncanny, pallid lights of luminous fish would dart back and forth across his view, faintly illuminating for brief instants a drooping jaw of translucent, milky teeth, or another blank, impersonal fish-eye staring back at him. After repeated viewings he realized that his host also could emit a feeble, greenish glow from tiny pits lining its body. These were "turned on" only when it was hovering over promontories of half-melted clay, where he assumed it fed. At those times he could see a weird lunar landscape outside—tall, wavy, vertical shelves of soapy dust-colored rock, sprouting grotesquely elongated antennae of coral, and motionless festoons of leathery, purple-green fronds like locks of hair. There were usually no other fish around—the only mobile life were the pale brown hag-worms, that would lash their long, long bodies violently whenever his host cruised by, throwing off heavy webs of mucous as they attempted to burrow into the solid rock and out of sight. He and the fish would take no notice, however, and slip gigantically past.

Once he noticed an indistinct patch of white, gleaming dully in the dark surface of the eye, just at the periphery of his vision. At first he had taken it to be a reflection from one of the lights behind him, but, of course, it was the wrong color. As he realized this he saw it move. A woman's wan ragged form, staring past him, with yawning black pits where her eyes should be. She had taken a step forward, and now, as he stood watching her, she remained there, gazing past him from a few feet behind him—and behind her, a gap opening back deep into the bone and completely dark. Her eyes seemed like holes descending into the deeper darkness beyond. From time to time, something black would well out from them and ooze down her streaked face. It seemed that, at any moment, she might gesture to him—her sticklike arms swung a little back and forth as if she was preparing to fly forward at him with terrifying suddenness. And then her arms did fly up, her hands contorted like talons, and she plunged her long fingers into her eyes, the white ridges of her knuckles vanishing inside, rooting and clawing in the cavities and black ooze gushed down her stricken face, effacing it entirely against the darkness, and, the next moment, she had pushed herself backwards into the gap, and disappeared.

Long hours of watching out that eye's window, his hands resting lightly on its clear, cold, fleshy surface, had acclimatized him to the frigid atmosphere inside the skull. Now he loved to sit up there, especially on the shelf behind the brain, and watch the slow connections flare in bundles of silvery threads lining the base of the brain and ringing the occipital plate on all sides. The filaments would spark like downed power lines, and the Golem's features would flicker in and out of resolution in their light. Sometimes a form of some kind would half-emerge from the surface of the fish's brain, and he liked to watch them out of the corners of his eyes while staring blankly down at his feet in front of him (the attitude that, for him, passed for sleep). They never fully disentangled themselves and stepped out onto the shelf, but they did seem to fall for his phony sleep routine. As time went on they were getting more and more accustomed to him, and he saw them more often.

Once, when he was exploring, he came across a long fleshy wall punctuated at varying levels by tiny pockets of air, trapped on either side by thin, translucent membranes. By pressing his ear to them, he could hear sounds welling up from deep inside the fish, thrumming through them. He would return there often, at different times, to acquaint himself with all the many different sounds the fish made, depending on what it was doing. On one occasion, he was walking down the wall when a face came into view on the other side. It appeared in the window as if someone had been waiting, leaning up against the opposite wall, and then had rolled over to stare at him out of the black pits of its eyes. He looked more closely—its mouth was moving in its blurred face, expanding and contracting like a leech as it tried to speak with him. Its eyes stared and stared. He could hear its voice buzzing through the membrane. He edged closer and turned his head, both to hear it better, and so as not to have to look at it. When it finished, he looked up, expecting the face to be gone. It was not.

WHY DID HE STAY? It was fully within his power at any time to leave. All he had to do was place his hand upon the holy book and whatever he needed would be given to him; he could sunder the fish apart and float to the surface safely, be conveyed on currents stirred by his own hand to the shore, and strike the city in half right down the middle, to hunt out Christine. Hand resting on the book, he could command her to do anything, compel her to surrender herself, and she would have no choice. But he is somehow prevented—and this, and Ollimer, as an example—how is he prevented? In whose power is it to prevent him?

Over and over, this refrain cycles in his mind like a skipping needle, and enmeshed with it is his sense of Christine. Opposing, stands his feeling that he can't act unless summoned to act, by the story he is living. And that anything she was compelled to do would be worthless to him, divorced from her by want of consent. In amongst these thoughts he reviews their last encounter, whether she had sought him out to lure him deliberately into a trap, or to: what should he say—surrender to him, parlay with him, capture him; the sense is somewhere in the overlap of them all. If she had meant to finally permit him to catch her, then why wear the mask that made it impossible? But still, he felt she meant him to catch her. He could never catch her without her consent, and while he could compel her even to consent, that nevertheless did not constitute "catching" her. The hide-and-seek waited on her leisure to end, and for that he would have to satisfy her of his patience. But if he did prove his patience, she would willingly come from her hiding place and give her consent to be caught. Everything, for him, depended on that. So he stayed, and did nothing. But was she going to send for him? He knew she could sense him down there, but was she expecting him to escape for himself?

In the end he thought of nothing but her, feebly hoping that somehow the constancy of his concentration would make him more difficult for her to ignore. Perpetually exhausted by all this thinking, he retired to the lower, darker chambers. There was a sort of pale, whitish egg-shaped room that he liked—he guessed it was superfluous and that the fish never used it. There were attenuated conical indentations in the puffy ceiling, supported at the top by rings of bone that held them open to the lighted cavity overhead, like skylights. He would collapse in one of the bright circles of light under one such skylight in the middle of the room and lie there, half-propped against the wall, with his legs sticking out in front of him and his heavy coat bulging out above his shoulders and around his head—thinking about Christine.

Consistent effort is its own best camouflage. It's only in moments of repose that one realizes how expensive it is, especially when there's nothing to show for it. The Golem was subject to intermittent palpitations of piercing longing and sentimentality, to stagger wounded up to Christine, and she would finally hold out her arms to him, and he could finally permit himself to collapse, having her to support him. She would buoy him up on her own warmth and breath, and when he thought of her he felt tortured and frantic. As time went by his exhaustion deepened and he allowed nervous helplessness to seep in. At his lowest point, he reached into his coat pocket and laid his fingers thoughtlessly on the torn cover of his book.

Instantly she was there, right at the border of the circle of light in which he was sitting. She was lying on her side, with her upper body raised, supported by her hands, one flat on the floor behind her and the other poised on its fingers in front of her, as if he had stretched out an invisible hand, swept her up out of the city and tossed her down again here. He stared at her, not yet completely aware of what was happening. She was disheveled and shocked.

"You're not going to *cheat*, are you?" she cried.

Christine was only dimly visible in the half light. She was pale and her face was framed by her dark, unruly hair so that it seemed to hover over her black dress. Her face was gleaming, and her features were shadowed as if they were folds in a single sheet of light. A shiny string of black buttons bisected her down the middle.

"How *dare* you bring me here!" she cried dramatically.

He took his hand away from the book resignedly.

She vanished.

There are props constructed to simulate banks of tiny lights, but that are actually just rows of holes in a board with a single light bulb burning behind them. Individual holes may be covered with tiny panes of tinted glass or plastic, but the "lights" are really only one, plain light. When that bulb is extinguished, they all disappear. The Golem was manufactured by design—he wouldn't attempt to destroy a desire when he could simply destroy himself. So he winked out, and all his desires vanished, too. His fingers had relaxed and released the book, and without bothering to see if she was still there, he pulled his hand from his pocket and let it fall with the other in his lap, letting his head droop down onto his chest.

HE HAD NOTICED ONE ghost in particular who seemed to be actively trying to attract his attention. It was a figure so eroded by time that he was unable to determine in it even the vestiges of its sex, circling around one corner of the long, low chamber with the "skylights," where Christine had appeared to him. Unfortunately, even when he became fully aware that it was trying to communicate something to him, it was so exhausted and dissipated that its message never reached him complete. The best it could manage was a series of apparently unrelated, attenuated pantomimes, but even this trivial effort cost it so much that its grey, flimsy substance was stretched to almost invisible thinness, and the Golem found it hard to distinguish the spirit's form from the background. Eventually, however, he came to know its schedule well enough to anticipate its appearance, and he would stand as close as possible and in such a way as to block the light from behind him, so that the ghost would be in his shadow, easier to see.

It would come then, preceded by dashing blows of vindictive, biting cold that spun out in horizontal arcs like the folds of a whirlpool from the spot where it was about to materialize. The next moment, it would appear as if it were being extruded from between the crushing weight of two dimensions into the limitless vampiric emptiness of three. The Golem would have to wait for it to pick up his presence, often for as long as half an hour, even though he was standing directly in front of it (as far as he could tell). Then it would instantly begin again the chain of inexplicable motions that it seemed so urgently to want him to decipher, but which were so vague that the Golem was unable to make out anything but a repeated cluster of similar hand motions, where it flapped its fingers and made a pincer of its two palms. All the while, it teetered back and forth as if it were standing on the deck of a ship, or an unstable chair. This would go on for something like an hour, then it would simply unravel before his eyes, as if unable to hold together any longer, still trying to repeat the same feeble gestures.

The Golem watched this display with increasing boredom and indifference until it occurred to him to search the spot where the ghost routinely appeared. He found a rumpled magazine concealed from sight in a pit in the tissue that had subsequently collapsed, creating a pouch in the floor.

The ghost never bothered him again, so he assumed this was what he had been intended to find.

The only thing in the magazine worthy of notice was a short fairy tale which went as follows:

"When Y was still very young she lived in a kingdom in the forest that was ruled by a Prince and Princess who were so similar that they could have been brother and sister. Their greatest passion was hunting, and together they would ride hard behind the hounds regardless of what the quarry might be, their eyes and teeth glistening like diamonds in the smooth, glowing planes of their pale faces. Their lances were so sharp they left a wake of severed branches and boughs behind them, cleanly cut without so much as a tug on the haft as they coursed past, holding them so that the blade hovered inches only above the ground. Their horses had been bred from horses and deer to make them as lithe and nimble in the heavy timber as they could be; the Princess' mount in particular, which had two small velveted buds of horn the size of walnuts, sprouting just below its ears. On one such occasion, the Prince nearly impaled Y on his lance, coming across her unexpectedly in the path of the hunt. She had been wandering on her own for days and was very weak and tired. The Prince swept her from the ground onto his horse with a single swing of his arm and carried her back to the royal pavilion, where he and his Princess would stay when they were hunting.

"The Princess and Prince both were enchanted with Y, and they looked after her as best they could. They gave her some food and drink, encouraging her to eat as much as possible, but they kept her talking to them and walking around the campsite when more sensible people would have realized she should have been permitted to sleep, being close to dropping with exhaustion. Y was so disoriented herself that she did not manage to tell them how tired she was.

"The two sovereigns passed the night telling Y the story of how they met, but she was too tired to really pay much attention. One of them had certainly come from a long way off, either searching for the other or at the other's request, and indeed it turned out they were related, although in what way she couldn't remember. Dawn broke unexpectedly, and in a flash they were up on their horses again, with Y riding behind the Princess in the same saddle. The Princess' body was fragrant and warm, soft even in its tight lacings and sturdy dress—unlike the Prince, who was all solid and hard as ice. Y slept fitfully with her arms around the Princess' waist and her head cushioned on the Princess' soft back. At one point, she asked the Prince, who was riding near, what they were hunting. He shouted back that there was a criminal in the vicinity who had been terrorizing the citizens, a kidnapper, murderer, and thief. From the Prince's description Y got the impression that this criminal was something of a general or usurper noble as well, with designs on the kingdom.

"A little while later, Y awoke to the sound of horns and a sudden jolting as the horse underneath her started forward at a full gallop. The dogs were baying in long, reverberating yelps that hung in the shimmering spaces between the trees. It was sunset, and the forest was swimming in a thick, golden light that made the buzzing midges and motes of dust look like flecks of gold swirling in the hot, soporific air. The sun itself emitted jabbing lances of light that stabbed into her eyes and made her squint, so that all she could see were tenebrous silhouettes with faint patches of color, as if she had a screen in front of her eyes. Apparently, they were catching up to the usurper. Like a reply, she suddenly jerked back at the sound of a scream from somewhere nearby. She looked around one side of the Princess' back, and at the same moment felt a jolt run down the Princess' other side, and there was a scream, exactly like the first, from right in front of them. She switched sides and saw a figure tumbling to the ground in tall grass between the trees in a small open space.

"The Prince and the Princess came together and began speaking eagerly to one another. From what she could make out, it seemed to Y that they had been chasing the usurper in different directions, and both claimed to have killed him. Then they dismounted, and the Prince took her by the hand, and the Princess' hand as well, and they all went together to look at the body. The Prince released her and knelt, while the Princess held her shoulders as if to force her to look. But when the Prince turned the figure over, it was a wooden dummy.

"'Look!' the Prince said, with no more wonder in his voice than if he'd just noticed something interesting in the newspaper, 'It's not a person at all. It's not even alive.'

"Nevertheless, they tied it to the Princess' horse and dragged it back to the pavilion. There the royal soldiers and attendants charred it in a fire, spitting on it and ridiculing it. After a while, Y could make out another sound murmuring below the insults of the soldiers. She listened closely and determined that it was the dummy, speaking. It was soliloquizing in a faint but steady voice that it was unvanquished, that it would take over the kingdom regardless of setback, that it would overwhelm them all, and so forth, on and on, in a continuous drone. The soldiers shredded its clothes, they tore out its hair, they spattered it with mud, and shat on it, and then threw it into a cart. Then Y noticed that the other attendants were packing away the last of the pavilion and camping equipment. She asked the Prince, who had been standing behind her, running his fingers through her hair, where they were going, and he replied that they were returning to the royal mansion, and that she was coming with them.

"The sun was setting again as they arrived at the mansion. It was a simple, square, stone building of two stories, sitting in the middle of a small, circular island, surrounded by a wide moat. A narrow ribbon of packed clay linked the island with the outer bank. As the servants filed into the building, Y stood by the walls of the mansion, watching the soldiers across the moat dumping the usurper, still soliloquizing, into the water. They tipped the cart up, and he slid slowly under the surface, vanishing altogether. The soldiers disappeared into the forest.

"Y looked up. She was alone on the bank with the Princess. The setting sun dazzled her, creating a flaming corona around the Princess' head, making her eyes appear to burn like hot coals, and her gleaming, sharp teeth spangle the air with white gleams. She explained that she and her brother looked nothing like what Y now saw, that in fact the two of them never left the mansion at all, being disfigured and not entirely mobile—her brother more than herself—so they resorted to projecting pleasing images of themselves outside the house, and so were able to live their lives vicariously. Now the Princess asks Y if she wants to come inside and see them as they really are, and Y says NO! The black door of the house opens wide and the Princess takes Y forcibly by the arm and pulls her in through the door, or tries to, with Y clinging to the door frame with all her strength, and pleading not to be taken inside.

"Copyright XXXX by Christine Dalman—dedicated to YOU KNOW WHO."

The Golem puts down the magazine and starts instantly out of the chamber, heading up to the fish's head again. He makes his way through the cold receding galleries as if a magnet was pulling him forward to the fish' eye—and, once there, he looks out, but he doesn't see anything. Turning around, he looks about the small cavity behind the eye, and then notices something flashing on the floor as he moves back and forth—an irregularly shaped spot of dim light, which he saw interrupted by his shadow as he passed before the eye. He drops to the floor and lays his head in the patch to trace the source of the light—it is coming from a very faint wavering expanse overhead, the surface, it's moonlight.

Now, it's time to go. He runs back through the gap across the room and up into the brain-case. With effort he forces himself down into the crevasse between the two hemispheres, his body buzzing in the low, grey thrumming force that arcs around him. He thrusts a hasty finger down his throat and disgorges a palmful of formaldehyde, smearing it on his hands; he then thrusts them deep into the walls of tissue on either side of him. The formaldehyde sinks down into the brain cells, darkening and spreading threads of embalmed nerves down into the fish's spine and along its control centers.

Suddenly, the thrumming abates, or no it doesn't abate at all but it changes character, because now it's behind him, and supporting him, like a locomotive pushing a train car, and he feels falling away from him on all sides the massive life of the fish in its cavernous organs and huge slow processes of bones and muscles. He can feel himself hanging suspended in a limitless void of icy black water that seems to move around him, not to be a medium to be moved through, as if he were absolutely still. Above all he can feel a kind of cold outside and a different, more active cold inside—a cold in which is nested a torpid will that vectors through the water. With the sense of turning a vast ship, he directs it to vector him up. Slowly, the fish begins angling its barn-sized head upwards, and he can feel its body creaking and protesting against the lightness of the pressure and the proximity of the dry air overhead. He guides it up and over toward the shore, the dim pilings of the deep-sunk piers of the city coming into view, like a forest of iron bars losing itself in the distance. The mucky slope of the shore comes into view now, and he opens his mouth wide and lets go, and water floods in as he flings himself backwards, down out of the skull and further down through into the gullet and a raging black surging of water gushing out, sluicing him from the gaping jaws of the fish as it backs out of the shallows and turns away, shocked and bewildered. Tumbling end over end he disappears in the water and a current that carries him toward the land.

He feels his body undulating forward on the waves, the water tapping against his eardrum. The air above him is dark and still, and he can hear the water lapping against stone walls on all sides as he comes in, floating on his back. Then candles begin to glow somewhere ahead of him, and around him, the flames start from embers and then grow to steady, unwavering fires, each with its own powdery ball of amber light, emanating from it. He can see now the walls of the chapel encompassing him, striped with shadows from the slender pillars upon which rest the Gothic arches that rib the ceiling. The Golem is being washed diagonally, feet first, across the floor and up the nave toward the altar. Gliding and spinning slightly, he flows over the smooth backs of the pews like worn river-stones, colliding with the floating hymnals and prayer books. As he drifts further in, he can see the night-dulled colors of the stained glass windows slipping past, and the bowed and veiled head of the statue of the Virgin in mourning, flanked by two gallant saints with flowing golden beards, protecting her from a group of menacing brown bears. The force of the torrent spins him slowly around on the surface of the waves, and he can see the candles lighting themselves along the length of the nave, their lights reflecting serenely on the agitated surface of the water.

As he turns around again, he can see that the Virgin has the Magician's face, and that she is looking at him from under her veil, smiling. The water stills, and she stares at him with her golden eyes, smiling. The Golem stops drifting and hangs motionless in front of the altar, and the formaldehyde permeating his clothes and skin spreads out in a film on the water. And from beneath the tombstones and markers, where the dead lie buried beneath the paving stones, tiny crumbs of earth are buoyed through the cracks and seams, floating up to the surface, rolling toward the Golem, and as they emerge they begin to shine like fireflies, drawn to the surface and to the Golem.

Soon he is haloed with shining motes in the formaldehyde, and one by one they transmit to him the sibilant, humming voices from beneath the stones, buoying him up with noiseless resonation like a thrumming gust, pushing him up, and suddenly the water goes as clear as crystal and the ground and paving beneath, and he can see them all lying in their graves in the dim orange light from the candles, reaching gently down the iron stalks of their stands and playing a gleam of false life across lifeless features lying supine only a few feet below him, and they are looking at him, smiling. The water is dripping down onto them through the transparent lids of their coffins, and all the while they gaze at him, smiling.

And rising in him the same feeling makes him fall back into the water noiselessly, smiling, shining with the wan twilight phosphorescence of motes of grave-dirt dissolving in formaldehyde, and painting his body with their eerie, sourceless, blue-green chemical light, and he rolls over in the water, staring down directly into something collapsed, blackened eyes gaping up out of a smudged face in a rectangular coffin, and then he rolls back upright again, and the windows lining one side of the church are blazing with sunlight and, on the other side, the windows have gone transparent, revealing a cobalt-blue sky with twinkling stars and a vast, full, white-and-grey moon. The pillars have become columns, carved in the likeness of gigantic reeds, and the stained glass tableau depict smooth-contoured profiles of caramel-colored figures in white linen and pharaohs' masks, and likewise the Virgin is wearing Christine's shining mask of blue and gold, and her guardian saints stare out at him through the eyes of a hawk's head, and a dog's head.

The Catechism and the Ten Plagues

From the causeway where she is standing, she can see him far below, crossing the square (it's actually a broad rectangular bridge connecting two large buildings, with a round planter in the middle). He lurches to and fro among the ghosts, who take no notice of him. She thinks a moment, and then from her purse she pulls a pair of binoculars which she raises smoothly to her face.

He jerks into focus and simultaneously stops walking. Even from this distance she can see the whites of his eyes flashing as he looks around, sensing her, trying to see where she is. In a moment he's going to glance up and notice her, and then his eyes will pounce on hers like an arrow shot along her line of sight. She quickly pulls from her purse, which is resting on the railing, an antique stereo viewer. With a steady hand she brings it into position under the binoculars, then very gradually begins to raise the viewer's frames up over the lenses, slipping the glass panels of the slides carefully underneath him, like scooping a spider up off the floor with the edge of a sheet of paper. Now the stereo viewer's panes completely cover the lenses. She drops the binoculars back into her purse without moving the viewer from her face.

He's wandering around in the viewer slide now, disoriented. The scene is a sepia-tinted museum gallery, near the wall, with a gargantuan doorway looming next to him. Titanic people glide by like icebergs, women in antique gowns passing with the rustling of silk skirts, a rustling amplified to him like the roaring of waves, and men tapping by with walking sticks the size of pier pilings. (At this distance the scale of the slide wasn't in exact correspondence with his size in perspective.) She adjusts the viewer, focusing the scene behind him like a rear-projection screen, and the next moment he's full size. He is slithering along the wall, craning his head in all directions, looking either for her or the exit. He can feel her nearby—she takes her eyes away and examines the slide from behind: a tiny figure, more like a man-shaped smear, creeps along the surface of the glass, hovering over it, separated from the slide by an invisible meniscus of surface tension in three dimensions. If she is careful, she can slip a different slide underneath him, then remove the old one and raise the viewer back to the light again, changing the scene.

With care she selects a park in San Veneficio and eases it into the slot in front of the museum slide. Then she whips out the museum slide with a flick of her ring and little fingers and brings the viewer back up to her eyes.

The Golem is standing on the outskirts of the park, just by the gate, blinking and rubbing his eyes at the sudden burst of preserved daylight. The moment he's able to see, he appears to recognize instantly where he is, and he darts through the wrought-iron gates and down the wide gravel path, threatening at any moment to vanish among the trees and bushes. He's moving fast, right along the edge of the grass. The pedestrians in the park drift unhurriedly down the lane, pay him no mind. Without taking her eyes off him, Christine's fingers flick smartly through the box of slides in her bag, plucking out another shot of the same park from further toward the center, including the same path the Golem is now taking. She holds it aloft over the viewer and waits. She waits without wavering or moving a muscle, smiling, enjoying herself patiently, watching his form shrinking, skulking at the verge of the path with his loping, crippled walk. Suddenly he drops neatly away to the right behind a sepia bush and disappears.

Without losing a moment she drops the next slide into place and withdraws the first all in one continuous motion, and then she can see him again, in the distance, weaving back and forth in the shrubs, trying not to be seen. She watches him coming, and as she does she has the strange idea that, although he is definitely coming toward her, his form appears to be dwindling away exactly as if he was moving away from her. Angling the viewer slightly from side to side, she notices that she can rotate her little window on the scene a full circle by turning around in place. At a roughly forty-five degree angle from his general position he seems to be approaching again—the shrinking effect is gone. Satisfied, she watches him coming slowly closer, hampered by his exaggerated strategy for not being seen. From time to time he stops completely, and his head swivels in all directions, trying to find her eyes. Every time, and the closer he gets, he seems to be guessing with greater and greater accuracy, and becoming harder to see as a consequence, since he is beginning to figure out in which direction he should cover himself.

He steps out from behind a tree into the square. She studies him intently, all at once he's not trying to hide anymore. Instead, he walks across to the fountain and stands with one hand resting on its lip, staring into it. The fountain is made of clear glass and its bottom rests on a huge kaleidoscope, flashing colored lights up from underneath through the water to spatter the trees and the faces of pedestrians with tiny panels of colored light, oozing into each other and refracting out of each other. Hovering motionless in the center of the pool is a freshwater octopus, shifting color and pattern to match the kaleiding from beneath, but always a little delayed, so that the last image lingers a moment above its replacement before fading altogether, never to be repeated, like a visual memory complete in one moment. The Golem's eyes are fixed on the octopus. They stand there a moment, his eyes on it, her eyes on him, the octopus standing still in the middle of the fountain, the Golem standing still at the edge, and Christine standing still by the railing with her viewer.

Then the Golem reaches into his pocket, eyes unwavering, and produces a small tin box. He opens the box and pulls out something brown and glistening—it looks like a shred of liver. With two fingers he tosses it into the water. The octopus extends a languid tentacle and plucks it up before it touches the bottom, curling it toward its beak, underneath. Christine looks more closely—what is he up to? The Golem suddenly thrusts his head under the water. She can see his mouth moving, distorted by the curved glass wall of the fountain into a wide black stain, evidently giving instructions to the octopus. She rocks a little back, feels the reins being tugged from her hands...

The octopus turns toward her. It can see her. It can draw her out of herself, as a favor to the Golem. In a moment the patterns change to splotch purple and yellow across its hide and everything around her goes dark except for a patch of light across the upper half of her face, across her eyes, where curling patterns of purple and yellow spangle her cheeks and glitter like embers reflected in her golden eyes. The colors get more intense and deepen, as if they'd been hollowed out and filled with light like paper lanterns, until her eyes are overflowing with them and they run down her cheeks in streaks of white-hot silver. She leans back as if a chasm had opened at her feet, but she's still falling forward, looking down at the scene in the viewer now and seeing the aperture between his hovering figure and the slide, and watching that aperture gape wide, and feeling it swing round like a frame in a revolving door, without the glass, flashing past her and swallowing her up, toppling past a mirror-frame into the picture. She turns around and then it's light again—but dimmer, domesticated light—she's not where she was.

The room is enormous, with a high domed roof over her head, and the city spread out far below, visible through the many small windows, small enough to be out of proportion with the wall. A hallway with a window and stairwell at the end stretches off in front of her. The viewer's gone—she's been sucked inside it. She turns around, looking at the roof, the pillars supporting it sprouting in the corners, turning toward the unusually high elevated stage at the far end. The Golem is standing on the stage. It's incredible: he's smiling at her! They stare at each other a moment. Then, with slow deliberation, he takes a step toward her, on the short flight of steps from the stage. She is so surprised that she can think of nothing better to do than turn and run as fast as she can down the hall.

From where he stands he sweeps the head of his cane across her feet (in perspective) and she is whipped to the floor, landing flat on her stomach, knocking the wind out of her. The gold mask flies off and out of her face and skitters across the floor. Breathless, she scrambles out onto the landing after it, pinwheeling her arms through the bars of the banister after it shoots through them, watching it ricochet off an open windowsill and go spinning off into the shadows, flicking spangles of reflected gold onto brick walls and darkened windows, plummeting down the shaft toward the black waters of the lake below. She runs down the steps to the window and pokes out her head in time to see the mask wink once more in the light before vanishing between the gaping jaws of a massive fish. It stares blankly up at her for a moment before sinking into deep water again with a faint gurgling sound.

The Golem's coming—slow, regular, ponderous footfalls. She turns without looking up and steps out onto the lower landing. Then she takes the next step more quickly, and then another and another until she's running down the stairs.

The stairs stop. She bounds down and finds nothing but floor where the well ought to continue. Overhead, the stairs creak slowly and regularly, a measured, heavy tread. She ducks out the door into the hall, heading for the stairwell on the opposite side of the building.

#1.) HANGED MEN: She's almost through the doorway when all the doors lining the hall crash to the floor. As she's moving through, a long silhouette swings up from the near right-hand doorway momentarily barring her path, bobbing on a gust of wind from the window in the room—a pair of legs, one with a brace, tied together at the ankles, swinging back into the room attached to a figure in a long black coat, with his hands tied behind his back, hanging from the ceiling just inside the door. There's one in every doorway, swinging back and forth on creaking ropes. Their heads are hooded with demure pink satin bags cinched tight around their necks, just inside the noose. She starts forward again but the roof splinters apart just above and ahead of her and more of them come slamming down directly blocking her way; she can hear the click of their necks snapping as the ropes crack taught like whips, but they're still twisting and jerking weakly back and forth, strangling. Behind her, Christine can hear the Golem creaking down the stairs and into the hall after her. She elbows the hanging men aside and pushes forward, but a whole broadside of gallows trapdoors burst open along the ceiling and more of them drop down snapping their necks, and their chins flop down flat on their chests, cocking their heads too far on either side: one after another but all more or less at the same time, the bound feet swinging down and bouncing back, all the same. She has to wade in among them, shoving them out on either side like a little girl forcing her way back into a closet full of heavy coats and stinking of mold and rot . . . The way they jerk and swing she can hardly pass between them, and the Golem is coming up behind her in the meantime. She's almost to the fire escape—she looks behind her: as the Golem approaches the hanging bodies around him whip sideways to let him pass, like hotel doormen or a phalanx of synchronized dancers, and he creeps through, spider-like with his cane and an evilly patient expression on his face. Now she's at the stairs—bolts down to the next floor and once again stops short at a blank expanse of concrete between her and the floor below. She barges out into the hall heading for the opposite stairwell like before.

#2.) LABORATORY SPECIMENS: This time the hall doors have been removed in advance, and in each doorway a different body falls swooning to the floor with exaggerated slowness. Gigantic fetal pigs, foals, calves, lambs, chicks, ducklings, monitor lizards, chimpanzees, etc, so large that each fills the room it's in, and swells as its head drifts past the doorframe and splats to the floor. Their tongues flap between their slack jaws or loll out one side of their mouths, their eyes are partially collapsed and scummed with white film, their flesh is grey and clammy and stinks of formaldehyde: each is already slit open down the front with two symmetrical flaps, exposing multicolored shapes with gleaming contours, that spill out across the floor in voluptuously spreading pools of blood and rubbing alcohol. As their heads hit the floor, perfectly circular sheets of stinking grey-brown fluid flow out from them evenly into the hall. Running from the Golem, Christine is involuntarily jarred backward—the specimens' blood bonds her feet to the floor like glue. Grabbing her leg, she tries to yank it free, and, meeting with no success, she is forced to spit around her shoes: the blood foams on contact with her acidic saliva and her foot comes free. From then on she is forced to weave in and out of the pools, finally hop-scotching wildly as patches of dry floor become more rare. All the while the bodies are swelling, the heads in particular, forcing her to leap around them as well, and finally to clamber over them as best she can, slipping awkwardly on their cold, oozing flesh and sodden hair or feathers.

The level of rotted blood on the floor is rising—she has to jump from head to head to get to the stairwell, where a low glass riser prevents the blood from spilling down to the next floor. If she falls in, she'll be stuck forever in blood amber. Behind her, the Golem is following effortlessly, if slowly, walking on the surface of the blood.

#3.) MOLD: From where she is standing, the light filters in through the opposite window through floating threads of spores, like tiny hooks at regular intervals on a line. They undulate together in minute draughts, forming semi-visible banners crisscrossing each other along the length of the hall, and in and out of the open rooms. More threads, finer than hair, ooze up from volcanic mounds of livid fungus heaped across the floor. Still more fungus creeps up the walls in ladders and gills and leprous stalagmites, and hangs in stubby icicles from the ceiling. In the rooms, it forms chains of gold and grey ringing the walls, chandeliers of pliant, clear puffballs strung together like bulbs of blown glass, and pastel-colored cocoons that hatch violet fireflies and hummingbirds whose wings are green and red and white, and who trail an exhaust of rust-colored spores. And here and there, people, looking half-melted, waving and murmuring, rooted to the floor, with rolling puffball eyes and cheeks rouged with blue and green molds.

Her first breath of the air in here clogs her throat like a wad of dry tissue paper. A mildewy stink, mingled with a rancid, meaty odor, flutters up from corrugated, fleshy funnels and veiny platters sprouting from the wainscoting. Clamping her hand over her lips, she struts disgustedly out onto the floor heading for the opposite stairway, as usual. But each step kicks up puffs of spores that rustle up the sides of her dress and begin tracing tiny filaments across her hands and face, like a butcher's map sectioning a carcass into cuts. A buzzing sensation starting behind her nose, in her sinuses, begins creeping back into her skull, and in an instant she feels the channels that connect her brain to her body being dammed, one after another. An indolent, pulsing, numb feeling spreads up her body, her momentum crashes down around her ankles and she begins to weave back and forth, dragging her feet through more spore-fronds and kicking up thicker and thicker ropes of spores that weave her up and down with tacky orange webs hovering a few millimeters above her skin.

Like waves pounding lazily down on her, she feels herself losing balance, a bloated desire to topple over backwards and sleep, would sense the mold first only as a momentary itch, followed by cool relief as it spreads and anesthetizes, neatly choking off the nerves like a gardener pulling weeds. In a matter of moments she would be sheathed in a safe, cool, fleshy envelope of lurid orange, blue, and purple patches further ornamenting her with fat leathery flowers and mushroom heads on long stalks like dangling lotus blossoms. Meandering in and out of one room after another, each with its own distinct color and texture now, where all was identical before, stumbling and drooping more and more as strings of spore feed into her nostrils and corkscrew into her ears, powdering her face and hands pale blue, and she totters to the Golem's metronomic tread. He's there in the doorway, but the spores don't bother him—the moment they land on his tainted flesh they shrivel and steam with formaldehyde poisoning. Even his shoes leave blackened scorch-marks on the springy floor.

Christine collects herself for an instant and thinks to drop one blue hand into her purse, from which she pulls a perfume bottle. She splatters it liberally on her face and hands, pulling off sheets of powdery blue lint melting in the perfume. Then she drops the bottle to the floor, shattering it on a fortuitously exposed bit of tile, and the coils of alcohol and perfume slither up in a cloud around her body, melting the spores and tangling the floating filaments up in impenetrable knots that drop to the ground twisting. The shock of the smell knifes through the buzzing in her head and she is able to reorient herself. She wipes her feet in the spreading stain, soaking her shoes thoroughly, meanwhile clearing blue tears from her golden eyes with her handkerchief, and then trips quickly down the hall and out into the stairwell, walking in a golden flame of perfume. The Golem is only a few yards behind.

#4.) GHOSTS: The moment her foot crosses the threshold, everything goes pitch black. Silence. No motion. No odor in the air. No temperature. No sense of the stairs behind her or the floorboards stretching out before her. The walls are invisible, and the rooms beyond visible only as patches of denser darkness against the dark. Without realizing it, she's taken several steps out into the room if it is a room. The sensation of her feet touching the floor becomes more and more remote, as if she were elongating up through the ceiling. But everywhere the darkness is humming, as though permeated by tingling nerves. It engulfs her without absorbing her, so that while the borders between all other things become blurred and intermixed, she and the dark stay discrete.

Nothing is preventing her from stealing down to the stairs, but she's wary to move, suspecting that she will begin to dissolve into the dark if she tries. But of course she's moving already, walking up and down in front of the doors first on one side, then on the other. But from high atop her shoulders, looking down at where her feet must be, far below, she feels she's only sailing along without effort. One by one she picks out the luminous figures that honestly were there all along. They shine with such diffused radiance that at least at first they're barely perceptible, but each appears to be brightening slowly, with each new pass, emerging at increments out of the dark.

As they come out, Christine recognizes who they are. It would be wrong to distinguish between them, they're all the same. Each is doing something in its own room, illuminating the few sticks of furniture collapsed in corners and casting dimly discernible shadows with their own light. They're pantomiming old routines, fixed in time to such an extent that their every motion has already become a circular preparation for the next repetition. As Christine recognizes them, she begins to hear them, baffled voices both reminiscent of her own and completely strange speaking fragments, coming to the door of the room and throwing up both hands, fingers drooping onto the palms, "... It can't..." a voice from the corner, saying, "... famine..." and other rooms, "... find me..." and, becoming aware of her, "... but, I..." and, coming up behind her, "... not for any..." muffled as if they were speaking through coffin lids. Sailing past the doors, she picks up every scrap and feels her court assembling around her on all sides. She stops in the middle again.

One of them draws very near. She floats silently forward, hesitates, then glides up, superimposing her immaterial skirt over Christine's. An indolent, numb feeling soaks into Christine's right leg, and then she's barely conscious of it anymore. Her eyelids droop, but then a moment later she jerks them open and looks—blue-black holes in a blue-white face smiling idiotically with its powdery smudge of a mouth only inches from her face, and her leg dislocated, numb and immobile, that this one is wearing like a stocking on her own ghost-leg. Around her, on all sides, there are others like this one, straining eagerly forward to ease in through the other leg, or an arm, to seize on her and dress themselves in her body. Feverishly, to fend them off, she thinks to bang herself hard against the floor, but she can't collapse—her right leg won't bend or tip. So instead she stomps on the floor with her left leg, jarring her up to her teeth, and flails out her arms, trying to smack them against the walls. She suffers to stay awake, and all the while a crude copy of her face grins oblivious at her, freezing her right leg to the ground. Finally, in a fit of desperation, she seizes the icy throat and squeezes it shut. The expression on the other face does not change, but for a moment it seems to be turning a darker shade of blue. The mouth opens a little and emits a mewling, reedy caricature of her voice. Christine shakes it violently by the throat. The shade appears to elongate a little, as if her head were trying to float off her neck, snapping back and forth. She's not sure what happens next—perhaps it slips? Suddenly pins and needles shatter up and down her leg and she's free.

Turning away a moment she can see the hallway stretching off into the distance, but now it blurs, turning into a bridge. The walls vanish, and a narrow lake appears, flanking her on both sides. The stairwell has become a flight of steps where the bridge joins an elevated walkway over the opposite bank. The ceiling is now a concrete dome, large enough to span an entire city, lit with colorless light evenly shining across its surface. The air is sharp and cold.

More of them struggle in front of her, closing around her, a knot sliding closed. They reach for her with coy gestures, pressing in to touch her. Behind her, there is nothing but an opaque wall of shadow, where the bridge trails off hanging in nothingness, no way out. She glances down at the water—it looks deathly cold and blue, poisoned. Finally, she simply throws up her arms and dashes between them, twisting sideways to avoid their hands.

In the middle of the bridge, she turns to see if they are following her—they're not. They're waiting. Christine stops, breathing hard, and watches them, straining her ears—what holds them back? One by one they come apart in fragments like silver dandelion heads, beads of white down that drift away to either side. Candles in squat blue bells of frosted glass float across the water, set in motion by long, graceful hands that retreat into gem-encrusted portholes in the bank, just above the waterline, their fingers weighted with heavy rings, wrists by pendulous bracelets, all set with big precious stones. Some of the candles drift lazily toward her, others race in straight lines raising tiny wakes behind them, only to halt perfectly still a few yards away from her. In their blue light that turns everything blue, she can see that the lake isn't water at all, but raw mercury, heaving like a living thing, throwing azure flashes back up at her.

A sound draws her attention back to the bridge. Standing where the shades had been, there is a black coach and team. The horses are black, and their skeletons have been painted on their bodies in thick streaks of white phosphorus. They have black plumes sprouting from their heads, but no bit nor bridle, no reins, because no coachman. She hesitates a moment longer, and then the horses and the front of the coach fade to transparency a moment, as if a jagged hole had been cut through them both, revealing the interior of the carriage. The Golem is in there, staring straight at her from his seat. His spectacles glint like a pair of dusty lamps as he leans almost imperceptibly forward. Then the vision fades, the horses and carriage reappear as before—the horses snort and start forward, rattling across the bridge toward her. She loses no time, but bolts up the stairs at the other end.

Here the bridge spans a pair of train tracks in a narrow gorge. As she runs across, a train rushes past not more than five feet below, and she glances down, still running, where she sees in the gully the windows flashing by. Inside they all are staring back, their eyes wide open, their mouths open and toothless in a sort of senile, fumbling expression, with their hands in their laps, strobing past all in the same posture as the train roars by behind her. As its noise dies down, she can hear the coach battering up the stairs to the causeway.

A path corkscrews among the trees, and after only a few steps she's lost. Overhead, densely interlaced branches scribble out the cavern-roof sky, and as she runs the trunks crowd in close on all sides, until she's practically moving through a tunnel—and then again, in moments a vista will open to one side or the other, revealing trees the size of cathedrals, with a span of branches big enough to shadow a small town—an underground forest. Spiders the size of barns rattle by on legs like oil-derricks, monkeys swing from tree to tree in barking shoals. Malachite branches and scored trunks of granite and basalt, limestone and porphyry, sheathed in coats of pumice-moss and ivy vines of soft lead, and wide beds of zinc grass.

Minute flakes of plagioclase feldspar sprinkle down from the boughs like dew and collect on the path in a thick layer of fine dust that billows in moon-colored transparent clouds behind her footsteps. Strange piping and chirping noises come shouting out of the darkness like birds being throttled, and others like the voices of parrots, ravens, or mynahs trained to speak by raving psychotics. They seem to be hunting her down, circling closer like bloodhounds. She gets a good look at one as it hops onto a branch hanging over the path ahead: it's actually a sort of clockwork, assembled around a small plastic figurine of a saint, with porcelain bird's legs emerging from its knees, tin tail feathers from the base jutting behind, wings on either side of the gears and cogs that protrude from its spine, and a painted metal beak affixed to the saint's face, which opens and closes to utter shrill, distorted cries and queerly-accented nonsense in the voice of a pull-string doll. More of them cluster all around her as she runs down the path, babbling incomprehensible words and groaning. The coach is still following her, ignoring the path, cutting toward her in a straight line. She watches as it vanishes behind a root the size of a freight car, and then appears again, mounting over the top and driving straight down the side perpendicular to the ground, the horses walking downward their hooves cling to the root like flies' feet, then bending backwards parallel to the ground once more to continue their pursuit. Around her she can see the Golem's skeleton reproduced in different sizes, the bones of the largest thrusting up among the trees in pallid and cracked columns, the ground littered with his bones, and leaping, yawping corpses flashing in the heather under swinging light bulbs that hang on long cords from the trees, kicking up clouds of fireflies and glow worms.

Angrily, she batters some "birds" from a nearby branch and sprints, nearly banging her knees against her chest as she runs. A moment later she turns a corner and confronts another "bird" standing beside the path, identical to the rest but fifty feet high, a colossal St. Roc, with his rigid loincloth and crutches sweeping back and forth, his yacking beak expelling thunderous fragments of words down at her. The next moment an impenetrable screen of trees interposes itself between them like a stage flat.

#5.) PUTREFACTION: Behind her the grisly coach is still coursing effortlessly after. A burning sensation is seething in her lungs, forcing her to stop running. The burning spreads to her face and across her chest and back, down her abdomen, but her arms and legs are cold. She can feel her skin turning red, then going green; her hands begin to shake; a violent throbbing surges up behind her temples. She feels as if she's been flushed through with mercury, a viscous green-black membrane intermittently clogging in her throat, and with it a rancid bitter metal taste in her mouth; sour, stinking vapors rustling up into her sinuses, her eyes are hot and red, wanting to water but too dry, curdling in their sockets and leeching color, becoming cheesy, crumbling . . . Something rifling through her, fingers and toes blackening, first sooting then blanching her face to bruise purple and green, like a steady-winding clockwork ticking out threads of burning bile down into her muscles and bones, and parching her skin until it's straining all over to split. Inside she can feel her heart collapsing and her shriveling organs quaking uncontrollably.

#6.) DISFIGUREMENT: Suddenly her right leg twists erupting gouts of sweet toothache pain as the brittle bone ruptures in three places. She clenches her teeth tightly down against it and staggers along the path, from tree to tree emitting little screams, and grinning as well: he's really laying it on, or if not him, *something*, something like the story itself forcing her to the end. A rustling from off the path—nearby she can see gleaming metal braces slithering in the bracken like predatory animals, waiting to spring, hoping to solder themselves around her shattered leg. Clinging to the trunk of her tree as if it were a life-raft, she inadvertently scrabbles at the bark—green crust crinkles under her fingernails and copper red beams underneath. With failing eyes she scans the border of the path and then, her mouth bubbling with horrible mirthless laughter as her leg yaws beneath her, she hobbles to another tree, hugging it to her chest as her knees buckle in splinters of exhausting pain. She presses one eye right to its knobby trunk—the "bark" is a thick layer of tarnish, but from the smell she knows it's silver beneath. Again her eyes twitch across the trees lining the path, and with her last ounce of strength she flings herself toward one that stands out—even through a blanket of pumice-moss and heavy shadows—from the surrounding trees that seem to huddle conspiratorially about it. She embraces the trunk, slumping forward, mashing her face against the uncorrupted gold, a fissure draining amber. As surely as silver follows copper, gold follows silver, and she knows this. A chemical mist steams off the tree from its roots, and she breaths it in, feeling the gold pouring coolly into her eyes, spreading cool and calm vapor from her lungs and rippling across her skin, through her hair, reddening her blood from green-black, driving the green from her face, drawing the corruption from her, since gold is hers. It plays numbing fingers along the ruins of her leg, aligning and knitting the bones back as they were, rotating her foot back into its proper position, easing wrenched joints back into their sockets.

She hangs there until she feels well again, her feet sound beneath her again. She peels some "moss" from the bark, exposing the rosy, reflective surface dripping amber here and there. She takes a single drop of amber on her tongue to refresh her, and steps back onto the path, crushing zinc blades of grass beneath her feet. But the coach is still approaching, almost on top of her, and she is forced to flee, though she wants to fight.

#7.) VERTIGO: There, beyond the trees, the path follows the line of the shore, running along white chalk cliffs and heaps of black rock down below. Stretching off to her left are low, dismal hills covered with clover, and sulfurous figures moving alone or in pairs dot the peaks and dip into the shallow valleys between. The ocean is purple like new wine, with roving patches of luminous emerald; the sky is still the same blank, glowing grey. The chalk path traces the contours of the cliffs. Glancing behind her, she can see the coach racing after her out of the middle distance. Her foot slips and she turns around again, staggering only a foot or so away from the cliff edge. The path is creeping steadily over toward the sea, until the brink of the drop becomes its right margin—but she doesn't dare leave the path.

The path is getting narrower still, and slippery. She's treading its left margin like a tightrope trying not to fall, but the ground is beginning to crumble. She looks below, and she can see the Golem, keeping pace with her down on the rocks, with a white sheet in his hands. The horses are each holding a corner of the sheet in their teeth, stretching it to form a crude equilateral triangle, ready to catch her when she falls. At every moment she feels as though she's tipping over toward them, and having a target only makes it worse. The Golem's face is impassive, unreadable, staring up at her with a plaintive expression, but the horses are nodding their skull-painted heads mockingly, lifting their hooves high and prancing jauntily over the stones. A chunk of wet earth crumbles beneath her feet and she swings round slamming into the slope, digging her fingers into the soft clay and fumbling for a firmer purchase. Her feet are waving in the air, but her fingers latch on to something like a buried pipe or a heavy tree-root (although there are no trees anywhere), and she seizes it with white knuckles. She can hear them flapping the sheet invitingly below. She holds on.

A sickening lurch and she can feel her feet beginning to angle upwards, away from the cliff face. The cliffs are falling forward. A moment later it stops, having tilted ninety degrees—small stones and clods of earth come skipping across the ground and ricochet past her into open air. The waves crash straight up just a little beyond her. Looking back, she can still see the Golem, standing sideways in midair holding the sheet at the same distance beneath her feet as before. With no cliff to lean on her arms are weakening, and she tries to worm her fingers deeper into the mud around the pipe, working her palms around it to support herself.

Another jerk and the cliff is plummeting forward again. She is hanging straight "up" from the ground, as if she were standing on her head, and the Golem and his horses are hovering immediately above her and upside down. If she lets go and misses them, she'll fall right up to the top of the dome, or perhaps straight through and out into the sky, into space. Now the fatigue in her aching hands and arms is becoming hot pain, her shoulders are straining to pop from their sockets, a hideous squeamish feeling ripples across the soles of her feet and in her knees at the thought of falling, and her palms begin to sweat. She wants to pull forward and curl up against the pipe and wait for things to right themselves. She closes her eyes, her mind racing.

She hangs there a moment more. Her face goes slack, and she relaxes. Then she flutters her eyelashes. Three tiny fountains of white butterflies sprout from the ground around her hands like gouts of living foam, looping around her in threads until she's cocooned herself in a cage of flapping wings. She releases the pipe, and then hangs there in her cloud of butterflies. They turn her right side up to the cliffs and carry her inland. Then, what light there is abruptly evaporates, and the butterflies with it. For a moment, she is completely swallowed by a shadow.

#8.) GRAVES: She can feel the cool powder of the path like finely sifted flour against her cheek. As she rises and takes a step, graves gape open to either side of the path where she stands, and out of the hazy distance a pair of tombstones come rolling up and plant themselves at the end of each grave. And something besides, hiding behind the stones or in the shadows down in the graves, moving opposite her to keep out of sight, crouched down, but also always aware of her, observing her from only a few feet away. Experimentally, she takes another step. Another pair of graves, another pair of rolling headstones, and possibly two others behind them, hiding. She walks quickly up the path and over the rise ahead, keeping her eyes fixed on the road and ignoring the graves, headstones, and whatever they conceal, like a pedestrian storming past a knot of beggars. They keep coming, two with each step.

Once over the ridge, she observes her path winding among a vast open landscape of graves, all as alert to her as if she was an actress just appearing after the overture. Nervous, she hesitates a moment before continuing forward, unsure even of what she's frightened will happen. It is always and only the sense that they're watching, and hiding. She strains her ears, cocking her head a little forward, thinking perhaps she might be able to hear them shifting about to avoid being seen, but they emit no sound, nor do they ever hide less than perfectly, invisible, but she is positive now that they are there.

The air is getting oppressively hot and freighted with the smell of fresh dirt from the graves and wisteria, whose vines embrace every stunted tree and every grave marker, growing fat on the fertilized ground. The branches are bloated and luxuriant, waving humid fresh leaves lazily at her and bobbing clusters of purple blossoms overripe with perfume. As she notices the wisteria she can see also a mausoleum sitting on a low hummock. The path brings its front around where she can see—one stacked inside another like Russian dolls, and each made of translucent, rose-colored marble panels that absorb and magnify both the light, turning it a glowing pink, but also concentrating the wisteria aroma into threads of purple smoke, wreathing it around on all sides like ivy, or incense. The doors of all the mausoleums are open, one within the other, and the Golem is hovering in the very center, hanging from the neck. Twisting there, precisely framed by the door, swathed in tissues of pink light, with his grimy coat and dirty, hanging hands, and the team standing to either side of the outer door, holding their plumed heads high and immobile like statues. As he rotates toward her, their eyes meet for a moment. His have been waiting for her with an expression of resignation.

But he has caught up with her already, she thinks, and has her in the palm of his hand right now. It is only a matter of closing his hand upon her, to capture her, but he hasn't—and now she realizes he won't. Even from this great distance he seems to say: "Isn't that enough? Aren't you satisfied?" She is tired, and tempted to explain—but then they both would have suffered for nothing, and the bargain would be vitiated. Behind him, the sky is turning pink in a perfect halo behind the mausoleum, causing the whorled, conch-shaped glass ornaments that line its roof to pulse with a violet glow. A sound like hundreds of crickets sawing uniformly back and forth rises all around her from the tombstones, and looking down she can see the graves are all linked together by a network of circular communicating passageways, lit by strings of Christmas lights embedded in the soft walls. She looks up again as the first rays of magenta light patter coldly across her cheeks and brow, dazzling her. The Golem's face is reduced to a watery grey smear with shining eyes, stretching diagonally as she squints into increasing radiance. Then her heart hardens. When the time comes—soon enough. He is harrowing her; she knew he would.

When she opens her eyes again, she is standing in a low-ceilinged chamber with cinderblock walls and greasy, oblong windows set high off the stained cement floor. A door covered with rusty sheets of tin hangs open on a concrete courtyard outside. A staircase yawns at her back, and further up—the reports of the Golem's leg hulking down after her? Without hesitation she strides quickly out the door and starts crossing the courtyard, a building looming up behind her, a brick wall, crumbled to the ground in the far corner, to one side, and cement walls opposite and ahead of her, a staircase leading to street level. Cities full of stairs.

#9.) PARALYSIS: Making straight for the stairs, she feels inertia gather numbly in her joints and jacket her limbs in lead. Like a great heavy hand pressing down on her she feels it slowing her, stopping her, freezing her in her tracks, and she is doggedly reaching . . .

#10.) DARKNESS: A cold, ruddy darkness closes around her eyes pressing them down into her cheeks, and as it rushes in to meet her Christine, with the greatest reluctance, resorts to an old substitution trick:

The Golem takes his hands from her eyes and turns her around. Miss Woodwind glares back at him with shining eyes, grinning. Christine is standing at the top of the stairs some distance away.

He makes to swerve around but Miss Woodwind seizes his arms with a grip like a vice—"Where do you think you're going?"

Christine is dwindling back into the shadows.

The Golem is trying to twist free, but Miss Woodwind matches him move for move.

"Go on, Christine!" she tosses gaily over her shoulder.

Christine is gone.

The Golem takes Miss Woodwind by the arms and tries to wrench her away, but she doesn't falter, still peering fixedly into his face, grinning gleefully.

Unable to restrain himself he leans forward and seizes her by her narrow waist. He can hear her throaty chuckle by his right ear, her perfume waft around his face to his nostrils as he lifts her off the ground and carries her to a corner. Presently, she has him with his head in her lap, sitting in the corner where the wall has crumbled almost to the ground, opening up a view of the park.

"What a simpleton you are!" she says glaring down at him, running her fingers tenderly across his face. Fine copper wires emerge, peeling back through the skin at his temples and weaving a garland around his head, which sprouts tiny brass leaves and clusters of berries, actually bulbs of glass flickering with minute jets of current. From time to time her fingers brush against the wires and the entire assembly vibrates with a quietly musical rattle. Oblivious, the Golem merely gazes back up at her with a contented expression, blinking stupidly. She seems to have him.

Off to one side, he can see a bronze figure standing against the horizon, with his back turned. He lies there, watching it, while she sits warm and dimly visible all around him, her face floating above him.

Although she's been speaking all the time, her voice only now rises to become intelligible. "Where does your power come from?"

"I don't have any power."

"Don't be stupid," she tugs one of his forelocks. "I've seen you do all sorts of unearthly things."

"I never do anything."

"You just sail along on your trapeze and everything else gets out of your way? Out of tact, I suppose?"

"No."

"Well then what?"

"I only make the gestures."

"But then who completes them? The Divinity Student?"

"Yes and no."

"He never does anything either—so then, his divinity?"

"Our divinity."

"And he passes it along to you?"

"Yes and no."

"And your strength, too?"

"The papers that fill my body cavity are lighter than your organs."

"But your body seems more ponderous, almost too heavy for you to carry."

"It is denser, for being simpler and more abstract."

"So then, when you threw me across the room," she scrapes a fingernail lightly across his eye, "it was your divinity reaching down to flick me away, like a fly? Or was it the Divinity Student?"

"I don't know."

"Doesn't he tell you anything?"

"There's nothing to tell."

"You're his agent, he must tell you things!"

"I'm not an agent like you."

Miss Woodwind looks down at him sharply.

"I know that Griepentrog sent you," the Golem says.

"He didn't—I agreed to go, for reasons of my own, and he offered to help, for reasons of his own."

"But Griepentrog can't get down here, while you can. He knew that, or you told him. He wanted you to come after me, or he wanted you to open the way for him to come down after me."

"I'm not an agent because I don't take orders. He and I have a bargain with your former employers. And you've evaded my question—how do you know what to do?" She's using her mysterious influence again.

"I'm his machine. I do what I'm supposed to."

"How do you know what you're supposed to do?"

"I can't do any different."

"How did you get that way?"

"He made me this way."

"Who, the Divinity Student or the divinity?"

"Both."

"One through the other?"

"Yes."

"And did he make me, too? And everything?" she holds out her hands indicating everything around them. "Everything we can see?"

"Yes."

"And are we all formed according to what we're supposed to do?"

"Yes and no."

"Not the same as you?"

"No."

"Or the Divinity Student—I keep forgetting he made you."

"He and I are the same."

"Same but different?" Not really a questioning tone of voice.

"Yes."

She sneers a little.

"Only the most trivial difference. We are essentially the same," he says.

He can barely see her face. Her mouth is only an irregular shadow; her voice seems to come from everywhere and nowhere.

"What makes you different from me, or Christine?"

"Christine is different from you."

Miss Woodwind ignores him. "Why did he make you different?"

"He needed a new body."

"Why?"

"I have no reasons."

"If his body was falling apart, why didn't he restore it? —Isn't it that he can't restore it? . . . And that he can't come down here himself?"

"Everything you say is perfectly true."

"You are your divinity, embodied? He must be a very abject god."

"It's possible—or perhaps he's abject because I'm abject—he and I— what he and I do affects him as well."

"But you do whatever he wants."

"Having it done changes things for him."

Miss Woodwind is silent a minute. ". . . But the Divinity Student is all but dead. Why leave him that way? Why not bring him back to life? Why cause you to be made in the first place?"

"He will be brought back to life again."

"Through you?"

"Yes."

"How?"

"I don't know yet."

"Through this?" she makes a vague gesture, indicating everything.

"Yes."

"Christine is going to be sacrificed to bring him back, isn't that it?"

"We will both be sacrificed. We are making our sacrifices right now."

"You and she?"

"Yes."

"How?"

"We exhaust ourselves."

"And when you are both fully exhausted? You will have sacrificed enough?"

"Yes."

"And then what?"

"We will be married."

"But won't that be a defeat for her? Isn't that what she's trying to avoid?"

"Christine can't be defeated."

"Then why bother trying?"

"We will stale-mate."

"I'll bet you will!" Miss Woodwind snorts. "—But what would fighting to impasse achieve?"

"It's the only way."

"Why?"

"Christine is that way, she needs things to be like that, and we need her that way."

". . . Suppose Christine isn't satisfied? Has it ever occurred to you that she might not want to be sacrificed?"

"She can't be defeated, no matter what she does. Whatever sacrifice is asked of her, she's making it now. We have a deal."

"What is she getting in return?"

"That's not for me to say."

"You mean you don't know."

"That's right."

"But suppose Christine doesn't help, won't the Divinity Student be dead forever?"

"Not forever."

Miss Woodwind grumbles for a moment. "Even if he was fully restored to life, won't he still be mortal? Couldn't he be killed again?"

"I suppose he'll always come back."

"And so on and on and nothing more? What good is that?"

"That's not for me to say."

"Does that mean your divinity is coming and going like that as well?"

"Yes and no."

"Then you're saying that your divinity is dying and living all the time."

"Of course."

"Well what is it that's killing him—other gods? Nature?"

"I don't know."

"What about the Divinity Student? After he is restored, what happens to you, to Christine? Do you die?"

"No, we will all live."

"Where will you be?"

"That's hard to say. We will all be in the house he is building for us."

"Never mind, that's far enough. That's too far."

Miss Woodwind pauses a moment and gazes out across the wall to the park. The wind twirls its petticoats in the trees, rushing like agile waves.

". . . And so he completes your gestures. Perhaps you might show me—do something for me then?"

"No, he won't do it like that. And he doesn't exactly complete my gestures. The gestures aren't wholly mine, and the intention is both mine and his. I can't make anything happen myself, at my whim."

She screws up her lips.

"You'll get your proof soon enough," the Golem says.

"Did he make you say that?"

"Yes."

"What proof?"

"I don't know. But I'm certain it's true."

"Is your god as ugly as you?" she asks peevishly.

"Uglier," he grins back at her.

Miss Woodwind snorts. "Of course, he would have to be more of everything, wouldn't he."

"I wasn't going to say anything," the Golem yawns.

She sits still peering intently down at him, playing with his hair, caressing his face, murmuring absently to herself with parted lips moist with venom. The Golem continues to return her gaze, dreamily looking around, out over the park. A breeze stirs through his wire wreath, blowing his eyes—Miss Woodwind's eyes, always probing, follow his gaze—the breeze comes down from the sky and blows his eyes over toward the park. The trees elongate and whirr together like rows of clockworks on stalks ticking down wound springs, so that their branches play out corresponding calligraphies, opening a deeper view. Something is scintillating deep within them, that dapples Miss Woodwind's face with roving gleams of faint light, blurred by the warmth and softness of her skin, the continual emanation of her perfume. They trickle up and down her face, distracting her, making it difficult for her to concentrate.

"So . . ." she says, trying to pull words up out of the stream always whispering between her lips like a thin trickle of smoke, "does your . . . divinity . . . ever . . . address you?"

"Hmm?"

"Does he ever . . . speak to you?" she says more forcibly.

"Yes and no."

"He never gives reasons?"

"Not what you would call reasons."

"Well then—what . . . what does . . . ?" she puts her hand to her head. Tiny lights seep in and out between her fingers and dangle in droplets from her eyelashes.

"You're like a horrible machine," she says, her voice stifled deep in her throat. "The trouble is finding the switch to turn—you—off!" punctuating the last three words by twisting his nose. His eyes are rolling slowly in their sockets, and she peers out into the dark to find what he's looking at. They circle round to the park again. Caught, she follows his gaze.

She looks again, against her will, out over the wall. She sees the fountain kaleiding among the trees, and the octopus hovering almost in midair, staring glacially right into her eyes, its own eyes, with their alien, bi-lobed pupils, icing out continual rays of grainy ocean-cold, framed on all sides by clammy boneless flesh, shimmering through delayed colors and patterns, fragments and coagulations along vectors like mirror-edges streaking along the planes and curves of her face, like frost-ferns of color and cellular divisions in pattern, dividing and consuming each other, flashing in her flinty eyes and showering sparks down her cheeks to her chin. Even as her features are going slack she's muttering, trying to speak to him as he coils upward onto his feet, and she stays seated, unable to follow, her face the axis for a spinning ring of reflected kaleiding. Her eyes flick to grey-gold, mustering her forces, and he knows better than to stay, turning for the last time to face the city and Christine hidden within it.

But paralyzed as she is, Miss Woodwind's hand, resting on her lap, feels the edges of the Golem's book through the fabric of her skirt's left hip pocket. She will disappear before he discovers the theft.

The Cathedral

Days go by and the Golem does not appear again. He seems to have gone. For Christine, he can only get farther and farther away. She's been staying in her enormous apartment with many small rooms. The days run by, watery and indistinct—no sign, and an intolerable derailed feeling grows and grows. The city rustles all around her, unmassed human shadows scatter like windblown cinders in the squares and along the streets, and dash against the bobbing foundations of the buildings. A terrible claustrophobia wrings her heart—she is stuck fast. She cannot return to San Veneficio. Given certain terms of her contract she is to wait the sufferance of certain signs, and these continue not to come. If they never do, she will never leave. When the fruit falls from the tree and is severed from its greater life, it isn't dead or alive: it's undead and potentially either, food for new flesh or new leaves. No Golem, and Christine fades away without a trace. After the Exodus a Pharaoh can only sit and stare bored and boring his half-empty empire, eventually to dwindle and to petrify into a million obsolete statues, mummies, museum exhibits.

Christine is now poised romantically at the water's edge—she leans on the railing of the floating dock and sends her thoughts out aimlessly over the tarry water. Grey slate dome dimly lit from below with a wan spectral light to the horizon, the air between water and "sky" is black. Suddenly Miss Woodwind is there, coyly smiling at her from the doorway of a shambolic bait shack whose decrepitude clashes with her stylish coat. She steps to the rail and stands by it.

"Hello, Christine."

Christine is hardening, her face glows white as paper, her coral mouth and green eyes light up.

"How dare you walk up to me and start a conversation like an old chum?"

"I have something—"

"*How dare you interfere?*" A slap in each word. Fireworks pop and crackle on the pier flash and jerk in the corners by the walls, and in the windows of the bait shack.

"Do you want to know or don't you?" Miss Woodwind replies pugnaciously.

"*Well?*"

"I took it while he lay with his head in my lap—I've hidden it in a safe place. I know you want it—I know why you came here—I overheard everything you told Magellan. I'll give it to you."

Christine leans against the rail, all her explosive vehemence gone, smiles a long slow smile. "Is that so?" Now she knows—he can't pursue her effectively without that book—that's why she hasn't seen him lately.

"That is so," Miss Woodwind is saying.

"You can't read his book, have you? You've tried and tried, for weeks now, and now it's on to plan B."

"I'll give it to you, if you'll tell me what it says."

"What makes you think I can read it?"

"You can't?"

"No."

"Well then, what are we here for? He's after you—if you had the book—"

"What do I want with a book I can't read?"

"What are you playing at? You're trying to keep away from him, aren't you?"

"Why, whatever gave you that idea?"

"Don't be silly, without the book he's slower, he's far less likely to catch you—"

"Then shouldn't you be talking to him?"

"—as I was saying," Miss Woodwind glares, "he's less likely to catch you, but he still could—he has all the time in the world, and you're trapped down here meanwhile—he's bound to catch up with you sooner or later."

"I suppose."

"Translate the book and we can both get out of here!"

"I've already told you, I can't read it. Only he can read it."

"Why?"

"Because only he has died and been brought back."

"I don't believe you—we could make something out if we tried—"

"Why should I help you?"

"Why should *you* help *me*?? Who stole his book for you? Who saved you from him twice?"

"I didn't ask for any favors."

"You won't help?"

"Why should I?"

"Are you honestly so stupid?! Or do you have a way out . . . a way out that I don't know . . ."

Christine's smile stretches.

"Don't feel bad—there are many things I didn't tell Magellan . . . and that I certainly wouldn't tell you. You came here thinking to profit yourself with some stolen knowledge, you came here on Griepentrog's behalf, and for the sake of the Seminary. You have meddled in something that was none of your business, and I have made use of you insofar as it pleased me to do so. And now in your ignorance you come offering me your worthless deals. I've already made a better bargain by far, and I have fairly earned what I was promised."

With a calm blast of rebuking force Christine vanishes as a low, thick, heavy wind is vomited from black air, icy black waves, walls and vaults of frigid stone, invisible horizon.

CHRISTINE STANDS IN THE cupola of a towering Victorian sort of building, railed along the roof with iron spikes which glow with a soft blue flame whenever lightning strikes the ground overhead—they are glowing now. A little wind trickles down from the vault and jabs into her with a shock with the thought of the Golem, whose vision lit her and made her dazzling, and her heart hardens as hard as a diamond brought fresh from the furnace sizzling against the air, the heat has not made it white-hot but clear-hot, so that its clarity burns back. She can see that this world is poised, even after all this time it is still poised in pain, waiting for her act, which can end the story. That is, the world of this story will begin and end with the pitch on one fulcrum, a diamond bullet flaring in her chest, lacing through every part of her a clear-hot stream of starry molten diamond. As the wind rises from across the dull black ridges of the water, she's ferocious, strong, diamond-hard and clear-scalding, she seems to loom to the roof of the vault.

Stepping into a ravishing white spotlight that carves its circle on the stones of the balcony, Christine shrugs, removes a scintillating feathered cape revealing a pearl white trapeze costume. She poses on the balcony, the light rebounding from her white skin and teeth and shines like a beacon over the city, her ivory arms, shoulders and neck emerging from her glistening white costume like lilies from a vase, all invoking the Golem.

Through the vault the great starry heavens are palpable, shrieking down through the stone, and what is howling further beyond that, where the light fails, is coming down somehow in soaring panic. Beyond the city lights the wall of the vault suddenly roars and splits, sending huge chunks of stone down into the water, raising waves to dash against the pilings and scatter them, pound them apart, the fabric of this flimsy, badly-realized city crumbling and tearing to shreds. In the growing aperture in the vault wall, Christine can see something huge, like a filigreed stone wedge, plunging down, parting the rock in a big V. From it issues a deafening pounding of bells, through which the ravings of a howling organ intermittently escape. She sees a tall bulb of neatly-fitting stone blocks and pierced just above center by a huge circular window of florid, furious colors. Christine rushes back into the cupola and hastily throws on her clothes—running out across the railed roof she sees this stone ram has sprouted two level wings, glittering with stained glass like a coat of mail. As she reaches the door, she witnesses the appearance of spire and the long shaft of the nave, copper medallions green with verdigris at intervals along the ridge of its peaked roof like a spine—when these appear she knows what she is looking at.

Christine flits out onto the street and down the length of a stone pier, wafted almost off her feat by puffs of hot air from slicks of burning oil on the surface of the water. The bells and the shriekings of the organ stop at once. The cathedral has disencumbered itself entirely of the wall and has precipitated itself onto the waves; the churchyard, crypts, and the slab of earth into which graves and apartments were sunk with the foundations, have been borne along with the building, and now form an island bristling with leafless, rook-haunted trees. Their sardonic calls rasp along the cavern walls to reach her. She sees colossal turbines of perfectly smooth-polished black stone attached to the sides of the cathedral like barnacles, and as she observes them, they start up, with a stern low vibration like the orchestra's trombones—with a noise like slowly splintering wood, the arc-lights crackle and ignite, one in each window and two in the spire, spreading their brilliant rays over the water. Softly at first, and as a snowy mist begins to rise from the foundations and spill out in all directions, the bells in the spire beckon to her. Their knells are so light, they sound as if they were being brushed rather than struck.

Christine looks around—finds a heavy iron rail lying jumbled in a pile of old tackle. She pries the pier loose with the rail, the moldering wood crumbles and spreads apart like stale hard cheese. The pier lurches free—Christine stands balanced in the center. The current bears her across the water, the current pulls her into the mist's clammy folds. Bump—stone steps. Christine climbs and the cathedral door is ajar before her, exhaling a smell of old cloth, leather, dust, wax, varnish. As she steps inside, the statues reach up and snuff the lights, the doors swing shut behind her, and the world outside the walls roars. There is an earsplitting crack and then a tumult of battering stone outside while inside all is silent.

Diamonds sparkling in her hair, she drapes her head in a gleaming white veil. Christine begins to make her way down the aisle toward the altar. About halfway there and she is brought up short by a sound. The Golem appears, mingled with the shadows at the end of the aisle, his joints creaking. They observe each other.

"Why did you call me? Have you changed your mind?"

His voice, ragged with valiantly-struggling hope, speaks from out of a well of sadness dark and cold; but all the same, she is ready to run should he take a step toward her.

"Miss Woodwind stole your book from you, and without it, you couldn't find me. Isn't that right?"

"Yes," she can see the glints of his moist eyes, and a rhomb of light across his brow, but the mouth that speaks is invisible in the dark.

"I didn't think that was fair."

"Thank you."

It's as though they are paralyzed and constrained to speak, although they still must improvise the words. Distant splashes are audible somewhere outside the walls, and another sound whose point of origin is more difficult to place, a whirring that seems to come from overhead, and might be very gradually growing louder.

"I'm curious—without your book, how can you go on, uh, living? You are a Golem—"

"The writing that keeps me alive is in here," he prods his abdomen, muffled noise of damp paper crumpling. "The writing in the book lends me its power, when it's needed."

He takes a step forward, and now she can see his face. His calm, measured speech belies the look of anguish this reveals. His features are drawn and seared with exasperation. Christine takes a step backwards.

"Why did you call me here? Are you teasing me?"

"I might be."

She is too hard to be broken, he is too inexhaustible to be consumed.

He takes another step—she tenses a little, but does not step away.

"Are you testing me?"

"I might be." She hears another splash outside.

"Our marriage was arranged. If you intended to break the engagement, I don't think you would run. I don't think you would have called me." He takes another step. She tenses a little more, but does not retreat.

"You wanted to know if I would suffer for your sake," he takes another step—he is now only a couple of yards from her. She leans a little backwards but does not take a step.

"Yes," she says, a little distracted.

He takes another step toward her—he is now so close she can smell his smell—formaldehyde, freshly-turned earth, wet wool.

"If you run again, I will not be able to find you. You should decide *now*."

From out of nowhere a tiny white card flutters down in front of Christine's face—in Miss Woodwind's sardonic handwriting it says "BEST WISHES ON YOUR WEDDING DAY." Miss Woodwind stands smiling at the end of the aisle by the door.

"I object," she says gaily. "The arrangement you mention is a sham. She has no intention of marrying *you*," she adds snickering. "She never did."

The Golem looks sharply at Christine.

"She's right, isn't she?"

Christine says nothing. Miss Woodwind snickers again. The echoes of her voice crinkle against the stones.

The whirring sound grows suddenly louder—and now Christine recognizes it: the flapping roar of an uncrackling fire. In the darkened recess of the apse's ceiling, above the altar, a gargantuan bell swings down, a metal ring of shade with a massive, swift clapper, and the moment before the clapper strikes the bells above begin to ring, the knells cascading into each other. The bell above the altar strikes with a crash that wrenches the floor, dashes prayer books and hymnals from the pew shelves and spins them in flurries like dead leaves. With an awesome hum the bell falls back and the clapper strikes again on the far side, the report blurs the pews, Christine and Miss Woodwind reel and grapple on to the pillars like sailors on the tilting deck of a storm-tossed ship, but the Golem remains braced upright. The mammoth bell bangs again and again. Christine, hanging onto the iron grillwork of one of the side chapels, feels its reverberations through the floor, her hands buzz and her bones stutter together and her ears shriek in chords.

Now the spaces between the chimes lengthen. The protracted vibration of its tones settles into the building. Christine ventures to release the grill work and stagger out into the aisle again, where the Golem stands unmoved, and Miss Woodwind, nearby, doggedly clutches a pillar behind her back. The long vibrations of the bell have altered the composition of the cathedral's fabric, making it less opaque. Through the transparent slabs she can see the dead bodies interred beneath the floor, each one clutching a jar of preserves in its hands against the time when their jars will in turn be opened and their sweetness enjoyed by the one who sealed them there. A thunderous crack, like a cannon-shot, rocks the floor—a shadow sweeps the cathedral, and when it passes, the statues have all acquired outspread wings of polished cherry wood, from each one new limber branches, drooping with clusters of glistening black cherries, have sprouted.

Color bleaches from the windows of the apse. The glass becomes transparent and clear, then evaporates. The leaded partitions that held the pieces together are the writhing, stiff branches of trees, which lean in through the windows and raise their bare boughs up into the shadows. Trembling sleeves of blonde flame slide down the walls of the apse, and the boughs become engorged, limber, and bristle with metallic black leaves. Black bulbs of flame, clustered like black cherries, dangle down from the shadows of the boughs. The volutes of smoke that billow from them, though dark as pitch, are cool like mist from off the ice, and possess only a weak, resinous odor, like frankincense. This smoke collects beneath the ceiling in a violently disturbed mass—the whirring sound now grows rapidly louder still—the Golem suddenly steps toward the apse, the altar, with a slow but not infirm step, and now the Divinity Student drops from the mass on telescoping metal rods, trailing tendrils of smoke from pockets trapped in his clothes. The two pools of smoke clinging to his eye sockets are the last to disperse, their dregs scattered to the surrounding air by the sudden fluttering of his eyelashes.

His body is as withered and wasted as a burnt log, white ashes flick from him and spin down like snowflakes. His face is a lurid white, the skin is tattered, peeling, and laced all over with tiny black splinters. His eyes are filmed with glistening black stuff, like cherry preserves, so that the whites, which are now yellow as cheese, are visible only in patches, and the iris and pupil gleam with a far-away starry, black-red glare. The livid mouth sags a little from obsidian teeth. He is looking at Miss Woodwind, who has released her grip on the pillar.

"Well thief," he says, his voice crumpled, his tone guttural, low but penetrating, "did you find what you came here to know?"

His manner indicates that he is not expecting, and would not welcome, any answer to his questions. Miss Woodwind stands paralyzed, appalled.

"Are you satisfied?"

His voice rivets her to the floor, stops up her mouth, squeezes her whole body in a press. There is more resignation in it than anger.

"Trying to steal the words I suffered and died for, to use *my* words to tell *your lies.*"

He swings toward her on silent, telescoping rods.

"Ruining my experiment with your selfish interference."

He is closer.

"All in order to steal secrets that you cannot understand."

With great boldness and effort, Miss Woodwind asks "Why not? Why couldn't I understand them?"

"You never paid their price."

"What price?"

He swings closer.

"What price?" she asks again, shrinking, frightened.

"What you try to steal, it will never be possible for you to steal. I brook no more interference from thieves."

The Divinity Student makes a vague, small, almost shapeless gesture with his right hand, and as he drifts backwards toward the altar Christine can see his right hand now holds the Golem's book. Miss Woodwind's hands fly to her now-empty coat pocket.

Without the slightest sensation, without so much as a jar, Miss Woodwind's vision just blurs for a moment; when her eyes focus again, she sees the cathedral's pale lights in the distance. She is standing on the soft, reedy bank of the lake, and the water, dotted with burning oil slicks, stands between her and the cathedral. Miss Woodwind, after the moment of her shock passes, rails and utters loud incoherent cries of frustration, kicking the ground. But the intervening barrier is mere water, and to a master of the element like herself, who can swim without being wetted, this is not an insuperable barrier. Miss Woodwind immediately flings herself from the bank into the water and swims furiously toward the island.

The Divinity Student, as he drifts back to the altar, drops the Golem's book. It falls at an angle, curving down past the Golem, who plucks it from the air with his right hand in a gesture like a man pinching up a bit of cooked rice in his fingers. The Divinity Student stops and descends a bit further, looking down at Christine with a more academic mien.

"I am ending this experiment; with Miss Woodwind's interference, it would no longer be possible to derive a clear result. Now I must ask you, were you able to love the Golem? Think carefully before you answer."

Christine looks down, not at the Golem. After reflecting a few moments, she looks up apologetically, "No." She turns to the Golem, again with an apologetic look.

The Divinity Student also turns to the Golem—"And were you able to love Christine?"

The Golem looks at Christine. She is immaculately beautiful in her veil, her shining hair, her gleaming ivory skin, her brilliant emerald eyes. She is magnificent, she is very admirable.

"No," he says, looking up at the Divinity Student.

"It's a shame," the Divinity Student says.

The Golem shakes his head, with a terrible sadness, "She is magnificent—she is admirable."

"Do you love her?"

"—I couldn't."

"All that is created here is a failure."

Wobbling lights play over the features of the statues lining the nave, until they all appear to wear the Divinity Student's face.

"These are elevated to saintly status because they are the valuable mistakes, and remain with the creator to remind and reprimand him. One must pursue every avenue in the labyrinth and discovering a cul-de-sac, while disappointing, contributes usefully to our knowledge—one goes on trying to be methodical but relying always on a judgment and patience that can neither of them be adequate, so relying too on luck—these experiments . . . trial and error.

"The Golem is an experiment of the Divinity Student and the Divinity Student is an experiment himself. Because not everything is known, and even one's own knowledge is seldom if ever perfectly understood, we experiment. Your principle purpose here was not to love, but to suffer, to live. The faculty of life that I lent you must now be returned to me with that interest you have accrued in your experiences down here."

He turns to Christine. "You upheld your end of the bargain admirably, and never broke our confidence—and, while it did not last long—long enough. Come forward, and receive your payment."

Christine approaches the Divinity Student, who drops down to just above the floor. He pulls something from the leaves of his book and hands it to her—a white card with a black engraving on it—as she takes it from him she sees it is undeniably a portrait of her, apparently of great antiquity.

"That's all?" she asks, looking at the card back and front. She opens it, and sees a smaller card, its corners pinched through slits in the backing, with two sentences written on it.

"Don't read that yet," the Divinity Student asks. "Not just yet."

Christine's face darkens, she looks up at the Divinity Student.

"It is more than it seems. Had you not suffered for them, you would not have understood these words. And had you somehow apprehended their meaning without having first suffered for them, that instant you surely would have died."

"But," she begins to ask, gesturing toward his book.

"This book is the book of *my* life, not yours. It would mean very little to you. What I give you will prove."

Christine looks up at his torn face and then nods. She takes a few steps away, and the Divinity Student turns his attention back to the Golem.

"May I stay and watch?" she asks a little hesitantly.

"No," the Divinity Student makes a small circular flip with his left hand and the door at the end of the transept to the left of the altar swings open. Through the open door, in the even orange light of four beautifully carved jack-o'-lanterns, she can see the gondola of a hot air balloon waiting for her. Christine looks at the Divinity Student, and with sympathy at the Golem, who stands leaning on his brace, his mouth a bit ajar. Then she strides through the door, which closes with a distinct thud behind her. The Divinity Student waves his stick once in the air and a fragile gust of wind disperses her scent, leaving only the smell of formaldehyde, dust, freshly turned earth, varnish, wet wool, smoke, wax . . .

The Golem looks up at the Divinity Student. "I never even had a chance."

"I have suffered more. The experiment is over, the city is gone, she is gone, there is nothing for you to do here, and nowhere you can go. You cannot return to the surface but through me. Without you, I will continue to rot forever," he holds out his hands indicating his pitiable condition.

"Will you kill me?"

"Of course not. You will live in me."

"How?"

"We will be someone else, to whose life the life of decay will only contribute."

"Haven't I got a choice?"

"Never. Stand—here," the Divinity Student points with his stick to a spot immediately below him.

MISS WOODWIND APPROACHES THE cathedral from the far side, through the trees, and its hulk obscures the gaudy, red and gold balloon that rises toward the roof of the cavern on the other. Christine looks up at the stone ceiling—a patch in the grey-black stone proves to be nothing but smoke laced with jets of flame, toward which she is ascending.

Statues and carvings to the roof at every elevation—the windows that faintly shine between the buttress ribcage dim and flare with irregular shadow flurries. Again, Miss Woodwind comes up to the open door, and slips inside. She looks this way and that, but dark sifts down from the roof like snow—there is no sound is there? She can hear something like cloth being crushed. Slipping her shoes from her feet, Miss Woodwind pads along the wall, under the arches, toward the altar. Now she can just make out a single, enormous figure, slumped on the floor before the altar in a single great mass. A shadow stretches across its upper half, the lower half is invisible under a heavy pall of damp black wool coat. As her eyes become accustomed to the dimness, she can see that the weak, convulsive movements have stopped, it is lying still, and there are two humps on the back somehow. The humps flip up to the sides, and the vast shadow that lay across the front half of the mass flutters, shivers, and rises from the floor.

As the balloon enters the cloud of smoke, Christine hastily opens the card and reads:

WE ARE ALL PHANTOMS
MANUFACTURED FROM WORDS

HOWEVER IT DOES NOT FOLLOW
FROM THIS THAT WE ARE NOT REAL

Miss Woodwind recoils a scream bursting from her mouth, as if utterance could be reflexive like a knee jerk. It has turned toward her, the face invisible in the shade of its great black greasy pinions, hooding the entire figure. Two braced legs slip backwards into their shade. For a silent moment Miss Woodwind lying on the floor and the sound of the greasy separation of sticky feathers. Miss Woodwind bounds to her feet and runs—but the cathedral is confusing—she finds herself darting into a narrow doorway by a peripheral chapel—stairs coiling up toward the roof. From the gushing wind and rattle of plumage she knows it is following her. She flings herself on the steps, straight up through hollow clouds of streetlights and tombstones hanging on rails, beams crisscrossing her course and weaving into subterranean tunnels, waving boughs shattered by its many wings spreading in lightless crystal spears peeling back layers of petrified earth, their colors fluorescing more and more brilliant as she nears the surface. In the first alcove she passes is deposited all her clothing, her skin and her hair. In the second, her eyes, her teeth, her bones. In the third, her muscles. In the fourth, her organs. In the fifth, her nerves and brain. And finally on the final turn—the desert, running away in all directions to the horizon and the ring of mountains black against the black sky pierced by white stars haloed with blue shadows the color of alcohol flames, the desert littered with pairs of reflecting lights reflecting back and piercing . . . The city describes its narrow circle around her feet so high up she is all of a sudden, standing in the highest place, on the pinnacle of the cathedral's tallest spire, at such an elevation that the city's walls appear no bigger than a tiny ridge of stone ringing her feet, she is thrust into the sky as the spire looms higher and higher, dilate the stars and lights all around her, not a dome but a field of stars above below and on every hand, and it still immediately behind her but nevertheless she shrinks back almost touching it recoiling in terror with her hands to her mouth, she cringes backward trying hysterically but unable to screw shut or avert her eyes, recognizing heaven as it engulfs her.

Acknowledgements

I would like to thank: Robert M. Price, Thomas Ligotti, Jeff and Ann VanderMeer, John Fenton, Harry O. Morris, Robert Parker and Karen Kahler, and the WORD of William S. Burroughs.

MICHAEL CISCO is a freelance writer and underemployed PhD. He is the author of *The Divinity Student* (Buzzcity Press, 1999), winner of the International Horror Writers Guild Award for Best First Novel of 1999. His other writings include *The Tyrant* (Prime, 2003), *The Traitor* (Ministry of Whimsy Press, forthcoming), numerous contributions to the *The Thackery T. Lambshead Guide to Eccentric and Discredited Diseases* (Nightshade Books, 2003), *Leviathans 3* and *4* (Ministry of Whimsy Press, 2002 and 2004).

Printed in the United States
210101BV00001B/122/A